KURAJ

KURAJ

SILVIA DI NATALE

Translated from the Italian by
Carol O'Sullivan and Martin Thom

BLOOMSBURY

First published in Great Britain 2005

Originally published in Italy in 2000 by Giangiacomo Feltrinelli Editore as *Kuraj*

Bloomsbury Publishing Plc, 36 Soho Square, London W1D 3QY

A CIP catalogue record for this book is available from the British Library

ISBN 0 7475 6534 1
9780747565345

10 9 8 7 6 5 4 3 2 1

All papers used by Bloomsbury Publishing are natural,
recyclable products made from wood grown in well-managed
forests. The manufacturing processes conform
to the regulations of the country of origin.

Typeset by Hewer Text Ltd, Edinburgh
Printed in the United States of America by Quebecor World Fairfield

To all those who try to make a life elsewhere

CONTENTS

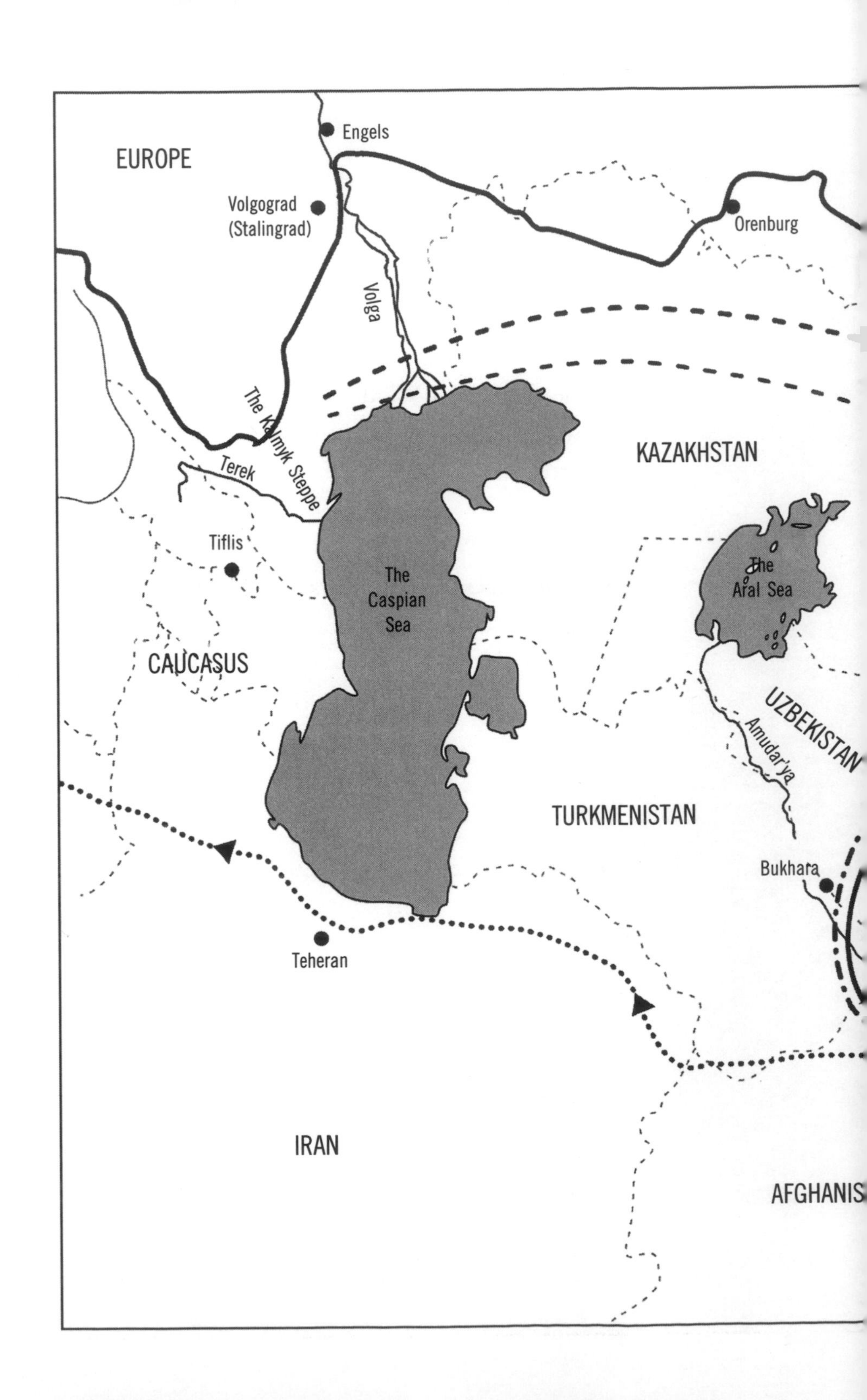

EUROPE
Engels
Volgograd
(Stalingrad)
Orenburg
Volga
The Kalmyk Steppe
Terek
KAZAKHSTAN
Tiflis
The Caspian Sea
The Aral Sea
CAUCASUS
UZBEKISTAN
Amudar'ya
TURKMENISTAN
Bukhara
Teheran
IRAN
AFGHANIS

Part One

THE GREAT WIND

I

AT FIRST I used to dream of Mai Ling every night. I know that I dreamed about her and that it was her, it was Mai Ling, with her almond eyes in her pale face, her plait hanging before her as she bent over me, and her smile. Above all it was her smile that I used to see, and her bending over me and talking to me. I would try to answer her; I would search for the right words, flounder about in the dream and yearn to speak but, try as I might, no sound would come from my throat. It was as though something prevented me from speaking. Then she would disappear, her eyes would disappear little by little, and so too would the half-loosened plait hanging before her as she leant forwards, until in the end only her smile remained, just that, a smile without those almond eyes and that pale face bent over me. Then that too dissolved into the darkness. And I would wake up.

It took me a while to realise where I was. My eyes searched instinctively for the brazier in the centre of the yurt, where the dried dung had become a dark powder. During the winter nights, when the cold threatened our warmth, Mai Ling would get up from time to time to add more dung; as she did so the brazier would emit a startling flash of light, the wooden lattice of the yurt seemed to come alive and the crimson of the carpets ignited for an instant, then fell swiftly into shadow again as the flame died down into the bottom of the pan. Then the air filled with that sharp smell I knew well, a mixture of burnt hay and earth, and with the thin smoke which caught in the throats of guests who weren't used to living as we did and made them cough. I looked for the gleam of the little oil lamp in front of the image of the Padma Sambhava, a glimmer which barely lit the lotus petals of the pedestal, the crossed legs and the fingers brushing the ground, while the torso, arms and ears down to the shoulders could dimly be made out through the darkness, as could the gilt which covered them. The lacquered cabinet in which the women kept their jewels and the few documents we had was itself red and gold, while the rugs draped on the rush walls and the fringed door were a glowing crimson, so that even the shadow inside the yurt seemed to have absorbed the reddish hues. And in the morning, when the first rays settled on the ceremonial saddle hanging on the wall, reflecting off its trim, its brass stirrups and its silk, the whole yurt seemed to fill with gold. In the evenings, lying in the place reserved for the youngest children, my eyes followed the winding of the carpets, the curve of deer horns and the course of a stream woven in a brighter thread. All around, everybody slept on their felt mattresses in their assigned place, the men on the right, on the left my cousins Haysce, Yesügen and Yesü, and my aunt Qada'an with her youngest son, Temüjin, who had not yet been weaned. In the winter, we put a small pen near the entrance of the yurt: the new-born animals slept with us, safe from the cold and the wolves. From time to time I would reach out an arm, slip it between the bars of the pen and touch the soft, silken coat of a new-born lamb. I would stroke the animal's warm body, feel it rise and fall, uncertain whether or not to trust the hand which fondled it. I was reassured by the breathing of all those bodies. Even though outside the wind blew and the dogs howled restlessly, the shadowy yurt was full of familiar presences and I soon closed my eyes.

Now I found it hard to open them and in the darkness I made out the whiteness of the furniture around me and of the eiderdown weighing down on me. I shook it off and raised my head from the pillow. Across the stiffly starched pillowcase there ran a sloping, embroidered inscription, which read *gute Nacht*. Every evening I sank my cheek into that embroidered goodnight, without understanding its meaning, because at that time letters were signs which I did not know. I fell into a deep sleep, the sleep of a little girl exhausted by too much emotion. I would wake suddenly in the middle of the night, lost in the mound of feathers, and wonder if I were dead, and if the white material covering me was perhaps the tunic in which my brother Ginchin had descended to the kingdom of Erlig Khan.

I would quickly wriggle out from the cave which I had hollowed out for myself beneath the eiderdown, set my feet on the bedside rug and venture out onto the cold floor. Then I would slip between the wings of the curtains, securely drawn over the window. Even the lace curtains were embroidered with writing. I pushed them warily aside, and found myself facing the freezing glass. I did not dare to open the window, for at that time I was always afraid of making a noise. I wished that I could move without touching anything or, better still, without being seen. I feared that the slightest rustle might cause the anxious eyes of my new mother, or the kindly but irritated eyes of one of the maids, to appear behind me. Their unexpected presence startled me each time, as though they were jinn come down from Mount Kuchi-Kaf at the ends of the earth to do me harm.

I used to gaze out from the corner that was free of the curtain and my breath would make a misty circle on the glass, which I rubbed out with the back of my hand. There were outlines of trees, so many that you could hardly see the sky. The sky was black, only a little lighter than the trees, while at home it shines even at night. It was an overcast sky. It was not only inside that one felt suffocated, in closed rooms where the breeze could not enter and where only from time to time did they allow it in, but it was also hard to breathe under that sky, closed as it was between rings of trees and roofs. I did not know then that the sky over Cologne had never been as open as in those years, or as vast, when there were no buildings to block it out. I did not know how a city was made in this part of the world. I knew just the cities of the oases, where the minarets are the only obstacle in the sky. On the steppes there is nothing to limit or oppose it, so that on foot or on horseback we have the impression that nothing is taller than we are. Here the sky filled me with dismay and the waving trees frightened me. Shivering with cold, I would return to the warmth beneath the eiderdown. Clasping my hands between my knees and drawing my legs up to my chin, I would curl up like a frightened animal and seek refuge from the jinn encircling me. Yet as soon as I closed my eyes I saw the red, gold-flecked glow of the yurt, and felt its warm breath and the bodies asleep beside me.

I have forgotten my own language. They say that it is impossible to forget one's mother tongue, but it is not true. Even language is lost, when it is linked to a childhood as far away as mine was. While my story appears before me in its entirety, the language which accompanied it is only a collection of shards which I am hard pressed to put together, bits and pieces rather than whole conversations. I have forgotten my own language. I no longer know the words with which we children called each other from one yurt to the next, the words which Mai Ling, who took the place of my mother, spoke to me, and those of my grandfather Bairqan, when he began his story and our story all over again, each time from the beginning: 'We Tunshan are the true descendants of the Tatars.' The words have escaped me, and what remain are occasional sounds, the 'rrrs' which came sonorously from the throat and the high liquid sounds on which the language occasionally took wing. Or was that the particular accent of Mai Ling, my grandfather's third wife, who was a Manchurian from Bukhara? I remember the care she took when trying to repeat the words we taught her, and the indecision before every 'rrr' facing her, as though the shaping of it caused her inner torment; I remember how, every time she had to pronounce her husband's name, we could read in her face her efforts to reproduce it with the proper sonority and the anguish of not succeeding, as though her way of liquefying the sounds was an affront to the dignity of the khan.

I seem to hear again the voices and cries of that time, but if I try to translate them into words all that comes out are sounds whose sense I can guess at, without being able to place vowels and consonants in the right order. It is as though I heard people speaking in the next room and I could recognise the voices and from the voices, the people, as though I knew what they were talking about but could not tell the words apart, with only a few emerging clear and whole on the surface of the dialogue. Some words have remained, survivors of the great shipwreck of my mother tongue – but is there anyone who still speaks it? Is it not now a vanished language, like the others which preceded it on either bank of the Amudar'ya?

One of the island-words I have saved from oblivion is *kuraj*.

I followed this clue, this one ordered and exact sound, wherever it led. I burrowed in dictionaries, letting myself be drawn into a game of circular references, penetrating deeper and deeper into a labyrinth of unfamiliar signs, and alighting on the shores of the most obscure meanings. How was I to retrace *kuraj* in the sea of language? I knew what it meant at home and I stubbornly searched for some written confirmation, as though I were looking for a buried civilisation, which ceases to be a chimera in the archaeologist's imagination only in the moment that a piece of wall or a potsherd is brought to light. I searched for the clue which would lead me to *kuraj*: steppe, plant of the steppes, herb of the steppes, bushes which in the winter lose branches and roots and give themselves up to the wind, thus spreading their seeds, *Salsola kali*, in Russian *perekatipole*, 'running field'. So, this was the clue I was searching for! I skimmed through the damaged pages of an old Russian dictionary, deciphering the characters with some difficulty, until a name emerged, and meaning and phoneme corresponded. The name was *perekatipole* or, in the language of the Kyrgyz and the other peoples of the steppes, *kuraj*. It was a kind of revelation, as though suddenly my past had been confirmed and ceased to exist only as the fabrication of memory, perhaps greatly distorted and reworked by my imagination over the years. Now *kuraj*, that one certain word of my language, was before my eyes, precise and indisputable on the page of the dictionary, and I felt moved and happy, as though I had found among those cramped lines of all-but-unknown signs the name of the clan I belonged to, the name of those who lived in my yurt, my own portrait with the long plait to my knees, the head-dress fastened at the nape of my neck with a long pin, the short felt boots sewn with seed pearls. The word was true and it confirmed my past irrefutably!

We gave the name *kuraj* to the dry bushes which the *afghanetz* picks up in spring and sends rolling over the steppes. Throngs of bushes move, and the steppe 'walks' or rather runs, enough to frighten the horses and give the impression, to someone looking from a distance, of a band of horsemen approaching at the gallop.

However, *kuraj* also means 'flute' and suggests a crude flute, a nomad shepherd's flute, made out of a simple reed; by extension, then, it designates also the flute player, and even a performer with a flute, a minstrel, a poet who improvised verses, a re-fashioner of ancient epics, or what you will – in any case a character dear to the peoples of the steppes and familiar also to me. But there is a third meaning, in some way contained within the others: a person without a fixed home and without a will of his own, who lets himself be dragged along by chance. More than a nomad, he is a rootless vagabond, at the mercy of the wind like a *Salsola* bush, in other words, like the *kuraj*.

But the word calls up yet another meaning, more mysterious than the others and perhaps only distantly connected to them. '*Kuraj, kuraj, kuraj*' said the shaman at the end of his incantations, and the word rolled over us, evoking the bushes racing over the steppe. Perhaps the *kuraj* of the shaman had no link with the other *kuraj* beyond its sound; perhaps different meanings had fused in time to become that one word which encapsulated them all and which, more than any other, takes me back to our nomadic existence.

2

WE LIVED AT the junction of the roads which have always linked west and east, north and south, the routes of the great caravans. We were, though we did not know it, at the meeting point between the great civilisations and the great religions, where the Greeks encountered Buddha, Zoroaster taught the Persians the worship of fire, Islam took on the colour of Chinese ceramics, and the Turks and the Mongols became one race. Languages and scripts were exchanged, or fed into each other. We ourselves, who claimed descent from the 'white bones' of Genghis Khan, were really a mixture of languages and tribes. Not all the Tunshan had, like my grandfather Bairqan, the physical characteristics of our Mongol ancestors: the broad face, the almond eyes, the flat nose of the nomads of the north-eastern steppes. To look at my grandfather in the yurt hearing disputes and meting out justice according to our code, seated on his throne, an armchair of painted wood piled with cushions, behind him the altar with its images of gods and ancestors, his legs folded under him and wearing his head-dress of felt edged with velvet which he never set aside, not even in the summer, he looked as if he had just stepped out of a Moghul miniature. He was the personification of the spirit of our ancestors and the respect he inspired was enough to placate the quarrelsome, to calm the rowdy, to reconcile the head families of the different clans into which the Tunshan were divided. Indeed Bairqan was not only khan, or head of a clan, a position which was handed down from father to son, he was also khagan, the great khan, the elected authority recognised by all those who pitched their yurts in a circle around his own.

Despite their common ancestry the Tunshan did not greatly resemble one another. Even among close kin, even among those who lived in the same village of yurts, some showed very few Mongol characteristics. Many had long thin noses, like our Afghan neighbours, or the brown skin and more rounded eyes of the Turkmens; many showed in their facial features alone the countless crossings that had shaped them, the casual or intended encounters and the forced or carefully arranged unions of which they were the unpredictable result.

There were not many of us: ties of kinship between our two hundred yurts were more or less close, and the men would discuss at length whether a marriage between members of the three clans was permissible or not; marriages within a clan were taboo. So women came from outside: contracted by the heads of the clans, they arrived wrapped in the veils of their tribes and brought with them, besides their dowries of sheep, camels and carpets, and their maidservants – if they came from rich or noble families – the physiognomy of their ethnic group and the words of their language. Little by little they began to say *ayil* instead of *aul*, to refer to the village of yurts, while in their turn our pregnant women began to offer bowls of *kumiss* to Momo, the celestial grandmother, because only when her shadow falls over the womb of a woman in labour will the birth be easy, and only she can keep the terrible Albasty at bay. Our pantheon was enriched by new spirits, our daily rituals by new gestures and our language by new expressions. Thus shape of nose, skin colour and words were intermingled: the language we spoke had ceased years since to be the language of the Mongolian nomads. I wonder if we would still have understood one other, if we had met, or whether we would have suffered the same fate as our Moghul neighbours in the Afghan highlands, also descendants of Genghis Khan, but left behind by the Mongol army at the time of the great race towards Persia: they spoke a Mongol dialect mixed with the Pashto of the Afghanis, a mixed language, which nobody but themselves understood, a language destined to be swallowed up by stronger idioms, like ours too, perhaps.

We lived at the crossroads of languages and ethnic groups: more Turkish than we were prepared to admit, Mongols in the eyes of our Uzbek neighbours, who indeed called us 'white Tatars', maybe because more than a century earlier we had come from Kazakhstan, which had been the territory of Genghis Khan's White Horde. We were different, and set apart for another, still more compelling reason. Out of all the peoples living on the banks of the Amudar'ya we alone were not followers of Mohammed. While our neighbours spread their prayer mats facing Mecca five times a day, and nearby villages resounded five times a day to the muezzin's voice, round our yurt little white flags fluttered to ward off evil spirits and approaching visitors spun prayer wheels. Each wheel contained six papier mâché cylinders filled with prayers, which multiplied as they turned, endlessly repeating *Om mani padme hum*, the six syllables of our religion.

We were Lamaists, which did not stop us from venerating local demons of all kinds and the spirits of our ancestors, or from reciting charms to ward off the jinn, after the manner of our Turkmen and Uzbek neighbours. Our faith was not coherent, any more than our appearance and our names were. Perhaps the many Alis and Hammans, as our cousins and neighbours began to call themselves, indicated more or less formal conversions, and represented the price which we paid to the Muslim tribes, together with livestock and sheepskins, in exchange for the women we lacked. We were tolerant, or perhaps merely eclectic: you cannot live at the crossroads of the caravans without absorbing the way of thinking of all those who have been there before you. It was as though in passing they had all left some element of their culture on the existing pile, much as travellers will reverently add a pebble or a bone or some other object in their possession to a cairn of rocks stuck with flags at a crossroads, an obo built in honour of the spirit of the place. We gathered up these legacies without really realising it and, having placed them within the felt walls of our yurts together with our other utensils, used them without thinking overmuch about them.

We were nomads but, unlike the Turkmen tribes, did not cover vast distances. We took down our yurts twice a year, in autumn and in spring, and twice a year we crossed the great river, the Amudar'ya, to return to where we had lived six months previously, to search out the three hearthstones where we knew we had left them and to build our yurts again around them. The river was the condition of our nomadic existence. In April, when the water level was high and the river difficult to ford, it promised the abundance and verdure of the north bank; when at the end of October it ran sluggishly, uncovering the sandbanks in the middle of the channel, it foretold the storms of wind and snow which were a little less violent to the south.

We had a relationship of respect and friendship with the river. This was the river which the Spanish ambassadors who travelled with Clavijo to the court of Tamerlane said was 'one of the three streams which flow from Paradise'. I do not know if this is true for the other two rivers, but in the case of the Amudar'ya it is altogether true. I thought so even as a child.

'Where does the big river come from, grandfather Bairqan?'

'Up there,' and Bairqan pointed in the direction of the distant and dizzying peaks of the Hindu Kush, 'there, right in the snow, sits an *arang* who is bigger than the other *arangs*. He sits right in the snow and when he gets too cold he blows on it and then the snow melts and comes down the mountain and runs over the plain to us.'

'And where does the river go then, grandfather Bairqan?'

'Can't you see, it goes west, to catch up with the sun and sink into it before going to sleep. But it never does catch up with it.'

Bairqan was clearly wrong, for the Amudar'ya curves around,

heads north and flows in the end into the sands of the Aral Sea. Or did Bairqan perhaps know that until the Middle Ages one arm of the river had indeed flowed west, as far as the shores of the Caspian Sea? Bairqan knew the river well, as he knew everything about our history and our homelands. 'When the *arang* gets angry, then he blows on the ice more fiercely than ever and the stream on the mountain swells, the water rushes down the mountainside; it runs, bounds, quivers, and when it gets down here it runs at full tilt, like an unbridled horse, and the banks can no longer hold it and it invades the fields around and the villages and then there are no more fords or ferries to cross the Amudar'ya and nobody can contain the river.'

'What do people do then, grandfather Bairqan?'

'Then the peoples of the two banks, those who live in felt-covered tents and those who live within walls of dried mud, kill a sheep and pour the blood into the water, so that the *arang* may be placated and stop blowing on the snow. Then the snow freezes again, the glacier stops melting and the *Naga*, the spirits of the river, make the water flow back between the banks and let the horses graze there in safety.'

How much history has flowed along the mighty river! And how many peoples has it seen arrive on its banks and cross over it! Armies who laid one side waste and made battlefields of the other, warriors on their way to conquer the lands to the north or south, nomads seeking pasture! We Tunshan knew that the earth, which we sprinkled with *kumiss* every spring, protected those ancient dead, as it did ours, and that our lives, on each bank of the great river, were adding new stories to theirs.

The Greeks called the river 'Oxus', a name which echoed the name given to it by the Turkmens, 'Oks'. The Turkmens lived at that time on the stretch of river which turned away from the main watercourse and flowed towards the Caspian Sea. The land round the Oxus was very fertile then; the banks on each side were green with grain, vines and gardens, and the houses of the Turkmens so close that a cat could have travelled comfortably from the Aral Sea to the Caspian Sea by jumping from one roof to the next. But one day the perfidious inhabitants of the khanate of Khorezm, who dominated the territory where the river branched off, dammed the left-hand arm of the Amudar'ya and it ran dry. Vines and gardens disappeared; the fields of grain withered; and the Turkmens, with nothing to sustain them, became nomad herdsmen and bandits so terrifying that even in my day they were still spoken of with fear.

On the banks of the Amudar'ya, on the plain of Balkh, Alexander the Great defeated Poros, the Indian king, and settled the borders of his empire. Fifteen hundred years later, in the autumn of 1220, Genghis Khan reached the river in his turn, this time from the north. At that time the stupas of the old Buddhist monasteries still stood outside the city of Termez, while within the walls rose the minarets, the domes of the mosques and the citadel where the sovereign's palace stood, decorated with alabaster reliefs. Once the city was in sight, Genghis Khan sent messengers ahead to deliver his simple but stark warning to its inhabitants: if you do not surrender, God alone knows what will happen. The city of Termez did not open its gates, and resisted the attackers for nine days, until rocks from the catapults breached the walls. Genghis Khan then ordered the inhabitants to come out – to count them, he said, and the deception too was part of the ritual of conquest – and lined them up on the open ground by the river among the flattened walls of the monasteries, men on one side, women and children on the other. Then officials passed through the silent throng and valued the prisoners one by one, separating the useful booty from the valueless, and at a sign from them the soldiers led away the strongest men and the prettiest girls. When the selection was over, and they had stripped the remaining prisoners of the jewels they wore, the soldiers flung themselves at them and cut them to pieces with axes. The story is told of an old woman, who when she saw her turn coming told the soldier whose weapon was already raised to strike her down: 'I own a pearl, a huge, magnificent pearl; I will give it to you if you spare my life.' The soldier looked at her, his arm frozen in mid-air, his eyes narrowed with greed. 'Give it to me and I won't kill you.' The old woman lifted a corner of her veil to her mouth, in the defensive gesture of a girl: 'I swallowed it,' she said, and her face twisted in mockery. Then the Mongol brought his axe down across the woman's belly and split her open. They say other soldiers followed his example and began to rummage through the entrails of the dead, hoping to find riches there, but perhaps it is only a horrible invention, designed to heap yet more sulphur onto the infernal reputation of the horsemen come from Tartary.

Less than two centuries later the empire founded by Genghis Khan no longer existed. Tamerlane, a distant relative of the great Mongol, succeeded, however, in assembling an empire which stretched from north of the Amudar'ya to the Ganges and to the Mediterranean, and was, though not as vast as that of Genghis Khan, not unworthy of the comparison. In the freezing winter of 1404 Tamerlane left his capital of Samarkand to strengthen the borders of his kingdom to the south. He halted at the Oxus. The river was a white expanse along whose edges clumps of reeds protruded like the standards of an army trapped in the ice. Tamerlane summoned his pontoniers and had them test the thickness of the ice in several places; they reported that the ice would take the soldiers' weight, but that a track would be needed. So the soldiers filled sacks and baskets with stones and earth which they tipped onto the ice, to make an improvised road. The army left a muddy wake in the white river, mirrored in the black trail of crows in the sky overhead. Tamerlane looked at the birds and his face darkened. It struck him that the crows would also be circling around the blue dome of the Gur-e Mir, the mausoleum which he had had built for himself, and that they would follow his funeral procession, over that same river, but proceeding in the opposite direction. He was not entirely mistaken: a year later the soldiers carrying his coffin to Samarkand forded a river, the Syrdar'ya, and it is likely that a trail of crows did follow them, because these birds always follow armies, as seagulls follow ships.

Fifty years later Tamerlane's grandson Babur Mirza, Emir of the region to the south of the Amudar'ya, stared at the river's raging waters and twisted the great ring on his index finger. The river had come between him and his enemy, who had occupied Samarkand.

Babur Mirza was in a hurry. The river had to be crossed in one way or another, even if they had only one barge on which to do it. There was no time to build bridges or to make rafts of skins to row across. After all, his Mongol ancestors, who knew nothing of boats, had crossed rivers of every size clinging to their horses' necks! His soldiers would do the same.

Babur Mirza was the first to set foot on the far bank of the Amudar'ya, carried to dry land aboard the only boat. His soldiers, on the other hand, took off their clothes and stuffed them in leather bags which they lashed to their horses' sides, then one after another they took to the water, like gazelles that blindly follow the leader of the herd and fling themselves after him into the jaws of the waiting crocodiles. From the opposite bank Babur Mirza saw soldiers and horses struggling against the current, the animals barely able to hold their heads above water, the men desperately clutching at their manes. He watched them disappear under the muddy waves. Often only the leather bag reappeared. Those who reached the far bank, men and animals, were soaked through and gasping for breath, their eyes wide with exhaustion and fear. When Babur Mirza regrouped his army it was difficult indeed to persuade them to close ranks and to instil fresh courage in them. Yet he reached Samarkand all the same, and without warning. From the safety of the walls his adversary sued for peace. 'Do you think that I have travelled all this distance to turn back now?' he answered. The loot from the rich city was his compensation to the surviving soldiers, but those who had been taken by the water became loot for the dogs, when the river grew weary of dragging them along and laid them down on the sandbanks in shallow water. They say that the fishermen of the Aral Sea were fishing up leather bags for years afterwards, and that they found treasures hidden inside. But it was no more than a legend, because inside there were just rags and rotted boots; Babur's soldiers, like others before and since, carried with them only their own miserable existence and the little that was needed to make them march and fight.

In my day the Amudar'ya marked the border between the Soviet Union to the north and Afghanistan to the south. But we Tunshan knew nothing of such things; if, when I was a child, someone had told me that there was another state on the other side of the river, I would have looked at them without understanding. Only later did we too start to talk about borders, but simply to say that soon they would be closed and that we had to hurry in order not to be trapped. Nestling against my grandfather's shoulder I listened to the excited conversations of the men gathered in a circle in the yurt. Moved by the solemn nature of the discussion and by my inclusion in it, I imagined that great gates had suddenly sprung up and that somebody stood ready to close them behind us with heavy iron chains like those of the Ulughbek madrassa in Samarkand. Before then (before, that is, the borders began to close), our one obstacle had been the Amudar'ya, which had to be crossed at the right time, it is true, before the river became a raging torrent of water and sand. Horses and camels crossed the watery border in a riot of splashes and shouts once in autumn and once again, at a ford further to the east, in the spring. To the north the banks were higher and quite steep, but the flat steppe was the same on both sides, only to the south the mountain slopes sheltered us better from the cold and the warm wind came more often to melt the earth in its hard shell. We pitched our yurts south of the river in winter, and in the spring we moved to the north bank. In winter the yurts of the village were pitched closer to each other. We children would clamber up the ancient steps to the caves hollowed out of the limestone and leaning out from our eyrie, we would see clear as day beneath us the geometry of our encampment, which spread over the steppe like a planetary system in space. In the middle was my grandfather Bairqan's yurt, easily recognisable by its size and whiteness, like a star blazing with light in the centre of other, dimmer heavenly bodies. The yurts of his wives revolved around his, and at greater distances but still gravitating round the centre, were those of his married children and of his servants. This first constellation of yurts, the basic unit of our individual and social lives, was what we called an *ayil*: for all nomads the *ayil*, or *aul*, means at once village and family. It was at once the place and the tie that bound those who lived within the circle of the yurt, protected, however, from the larger circle of the *ayil*. The other villages gravitated round my grandfather's *ayil* like minor planets round the principal star and their distance in space corresponded to their distance in blood. Together they formed a clan whose members were all to some extent related, though the distance in time and the distance from the main family tree made these relationships very difficult to untangle. The other two clans of the Tunshan were encamped a few hours from our villages.

We Tunshan continued to call ourselves *ulus*, as our most distant ancestors had done, and to display the banner with the eight snakes entwined, even though we had long since been reduced to just three clans. Our villages were no longer as populous as they had been in the days when each yurt was home to up to ten people and, given that the number of yurts in an *ayil* varied from five to ten, a village, a whole community which lived and worked together and owned tools and livestock in common, might number up to a hundred people. Although we were fewer than we had once been, we clung all the more stubbornly to the established geometries, so that space, which was expanding around us, would be constrained by our order, and remain measurable, as was the finite space surrounding the individual yurts, which were centres and circumferences at the same time. Every yurt was in fact a little planet in itself, around whose central point, the dome, or rather the smokehole, the inhabited space extended. There was then a patch of cleared ground where the household tasks were carried out, occupied only by the hut which contained the stores of dried dung, and by the rails to which we tied the horses, the milking mares and the foals.

Despite their basic similarities, yurts differed from each other. These differences were particularly obvious when seen from above: the yurts of the newly married and those of the rich could be picked out because they were paler than the rest, the former because their felt covers were newer, the latter because their covers were made entirely of white wool and changed more often, while the yurts of the poor were grey or black and often patched. Naturally there were other differences too, but these were invisible from a distance. We children knew them well, because in the summer we were free to enter any yurt, to eat wherever we were offered food and even to sleep where we pleased. In winter, however, distinctions were more sharply drawn, because food was scarcer; then the servants and our poorest neighbours came to our yurt to eat. They had the right to fish with us for the pieces of meat in the pot, though only after everybody else had helped themselves. In winter each of us took our proper place in the yurt and we slept together to keep warm. In summer the distances between the villages and even between the individual yurts were greater; whenever possible, each one was pitched on higher ground, and often separated from the others by a stream. But both in winter and in summer a plume of smoke issued from the smokeholes of the yurts, a sign that the hearth fire was lit inside, and this could never be allowed to go out, at least not by accident. So the fire in the yurt, a symbol of the continuation of our families, crossed the river with us.

At that time there were no bridges over the Amudar'ya. There had been a bridge in the days of the ambassador Clavijo, a wooden bridge which arched over the deepest part of the river, but they could not count on its being there, because Tamerlane had it built when he wished to cross the river and then destroyed after he and his retinue had passed. So that bridge, built and rebuilt as and when the king wished it, did not simplify the river crossing, which anyway was hedged about with bureaucratic difficulties, at least for those who wished to leave the country to the north of the Amudar'ya. Indeed, contrary to what happens today, you only needed to show travel papers if you were leaving the territory, but if you wished to enter it you didn't need to observe these formalities. That is how it was in the days of Tamerlane. In my day, crossing the Amudar'ya did not present bureaucratic complications. The old fords were there, as were the Afghan ferrymen squatting like pelicans beside their flat barges, with nothing to do but unwind and rewind their turbans. When a client approached, they would first wind the yards of tattered material round their heads, then they would rise calmly and with dignity, secrete the obol for the crossing in roubles or rupees in one of the deep pockets in their tunics and eventually they would sink their poles into the sandy river bed. They did not ask for travel papers, but often, following a sudden whim or their own sure instinct for gauging the depth of the potential client's purse, they would ask double the price or even more, well aware that they were indispensable. For those without a horse or other long-legged animal, the ferrymen provided the only way of crossing the river dry-shod.

The river was subsequently bridged by Soviet engineers, and then ferries and turbans were replaced by reinforced concrete piers, and by eight hundred metres of 'friendship'. While it was perhaps not foreseen from the outset that the bridge would be crossed by tanks and armoured divisions, it is certain that they too crossed it in the name of friendship on their way to Kabul. When there was no more talk of friendship, only the name of the bridge was left to recall it, thrown up as if in mockery to link the two banks in sullen enmity. Today the bridge is closed by a barrier with a notice over it in two languages, Russian and English. Anyone wishing to cross must have a special travel permit, and in addition pay a toll of five dollars if on foot, ten if in a car, fifteen if driving a truck. The triple obstacle, barrier, travel permit and toll, means that very few venture onto the eight-hundred-metre stretch of deeply ambiguous friendship. The Amudar'ya has become the bridge's prisoner, guarded by rows of missiles and panzer tanks, and kept under surveillance by radar and sentries. The mighty river now runs between two armoured banks, virtual fronts in a war suspended above the bridge. Even the tumbled walls of the old Buddhist monasteries and the crumbling stupas have been imprisoned behind barbed wire. In my day, sheep grazed there as their shepherd sat in the shade of a pagoda built of tufa, at the feet of a bodhisattva whose head had been eroded by the wind.

There are no nomads left north of the Amudar'ya. We were among the last; indeed the Tunshan were also the last to cross the last open border to the east, so stubborn were they in their refusal to settle down and become farmers. The other nomad tribes, which had remained within the borders of the Soviet Union, were forced to yield to the inflexible plans of the bureaucrats. They pitched their yurts beside new brick houses and never dismantled them again. These yurts can still be seen scattered across the high ground beyond the cultivated strips of farmland, but now they serve merely as summer pavilions, because they are cooler and airier than houses in the summer.

Perhaps the Tunshan still pitch and strike their tents beyond the Pamir, in Sinkiang, and perhaps there are other rivers for them to ford with their horses and camels. If I have not been able to follow them on their great journey to the East, but have had to take the path to the West alone; if today I no longer bear the name of the Tunshan which was my father's and my father's father's, but that of Berger; if the river I can glimpse from the roof terrace of my house in the city is the Rhine; if all of this is so, it is because during the years of my childhood a more violent wind than the *karaburan* and the *afghanetz* together dragged millions of lives along with it, brought them crashing down and entangled them one with the other, like *kuraj* bushes when the wind rolls them into an inextricable tangle of branches and then abandons them in the vast emptiness of the steppe.

3

IT WAS THE morning of my tenth birthday. In fact at that time I was still ignorant of exact dates; the days unfolded before me with no need of a written calendar, for they were marked by the phases of my nomadic life. Not that we ignored a date as important as that of a birth. On the contrary, the midwives carefully noted the day and the hour of the birth so that the lama could predict the baby's future. However, they kept secret the place where the placenta had been buried, so that evil spirits could not find it out and harm the child. I remember how, three days after my cousin Temüjin was born, I came upon Qada'an crouched down by the threshold inside the yurt. She had lifted the layers of felt and carpets that made up the floor and was digging a large hole in the bare earth. I looked at her in amazement, unsure whether I should come in. 'What are you doing, Qada'an?' As though seized by a sudden doubt, my eyes searched for Temüjin, but the inlaid cradle hung motionless in its usual place over Qada'an's bed; the baby could just be seen inside, all wrapped up in his coverlet and held down with cords to stop him falling out, but he was certainly asleep. 'What are you doing?' I asked again but Qada'an went on digging with the anxious air of someone who fears being caught out in a secret activity. She did not answer, but only gestured towards a little basket on the ground near her containing an object wrapped in felt. She placed the basket carefully in the hole and covered it with earth, then, as she was replacing mats and carpets, she looked round, as though worried that she could be overheard. She said to me, 'It is part of my baby. I put it in the lap of the earth. May Golumta-eke protect it!' Golumta-eke, the mother of our hearth, protected the yurt and those who lived in it. Qada'an was entrusting her son to her and I, present by chance at the rite, was let in on a secret intimately connected with the baby's birth and became in a sense responsible for its protection, more than I already was by virtue of our kinship. I kept the secret and told nobody where Temüjin's afterbirth was buried. I don't know on the other hand where the burial place is of the placenta which surrounded me at birth, but it was certainly committed to the earth at our winter campsite, south of the Amudar'ya, where the plain meets the valleys of the Hindu Kush, which roar with melt water in March.

The people in the nearby villages called the place 'Birbesc', the five fountains. Indeed, not far from the river, which disappeared in the summer heat, there were five springs of crystal-clear water, which flowed out into five natural basins, white as chalk. In the sunlight they were the colour of the tiles on the mosque of Mazar-e Sharif, as though its domes had been turned upside down and filled with water. A long time ago someone had dug an opening in the rock and made a channel with crudely piled stones cemented with lime, to catch the water. In summer the place became a drinking trough. The ground all about was trampled and chewed up by thousands of hooves, and resembled the surface of a lake disturbed by a constant breeze. The water which overflowed from the channel disappeared instantly under the layer of dung into which it sank as though on a heath. Not a plant or a bush grew there, for the insatiable hunger of all the passing ruminants had turned the area into a desert. In early March when the green of new growth crept over the steppe the ground around the springs remained bare, except for little plants with tough stems and small yellowish flowers dotted about. I vividly remember Bairqan bending down to break off a stalk to examine it more closely and then shaking his head and turning to Borrak, his youngest son, who was following on foot leading his horse by the reins, and to me, the favourite among all his grandchildren, who was hanging about him as usual: 'There are more of them every year,' and he showed us the stalk in confirmation of his words. 'They come up through the dung and can survive anything,' Bairqan said, 'even twenty years ago there were none around here.' Now it is Borrak who picks up the plant to study it, and throws it away with the same disdainful expression as his father's. Of all his sons, Borrak was the one who most resembled him, in face, gestures and voice, so much so that he might have been a reincarnation before his time.

'If animal numbers go on rising we will end up being eaten by the sheep.' Anybody who has been close to a grazing herd as it approaches will understand how much of a threat lies hidden in the harmless appearance of sheep peacefully at pasture, how much noise is caused by the shuffle of restless hooves and what an indefinable panic can be caused by the buzz of jaws tearing at the grass. My grandfather Bairqan was right; the herds of Karakul were a scourge to us. They spread over both banks of the Amudar'ya like felt mats drying in the sun; they fouled the drinking holes and they took over grazing traditionally reserved for horses. There was bad blood between the shepherds and the breeders of horses like us. In winter, however, the damage caused by all the grazing and trampling was less obvious. The sods of turf kicked up round the drinking trough at Birbesc hardened and the limestone basins blazed clear blue like a mirage in the desert. The surface was often covered with a layer of ice and underneath the bubbles rising to the surface formed kaleidoscopes of currents.

We children threw stones as far as we could, and the winner was the one who succeeded in breaking the ice nearest to where the water gushed up into the basin. My cousin Malik was a superb shot and often quarrelled with his younger brother Ali, who would ignore the starting line even though it was clearly visible against the whiteness of the snow. When it was my turn I would concentrate long and hard, calculating the distance, lean in the direction of the basins as far as I could without losing my balance or overstepping the mark on the ground, and then I would throw my stone, but I hardly ever succeeded in hitting even the edge of the basin. Then Malik would laugh, sure of his victory.

I was born at Birbesc on the thirtieth of January 1938.

The yurt was full of steam and smoke. Flames licked at the bottom of the cauldron, and the women around it fed the fire constantly. The smoke flowed sluggishly through the hole in the middle of the yurt, blown back in by the wind outside that lashed furiously at it, and hung in the air inside. The women sweated with the heat and the damp which had built up during the days of continuous waiting; only my mother Börte trembled under her sheepskin covers. Shivers racked her as Mai Ling lifted her head and held the cup of *kumiss* mixed with the infusion the shaman had made to her lips. My mother managed to swallow a few drops, then fell back on the mattress, racked with fever. 'There are two of them,' Ügedelegü had pronounced some time earlier. He was the man with most offices in the three clans: tamer of spirits and doctor at the same time, he was called when a child had the fever or stomach ache and it was feared that jinn were involved, or worse, Albasty; when a birth was expected, to pray for a happy outcome; when some obscure sickness threatened the livestock; when someone became suddenly disturbed and began to speak senselessly; when anybody wanted to go on a journey, to know if there were demons opposed to it; to plan a good marriage. Ügedelegü was always ready to hasten over, to recite the occasional simple charm, to preside over a ceremony or to administer potions. Each time he brought with him his baggage of drum and sacred book and, above all, the aura he had of being in direct contact with the spirits of heaven and earth. To look at him moving around the *ayil* and going about his daily tasks like the rest of us, nobody would have perceived such exceptional abilities in him; but his face, which was broad and lean, sometimes darkened, as though a winged demon had passed before it, and when we watched him walk we sometimes had the impression that an invisible throng followed him everywhere, jostling him, importuning him to the point where he had to flail around with his arms, as though to drive away a swarm of flies. Given his authority in the most diverse areas, Ügedelegü's yurt was pitched right opposite the khagan's and therefore near that of the women, where my mother sweated and trembled in the throes of puerperal fever. Ügedelegü had been right, when he touched her prematurely distended belly and predicted that 'there are two of them and it will be a difficult birth.' I, Naja, had come into the world first, followed an hour later by my brother Ginchin. When my father saw the newborns he made two cuts in the central weight-bearing pole of the yurt at the point where it forked: the two lives, first joined in my mother's body, were now separated from her. From this moment we would be two and at the same time one in the blood we shared.

After the birth, however, had come the fever, unexpected and tenacious; the women around my mother spoke in low voices. Ukin, who was the oldest and knew what words to whisper to the spirits, repeated as if to herself: 'If ever I offered you the *kumiss* of the first milk, if ever I sprinkled the ground before my yurt for you, if ever I gave you meat from the lamb of the first milk, Momo of the white hair, Momo who walks on the Mountain of Dawn, Momo who rides a grey mare with not a dark hair, a mare who has not yet given birth, Momo drive the fire from the breasts which have not yet been able to give milk, Momo drive your enemy Albasty back into the kingdom of the black *Tengri*, Momo, oh, Momo, relieve the suffering of these children who have not yet tasted their mother's milk.' But Momo the celestial grandmother was not listening, and the women shuddered as though they heard around them Albasty's coarse laugh as she shook her yellow hair, knotted like felt cords, and tossed her pendulous, dry dugs over her shoulders as though they were the flaps of a tunic.

Ügedelegü was summoned. For three nights running the shaman wore his ceremonial dress laden down with bells and the falcon feathers over his eyes, and pleaded with the spirits and pursued them on his drum into the beyond. For three nights he filled the yurt with his cries and with his impotent fury. He had a live lamb placed on my mother's belly; he had the blood of a dead lamb poured over her forehead as she burned with fever; he ordered wild tulip bulbs to be mixed with powdered bone, and in the end, quite drained, he collapsed onto the carpets by the bed of the sick woman, his goatskin drum between his knees, his eyes closed. Then as though he remembered suddenly that he had not finished his task, he began to speak again in fits and starts. His voice rose on higher notes, to fall then into a monotonous chanting, accompanied by the shiver of the bells sewn all round the rim of the drum. Every now and then Ügedelegü rose and felt my mother's forehead, then resumed his post and his voice, fired up again by one last desperate act of will, soared for a moment, expressing a command rather than a prayer or a plea. My mother asked for us, and Mai Ling obediently picked us both up and, holding a baby in each arm, smiled as she showed us to my mother: 'They are beautiful, Börte, they are healthy.' My mother, in her fever, seemed to smile the ghost of a smile, and tried to say 'Take care of them!' but she could not get the words out, and trembled. And meanwhile somebody in the yurt held me to her warm breast, but it was not my mother.

It had been a particularly cold winter. The ground was covered with a frozen crust which the horses tried in vain to nuzzle aside to get to the few blades of grass trapped underneath. They were on edge and would jerk their long necks backwards and whinny with hunger. A third of the sheep were butchered early. The hay which we carried with us in reserve for the winter was not enough and we had to go looking for more in the villages of the Uzbek farmers, several hours' journey from our yurts. They usually refused, as they too were short of provisions, but somebody, perhaps with a daughter to marry off in the spring, would accept the exchange which necessity made so favourable: a woollen wedding saddle-cloth, woven in the warm red which our women knew how to extract from madder and in the patterns which they had learnt from their mothers, in exchange for a few sacks of straw, so that the horses at least might be saved.

It was difficult to find enough wood to make a pyre worthy of my mother. The men went in search of it as far as the valley of the Surk, where the valley steepens and narrows towards the Hindu Kush and the first woody bushes appear, twisted and barely clinging to the rock and with their roots sticking out into the air like fossilised snakes. As they walked up the stony river bed, my father's horse Dari, so called because his coat was tawny like a deer's, went lame. To part with your horse before time, or worse still, to have to end his life with your own hands so that he does not suffer, is almost as serious for a nomad as the loss of a near relation or a friend, because a horse is a carefully chosen friend, lovingly trained. When the choice is well made and the training complete, horse and rider are one being, each profoundly sensitive to the most minute vibrations in the body and mind of the other. My father returned to the village suffering from this double loss and tormented by the most grievous forebodings. Not even the presence of the newborns could cheer him. It is not impossible that the decision he took so soon afterwards, and which would so irrevocably change the course of my life, though it had only just begun, was in some way linked to that fatal succession of sorrowful events.

For days the snowstorm prevented us from lighting the pyre on which my mother waited to begin her journey to the kingdom of Erlig Khan. When my grandfather told me all this, the child that I was saw my mother in front of me, white as a statue in the middle of the snow-covered plain. I saw her wrapped in a mantle of fire, and I imagined her spirit flying to take refuge in the warmth of another being, perhaps inside an unborn foal who would welcome it and hold it in itself and in April would give it new life. I liked to think of her in this new body while I stroked the velvety neck of the filly born a few months after me, and whispered in its ear; she turned her head and nodded in answer. I was firmly convinced that she contained my mother's spirit, but of course I did not reveal to anybody, still less to my cousin Malik, this childish interpretation of a complicated doctrine, which very few of the Tunshan would have been able to explain anyway. 'I will call her Börte,' I had announced proudly, as I knotted ribbons of coloured silk into her mane to make her beautiful for the festival of *julag*. 'That's no name for a horse,' Malik had argued. He was a year older than me and since he had started sleeping on the men's side he had assumed this knowing air, as though the initiation into the privileges of the male sex conferred ultimate authority on him in all spheres of life. 'Horses are called Erleg or Üle, or Bughural or Boro. Börte's no name for a horse.'

His tone was categorical, but I stood my ground: 'I'm calling her Börte all the same: she's blue-grey like a wolf and "Börte" means exactly that and if you don't know that it means you weren't listening when grandfather Bairqan told us and if you don't stop acting like a khagan I'll tell him.' My cousin shrugged: 'Call her what you want, but it's no name for a horse!' Exasperated, I had to let him have his say, and he took the opportunity to tell me again that that wasn't a horse's name. Fundamentally, I suppose he was right. After all, Börte was much more than a mere filly with a grey-blue coat, since she was mother and friend at the same time, and returned my affection and the trust that I placed in her.

I wanted to be the one to milk Börte and when they let me do it I carried out the task with the pride of a child who feels itself to be participating in an adult rite. I performed the gestures I had seen so often with the meticulousness of somebody who is aware of their importance and who knows that the outcome depends on exact repetition. I tied Börte to the highest rope and her foal to the one on the ground so that mother and son were touching, but the foal could not reach her teats; I squatted down by the horse's flank, balanced the wooden bucket on my left leg, with the handle over my wrist, so as to be able to hold it and direct it, and finally passed my right arm behind the horse's leg. I thus hugged Börte's hind leg and leant my forehead and nose against her thigh, as though we were a couple discovered in a tender embrace. In that position my fingers searched blindly for her nipples and I squeezed them with all the strength and at the same time all the tenderness of which I was capable.

It was Börte who accompanied me on my last journey, the journey west, on paths known only to nomads and smugglers. When Bairqan, my uncle Borrak and I boarded the train at Nusaybin, the last Turkish station on the Baghdad Railway, I handed the reins to Malik, who was staying behind with the others: 'I am giving you my Börte, treat her as though she were yours.' My cousin nodded and, because he was afraid he would betray the unmanly emotion he felt, said nothing; he didn't even remind me how unsuitable that name was for a horse but bowed his head, clutching Börte's reins along with those of his own Erleg. For a long time I watched them from the train as it moved slowly westwards, the boy standing by the platform, holding both horses by their bridles, and Börte rubbing her muzzle along her neck and making it swing gently from side to side as if to say farewell.

4

COLOGNE WAS BURIED deep in the chill. It was one of the coldest winters in living memory. My father had taken me by the hand and we had walked down the avenue of limes to the banks of the Rhine. The river, a long white strip clasping boats, ferries and barges firmly to its sides, was covered with sharp-sided blocks of ice, resembling waves that had been petrified in the midst of a violent storm. My father was in high spirits, as though the freezing weather had melted old memories of his; he waved his arms, pointed at the river and explained to me, who understood so little, the races he had taken part in as a child, jumping on the ice and letting himself be dragged along for a little while by the still flowing current. Children dared each other back then, too, and used to jump in small groups from the bridge onto the floating lumps of ice. I had seen the Amudar'ya frozen only once, but the surface of the river was smooth and when you crossed it on foot you felt as though you were walking on a white carpet spread out between the banks, bringing them mysteriously closer together. This river was not so wide and anyway there were bridges between the banks. Bridges? The one my father was pointing to was sinking into the river. It seemed to have plunged into the water and now it was trapped in the ice and could not get free. Twisted steel cables coiled and curved out of it, trying in vain to reach the other stump on the right bank. Further away, towards the north, another bridge, an identical mass of iron and steel, hung motionless in the middle of the river. I looked at them in astonishment and my father explained, while I, not understanding his words, imagined the catastrophe hidden under the tangle of metal.

The frost had redesigned the gate in front of the Mendel family villa. I remember stopping to look, so pretty was it, with the sun shining and reflecting the curves of the tulip shapes in the wrought iron. The gate was barred, like the villa, which had been closed since the family disappeared one night, but the two white cherubs on either side of the gate were still there, plump and laughing; the plaster decorations round the windows were undamaged and even the grey tiles on the steep roof were all in place, neatly arranged one over the other like fish-scales. The war had passed over the Villa Amélie without harming it. Only the people weren't there any more and no heir returned to open doors and windows. We lived nearby; the garden of the villa was on the corner of the Schiller-strasse, and the Bergers' house was two or three gates down from the corner. Our gate, which was not as beautiful as the one belonging to the villa, but which was iron too, left an arc in the hard snow as it opened, which became a bit harder and shinier every time it swung open. Marianne had sprinkled large handfuls of sand and pebbles or gravel on the path leading up to the door, as though she were sowing grain; every time I came in she warned me to clean the soles of my boots well and to take them off straight away and she helped me by pulling, while I held onto the seat so as not to be dragged towards her chest along with the boots. Then I would sink my feet in their hand-knitted woollen socks into felt slippers that reached to my ankles, because the floor was cold despite the carpets and my mother lived in fear of pneumonia. We couldn't heat the whole of the large house, for fuel was scarce that year and briquettes of coal arrived at the house almost in secret; they were sent to us by our grandfather who was a district medical doctor and had an extremely wide acquaintance, outside the city too. The Bergers didn't need to attack the wagons waiting at the station, as many people did in Cologne, to fill sacks and carts with coal. In any case, 'organising' was the only way to survive in the ruined city and everyone, man, woman and child, was involved in it in some way or other, to such an extent that Bishop Frings had given a general absolution to all those who organised. 'Now you can steal with the Church's blessing,' my mother had commented indignantly. Our grandfather's blessing and that of my father's friends were enough for us to light the stoves even in those cold months.

In fact only the rooms on the ground floor were warm: the little dining room, my father's study, my mother's sitting room and the kitchen; the drawing room was not heated, and so stayed closed throughout the winter. The rooms on the first floor, where we slept, and on the second floor, where Hannah, Marianne and Käthe slept under the steep mansard roof, were always cold. Every evening Marianne would put a hot-water bottle in my bed so that I would have a little warmth in which to curl up. She was convinced that I came from a hot country and that I couldn't bear the cold, and even later never failed to give me knee socks for Christmas which she knitted herself; they were warm but so stiff that I could hardly get my feet into them and so rough that they left my skin red all over; furthermore they were always the colour of egg yolk, halfway between white and bright yellow, because the wool was undyed. I was resigned to putting them away in a drawer along with other unusable objects which I amassed in those years, and to remembering the good intentions of the woman who had made them. Marianne did not know that it is not temperature that counts, so much as the way in which one is used to dealing with cold or heat. The winters were harsh at Birbesc, but I would be wrapped in lambskin, my feet warm in leather boots covered with felt, and I did not feel the wind cutting my face and spitting crystals of frozen snow at me. But in Cologne, wearing a dress which did not cover my legs and a little woollen sweater which restricted my arm movements, I did not feel sheltered. The rooms had high ceilings, too, as well as cold floors insufficiently covered by thin carpets. The house never held the cosy heat of a yurt. There were warm places and cold places and doors separating them, and there was always somebody shouting at you to close the door, not to let the heat out. In that house, heat and cold were two demons which we had to keep in and out, respectively, and there were precise rituals for doing it.

I had instinctively chosen for myself the warmest and cosiest place in those rooms where everything was strange to me and I had no place to be. In the dining room, in the middle of one wall, there was a large white porcelain stove, which was lit in the mornings. I would snuggle down beside it, having decided that this might be the place where the spirit of the house lived. I put myself in a sense under the goddess's protection and curled up the way I would in the yurt in the place set aside for the youngest children, my left leg folded under me, my right knee under my chin. I would stay in that position for long stretches of time, looking from the corner by the stove at what was going on around me, as the heat spread sweetly through my limbs. Every now and then Marianne would come up to me and bend over me with her knees slightly flexed, her hands on her thighs. She would say something to me, speak to me and I would understand by her tone that she was trying to persuade me to move. Sometimes she lost patience and would pull me up by one arm, make me sit at the table and put a plate in front of me. But I would hardly touch that food, because I did not recognise it and not even hunger could overcome the suspicion that it was black food. Moreover I didn't know how to get it to my mouth, because I didn't know how to use cutlery. Marianne would shake her head and bring me a glass of milk with lots of sugar, the only thing I would accept. My mother would appear briefly from time to time at the door of the dining room and disappear again immediately, as though the sight of me terrified her. I thought that she did not dare to approach me because she believed I was a harmful being and I would curl up even smaller in my corner between wall and stove, and stay there even longer. I must have felt then like Princess Toli Gö Dagina, who lived in the land of Aikhan, on the banks of the River Sün, when she woke up one morning and wasn't in her white yurt any more, but in an unknown tent, in a country further away from where she lived than the place you get to if you travel for ninety-nine years. Erkhem Khar, the son of a powerful *Tengri*, had brought her there in the night, wishing to make her his wife. But the princess knew the art of shortening distances and making far places near, and she shortened the distance of ninety-nine years into ninety-nine months, then from ninety-nine months into ninety-nine days, then from ninety-nine days into ninety-nine hours, until Toli Gö Dagina returned in a single night to the white tent of her father Agi Bhran Khan. But I wasn't Princess Toli Gö Dagina, and I didn't know how to join the sun and the moon and stop them in their courses, or how to wake the dead and make fruit grow on the branches of a dead tree. I didn't know how to shorten the road home and my country was much, much further away than the ninety-nine years of the fairy tale.

The day of my birthday I knew nothing. After lunch my grandfather had come to collect me, and side by side we had walked down the avenue of limes to the park, then down to the Rhine; then grandfather had pulled his watch out of his pocket and we had hurried back. Marianne put my felt slippers on and then took me by the arm and pushed me firmly but affectionately towards the dining room. On the other side of the frosted glass door I could see lights and hear voices. I hesitated and my grandfather beckoned me in. Marianne gave me a firm push; I went in and my first impulse was to run away. Everybody was looking at me from where they sat round the table covered with white linen; my mother stared at me with that anxious air she had, my father with his usual hesitant expression, my grandmother, a German from the Volga, spoke to me in Russian; she was convinced that I must understand at least a little of that language, because I came from Stalin's country. *Ach ty bedny rebyonok*, she said to me, poor sweet child, and though I did not understand I sensed the compassion in her voice, felt tears come to my eyes and longed to run away. Beside her sat Dr Wallatz, whom I did not yet know, scrutinising me like an art critic faced with an old painting whose period and value he is to estimate.

I did not know the reason for this meeting, and, more perplexing still, I didn't understand the seating plan. Why was my grandfather not sitting at the head of the table, but pointing me to it, why were my mother and my grandmother sitting opposite rather than beside each other, why was the stranger with the authoritative air sitting at the other end beside my father? I sat where I was told to and everybody began all together to try to make me understand; my father showed me the paper I had had with me in the leather bag around my neck when I arrived, and pointed with his finger to a date, forgetting that I did not know the meaning of written signs. An impatient Marianne repeated several words over and over breaking them up into syllables so that I might understand better: *Es ist dein Geburtstag*, it's your birthday, don't you understand, *dein Ge-burts-tag*.

I knew the year, the day and the hour when I was born, but at home it is not a particular cause for celebration. When we celebrate the beginning of the new year, in February, everybody adds a year to their own age and the animals too are not excluded from this collective birthday. But while the exact date of birth is important for each individual, because it determines his earthly fate and even the manner in which he passes over to the beyond, it is of little importance to the clan whether he saw the light on the first day of the waning moon, in the month of the mouse or the dragon, in the month when cows begin to give milk or when the snow turns to water on the threshold of the yurt. The number of years, on the other hand, affects everyone. When I neared nine, at the approach of the new year they began to talk with growing agitation round the yurts of our *ayil* about Mongotai, an uncle of Bairqan who was almost eighty-one years old. They talked about it in lowered voices, not so much because they were afraid that their words would reach the old man's ears, which were by now weak, but rather because at home we don't talk about things that bring bad luck, or we talk about them in low voices, in order not to summon the spirits. The eighty-first year was considered unlucky not only for the person who reached it, but for all their family and for all the clan, because the cycle of nine had then repeated itself nine times. Every nine years we had to follow a particular ritual. I, who would turn nine at the beginning of the new year, would have to look for nine black stones and nine white ones, spread a white and a black sheepskin out in the yurt and pour river sand over them, while Mai Ling prepared a little doll made of dough. Ügedelegü's incantations would transfer the bad luck from the assembled objects to the little doll and would make the doll suffer the misfortunes which awaited me on the threshold of the ill-omened year instead of me.

If the passage from the first to the second cycle of nine required such an expense of energy, how many and what kind of objects would Mongotai now have to gather? How many words would it take to expel such a powerful multiple as eighty-one? Luckily the Tunshan knew that when maleficent influences cannot be exorcised, the only way out is to get rid of what caused them. But how would one get rid of a year of life? The Tunshan did not lose heart so easily. Time belongs to men, who therefore have the right not only to measure it, but also to shorten or lengthen it as required. In the case of my uncle Mongotai, they had to carry out a rather delicate operation on time which required cunning and a great deal of tact, given that they had to confuse the spirits, shortening the current year so that they could bring forward the old man's birthday and reduce the unlucky eighty-first year to a period of just a few weeks. The devisers of this plan did not underestimate the risks inherent in such an operation, because if the spirits happened to notice the deception, they would certainly fill the brief time available to them with even greater disasters. The preparations were made almost in secret and only the closest family members knew what was going on.

A few weeks before the end of the year we went to Mongotai's *ayil*. His children and grandchildren were already gathered in his yurt; presents were exchanged and everybody took their places according to etiquette, then the ceremony began, which consisted according to Tunshan custom of a large dinner. When the guests went back to their own yurts in the dark of the night, Mongotai's birthday had happened before everybody else's. As they left, everybody wished him luck for the short time still to run before the end of his eighty-first year, their wishes made warmer and more sincere by the vodka they had drunk. A few weeks later, Mongotai had his birthday along with everybody else and everyone congratulated him on getting through the terrifying tangle of nines unscathed.

That memorable birthday party was the only one I could remember. How could I understand the reason for this celebration now? And even if I had understood that it was my birthday, why take so much trouble over such an unimportant year as the tenth?

Sitting at the table, in the place of honour which in my opinion was unsuitable for the youngest person present, I thought that this was the feast of the beginning of the year and I wondered why in that case I was the centre of attention, and I was even more astonished when my mother held out a big box to me with a pink bow on it. I felt everybody's eyes on me as I untied the ribbon and looked at what was inside the box without daring to take it out. A blonde doll looked out at me with blue glass eyes. She wore a wreath of silk flowers in her hair, a pink frilly dress, and little silk slippers. At the slightest movement of my arm, heavy eyelids closed over the glass eyes and the doll, snug in her cardboard box, seemed to be lying in a coffin. In my embarrassment I continued to shake the flowered box and the obedient doll lowered and raised her eyelids, looking at me with her glass eyes. My mother gestured to me to take her out. She was watching me more anxiously than ever, so tense as she waited for my reaction that she was almost trembling; I was afraid she would burst into tears. In the confusion of sounds I heard at that time without fully understanding their meaning, I searched for a word which would help me; I rummaged through the images I had accumulated. I remembered the postman holding out a parcel to Hannah, and Hannah putting coins into his hand, saying '*Danke*'; the boy coming and going from the gate to the kitchen door at the back of the house with big sacks of potatoes on his back; every few steps one of his clogs, which were too big for his feet, would fall off, and he would have to turn round again to put it back on. Marianne had filled his pockets with potatoes and the boy had said '*Danke*' to her and had clattered off, hunched inside his military greatcoat as though he still had the sacks of potatoes on his back. Then I too said '*Danke*' and saw my mother's eyes light up suddenly. For the first time since I had come to the house, the anxiety left her face and her lips curved in a faint smile. The others became convivial, as though an unexpected order had freed them from the awkwardness that had restrained them until that moment, and they released the tension in a round of applause for the cake that Marianne put down triumphantly on the table.

The cake, with its topping of whipped cream bristling with candles, held everybody's attention. 'I haven't seen a cake like that since before the war'; my grandmother's comment was an offer to cut into this soft and sugary vision, and with the gesture of a high priestess sinking the knife into the throat of the sacrificial lamb, she dug the silver cake slice into the orange-white confection, cut it into slices and loaded up the plates which were held out to her one by one. I found myself facing a large slice, lying languidly on the porcelain plate, displaying its insides in alternating layers of biscuit and vanilla cream.

I don't know if I noticed the taste, concentrating as I was on carrying the spoon to my mouth without letting the mass of quivering gelatine slide off, and on holding the cup of chocolate by the handle and raising it, without letting even a drop fall and sully the whiteness of the tablecloth. Having to sit on a chair at table and to use cutlery made mealtimes with the others a torment. I couldn't taste the food; I barely ate a thing, and if without thinking I stretched out a hand towards the dish in the middle of the table, my mother's 'no' would stop me in mid-air and I would pull my hand back in shame, like a puppy caught sniffing at his master's plate and being slapped back to his place. And yet I had been dexterous at using my knife to cut meat, which at home was presented in large pieces on a communal plate; everybody helped themselves when it was their turn, lifted a piece to their mouth and cut it with their own knife. My cousin Malik proved to be particularly skilful at this too; holding the meat in his teeth, he would slice it with the knife so close to his lips that we smaller children would watch with bated breath, afraid that we would see him dripping blood from one moment to the next. Bairqan laughed: 'If Malik had a nose like his cousin Haysce he would cut a slice off it every time.' Malik, who had the short nose of the Mongols, pulled a face in reply to the jest, while Haysce, who was proud of her Greek nose, shrugged and didn't laugh. Our table manners involved knowing how to use a knife. I remember my aunt Qada'an repeating to Temüjin, who preferred to rip the meat off the bone with his teeth: 'Are you a dog, then, that you can't use a knife?' When stubborn Temüjin still refused to use it, my aunt lost patience with him and hit him with the bone that he had just finished stripping with his teeth.

The pink doll went to join her sisters on the white chest of drawers in my bedroom, and she had to wait a long time before finding arms to cuddle her. I didn't play with dolls. At home, as soon as little girls reached the age at which they are sent to school elsewhere, or even earlier, they have little brothers or cousins to look after. They don't need pretend children. I didn't even look at those dolls arrayed on the chest of drawers, some sitting, others standing with the eternally serious look of good children, all occasionally dusted by a distracted Kathe. They were important to my mother, though; sometimes she would come into my room, and perhaps because she thought I was too shy to play with them or afraid I might break them, she would encourage me. Once she tried to show me how; she reached into the pushchair and pulled out a fat little baby doll wearing a lace robe and a nappy between her legs, held together with a safety pin, and she took her in her arms and rocked her. As she did this, my mother's face filled with tenderness, as though she were holding a real baby. Lost in the sweetness of the act, she remained like this for a little while, oblivious of me as I looked at her in astonishment. Then she came to, blushed a little, and with a gesture at once embarrassed and imperious, held the doll-baby out to me, inviting me to do the same. This time it was I who was confused, holding the doll in my arms, undecided as to whether to imitate my mother. Suddenly I thought of Temüjin, and how I used to carry him on my shoulders as we chased each other round the *ayil*. I put the doll on my eiderdown, looked around and saw the embroidered cloth on the round table by the window. I moved the vase of silk flowers, folded the cloth into a triangle, put it on the bed and arranged the doll on it, in the middle, so that only her little curly head stuck out. Then I folded the point of the triangle over between her plump little legs, tucked the edge into her nappy, so that it would not slip, leant over with my back to the doll and knotted the corners of the material around my chest, running it under my armpits. Then I put my arm under the doll's bottom and stood up triumphantly, looking for the approval on my mother's face. Her eyes widened in shock, but immediately regained the fearful expression I was familiar with, as she adjusted her hair with a long white hand, disconcerted by this evidence of my irremediable otherness.

5

A FEW DAYS after my birthday, Kathe plaited my hair with special care and my mother pressed a slate and a wide-lined exercise book into my hand, put on her bell-shaped overcoat and took me to see Dr Wallatz. Dr Wallatz lived nearby, a little way round the corner onto the avenue of limes. At that time of the morning the area had an air of chilly desolation, and my mother did not speak. Every now and then she glanced at me and her lips seemed to let out a sound, but they stiffened immediately, as though the words froze even before they were breathed. I began to fear those lips that refused to emit sounds and that nevertheless by this refusal exercised over others a power more subtle than words, forever forcing them to interpret the unsaid. I too began to fall under the doom of those silences, to observe my mother's gestures with apprehension, out of the corner of my eye, searching her face for what her voice did not reveal. That morning, walking beside her, with my slate clutched tight in my hand, it seemed to me that I was reliving the scene of the previous evening, when I had passed in front of the half-open door of my mother's room, heard her call me, and hesitated outside the door, with her beckoning me to come forward.

I had never been in my parents' bedroom before and had seen it only in passing, as Kathe made the bed. It had not been the room itself that struck me but the girl's movements as she moved around the bed with the belligerence of an Amazon, seizing the eiderdowns by two corners of the cover and shaking them violently in the air, as though her intention were to expel the demons imprisoned in them overnight rather than to tame the goose feathers, restoring them to their usual rounded pagoda shape. Now the room seemed quiet and welcoming to me in the light of the lamp on the bedside table. The peach colour of the bedspread softened the dark furniture. My mother was wrapped in a dressing gown of heavy pale pink silk which flowed in royal abundance down to her feet. At home the women wear silk dresses, but only on feast days, when they take off their tunics and leather trousers and wear dazzling *chalat* made of the fabrics that their men buy for them at the market in Bukhara and in the bright colours we cherish. In the Bergers' house, however, brilliant colours such as red, blue and emerald green were banned, and we lived with muted colours in uniform shades, carefully chosen to orchestrate a perpetual harmony of curtains, tablecloths, carpets and fabrics of all kinds.

My mother Siglinde was thirty-four then; her bosom swelled generously under her dressing gown and her waist was slim. Her hair falling loose over her shoulders was a dark chestnut colour, inherited from her great-grandfather Tamburino, who had come from Bergamo nearly a century earlier with nothing in his baggage except the art of casting tin. Great-grandfather Tamburino practised this art with such skill that in the thirty years of his career he never lacked for customers, many of them ecclesiastical, so that he had produced a great number of objects in chased tin and brass for the altars and the private houses of Cologne. As well as the foundry and a remarkable quantity of plates and dishes, many of which were displayed in the Bergers' drawing room, he had bequeathed to his descendants his chestnut hair, which had lightened with the generations but which still appeared every now and then on the head of one of his descendants. Then grandmother Christa would say 'you're the spitting image of great-grandfather Tamburino!' and she said it gaily, but the child would look around lost, as though feeling the weight of some hereditary taint. My mother must have felt like that too, since her sisters were Brunnhildes one and all, while she alone reproduced the image of her great-grandfather, dark and rather short. At ten years old I was almost her height, as our reflections in the dressing table mirror revealed.

'Look, Naja,' said my mother, pointing to the throng of portraits displayed in a semicircle on the chest of drawers, 'do you recognise her?' She pointed at the portrait in the centre, in a heavy silver frame, and handed it to me. A little girl of perhaps twelve months or a little older, sitting on a cushion, one leg folded under her little embroidered dress, a big bow in her fair hair, eyes whose blue could be guessed at. 'Do you know who she is?' She brought the picture nearer so that I could have a closer look and as she did so she glanced from me to the picture, as though to assure herself that she had not missed any hint of an even remote resemblance. But there was no doubt about it; I looked nothing like her. I had nothing in common with that chubby fair-haired child, nothing except the coincidence of our birthdays. I received, however, the confused impression that my mother was comparing me to the portrait; I could sense the disappointment with which she put the picture back in its place, amidst the ranks of framed shadows, and felt how offensive the comparison was.

The feeling I had of having suffered an injustice flared up again that morning too, rekindled by the facial expression my mother seemed to have retained intact since the day before, as though she had done nothing all night but feed it.

* * *

Our arrival at the gate of the Villa Flavia was announced by a pair of lions sitting on pillars on either side of the entrance, holding two shields in their right and left paws respectively which said 'Villa' and 'Flavia'. In order to read the names one's eyes necessarily lighted on the mild, resigned expressions on the faces of the two lions, which were more like tame animals than wild beasts. My mother pushed the gate open to reveal a garden shrouded in frozen snow. I was instantly struck by the tree in front of me, a huge cone, tapering towards the top and so intensely green that winter seemed to have no power over it. It appeared to be carved by hand, and in a sense it was, but since I was not yet acquainted with Dr Wallatz's secateurs and the precision with which he attacked unruly twigs that dared to disrupt his geometrical designs, I didn't understand the phenomenon. In any case it wasn't the only plant to be such a peculiar shape, since all the trees and bushes in that garden had been made to measure, manipulated and forced by Dr Wallatz into the most artificial shapes. 'A garden is a living work of art, and the gardener is at once a painter and a sculptor; the secateurs are my brush and nature provides my palette.' Dr Wallatz's artistic judgement was clearly reflected in the box hedges in the shape of parallelepipeds and spirals, in the little cubes of glossy leaves lining the path to the front door and in the abstract geometry of the yew trees. Dr Wallatz had set out to create an Italian garden, under the illusion that this would bring him closer to that beloved and admired country, which historical circumstances had rendered unattainable. 'We Germans are like the Pompeiian faun,' and Dr Wallatz pointed to the little porphyry statue in the middle of the fountain, a copy of the original, acquired on one of his trips to Italy. 'We are always about to take flight, but something always holds us back.' The faun stretched out an arm draped with icicles towards a blank white sky, ready to leave the earth, but held back, or so it seemed, by the transparent mantle hanging from his back and keeping him firmly stuck to his pedestal. So naked in the cold air and so clearly ill at ease, he exuded an air of pathetic impotence rather than of untamed wildness.

* * *

But Maria had already appeared on the doorstep and Dr Wallatz was there in his loden waistcoat. My mother was invited to take off her coat and come inside, but she smiled blankly and walked away down the garden path, the bell of her overcoat swinging around her at every step. My mother was elegant. And I was already being shown in to a room full of books and antiquities, which Dr Wallatz called in Italian 'il mio studiolo'. It was clear that he was particularly attached to this word, not only because he used it frequently, but more than anything because as he said it an expression of inward bliss spread over his face, which was not only satisfaction at his own erudition, but also a kind of childish happiness at successfully sliding down such a cascade of vowels without slipping.

I sat shyly in front of him – seeing my slate reflected in the polished surface of the cherrywood table – and my eyes ran over the bookshelves, crowded with books standing vertically side by side or lying horizontally in untidy piles, and at the big picture in the gilt frame of a landscape with a river in the background and a shepherd in the foreground, with a long thin flute in his hands, and sheep around him. Green like the steppe in spring. But I was even more interested in the picture directly opposite me, which was a portrait of a little girl, more or less my age, executed in soft pastel shades. There was a blue ribbon in her blonde hair and she wore a blue dress with a full skirt like a bluebell. She looked at me with a serious, intent look, from amidst all those bows and that blue. I felt I was being watched. It occurred to me that little Ilse would have been like that at my age, if she had not already been carried away by pneumonia, and she would have sat there plumply on the velvet cushion like a blue-blonde promise. The girl in the picture must also have stopped there, where the portrait had caught her, just as Ilse had not gone beyond the photograph. Maybe she too had remained an unfulfilled promise, trapped amidst lace and bows like Sleeping Beauty in her glass coffin with nobody to wake her. Now she was watching me, with the intelligent eyes of a little girl who knows it all. As for me, I sat there, with my black plaits hanging down the back of the chair, with all those books around me and my black slate in front of me, whose purpose I didn't understand, and I felt awkward and superfluous. My ignorance too began to weigh on me like guilt.

Dr Wallatz stroked the rim of beard round his smooth cheeks and said at regular intervals: 'Well, well,' as though he were summing up our situation and looking for one end of the skein. At one point he got up, saying 'Naja . . . Naja . . .' but not to me, rather to the books on his shelves. He ran his eyes quickly over them, as though expecting an answer. 'Naja . . .', he said, and began to leaf through the book: 'Here we are. *Naja*. Cobra. *Königshutschlange*. Found from the fringes of the tropical forest to the thorny bushes of the steppe.'

'*Naja . . . Naga*', Dr Wallatz went on. 'In Indian mythology the *Naga* and the *Nagini*, king and queen, have since time immemorial been protective spirits of household altars, half-human or entirely human figures, with a great head-dress in the form of a cobra . . .'

Dr Wallatz opened and closed books, oblivious to my presence; he seemed to be following the trails of all the *najas*: '*Naja naja*, common throughout South Asia . . . *Naja sputatrix*, spitting cobra, Indonesia, *Naja nivea*, South Africa and Namibia, bright yellow or dark brown in colour. *Naja oxiana*, Central Asian cobra, Central Soviet Asia, found from the north-east to Kazakhstan. Two, three months of hibernation. The northernmost species of cobra.'

Here was the trail that Dr Wallatz was looking for: the trail of the *naja* that lives on the banks of the Oxus. It had been discovered by a fellow-countryman of his, Eduard von Eichwald, Dr of the Most Excellent University of Heidelberg, more than a century before, on a journey round the Caspian Sea in 1831. The celebrated biologist and ethnographer had made detailed notes on this reptile, which he had come across by chance. Its body was striped in purple/pink, its throat pinkish, its eyes blue: it was a species of cobra hitherto unknown to Europeans, whose habitat was to the east of the Caspian Sea along what had at one time been called the Oxus river.

Dr Wallatz stopped reading, raised his eyes from the book and wrote in ink on a piece of paper: 'Naja', the N tall and winding, the j like a thread looped round itself. 'N-a-j-a,' he enunciated solemnly, separating the four letters from each other, 'we will start here, with *naja*.'

So this was the sign my name left on the paper, a winding blue sign. I who bore that name knew that it came to me from another sign, which had been traced on sand, but which also carried the evidence of its meaning in itself and revealed it to others. Furthermore, as the bearer of that name, I also knew that it was only the outward form of my being: this name had the properties which were in me; it was my nama-karma, which, for reasons which I was not given to understand, linked me with a real and supernatural being like the *naja*.

At home children learn to ride even before they learn to walk or they learn to do both at the same time. They are not yet steady on their legs, they still cling to their mother's skirt and they still fall often, when they are put on a horse for the first time: for the nomads of the Turco-Mongol tribes, a horse's legs are a kind of extension of their own. I was not yet two and it was summer when strong hands lifted me onto the back of a particularly placid mare. 'Ride.' I held onto her mane and I squeezed my legs against the animal's flanks; she moved off slowly, guided by sure hands, but I slipped on her smooth back almost immediately and fell backwards. Freed of my slight weight, the mare walked on calmly down the slope, while I tried on all fours to reach her and left a winding trail behind me on the ground, like the trail of the *naja* when it darts away and if you see it you know the snake is nearby, waiting to strike. The people following me, laughing at my efforts, saw the sign on the ground and knew that my name was Naja.

6

MAYBE THERE WERE *Naga* too in the Bergers' garden, hidden under the bushes stiff with frost, or lurking round the frozen pool, where the paths met. I roamed the lawn warily, watching where I put my feet. Of course I knew that in the winter the *Naga* stay in the warmth of their burrows, and only come out when the sun becomes warm and the ground soft, but I no longer trusted what had been certainties for me until now. In this strange country, perhaps the *Naga* too had other habits and were waiting under the frozen turf for me to pass so that they could bite me. Perhaps they were spying on me. What duties were entrusted to these unknown *Naga*?

At home there were *Naga* who guarded the abodes of the gods, flying *Naga* who ruled the winds and the rain and earthly *Naga* who were the keepers of hidden treasure, but because we lived in the desert and the steppe, the most important for us were the *Naga* who protected the springs, lakes and rivers, the feared and respected guardians of our life source. They were easily met in damp places, but I knew also that the *Naga* did not always show themselves in the guise of snakes. To those whom fortune favours they reveal their true being: princes and princesses who live under the surface of the water or on riverbanks in palaces studded with precious stones. But woe betide those who arouse their anger by treading, even inadvertently, on places sacred to them, and woe betide those who cross their path. The first punishment of the *Naga*, even before the cobra's curved teeth inject their poison which paralyses the limbs and stops the breathing, is terror. Terror paralyses the victim, turns him to stone, blocks the instinct for flight and compels him to stare into the reptile's eyes and suffer the fatal bite.

'Take care,' the children were told, 'where the bushes are thickest and the grass greenest, where water is near and the earth sucks in its moisture and becomes soft, for the cobra nests there, puffs out his chest, hisses, sinks his teeth into your flesh and carries you off to the kingdom of Erlig Khan, as he did with our ancestor Alcidai.' It was true, Alcidai had come back, but, in order not to risk the same fate, we stayed clear of wet grass and marshy banks, while our mothers, to protect us from real *Naga* and to win us the favour of the supernatural ones, cut little elongated figures out of felt, sewed strips of red or blue cloth onto them, attached seed pearls for eyes, and then pinned the little figures to the edges of our clothes, or hung them on a string round our necks. Snakes, and especially cobras, are common where we live, and it was not unusual for them to come into the yurts. For this reason also there were similar amulets tucked inside the wooden lattice of the walls or over the lintels of the doors, where, along with the images of our ancestors, they served to protect possessions and children, to appease the spirits, if they should cross the threshold with malicious intent, and above all to win the clemency of these easily offended beings by demonstrating the respect in which we held them. The *Naga* were part of our lives: we never failed to offer them a taste of our food and of our drinks in little wooden bowls; we made sure to sprinkle them abundantly with *kumiss*, and, at times, to pour melted butter over them.

In May, when we milked those mares who had dropped foals and fermented the milk, we offered the first of the *kumiss* to the spirits of the *Naga* and to those of our ancestors, as we did to all the others we invoked for our protection. This was a special ceremony called *julag*, one of the most important feasts of the year: we counted the months of the year beginning at *julag*, those which had passed since the last one, and those which still remained until the next.

I too tried to count them on my fingers, but I lost count immediately. How many months until the next *julag*? From March onwards we would wait for the lamas to arrive. It was their task to fill the flat wooden basin with the nine channels and sprinkle the first *kumiss* towards the four points of the compass. We all gathered in a circle before the khan's yurt and in the middle of the circle somebody held a recently born foal, all white, which we had decorated with coloured ribbons; its mother, tethered nearby, watched it anxiously. The lama held the basin of *kumiss* and shook it around him, and as he did so he recited, as though singing a litany, the invocation to the gods:

The sun rises through a gap in the clouds,
leaves and flowers grow from an opening in mother earth,
a blessed filly gives birth
and a tender foal tastes

that which no mouth has yet tasted,
a foal just born
tries that which no tongue has tasted!
first kumiss of a strong filly!
first kumiss of a young filly!
first milk of a filly which has borne
her first foal!
A filly has given birth and a foal is born with no dark hair,
she has borne a new being and milk has flowed from her!

Gathered around the lama we watched closely as his arm lowered to dip the ladle of libations in the container and then rose sprinkling white spray around him; as he did his red tunic slid aside and revealed his taut, tanned skin. Gods of the Lamaist pantheon, divinities of nature and the spirits of our ancestors were all named, one after another, as though this prayer were a general address, a kind of annual parade, in which nobody, god or spirit, could be left out. The gods of the tantric paradise passed before us, the buddhas of present, past and future, all the bodhisattvas, the enlightened ones who agree to be reincarnated to teach the doctrine to others, the gods of the afterlife like Yamantaka, god of death, and powers like Esru-a, god of the earth, and Qormusda, god of the eternally blue sky. Then it was the turn of our great ancestor, Genghis Khan:

I, your descendant, make an act of obedience
and I offer this libation
to the lord of the white standard, Genghis Khan,
born by decree of the eternal heavens,
tutelary spirit of all the Mongols,
to him, adorned with silver, with gold and jewels,
who took on the rule of all the earth,
to him, who bore the name Temüjin-bagatur,
to him, born on the banks of the river Onon,
who became head of the uncounted nations,
to Genghis Khan of the illustrious ancestors
who runs without allies

to him kissed by fortune
who had four beautiful wives
and above all the wise Börte
and became lord of all the nations of the earth.
To Genghis Khan, born of the light of a ray of sunshine,
to Genghis Khan, born with power.

The lama spoke in all our names, for we were all descendants of the great khagan, and we listened meekly while all nature passed before our eyes: Mount Sumeru, king of the mountains, saffron, king of plants, Garuda, king of the birds, the panther, queen of fierce animals, and finally the eight *Naga* kings. The shaman offered three times nine libations to all the lakes, mountains, and streams of unknown lands and of lands known to us, as well as to the wells near which we pitched our yurts. He addressed his entreaty to all:

Grant that the foals tethered with rope
be more numerous than the gazelles and the wild horses,
grant that the foals reined in by the bridle
be more numerous than the ducks and the geese.
Grant that they be lords of the green grass
that withers beside the stream.
Let them not fall into wells!
Let them not meet thieves and brigands!
Grant that the master who cares for and rides them
live serene and in peace!
Let my mares have overflowing teats!
Grant that the barren become gravid!
Grant that my foal be at the head of a herd of a thousand
geldings!
Keep sickness and want far from us!
Grant that I, who have adorned this foal and who ride him, have
peace and prosperity without end, until my old age.
Kuraj! Kuraj! Kuraj!

These were the final words, and when the lama spoke them it was a sign that the ceremony was at an end and that our turn had come to taste the first *kumiss*; when the gods and spirits were appeased, we could devote ourselves to feasts and races. Then the white foal was allowed to return to its impatiently waiting mother and seek her teats, while the mare licked its back with her rough tongue and nuzzled at the ribbons adorning it, trying to remove them.

There was no one in the three clans of the Tunshan who did not know the story of Alcidai and of the eight *Naga* kings, and no one who did not know their names by heart, though of course no one could explain why there were exactly eight of them, eight like the spokes of the wheel of life, like the steps by which one climbs to salvation, like the clans of the Tunshan in the distant beginning of their history. We learnt this story when we were small. Children were told that 'the man who does not know his own history is as the monkey who spends his life in the forest; the man who does not know the genealogy of the clan he belongs to is like a dragon carved in jade; the man who does not know the writings which have been passed down and speak of his ancestors is like an exhausted child who is lost.' In order not to seem like lost children, we learnt the genealogy of our people by heart: it was our school.

7

I WHO COULD name all the most celebrated Tunshan and the most famous events of their history felt like that lost child who knows nothing of his people. In those days of endless solitude I repeated to myself the story which Bairqan my grandfather had told us; it seemed to me that by calling to witness the many ancestors who had borne my name I would not be entirely lost. I searched for their presence and that of Bairqan telling stories and that of my cousins, standing around him listening. I went over names and deeds, trying not to leave any out; every detail seemed important to me, as though the mere fact of reciting them from memory made them more real and close. I was not alone in the Bergers' garden or beside the big porcelain stove; I continued to exist and would remain myself as long as I was able – so I thought then – to remember my people.

'We Tunshan are descended from the Tatars . . .' Bairqan told us. We were the Tatar-Tunshan, descendants of the powerful Mongol tribe of the Tatars, the original Tatars, those whom the Chinese called Ta-Ta, not those whom the Europeans later called 'Tartars', mixing sound and semblance, mixing the assonance with the Chinese name and the resemblance to infernal beings, because the nomad hordes seemed to them to have come from Tartarus.

So we were descended from the Tatars, who lived on the banks of the Orsun and grazed their herds on the banks of the blue lake, on the yellow steppe. They were bitter enemies of the tribe from which Temüjin, the future Genghis Khan, was descended. There were ancient enmities between them. Temüjin's father had been killed by the Tatars and it was said that, as he died, he had left his son a legacy of revenge: 'Do not cease to seek vengeance until you have shivered the nails of your five fingers, until you have worn your ten fingers to the bone!' Temüjin did not rest until he had obeyed his father's will. One day his men surprised the enemy tribe at the river Ulz, attacked them from two sides, destroyed their yurts and killed the enemy khan together with all his family. They even carried off the silver crib and the pearl-sewn blankets of his youngest child. In the end, though, among the ruined tents, they found a child, forgotten by the others in their flight, who had a gold ring in his nose and a silk *chalat* lined with ermine and embroidered in gold. They took him to Temüjin, who in his turn gave him as a gift to his mother Hö'elün. She took him with her, named him Sigi Quduqu and raised him as though he were her own son. Sigi Quduqu, the youngest of Genghis Khan's brothers, is the ancestor of the Tunshan.

When Temüjin brought peace to the peoples who live in felt-padded tents, Sigi Quduqu was at his side and was with him at the source of the Onon river, where the Mongols gathered, planted the white banner with the ninety points and gave Temüjin the title of Genghis Khan. Sigi Quduqu followed him when Genghis Khan organised the army in *tümen* of ten thousand men each and began his march of conquest towards the steppes of central Asia, and was at the head of the vanguard when the Mongols crossed the Altai mountains in their push towards the West.

On the Altai pass Sigi Quduqu reined in his horse and turned to look behind him at the line of horsemen trudging up the path along the mountainside. At the bottom he could see the main body of the army, dark against the green of the plain. Further back still, days away, the carts were following, drawn by oxen and camels, and the women and slaves, the rest of the advancing horde. They had left behind them the valleys of the Kerulen and the Onon, the rivers of their ancestors, and though they carried with them, in bags which bumped against their horses' flanks, their spirits and everything they needed for the journey, Sigi Quduqu was troubled in his mind and wondered if he would ever see the plain behind him again, and if the steppes which opened out in front of him would be greener than those he was leaving behind. He looked up to where the mountain rose sheer, still white with snow, and a shiver of a pain he had never felt before shook him: was Genghis Khan not daring too much in his will to conquest? Was he not offending the spirit of this unknown mountain by crossing it? Who were the divinities who protected this unknown country stretching out before them? He only knew the name of the pass and of the river, still young, which burbled to the right of the path down the valley towards Lake Zaysan. It was the Kara Irtysh, the black Irtysh. That name, which bore the doom of an unlucky colour, did not augur well. I will have to make an offering to the spirits of this place when we have pitched the tents, thought Sigi Quduqu to himself.

The rich cities of Transoxania fell. The Mongols, who knew no other way of living than their yurts, stared with a mixture of disbelief and contempt at those who lived in buildings with wooden doors and, closed within walls of dried mud and in immovable houses, spent their lives in one place, like stones which a river has thrown onto the bank and which have remained there.

How easily they burned, the straw roofs of the barns, the wooden lattices of the buildings and the carved pillars holding up the roofs of the mosques. Peoples who could build roads and palaces, but who did not know how to defend themselves, deserved their contempt. At the same time, however, the nomads' greed and fury were aroused by rumours of the riches hidden within the red earth walls, behind the arches in the courtyards of the merchants, under the octagonal roofs of the bazaars, inside the citadels where the palaces with their majolica-tiled walls nestled, and where, behind the windowless walls, storehouses overflowed with goods and in room after room the women huddled. Everything, be it gold, carpets, sacks of grain and rolls of silk, or animals and terrified women hiding behind their veils, everything belonged to the nomads of the eastern steppes, who seized it and carried it all off, to divide it up fairly among themselves later, with some for each *tümen*, some for each general and some for the soldiers escorting them.

Genghis Khan camped on the right bank of the Amudar'ya that autumn, and waited until he could cross the river in spring. He was in no hurry. The winter, which slowed down the headlong race of his soldiers, was the season best suited to government. The great khagan gave audiences in his nine yurts covered with white silk. Seated on a low throne of gilt wood, his legs folded under him, wearing the blue silk *chalat* with the gold ornaments, Genghis Khan gave orders, received messages, distributed honours and rewards.

Sigi Quduqu sat at his right hand, and when Genghis Khan called the commanders of the *tümen* to him to reward them, he said to him, 'Great Khan, you reward your generals, but have my services to you perhaps been of no value? Was my courage worth nothing? From when I was in my cradle until the first hairs grew on my chin I have grown up on your noble threshold. Your mother Hö'elün placed me at her feet, she treated me as a son, she had me sleep beside her, she raised me as your younger brother. How will you now reward me?' Genghis Khan answered: 'Are you not my sixth brother? Here is your reward, little brother: take your share of the spoils, as is due to younger brothers!' This he decided and he went on: 'When we, protected by the eternal heavens, conquered all other peoples, you were my eye to see with, my ear to hear with. Therefore it will be for you to divide these conquered peoples into fair portions, some for your mother, some for your younger brothers and for our sons – according to their rank; you must be the one to divide the people who live in felt-lined tents from those who live behind wooden doors! And let no one disobey your command!' This was Genghis Khan's decision. Then he gave Sigi Quduqu the task of judging according to the law: 'Punish theft! Resolve disputes! Kill those who deserve death, punish those who deserve to be punished!' And he added: 'Furthermore, you must write down on a register all the decisions you make regarding the division of spoils and the law; you will write it in blue in a book and let what Sigi Quduqu has decided in agreement with me and what he has written in blue writing on the white paper of the book not be altered unto our sons and our sons' sons! May any who alter anything in the book be punished!' This was decided by Genghis Khan and he made his younger brother a judge and master of the law, because Sigi Quduqu was, among his loyal followers, one of the few who knew how to write with a bamboo stick.

Sigi Quduqu wrote in the script of the Uighurs, a Turkish people who lived on the border with China, who had learnt this in their turn from the Iranian tribe of the Sogdians, who had learnt it from the Aramaeans. The Mongols on the other hand wrote as the Chinese did from the top of the page to the bottom. The books compiled by Sigi Quduqu contained long vertical columns of linked blue letters, with marginal notes to the left or right. To Genghis Khan, who had never learnt to use them, these letters must have had the none too reassuring appearance of worm-shaped beings which, having debated in vain from one side of the page to the other and left smudges and crossings-out in blue, had remained imprisoned in the paper. Despite the trust he placed in Sigi Quduqu, the great khan continued to regard these signs with suspicion, as though they were perpetually on the point of becoming spoken words again.

*   *   *

Sigi Quduqu followed Genghis Khan from city to city, from conquest to conquest; he pitched his yurt beside that of his brother, transcribed his orders in the book of the law, divided the loot into fair shares for those who had earned it and calmed disputes between the generals of the *tümen*. Genghis Khan was grateful and gave him the hand in marriage of his youngest daughter, Altun, whose step was as light as a filly foal's, and Sigi Quduqu's sons were born one after the other, between a battle and the sack of a city, on the Amudar'ya and at their winter quarters in Samarkand.

When Genghis Khan set off again towards Mongolia, Sigi Quduqu followed with his wives. And sons and daughters were born on the return journey, in the Talas valley and on the Chu river, in the green dales by the Ili and on the banks of Lake Alakol. Here Genghis Khan ordered Sigi Quduqu to stop: he was to remain with his khans to guard the laws of the Mongols and at the same time to keep those peoples who had been most recently conquered at bay. Genghis Khan embraced his brother, took the knife with the gold scabbard from his own belt and gave it to him.

From that day Sigi Quduqu stayed with his people in the land occupied by the White Horde, between the Kyrgyz steppe to the west and the plateaux of Dzungaria and Sinkiang to the east. This was the land scored by the river Ili; the Chu and the Talas bordered it to the south; to the north it was crowned by Lake Alakol and to the west by Lake Balkhash, while the Alatau mountains protected it to the east and the Karatau to the west. This land was scored by rivers and streams which flowed from a thousand springs; it was the land of seven rivers.

8

I TRIED TO guess what was at the end of the street which I could see stretching out, nearly always deserted, beyond the garden. Those few times that someone walked with me to the river we always took the same route; we turned the corner in front of the

Villa Amélie and we went on a short distance to the short cut down the steps which led directly to the riverbank. I wondered if another road began after the Schillerstrasse, and then another, and then another, and so on to infinity, every one the same as the one before, perhaps a little bit wider, because this city was not like Bukhara, where the houses are close to one another and the lanes so narrow that a cart can hardly pass; the people here seemed to want to stay as far away from each other as possible, and to hide from their neighbours' gaze. Winter made them vulnerable, for it revealed their houses behind their walls and gates, and allowed curious eyes to gaze at the arches of the windows and to uncover the nakedness of the statues in the parks. Spring would make them inaccessible again, restoring the intimacy which winter had stripped away to houses and gardens; but spring was still a long way off. The few people who appeared from time to time on the Schillerstrasse seemed to be anxious to get back inside their houses. If they met a chance acquaintance they greeted them hurriedly, rarely stopping to talk. I thought that their haste could not merely be due to the cold, and that their posture did not allow longer conversations. It's uncomfortable to talk standing up, yet nobody hunkered down on the balls of their feet, as we did at home. Here they needed bulky chairs or sofas to be comfortable. When there were none to hand, they stayed standing, but seemed ill at ease, as though this chance meeting prevented them from reaching a longed-for destination and they had to try to extricate themselves as quickly as possible. Marianne and Kathe too, those few times that I saw them exchange a few words with a neighbour on the doorstep, put their bags on the ground, but it was as though they expected at any moment to be called inside, and as they spoke they kept glancing uneasily at the door. Perhaps people met in other places, where I couldn't see them, at the bazaar, which couldn't be far. The women, indeed, never stayed away for long, but came back home before the end of the morning, bent under the weight of baskets and bags which they then emptied onto the kitchen table, as though trying to prove that they had not been out to no purpose. They brought home vegetables, eggs, bread; they didn't have to worry about water as our women did, who came and went with the pitchers on their heads, straight-backed, as though the water weighed nothing at all. Here the water arrived by itself and I wondered if there was somebody underneath pushing it along the pipe. Certainly the other houses each had their own well. This was a fortunate country, I thought, in its own way this too is a land of a thousand springs, even though it is very different from the land described in Bairqan's stories.

The land of seven rivers! At that time I made no real distinction between reality and story. I could have described the plain around Birbesc, where I was born, and the mythic land of the Tunshan, with its rivers and its springs, with the same precision and warmth; not only that, but little by little the countryside round the Amudar'ya, which I had left only a few months before, and the lost land of my ancestors became one and the same in my memory. I shut my eyes and I could see Lake Balkhash appear before me, so huge that the horizon was lost among the reed beds. The Tunshan had lived on its banks, in the valleys which descend along the flanks of the Alatau, a long time ago, and they had left there one day to go down as far as the Amudar'ya.

Sigi Quduqu's yurts were pitched on the banks of Lake Balkhash when one day Alcidai, his eldest son, climbed up into the heights of Em to hunt. There he saw a three-year-old stag and set off after it. He followed it all day and when evening fell and the animal seemed near enough he took an arrow with a tip of cypress wood and shot at the beast. But the stag disappeared in the dense undergrowth around Lake Alakol and vanished from the boy's sight. Alcidai dismounted and explored the grasses, looking for his arrow and for the animal. As he walked along looking at the ground he did not notice that he was getting closer and closer to the water, the ground was becoming wet and his feet were sinking into it. And suddenly he saw a snake in front of him with a flat head and blue eyes. The snake darts at him, bites him, and bending its head backwards, sinks its curved fangs into the young man's warm flesh. The poison comes out of the channel behind its fangs and spreads through Alcidai's body. His strong legs will no longer obey him, nor will his muscular arms; his tongue stiffens against his palate. Then the boy's soul leaves his body and arrives at the kingdom of the eight *Naga* kings, who live beneath the waters of the lake.

Under the surface of Lake Alakol the *Naga* princesses sang to the sound of a twelve-stringed lyre. When Alcidai arrived they stopped singing and said to the princess who had sent him:

'Sister, why have you made this young man come to us before the appointed hour? Can you not see that there is fire in his eyes and splendour in his face? Though he has trodden on the sacred ground of Lake Alakol, his heart was without malice.'

And they turned to Nandi, the first *Naga* king, and said:

'This young man has fire in his eyes and splendour in his face. Let him return to his own people.'

And Nandi turned to Ubanandi, the second *Naga* king, and said:

'This young man has offered us libations of *kumiss*; he has given us his food to eat and the milk of a filly milked for the first time to drink. This young man has invoked us during the feast of *julag*. His face shines; his soul is pure. Let him return to the yurts of his *ayil*.' Then Varuna, the third *Naga* king, said 'Go back to your own people, Alcidai, because it is given to no man to sit among us before the appointed hour.' The fourth king said 'As compensation for the fear he has suffered he will have the eyes of the *Naga* to see in the days which are not yet come; he will be the one who can melt the silence of the future.' And the fifth king said to him: 'In exchange for the injustice you suffered you will carry on your tongue the gift of the *Naga*.' And he pressed into his tongue the gift of speaking what would come to pass. And the sixth king said: 'As compensation for the pain you suffered you will put on your standard the emblem of the eight *Naga*.' And the seventh said to him: 'You will be khan of your people and the *Naga* will protect your white yurt. As long as your descendants are united, they will live in the fertile pastures of the land of seven rivers, where the *Naga* live.' The eighth king said to him finally: 'Because you have listened to the song of the *Naga* you will carry their music with you.' He placed in his throat the song of the *Naga* princesses and led him back to the path down which he had come, towards the surface of Lake Alakol.

The wolves were already circling Alcidai's body where it lay in the grass by the lake, and they were stretching out their hungry muzzles, when suddenly warmth returned to the boy's limbs; his blood, which had stopped, began to flow again; his tongue stirred in his mouth and his eyelids opened to the sky. Alcidai went back to his yurt and when he played the horse-skull violin he enchanted the people who lived in the felt-padded tents and the spirit people in equal measure.

One night Sigi Quduqu dreamed of Genghis Khan. He was riding a white horse caparisoned with gold and holding in his left hand the reins of another horse, also white, caparisoned with silver. 'My younger brother,' he was saying, 'can't you hear me? I'm calling you. Don't you recognise my voice? Your destiny is sealed. Follow me.' And as he said this Genghis Khan held out the reins of the horse harnessed in silver. In his sleep Sigi Quduqu tried to seize them, but could not. He woke instead and managed to get up in his mind, but his legs wouldn't move and his arms were as heavy as granite. Sigi Quduqu managed with difficulty to attract the attention of a servant. His son Alcidai was sent for. Alcidai brought his ear close to the scarcely moving lips, his breath warm against his father's struggling breaths: 'Keep your people united, my son, let them live in harmony according to the laws of their fathers.' When he had said this Sigi Quduqu died.

Alcidai had the news brought to his father's wives and children, and ordered the eight clans of which he was now the head into mourning. He had a tent raised and Sigi Quduqu's body placed inside, wrapped in silk, laid out on wooden trestles. In front of him they put a table loaded with food; a white horse, caparisoned with jewelled harness, was led into the tent. Before everything was closed inside the cave chosen for the burial, Alcidai prostrated himself three times in front of his father's body, then stood up, and, with the snow-capped peaks of the Alatau behind him and the fan delta of rivers widening towards Lake Balkhash in front of him, intoned the song he had learnt in the kingdom of the *Naga*:

You who knew the word of the law, O father,
why are you silent now on your golden bed?
You who knew how to trace the blue signs,
why is your hand now white, O my father?
You who brought us to this land shining with rivers
and damp with pastures,
why abandon it now, O my father?
The streams which flow down from the Alatau
and those which flow down from the Karatau
stop to pay you homage,
the long-legged foals
cease chasing across the meadows
and the Tunshan crumple in sorrow,
like the reeds heavy with rain
on the banks of the Ili.

The cave was closed with the tent inside it and in the tent the body of Sigi Quduqu and the horse caparisoned for the journey; sentries were posted in front of the cave so that nobody would dare to approach it. The Tunshan returned to their yurts further down the valley, in their summer quarters, and after nine days of mourning Alcidai was declared khagan.

Alcidai had the banner with the eight knotted *Naga* raised in the middle of his *ayil*, and he gathered the princes of the eight clans around him and said: 'Look how the eight *Naga* writhe in the wind! Even if the wind buffets it, the knot of snakes is not loosed. So must you also be. Be faithful to your name: Tunshan, those who are united and in harmony. Make the knot tight and let none loosen it!' The khans swore fealty to each other, but Alcidai, as though lost in other thoughts, now spoke a language which was different from theirs: 'The day will come when the Tunshan must choose between the bear and the tiger and go their separate ways; the day will come when they will have to leave the land of seven rivers. But when another Tunshan returns to the kingdom of the *Naga*, then they will choose the tiger and they will pitch their yurts to the left of the Alatau, in Ṣinkiang.' The khans round Alcidai looked at each other in astonishment as the khagan, his eyelids half lowered over his eyes, his body streaming with sweat, withdrew into himself, as though exhausted by the weight of his own words.

At this point in our story Bairqan stopped and leant forward. Then he looked around, as though to assure himself that his listeners too had understood the gravity of the prophecy. The mothers said to their children: 'May it not be you who returns to the kingdom of the *Naga*!' The men, at the time when I was among the Tunshan, still discussed whether it was better to choose the bear or the tiger and somebody always argued in favour of China, while others defended Russia and still others maintained that the promised land was the region to the east of the mountains, Sinkiang. The Tunshan enjoyed discussing their past and speculating about their future, but who would have said then that Alcidai's prophecy would come true and that it would be my own brother Ginchin who would bring it about?

9

THE PROPHECY WAS in one way or another at the bottom of everything, even my own story. There had been other reasons which brought me to the Bergers' house, but those too were obscurely connected to Alcidai's prophecy, or so it seemed to me. At that time I couldn't explain exactly how they were connected, just as I didn't know exactly what had brought me there. I only knew that there was some insurmountable enchantment between me and the Tunshan; that an impassable gorge had been placed between us, like the gorge of the Talas, and I was on one side, and they were on the other, and in the middle there was a demon barring my way, and the gorge had become longer, terribly long, and I couldn't see the Tunshan any more, and the din of the river and the rocks rolling down the walls of the gorge deafened me to their voices.

The gorge of the river Talas was one of the most feared places in our history, precisely because to the south it marked the border of the land of seven rivers, and beyond it lay a world which was entirely foreign to the Tunshan. The missionaries of the Prophet had stopped at the gorge of the Talas; this was the only crossing point over the Karatau, the gate from Persia to China, of necessity the route that the caravans took for Merv, Bukhara and Samarkand, and on towards the rising sun. The mullahs turned about at the entrance to the gorge; perhaps they were afraid of the walls plunging steeply into the river and the legends of the jinn who were said to inhabit those rocks, but it's more likely that they were put to flight by the archers of the White Horde, posted to defend the pass, or the customs officials who extorted substantial tolls from anyone who dared to enter the gorge.

Safe behind the double chain of mountains and the sands of the Karakum, the clans of the White Horde watched the swift rebirth of Transoxania with hostile disdain. In their turn the inhabitants of the south regarded the nomads beyond the gorge of the Talas as barbarians ignorant of any civilisation. While to the south Tamerlane's engineers built daring domes, which broadened out into hemispheres, suspended from their keystones; while his artisans mixed cobalt salts with copper oxide to obtain the blue of their ceramics and placed mosaic tiles in relief on glazed tiles to cover the façades of mosques and mausolea to the north of the Talas, the Mongol tribes were still stretching the ring of poles around the circle of smoke and covering the domes of their yurts with layers of felt. The very form of their dwellings, so perfected that improvement was impossible, made conservatives of the Mongols who lived in the land of seven rivers, and who still preferred their nomadic existence on the great plains to a life closed inside city walls.

Not that the land of seven rivers was without cities; there were several, which were very ancient indeed, like Talas and Otrar, Togmak and Sighnak, all of which had sprung up at the edges of Transoxania, the very last ramifications of roots which led from the centres of culture further to the south, as though enough lymph to feed the cities had only got so far and then run out. The cities further to the north are recent cities, forts built on the Tsar's orders to defend the new borders or centres springing up around the prison camps – cities, in other words, with a none too glorious history. On the other hand, the cities which arose where the tributaries of the Syrdar'ya met had been rich in property and culture, but they had suffered the same fate as the rivers which lapped against their walls: as their strength waned, they could no longer reach the bigger rivers, exhausted their vigour before they reached their destination and sank into the sand. Even Sighnak, the once famous capital of the White Horde, has vanished without trace. They used to tell a blood-curdling story about Sighnak which the Tunshan never tired of hearing.

Sighnak stood on a river which flowed like the Talas down from the Karatau. They say that the city was abandoned by its inhabitants, so suddenly that they left food and jars full of oil in their houses, and that the cause of their flight was an invasion of snakes. It must have been a hitherto unknown species of snake, short, black, extremely venomous reptiles which seemed to have come from the Kara-Ichuk. When the river dried up it left a huge expanse of mud open to the air, from which came swarms of black snakes. They slithered up the bank towards the city, and were so fast that they reached the first houses in Sighnak in a day, slipped through cracks in the walls and under doors in search of shade, hid in chests and beneath carpets, and nested in earthenware vessels. The inhabitants of Sighnak were petrified, and tried to get rid of the snakes, but many succumbed to poisonous bites; and the rest, convinced that the infestation had been sent from hell, fled and took nothing with them, for fear of bringing the snakes with them too. The fame and the terror of that invasion were such that not even robbers dared to defy the curse. The city was not sacked, and the wind was held to have made it disappear in the end, eroding walls and roofs, filling houses and courtyards with sand, obliterating every trace of life in its fury.

But the Tunshan knew Sighnak and the other cities only by hearsay; like their Mongol ancestors they lived on the steppe and the river-carved plain, and they continued to pitch their yurts along the banks of the Ili and on the shores of Lake Balkhash. The land of seven rivers was fertile and the White Horde would have lived in peace and happiness if it had not been for the frequent disputes between clans. For example, there was the occasion when the powerful Ulus Khan laid claim to the pastures belonging to Toktamish's family, and the latter, in search of allies, turned to the Tunshan.

The khans of the Tunshan were gathered in the yurt of Jintai Khagan, passing each other tobacco in silence and sipping tea. Toktamish's ambassadors sat on the khagan's right draped in their heavy silk *chalat* with the embroidered dragons on the cuffs, after the new fashion that the caravans had brought from Bukhara and from Samarkand to the bazaar in Sighnak. Not only their clothes but also the affected way they had of lifting the cups of tea to their lips marked them out as city people, whom only the necessity of the moment impelled to seek friendship with the nomads of the steppes. When enough time had gone by, the khan put down his bowl and said: 'You who have come in Toktamish's name will know that the Tunshan are bound to his family by ties of alliance. Didn't Toktamish's brother's daughter Altani marry my cousin on my father's side? You will know what Hö'elün, Temüjin's mother, said to her four sons? Hö'elün gave them each an arrow and said: "Try to break it." Her sons broke the arrows effortlessly. Then Hö'elün took four arrows and made a bundle of them. "Try to break it now," she said. But none of her sons could do it. May our families be like wise Hö'elün's arrows. Two thousand Tunshan warriors will come to your aid.' The khans of the Tunshan nodded, the ambassadors bent their heads in sign of gratitude and together they devised a plan.

But they little knew Ulus Khan, an ambitious and mistrustful man. He could not delight in a victory that was only half-won, and took no pleasure in drinking with the others in the palace at Sighnak. On the faces of the relatives and friends laughing around him, flushed with wine, he saw the will to betray him. Already their mere capacity to formulate ideas that differed from his own made them guilty in his eyes. Ulus Khan had sent spies in disguise around the land of seven rivers, spies more numerous than the thousand springs of the river Chu. The preparations the Tunshan were making did not go unobserved; two herdsmen looking for a missing camel, so they said, ran to report what they had seen to the khan.

Toktamish had pitched his camp on the left bank of the Talas and his warriors were sleeping unawares. Under cover of night, Ulus Khan's army came to them and massacred them in the dark. When the Tunshan arrived at the appointed place the next morning and climbed the steep bank, they saw with disbelief that the valley on the other side of the river was all covered with tulips. But they were splashes of blood, not flowers, which coloured the grass and the banks of the Talas.

Toktamish and a few companions succeeded in reaching the gorge of the Talas and did not stop until they were in Samarkand, where he placed himself under Tamerlane's protection. Tamerlane sent his soldiers beyond the Syrdar'ya, but Ulus Khan sent his own soldiers against him. The two armies were already close when a terrible storm broke over the plain; the soldiers of both sides looked fearfully at the sky riven with lightning while the horses neighed and stamped at every clap of thunder. Ulus Khan returned to Sighnak, but Tamerlane's soldiers had to take shelter where they could, poorly protected by their travelling tents, soaked and frightened. The air had cooled suddenly, so that even before the rain hit the ground it had turned to hailstones that stuck like locusts to the horses' flanks, to the weapons, to the soldiers' clothes and to the tents. The ground had become slippery, the river unnavigable. The road home was closed to Tamerlane's soldiers. Then the khagan ordered an immediate attack on the enemy, taking advantage of the night. But Ulus Khan's soldiers were not sleeping either.

The battlefield was lit only by the moon; the thin layer of ice which shimmered eerily soon became a marsh under the horses' hooves and the fallen bodies, and under the mud-encrusted boots which trampled it. Tamerlane's warriors outnumbered those of Ulus Khan and forced them to retreat. It was then that Toktamish saw a lone horseman, fleeing the field of battle at speed. Toktamish caught up with him and headed him off. He drew his bow and hit the other in the shoulder with an arrow. It was then that Toktamish recognised Ulus Khan. He spurred his horse, but Ulus Khan, without even trying to pull the arrow out of his shoulder, turned his horse towards the river and forced the horse to enter the water. The water was soon above the animal's chest and overwhelmed him, dragging him into the darkness beyond the strip of slanting moonlight which shone on the river.

10

'NAJA! NAJA!' MARIANNE was calling me. I saw her appear in the doorway, wrapped in the crocheted shawl she had thrown around her shoulders to come outside and which scarcely covered her bare arms. In her haste she had not put on her shoes and now she didn't dare to venture into the garden in her slippers. So she was only looking for me with her eyes, without leaving the threshold, but I was familiar with her vexed and anxious expression. I ran over to her and she greeted me with a 'Heavens above, Naja, in this cold . . .', frowning. Marianne didn't feel the cold, she said she was 'warm inside,' but standing outside in that cold she found somehow disgraceful. I hurried into the house after her, but not before carefully wiping my shoes on the mat. I was imitating Marianne's reflex action, repeated this time out of habit, forgetting that she was wearing slippers. It was a ritual gesture, for when one crossed the threshold one was supposed to leave every trace of the outside on the outside, even if it was a pebble stuck to the sole of a shoe or a lump of soil wet with snow, just as the men at home, before they crossed the threshold of a yurt, took their weapons off and leant them against the outside wall of the yurt, in order not to offend the spirit who guarded the home. There was a house spirit in the Bergers' house as well: the signs carved in plaster right over the door were certainly addressed to him and to the evil spirits, to keep them out. But I was afraid inside that house too. I jumped when the telephone rang, when the doorbell rang, when doors slammed, when a voice issued unexpectedly from the radio, when the kettle whistled or when its nostrils spat smoke like a dragon. I started when flames leapt to meet the gas coming from the ring on the stove. Marianne must have been afraid of fire too, because she held the match in the air with her arm outstretched and sprang back bodily as though in fear of being attacked by it. That house was full of danger. Who protected it? My eyes sought out the lintels of the doors, where I expected to see an amulet or an image somehow declaring its celestial nature, and I looked to where the walls met, the best place, I thought, to welcome a god. And almost immediately I caught sight of a little statue of coloured wood standing on a wooden bracket on the wall in a corner of the kitchen, a woman holding a plump baby in her arms. I was struck by how sinuous her body was, as though the baby's weight had forced her into an unnatural contortion, and she was about to lose her balance and tumble off her high shelf onto the kitchen table. She was wrapped up in a cloak, like the brides at home who come from outside, and she was looking around her meekly, almost shyly. She was without doubt a goddess, because at her feet, stuck to the plinth, was a little metal vase containing sprigs, which the women changed every so often. The little statue reassured me a bit. But how was I to talk to her and win her favour, if I did not know her language? The gods too speak different languages and you have to know the words with which men address them. I did not know the words any more than I knew anything else, and Marianne did not speak as she was putting mistletoe in the little vase at the feet of the statue. Perhaps here they talked to the gods in silence.

One afternoon my eyes lighted on the white pebbles that decorated the main garden path which, like all the smaller paths, ran into a large flowerbed. I don't know if I had a plan or if I was given the idea by my restless hands, but I began to collect the stones and to make a nice pile of them in the centre of the flowerbed; when I thought it was high enough I stuck a dead branch into the middle of it. I looked around in search of an ornament of some kind, a piece of material or a thick flexible stalk, but there was nothing in the garden that would serve the purpose. The only object worthy of decorating my creation was the red silk ribbon at the end of my plait. I thought for a moment, then untied it and put a bow on the branch. I stood up to admire my handiwork; the dull wintry afternoon light blurred the edges of things, but the pile of white stones with its ribbon stood out like a bonfire against the snow. If there was a homeless spirit anywhere about he would immediately understand that it was an obo, Naja's obo. The branch stuck out of the dome of stones like the smoke from the opening in a yurt; I was offering a home to the spirits of the place which was in no way inferior to the other, larger obo I used to know, which generations of nomads and travellers had erected on the Talki pass.

The Talki pass, one of the few passes linking central Asia with China, marked the border between the land of seven rivers and Dzungaria. For the Tunshan it marked the boundary between the known and the unknown and as such it was a source of danger; that pass made the land of seven rivers vulnerable, opening it to the east. It was no coincidence that many calamities had reached us from there and it was that pass that decided the fate of the Tunshan.

From their summer camps on the slopes of the Alatau, the Tunshan had seen the first handfuls of Oirats coming over the Talki Pass. They doubled the guard on their livestock and posted sentries to watch the mouth of the valley. The Tunshan were on the alert. And one morning the sentries galloped up: at least a *tümen* of armed men was coming down from the Alatau, and the valley of the Boro-tala on the other side of the Talki Pass was already full of warriors and horses heading south at speed. Then Baatur Khan ordered the trumpets to sound and called the Tunshan together.

The heads of the eight clans were already crowding round the khan's yurt, getting ready to go in, as the servants hitched their horses to the rail; Baatur was about to lift the felt carpet into the yurt, when his mother Örbei Katum called him. She was standing not far from the entrance and behind her stood Nan Khoga,

Baatur's beautiful bride, her hands resting on her belly which was already swelling under her *chalat*. Behind the two women was a crowd of silent, straight-backed women, the mothers and wives of Baatur's brothers, and of his cousins on both his mother's and his father's side. The khan looked in surprise at the group of women: 'I did not send for the women,' he said in annoyance. 'Don't you understand how urgent this is?'

His mother Örbei Katum answered: 'It is the urgency which brings us here. It is precisely because you didn't send for us that we came to talk to you, Baatur. Don't be in too much haste to go to war. Don't let anger lead you. Beyond the Talki pass the Oirats have nine times as many *tümen* and their warriors are more numerous than the herds of wild horses on the yellow steppe. Mind you do not attack them! Come to terms with them! We did not give birth to you so that you could end up skewered on Oirat arrows. Nan Khoga does not carry a son so that he can come into the world fatherless!'

So spoke Örbei Katum, who knew her son's heart and knew how much more powerful his rage was than the counsels of his mind, and how it impelled him to act rashly. But Baatur was already gazing at her in anger: 'Is my name not Baatur, the hero? Did you not give me this name? Am I not destined to avenge the insults to the Tunshan? Why have you come to talk to me of terms, when an armed enemy is crossing our pastures? Has he come down from the Talki pass to sit as a guest at my right hand? In that case, why has he not first leant his weapons against the wall of the yurt?' Baatur's mind was by now ablaze with anger and Örbei Katum was silent, regretting her words, while Nan Khoga bent her head in confusion. 'How long has this cowardice dwelt in your heart, mother?' Baatur finished, and, raising the felt carpet, he crossed the threshold of the yurt followed by the group of khans.

The Tunshan were already prepared for the Oirat attack. Their war cries rose through the air: kru kru kru, thrown from one soldier to the next, louder and louder. Kru kru kru, the Tunshan warriors repeated and the battle cry united them and bolstered their courage; kru kru kru, like a flock of crows ready to swoop down on their solitary prey on the steppe. Every Tunshan felt like the winner who beats all his adversaries in the wrestling competition and now gives vent to his triumph alone in the middle of the ring by imitating the movements of the eagle. Kru, kru, kru the Tunshan repeated louder and the banner with the eight *Naga* knotted together fluttered in front of every line of warriors and it looked as though the eight heads were tossing in the wind, ready to throw themselves on the enemy and kill him.

From a height Örbei Katum looked around and saw only women, old people and children left in the village. On the heights, in front of the empty yurts, there was silence. Not even the children dared to move or run about.

A few days later the women of the Tunshan saw a horse arriving at the gallop in the evening, alone. It was Urruk Schiorchal, Baatur's magnificent destrier, coming back in a lather of sweat from his long run. As soon as they recognised him, the women understood what had happened. Nan Khoga threw herself against the horse's neck, hugging him, and leaning her forehead against his soft coat she said: 'Urruk, why did you come back alone? Where did you leave your master my husband?' And she wept. But she pulled herself together instantly, turned to the women who were crying in desperation round her and said: 'Why do we stand here weeping? We too can bend a bow and use a dagger. We too can ride geldings and certainly no worse than men. Perhaps we can yet come to their aid!' At these words the women roused themselves; the mothers left their unweaned infants with the older women, and sought out helmets and swords, gathering what weapons were left in their yurts and saddling the horses. Nan Khoga leapt on to Urruk Schiorchal's back, and he showed them the way.

When the women came to the Ili valley the sun had not yet risen over the peaks of the Alatau, but the shadow was not enough to hide the massacre from their horrified eyes. They could make out the bodies of fathers, husbands and brothers scattered along the riverbank, stiff as the horses lying beside them. Yet the women kept the silence they had agreed on, and rode among the bodies without making a sound, as though they were ghosts and the men on the ground among the horses' hooves but shadows. On the opposite bank of the river they could see the enemy yurts whose inhabitants were sleeping peacefully, weary after battle. The river was low at that point, and pale stretches of dry sand could be seen rising from the water. The women leant over their horses' necks, whispering soft words in their ears to calm them, urging silence on them also. The wind had risen and mingled the sound of the rustling of leaves with the lapping of the water. Once they had reached the opposite bank the women lost no time, but fell upon the tents, plunged their weapons into the sleeping bodies, loosed perfectly aimed arrows at their fleeing enemies, and spared none of the wounded who were trying to strike back. Silence soon fell also on the left bank of the Ili. The Oirats, who succeeded in reaching their horses and fleeing, would later say that a flock of demons had fallen on them and that their officers had certainly been mistaken in choosing that place for the battle, because it was protected by powerful spirits.

When the women of the Tunshan crossed the river again, the shadows had retreated towards the foothills of the Alatau and the white light of morning revealed the well-known faces and displayed, despite their obscenely twisted limbs, the bodies which had been touched and caressed when still alive. Like a flock of seagulls scouring a beach for the fish thrown up on the sand by the tide, the women scattered over the field along the riverbank and there was no one there who did not recognise a relative or a neighbour. They were all there, none of the Tunshan had missed the call.

Nan Khoga bent over Baatur, beside herself with grief, and repeated: 'Was it for this that your mother Örbei Katum bore you? Was it for this that I left my family for your yurt? Was it for this that you put your seed in my womb?' Such was her despair that she did not notice at first the stab of pain in her belly. It was only when the pain became sharper that she remembered the arrow that she had wrenched from herself without thinking in the heat of battle. The wound was bleeding now. Nan Khoga panicked and ordered them all to return to the yurts. 'May our sons not be left without mothers too!' she said as she spurred Urruk on.

Nan Khoga was young and the son she carried inside her was bound to her by a rope stronger than the rope which ties the foal to the rail in front of the yurt. When the moment came a boy was born lively and healthy, but lacking a thumb on his right hand. So they called him Muchor Lousang, Lousang No-Finger.

I I

THERE HAD BEEN a time in the history of the Tunshan when the women had made the decisions. We children were amazed. Why isn't it like that any more, Bairqan? My grandfather Bairqan answered, it is not in the order of things that women should decide clan affairs. Women were absolute mistresses of the left-hand side of the yurt and of the space around it, used for milking the mares and for other household tasks, but it was the men's council who decided when to go to the bazaar at Bukhara and which was the right day for striking the yurts and crossing to the other side of the river. It had always been like this. But I knew that inside the yurt, when nobody else was listening, Mai Ling spoke with her husband at length, gently coaxing him. I could hear them whispering, she with her high voice trying to win him round, Bairqan's deep voice becoming less and less certain as Mai Ling spoke. In the Bergers' house it was hard for me to work out who was supposed to make the decisions. Was it my father, Günther Berger? When he came home the women lowered their voices and they bobbed their heads when they met him in the hall. But my father was hardly ever at home and I had never seen him give an order to the maids. When my mother's parents were expected, conversation in the kitchen fell to a whisper; the women's movements became a little agitated, and they glanced reproachfully at each other if the cake came out browner than usual, or looked at each other aghast if its top sagged. But my grandparents never stayed long and when they left the atmosphere in the kitchen would clear, and chatter and laughter would break out again. It was not my grandparents who made decisions about household matters, but then neither did my mother, who rarely set foot on the ground floor, except to go and shut herself in the little sitting room: then she would appear in the kitchen, just to say a few words which bore no resemblance to an order, or to ask a question. She would disappear again immediately, but her scent lingered and mingled with the smell of soap permanently given off by Marianne's hands and which came from dish-cloths and tablecloths. As time went by I became convinced that it was the staff who made the decisions in that house. Marianne, Kathe and Hannah were the real mistresses, even if they slept in two dingy uncarpeted little rooms under the eaves. It was the women who divided up the chores, according to an entirely understandable hierarchy. Marianne, the oldest, was in charge, but the others had the right to challenge her. Indeed, the kitchen was often the setting for a succession of quarrels and verbal spats, until Marianne or one of the others glanced at the clock on the wall and exclaimed in fright, '*O Gott, es ist schon spät*', and as though all three repented at that '*spät*', they rushed to make up for lost time. When all was said and done, they got along well enough. Women are more reasonable than men; it wasn't only Mai Ling who said it, Mai Ling who knew how to defeat the khan's stubbornness with smiles; the others, men and women, knew it too, and the history of the Tunshan offered a plain and irrefutable example of female reasonableness in the figure of Nan Khoga the warrior. It is true that her story was followed by that of the unreasonable Bigeci, but this did not alter the opinion of the Tunshan.

The Tunshan never lived so peacefully as when Nan Khoga was head of the clans and sat in the middle of the yurt, surrounded by cousins and sisters to advise her. Peace was made with their Oirat neighbours and as a pledge and a strengthening of that peace, the alliance was sealed with a marriage: Bigeci, daughter of the khan of the Oirats, was to marry Nan Khoga's son Muchor Lousang, the boy missing a finger. When the first hair appeared on Muchor's face his mother sent messengers to the Oirats with scarves of white silk and a leather bag full of gifts, to remind them of the promise. The messengers returned with the nuptial agreements.

Bigeci was thirteen, with eyes like swallows' wings and silken hair down to her ankles; her forehead and her neck were hung with turquoises, and coral earrings brushed her shoulders. When she found out that her future husband was missing the thumb on his right hand Bigeci became sad and said to her younger sister: Ülen Solongo, my sister,' she said, 'why has our father chosen a mutilated man for me? Am I not pretty enough to merit an able-bodied man?' Ülen agreed and together they hatched a plan. In the utmost secrecy, they summoned some faithful servants and ordered them to take up a position below the Talki Pass and lie in wait there for the wedding procession coming to take Bigeci. There they were to take the groom prisoner.

Meanwhile Muchor Lousang had adorned his horse with rich harnesses, hung his knife and the little silver-studded casket of flint on his belt, and slipped the carved coral snuffbottle into the sleeve of his *chalat*. Equipped with all the trappings of a man, Muchor rode gaily towards his future bride's *ayil* on the other side of the Alatau. Gradually, however, as he approached the pass and the path became steeper and stonier, Muchor was assailed by doubt. 'Will Bigeci accept me for a husband, though I lack a finger?' Muchor looked nervously at the hand which held the reins and suddenly the scar that twisted his skin where the thumb was missing looked deformed and horrible to him. His disgust grew and turned to sweat on his brow. Muchor could not believe that he had never thought about it before. How had he lived all those years with such a disfigured hand? How had his mother not made him hide this calamity of fate which he carried so clearly in sight on his right hand? Muchor could manage a bow and handle a knife as well as anybody else; he had even come first in the horse-race that year and could keep guests entertained with his lively stories and his ready wit, but at that moment the gifts he was so proud of seemed paltry, and his hand a monstrous thing. Soon Muchor felt himself to be nothing more than a hand, a hideous, thumbless hand. Tormented by these thoughts, he turned to his escort and, scrutinising his cousins' faces, believed that he could read these same thoughts in all of them. Why else were they silent? Why did Jagobon look so unhappy, who usually laughed so readily? The hatred he felt for himself spread to his companions. They were surely laughing at him among themselves, for they all knew his bride would reject him, mutilated as he was.

When they got to the top of the Talki pass, with the Borotala valley stretching before them, they were all sweating from the climb and dismounted to rest. Muchor would rather have turned his horse round and gone back the way he had come or run from his men's sight. He glanced almost unwittingly at the rock walls to see if by chance there was a feasible path or hiding-place. Then his eyes lighted on the obo: the stones looked like crystal in the sunlight and the rags on the branches looked like newly knotted white silk ribbons. The cairn shone as though a fire had been lit inside it and heat streamed from it to merge with the surrounding air. The whiteness attracted Muchor and drawing nearer he saw, seated on the stones, an old man dressed in white with a snow-white beard and long hair which was also white. He held a stick which ended in a dragon's head. Muchor recognised him as Tsagaan Ebegün, the Old Man in White.

Now he was sitting in front of Muchor, white as the stones of the obo, and talking to him. The boy came closer to listen. 'Muchor Lousang, why do you suffer?' the old man whispered. 'Is the part you are missing also the whole? Is a horse's value measured only by its hocks? Is a man's worth measured only by his appearance?' As he said this the old man opened his hand and held something out to the boy. Muchor went to take it, but just before his hand touched the old man's, the latter disappeared. In his place a little terracotta object lay on the obo. Muchor picked it up and looked at it: it was thick and triangular in section, with three holes on each side, a whistle, like the ones you can buy for a small coin in the bazaar, that shepherds use to call dogs, and children use to call to each other in play. Muchor looked at it for a moment, holding it on his open palm as the old man had done shortly before, as though it were a butterfly. Thoughtfully he slipped it into the sleeve of his *chalat* next to the little snuffbottle and forgot all about it.

Meanwhile the cortege was proceeding down the Borotala valley towards the yurts of the Oirats. Muchor, who was still deep in thought, had ridden on ahead of the others. Towards evening he found himself alone in a clearing among great patches of holm oak. Suddenly three armed horsemen sprang out of the shadows and surrounded him, one of them grabbing his horse's reins. As though obeying a flash of intuition, Muchor put his hand into the sleeve of his *chalat*, pulled out the whistle and brought it to his lips. A long, blood-curdling whistle sounded over the clearing. Birds flew up from the branches of the trees and his attackers' horses reared up, unseated their riders and trampled them. When his escort arrived at the gallop, Muchor was still in the middle of the clearing looking uncomprehendingly at the bodies of his adversaries, slain by a whistle.

Muchor Lousang never found out who had laid the ambush. It is certain, however, that Bigeci was very happy that her own plan had failed and over the years that followed, she showed particular devotion to Tsagaan Ebegün. Muchor thought that she was especially grateful to him for saving her bridegroom, but Bigeci was not only thanking the deity with prayers and offerings for preventing the carrying out of her wicked intentions, more than that, she was trying to insinuate herself into his good graces. What would her married life be like, indeed, in the afterlife, when the Old Man in White revealed the plot to her husband? For the Tunshan, the same rules and customs obtained among the dead, the living and the immortals, as did of course the same ruses that existed on earth. The lamas in their red tunics had not yet come to the land of seven rivers to put an end, at least officially, to the corruptibility of the immortals and the profit that the living could derive from it.

I don't know exactly when the first monks in their yellow hats came down from the Talki pass to the yurts of the Tunshan, but I remember the names of those who came down to us on the Amudar'ya at the beginning of April for the festival of *julag*, and at the end of September; they were Tsogtu the Tibetan and Mergen the young Mongol. They came over the passes of the Hindu Kush and arrived tired and dusty, their faces tanned, their tunics faded by the sun. When they arrived at the yurts of the Tunshan, we children would run towards them and surround them shouting '*Manaski, manaski*!' This was what we called the Kyrgyz minstrels who travelled around reciting the deeds of the hero Manas, but it had come in time to mean all the different kinds of wandering storytellers, rhapsodes and improvisers and it had become a formula of welcome among the Tunshan. The two *manaski* who came from somewhere beyond the Pamir, perhaps from Sinkiang, or even from distant Tibet, were of a different kind; they did not bring heroic verses and brave tales, but pious legends and holy teachings. Nevertheless the Tunshan who gathered round the newcomers greeting them with joyous respect, were glad of their coming. They loved stories, and words, all the more if uttered by such venerable mouths.

Everybody would gather in Bairqan's yurt, which was the biggest. When everyone had taken their usual places, the men on his right and the women on his left, the children sitting higgledy-piggledy between the grown-ups' legs, when everybody was finally quiet, the boy Mergen would present a roll of paper to the lama, holding it like an offering on the flat of his palms and describing a bow. Tsogtu would receive it with a ritual gesture and begin to unroll it and separate the paintings. He would choose one with particular care, as though the decision were not part of an established routine, but sprang from an impulse or was the result of a change of mind. Then he would make a sign to the boy, who would get up again quickly and take charge of it. Only then would he open it and show it to the audience, and he would shuffle round the circle of seated Tunshan raising or lowering his arms at the request of his public, so that everybody could see the picture. When he was quite sure that everyone had seen enough, Mergen would sit down by Tsogtu, keeping the canvas open, and would stay quite still, like a living lectern. I admired this capacity of his for staying still and thought it must be one of the virtues to be learnt at the monastery they both came from, master and student, and of which I only knew that it had whitewashed walls and stood to the left of the Pamir.

Everybody's eyes were on Tsogtu, who was sitting under the central pole of the yurt as Siddhartha Gautama, the Buddha himself, sat under the Tree of Enlightenment. The story he was readying himself to tell was not in fact new to the Tunshan, but for precisely this reason they were already looking forward to the climactic moments and preparing to relive them. The story was the famous Indian legend of Holy Molon-tojn, who crossed earth and the afterlife to save his mother from eternal damnation.

The audience never took its eyes off the lama except to look at the painting in Mergen's arms to see which character was being depicted. The audience underlined the most moving parts with long oohs and aahs and interrupted the narration with repeated *uukai*, which approximates to 'And then what happened?' Through scene after scene the Tunshan gathered in the yurt followed Molon-tojn and his master Tsongkha-pa from one level of hell to the next, right to the bottom, where Holy Molon-tojn's mother was condemned to be crushed between great stones behind impregnable rock walls. When her son finally found his mother the sinner and freed her, when the latter repented and was reborn, then Mergen unrolled the last painting, which was of paradise, naturally, and held it at shoulder height, turning his torso round, like an athlete on the podium showing the victory pot to the applauding public.

Little by little the *uukai* died away, then the lama sat down, accepted the cup of *arrak* he was offered and took a lingering sip, while the spectators bowed before him, thanking him and praising his performance, and left the yurt carrying their younger children asleep in their arms.

Night after night, *ayil* after *ayil*, the lama and the boy transmitted their repertoire of legends and Buddhist doctrines to the Tunshan.

When Tsogtu and his young companion left, a kind of imperceptible bustle could be sensed in the yurts, almost a subcutaneous activity behind the felt walls. Everyone began to tidy up and fill in spaces which had been so suddenly and so zealously emptied. The women pulled rag dolls and stumpy figures carved from birchwood out of their hiding places and put them back in their places on the altars of the yurts. They were humbler than the ancient *onggod*, the spirits of our ancestors, who used to stand guard on either side of the house altar and who had first brought the wrath of the Buddhist monks down upon themselves. They were also handier and therefore easier to hide in case of an inspection by the lama. When indeed the snow melted and the two monks were sighted on the mule track which led to the valleys of the Hindu Kush, the previous season's movement was repeated, but in reverse: little cloth and felt idols disappeared from the lintels of the doors and were concealed inside felt carpets rolled up by the wall or inside the red lacquered chest, and only the icon of the bodhisattva on his lotus pedestal was left on the household altar, in front of serried bowls of rice and *kumiss*. It sometimes happened that when the lamas entered a hastily depaganised yurt, some old person would still be stubbornly gazing at the roof-pole or the corner of the wooden lattice where an ancestor had hung only moments before, and scowling at the daughter or the daughter-in-law; but the latter would pretend not to notice and would touch their clasped hands to their breasts and their foreheads to mark their respect. As for the lama, if he did happen to catch sight of an idol here or there, left in plain view through haste or stubborn superstition, he would behave as if he had seen nothing at all, faithful to the principle that it is better to have an extra god in the Lamaist pantheon than one less of the faithful in one of their temples.

12

'ON THIS SIDE of the Talki Pass and beyond, the Mongol tribes continued to fight each other, to the point where one day even the powerful Oirats were forced to leave their lands and take refuge on the banks of Lake Balkhash, at the edge of the land of seven rivers. Little by little they began to speak of moving West . . .'

When he got to this part Bairqan used to pause for breath before continuing. The journey West was too important a caesura in our history to be rushed. Bairqan was an accomplished storyteller and knew how to measure out pauses, how to keep us in suspense, how to carry us with him on the great ride that the Tunshan were about to set out on over the steppe, first heading west, then south. They would not stop until they got to the Amudar'ya, where we were waiting for them, sitting in a circle around Bairqan as he told the story.

A thick cloud of smoke hung over the central dome of the camp, the yurt of Khan Cho Alek, where the heads of the Oirat clans had been in council for hours. The pipes went round the yurt without the usual compliments; indeed they were sucked fiercely, as though to draw the last breath out of them. Mouthpieces clenched between their teeth, the men clung to the smoke as to a life-raft. The debate raged so fiercely and the air was so suffocating that the khans had forgotten precedence and were all talking at once. They were discussing the pros and cons of an adventure whose outcome was uncertain, assessing their own strength and that of their possible allies, and speculating about the possible reaction of the Russians: would they allow the refugees access to their territory? Was it wise to come to terms with them? How should one weigh up the plans of their nearest enemies, the powerful Khalcha, who were pressing towards the south of the Altai? Between one lungful and the next, a spectre was little by little taking on a definite shape, as though it had come from the bowl of one of their pipes and begun to grow, to expand like a jinn from a bottle, to swell until it filled the whole space of the yurt from door to smokehole. By now those present could no longer tear their minds from the shifting shapes, as though the spectre had glided back down the stems of their pipes and into the folds of their brains, sluggish from the increasing warmth, from the debate and from the *arrak*. It was a mermaid, but she had no seaweed for hair, rather long green grass, and her sinuous body which took the smokers' breath away was like the swaying of the meadow grass when it bends in the wind. She was the Siren of the Volga. Many times the nomads of the steppe had heard the lands between the Don and the Volga described, and had imagined seas of grass, with herds of horses rising out of the grass like islands. The mermaid had assumed so definite a form that no one in the yurt would have doubted they had seen her, if as they left they had looked westwards: she was certainly reclining on the edge of the steppe where it meets the sky in a haze of burning air.

The mirage was infectious and spread to the yurts surrounding that of the khan and gradually to all the others; no one seemed able to escape its enchantment. It spread through the line of women returning from the well and among the servants who watched the horses, it distracted the sentries who scanned the horizon, it seized hold of the children, it set horses and camels stamping and sidling and threw the sheep into turmoil. Even the heaps of *kuraj* lying on the steppe seemed only to be waiting for the wind to remember them, to set off again on their journey westwards.

The Oirats were not, however, the only people facing momentous decisions in those stifling days. On the other side of Lake Balkhash the Tunshan too were assembled in council. The ceremony and the theme of the discussion were the same in the yurt of Tok Timur Khan; the Tunshan were in similarly heated debate on the subject of the advantages and disadvantages of a journey west. In truth, only two out of the eight khans of the Tunshan were in favour: Mongotai and Bairqan, the heads of the clans related to the Oirats through the marriage of Muchor with the lovely Bigeci. The matrimonial alliances of a century earlier, reinforced by later marriages, had sealed the destiny of the two clans forever, linking it to their more powerful Oirat neighbours. In the yurt of the khan, Mongotai, the youngest man present, was advocating flight. 'To the south, beyond the gorge of the Talas, there are peoples who touch their foreheads to the ground in honour of Allah, peoples quick to raise sword and scimitar against those who do not share their faith. When the Oirats leave, we will no longer have allies. Let us join the journey westwards, and reach the green plains of the Volga with them!' When Mongotai had fallen silent, Bairqan spoke up. He bowed low towards the centre of the yurt; as he did, his beard, which fell in two tufts from his chin, touched his *chalat*, and the silver hair against the dark blue material conferred truth on his words, even before he spoke: 'Tok Timur, khan of the

Tunshan, you are too young to remember what I have seen and remember; you know this land only as it is now, you do not know what it was like when I was a boy and my father and my grandfather before him. You do not know where the rivers ran that used to furrow our land. Consider the Chu, for example: when my grandfather's father was a child, the river reached the Syrdar'ya, albeit with difficulty, and merged with it, where now only an empty ditch stands to remind us. Think of the Ili: every year the water's flow becomes shorter, as though the river were growing old and lacked the breath to flow onwards. Where two years ago the water still came up to the wrinkled knees of a camel, today a six-month-old lamb can cross it without wetting more than its hooves. But the rivers are not the only things to be touched by this fate. In the time of our ancestor Alcidai Lake Balkhash was joined to the other lakes and ponds around: today they resemble the stumps of a lizard's tail pulled from its body. You will have noticed how the lake is shrinking, and how it is stifled by reeds, whose bite squeezes tighter every day. This is the fate of the land of seven rivers. Within two or three generations it will have become like the Kyrgyz steppe, where only the *salsola* grows, and the rivers which you see foaming today will only be skeletons of rivers, which not even the melt-water from the Alatau will be able to revive. For this reason, Tok Timur, and you khans of the Tunshan, let us leave this land before the curse looming over it dries up even our eyes, and before it breaks our hearts like dry clods of earth as we watch the ground we love dry up beneath our feet. Let us find new springs for our children, let us follow the Oirats to greener lands, where the rivers are not losing their vital force.' When he had said this Bairqan fell suddenly silent and withdrew into himself as though the flow of his speech had dried up and leached away the vitality that had kept the speaker upright until then. He bowed his head and it was noticed how his beard, which poured abundantly from his chin, became thinner until it ended in a thin stream of hairs on his chest, as though his beard too was drying up like the rivers of his speech.

Now it was Tok Timur Khan's turn; his task was to refute the earlier arguments and propose a solution. And this is what the khan said: 'The peoples who live to the south of the land of seven rivers, and whose faith makes them warlike, have never dared until today to venture behind the Talas gorge, nor will they do so in the future, given that even more than the words of the Prophet they fear the Kazakhs, who have thus unwittingly been our guard dogs. We will come to an agreement with the other Mongol tribes. Have we not treated with the Oirats in the past? Are you yourselves not living testimony of what I say? As for you, Bairqan, though I do not deny that your forecasts of catastrophe contain a grain of truth, they are as a whole exaggerated. What wisdom is there in leaving a safe land which can feed us to seek out a distant and none too safe land?' After this show of rhetoric in front of his silent audience, Tok Timur looked around for agreement and wondered if he should add further arguments. Since nobody seemed to want to contradict what he had said, he thought that the moment had come to force a decision; also he understood that the other khans, like him, wanted to bring the meeting to an end so that they could be off about their own affairs. So he produced his final argument, which in his opinion would defeat any remaining resistance: 'Do you remember the prophecy of our ancestor Alcidai? The *Naga* on our standard will be able to stand up to our enemies only if we remain united! If any of you decides to choose a different path for himself and his own clan and refuses to be ruled by our group decision, that man will strike a crueller and more abject blow against us than these unlikely enemies of ours!' As often happens, Tok Timur's words made an impression only on those who had been in agreement with him from the beginning, while the two khans who were not remained unmoved, even by the last terrible accusation that the khan had levelled at them. When Tok Timur asked the final question, with the aim of putting his opponents on the spot: 'So who among you wants to follow the Oirats and their allies in their flight westwards?' Mongotai and Bairqan rose to their feet as one, bowed to the khan and those present and walked towards the threshold of the yurt together, raised the embroidered felt carpet one after the other and went outside.

* * *

The Mongols who were preparing for the journey to the west, guided more by a mirage than by precise information and even less by maps or compasses, belonged to different tribes who had origins, language and religion in common, but no name which described them as a group. Yet the travellers of this time called these Mongol tribes 'Kalmyks'. The name probably comes from the Mongol word *qäli-mag*, which means: 'those who cross the riverbank', or 'those who come from the other bank', and this is why. Not long after the Oirats crossed the Emba river they met a caravan heading for Astrakhan. When the Russian merchants asked the Mongols who they were, the latter, either because they had misunderstood the question or because they were at a loss, not knowing what to answer off the top of their heads, answered as I have said. The Russians understood *kalmyk* and since then the name 'Kalmyk' has designated the nomads who settled on the Volga.

The name 'Kalmyk' may also come from the Turkish word *qalmuq* which means 'the ones who stayed behind' and by the same token, those who are backwards, primitive, who are, in short, barbarians. The name might seem to be justified by the savage appearance of the fleeing Mongols, due above all to their hair, because they shaved their temples and their foreheads, leaving only a circle of hair in the middle of their skull, which they kept very long and which fell in plaits down their backs. To the eyes of the highly civilised Russians and their Turkish subjects, that plait invited the adjective barbaric, which came by extension and very unfairly to denote also the person who wore it. The intention behind such a hairstyle was, however, anything but warlike; rather, it expressed the admiration and even affection felt by the Kalmyks, who were superb horsemen, towards the animal they rode and which they tried quite openly to resemble: seen from behind, tail and plait fluttering together at the gallop, rider and horse must have offered an image of perfect symbiosis. But these peaceful intentions were entirely misunderstood by the peoples who lived on the eastern border of the Russian empire and who were very frightened when they saw the horde of plaited nomads, determined to settle on the grasslands bordering on their own fields. This is how the name 'Kalmyk' with its disparaging connotations was adopted by the whole of the West. But the Turkish word *qalmuq* may also go back to the final phase of the flight, in other words the return. The Mongols who lived to the west of the Volga camped along the river waiting for it to freeze so that the other tribes could catch up with them. When this did not happen, they went on alone. The Mongols 'left behind' were called 'Kalmyks': the others, who left, remained nameless. But in the story passed down to the Tunshan, those tribes were also given the name 'Kalmyk' on the journey out and kept that name also on their journey home.

Bairqan, who had spoken with such fervour in favour of the journey west, never reached the Volga, but died exhausted by fever at an unspecified point between the River Emba and the River Ural. One of the lamas then took the funeral manual out of his travelling bag, and established on the basis of the details of his birth and of his death that Bairqan should be wrapped in a white felt shroud and left on the steppe, with his chin pointing west. A natural grave was found, which by chance faced in the required direction. There Bairqan's body was laid and there it stayed, in his sarcophagus reflecting the sunlight, like a dead man who forgot to reawaken on the day of judgement. All around the ditch, wands were planted in the earth and blue silk flags attached to them, which the lama sprinkled with holy water, but above all with words. The Tunshan set off again, gazing often in the direction that Bairqan was facing. The sight of the blue flags fluttering menacingly in the breeze caused them to step up their pace, for fear that Erlig Khan might catch up with them, and they did not slow down again until that blue marker had faded and finally disappeared from view, like a balloon lost in the yellow sky of the steppe.

Mongotai on the other hand was among the first to reach the Volga; he reined in his horse on the bank and waited for the rest of his family to arrive. In a little while he saw Ka'an approaching on horseback, half-hidden by the veil with which she shielded herself and the baby at her breast from the sun. When she got close, Ka'an looked up, with the baby still suckling, and looked blankly at the river, because she was so tired. Mongotai noticed there and then how much her face had aged in the course of the flight, as though the race west had speeded up the passing of the years. When he had taken her as his wife in the land of seven rivers Ka'an had been little more than a child, with breasts that were smaller than green pomegranates, so that Mongotai had wondered more than once if they would be able to nourish a baby. Now the breast which Ka'an held out to her son under the veil was swollen like a pomegranate whose seeds are about to burst out, but her body was dried and withered, as though all the vital lymph had flowed into her milk channel, leaving the rest dry. The expression of still slightly childish curiosity had left her face, and had been replaced by a look of infinite tiredness, which made her seem old. Ka'an displayed no emotion on seeing the Volga, while the Kalmyks around her were wild with joy. Men and boys leapt from their horses and ran down to the river, where at that point there was a small pebbled beach, and jumped among the stones; the more daring tore their clothes off, waded into the water and let themselves be dragged along for a stretch by the current. On the bank mothers were restraining their clamouring small boys and the girls were bending to touch the water and bathing their faces, not caring if they splashed clothes and boots, and shrieking with happiness, so that the river was full of shouts, echoed by the shrieking of frightened birds in the grass and among the reeds.

Meanwhile, as it got nearer, the caravan of Kalmyks broke up and divided like a current which meets an obstacle and turns on itself, swirling in circles: families came together and busied themselves unloading the animals and pitching the yurts in a circle, while other side branches broke off from the column as it arrived, and made for the Volga at points ever more distant from that place where the *ayil* of the Tunshan was already rising.

The news of the horde's arrival had reached the city of Tsaritsyn, later called Volgograd, before receiving and losing the name Stalingrad, and which was further north, a day's ride away.

Everyone in the city who possessed a boat, a raft, a vessel of any kind, anything that floated, set out, by water or overland, and offered it to the Kalmyks in exchange for kopeks or for bartered hides and livestock. It took more than a month for the Kalmyks to reach the opposite bank, where the land opened out in front of them and seemed to correspond in every detail with the tempting promises of the Siren of the Volga. The valleys to the west were green with pasture even at the height of summer, while to the south stretched the steppe which would be known as the 'Kalmyk steppe', a huge, sparsely inhabited area, suitable for flocks and herds of horses. One can hardly be surprised at Cho Alek Khan accepting without cavil the Tsar's conditions, which were for men and horses in exchange for right of pasture. He would have treated with Erlig Khan himself in order to stay, let alone the Tsar. However could he have imagined that the Tsar was even busier carrying off souls than Erlig Khan was, but much less scrupulous than the latter as to treaties and wholly unmoved by spells? As for Mongotai, only a quarter of a century later, when his second son too had been sent off to fight in the Crimea, never to return, he began to think that it would have been better to stay without allies in a land which was drying up rather than let himself be bled by such an insatiable ally.

13

EVEN IN THE land of seven rivers, the grumbling of the discontented was more and more often heard. Some of the grumblers regretted not having followed the Oirats on their journey west, others were afraid that the Tunshan would be crushed between the jaws of the Russian and Chinese empires. To choose between the tiger and the bear was by now merely to choose between the frying pan and the fire. It was then that the general assembly of the Mongols was convened, the most famous *quriltai* ever, after the legendary assembly which had acclaimed Genghis Khan on the banks of the Onon.

It must have been an impressive spectacle for those who arrived over several days in the place determined for the meeting, in the foothills of the Altai, on the banks of the river Irtysh. You could see from far away the white dome of the palace-yurt of the prince of the Khalcha, big enough to contain more than three hundred people, while the yurts of the delegates of the Mongol nations rose for miles around, all dazzlingly white because the delegations were flaunting the purity of their origins and displaying their wealth. Around the yurts grazed the finest horses ever raised by the nomads and camels caparisoned as though for a fair in Dzungaria. Flags of all colours and shades fluttered among the yurts and the people bustling about, even those who were only servants looking after the livestock, wore clothes that would not have disgraced a gathering of kings. These, however, were the noble representatives of tribes and clans which now paid tribute to the Manchu emperor or to the Tsar, people who were becoming poorer by the day, and who were threatened on both sides by the advance of the settlers. But when the khagan of the Khalcha, after officially opening the proceedings of the *quriltai*, rose to speak and saw around him a triple circle of seated men wearing the silken *chalat*, and when these latter, as they bowed low in homage to him, endangered the dignity of their headdresses and revealed over their bent shoulders the silver hilts of their knives, the khagan thought for an instant that he was back on the banks of the Onon and almost felt his illustrious ancestor's spirit descending on him. But he pulled himself together immediately and began to declaim the speech he had prepared:

'When the tiger and the bear ran into each other in the middle of their hunting grounds, the tiger turned aggressively to the bear and said: "Beware that you do not hunt on my steppe! The herds of gazelles and wild asses that graze here belong to me, woe to you if you hunt them! To avoid misunderstandings, I will now trace the border between our territories and if you cross it you will be torn to pieces!" And as he said this he drew such a deep furrow in the ground with his claw that it could not be erased from the sand. The bear was not about to back down either: "Mark my words: I too have claws with which to grab you if you ever venture over the border and catch even the tiniest mouse which belongs in my territory." The animals who were following the discussion from a distance and who well understood the significance of this pact were thrown into panic. The terrified gazelles jumped over the furrow and back again and ended up between the jaws of both beasts; the wild asses thought that the bear was preferable to the tiger and rushed over the border, straight into his clutches; the wild boars, who usually snuffled about the bear's territory, ran snorting wildly to the tiger's side, and were slain in great numbers by him. But the eagle, who was watching the scene from a height, screamed to the maddened animals: "Fools, why are you running from one side to the other? Do as I do; I stay above them both and nobody can take me!" A nanny goat who was perching on a spur of rock, right in the middle of the border between the two hunting grounds, heard these words and answered: "What you say is all very well but you have wings to fly over both sides! I who have no wings, know, however, the art of balancing in the middle where neither tiger nor bear dares to venture!" A wild ass, who had been following the conversation from below, turned then to the other animals and said: "If we all decide together where we want to go then our numbers will give us some strength; neither the tiger nor the bear will be able to eat all of us. Let us declare ourselves subjects of the tiger, and he will be flattered and will reward us by sparing our lives."

At this point the khagan turned directly to his audience. 'What would you prefer? Will you be like the panicking gazelle or like the goat, balancing on her spur of rock? Do you perhaps have wings which allow you to fear no one? Or do you want to follow the wise ass's advice and come to terms with the tiger?'

This, then, was the substance of the speech given by the khagan of the Khalcha, and the reason why he had called the assembly: to convince the Mongols to submit to the Manchu empire, which he believed to be the lesser of the two evils. The delegates approved his proposal by acclamation and the assembly concluded with the same pomp with which it had opened. But when everybody had gone home and the moment had come to adopt the unanimous decision, the Mongols behaved like the animals in the story, who were seized by panic and ran from the claws of one predator to the jaws of the other. Many of the Khalcha went over to the Tsar, while other Mongol tribes, who were Russian subjects, declared themselves vassals of the Manchu. Only the Tunshan followed the tactics of the goat and remained, as in the fairy tale, clinging to their foothold of land which became every day more dangerous and more friable beneath the weight of the hooves and boots competing for it.

It was Chinese arms which decided the Tunshan. On the right bank of the River Ili there was a stone stele which bore a date, one of the few precise dates remembered in the history of the Tunshan, 1755. The Manchu emperor had had the date carved into the stone in remembrance of the conquest of the land of seven rivers, and it was written in four languages: Chinese, Manchurian, Tibetan and Oirat, so that the peoples on either side of the Talki pass could read it and hand down the memory of it. In my time there were still some among the Tunshan who knew that text and could recite it from memory. The emperor praised his undertaking: 'I have given precise instructions to a strong army: bring sufficient provisions with you for several months! Do not think that you are going there to sack cities! A light rain appropriate to the season was falling as the army set out, with the men well rested. The Imperial troops marched in strict formation; no river in full spate barred their way. The man on the left drove the chariot, the one on the right held his lance straight. The Imperial army advanced calmly, the divisions finding no obstacle in their path. We reached the Borotala in one bound, and from there, without stopping, we crossed the Talki. The armies met; we attacked from behind. In only one day the enemy was put to flight, thrown down into the dust, beaten. The Ili is pacified and I, calling to witness the millennia to come, have had these lines cut into this marble,' the Emperor concluded to his own glory.

The khan who pronounced the submission of the Tunshan was called, ironically enough, Genghis. This name had made him uncomfortable all his life; now, however, as he bowed before the Chinese official and placed the banner of the eight *Naga* under the protection of the Manchu emperor, Genghis Khan would willingly have borrowed his horse's name, rather than pronounce his own, so dishonoured and mocked was it on that day. For the rest of his allotted span, until he died none too heroically covered with the oozing pustules of smallpox, Genghis wondered what sins he had committed in a previous life to deserve the punishment of such an inappropriate name. And since he was by nature more compassionate than cruel, in this too quite at odds with the name he bore, Genghis had good cause to torture himself. But the greatest pain he suffered was caused by the events of the year in which the Kalmyks embarked upon their homeward flight, and was connected with this flight.

'The flight of the Kalmyks was one of the most stirring episodes in our history. I say ours, because, as you know, the Tunshan, who had themselves once left the land of seven rivers to follow the Oirats, played a part in it. So stirring an event – when in history did so many people set out to return to the land of their ancestors? – was bound to have consequences. And indeed it marked the history of the Tunshan for ever.'

The flight. A people is on the move, a column is lost in the desert, and the beginning cannot be seen and the end cannot be made out. I still saw that column in my dreams, curled up in my white bed in the Bergers' house, and it became confused with other columns. There were so many people fleeing through my story.

Unlike the original journey, the flight of 1771 was not the fruit of a collective decision; on the contrary, it was meditated, discussed and planned in the khan's tent, without any word leaking out among the people. Agreements were struck in secret with the Chinese emperor; ambassadors were sent in secret to the Dalai Lama, so that he could give his blessing to the undertaking from afar; seers were consulted in secret to decide the most propitious moment for the departure.

* * *

It was the beginning of June when the men who watched over the herds not far from Lake Balkhash saw the column of refugees appear and went to warn the others. Then Genghis Khan ordered his son Urus to go and look. What seemed from above to be an ordered procession, following fixed instructions, proved at close quarters to be a stream of people driven forwards by a will whose original impulse had been forgotten. The faces were empty of all thought and marked only by the determination to push on, shared by men and animals alike, made similar by fatigue and hunger. Many Kalmyks abandoned their heavier baggage and loaded their children and those who could no longer walk onto their animals and themselves walked, beside the animals, carrying whatever was indispensable. One would have said that their own weight was too much for them and that they would happily have given up that too, even though under their faded *chalat* there was little more than skin over their bones. The animals were in no better state. The horses' ribs were bent like bows about to burst through their skin; the camels' humps hung wobbling like Albasty's empty breasts and gave them a pitifully melancholy appearance, while the cows seemed to have suffered seven lean years. Only the sheep hid the hunger they suffered under their tangled coats. Seven hundred and fifty miles of desert steppe, crossed in a few months, had reduced the robust Kalmyks to a horde of spectres, so much so that Urus wondered whether a gust of the *karaburan* would not be enough to scatter the column.

When Genghis Khan learnt of the identity of the refugees, he sent them animals, livestock, provisions and yurts and invited them to stay on his lands until they were able to continue their journey. But not all the Tunshan approved of this generous welcome and many protested. Genghis Khan was angry: 'The steppe has no border; borders are in men's minds. While I am khan of the Tunshan, we will not deny these refugees our warmest welcome, even down to our last bowl of *kumiss*.'

Genghis Khan slept badly that night. The morning breeze had not yet risen when loud shouts and a hubbub of people and horses brought him running out of the yurt. Straight away he saw that tongues of flame were rising from the Kalmyk camp. The air was so still that the fire seemed like an ordinary campfire, only higher and strangely still, while around it everything was in motion. Some were trying to smother the flames with felt carpets; others were digging a ditch to stop the fire spreading; still others had formed a long line and were passing containers of water from hand to hand.

Where a yurt had stood the evening before, there remained three hearthstones, the brazier and a few objects spared by the fire. But a dead foal, which had been tied to the fire, was still lying inside the blackened circle. Genghis Khan went to the yurt where the victims' family had taken refuge, carrying gifts, but when he heard that a child had been trapped by the flames inside its cradle, hanging from the ceiling, and when he saw its mother's face, he felt as though he were choking and hurried out.

Genghis Khan wondered again why the gods had burdened man with the capacity for compassion. 'Perhaps even my ancestral namesake cried at the death of his mother Hö'elün,' thought Genghis Khan. And yet how to imagine a man in mourning who had arranged to have his own son put to death? Had he not declared that his greatest pleasure lay in defeating his enemies, driving them before him, stripping them of all their possessions, seeing their loved ones in tears, riding their horses and forcing their wives and daughters to his own bed? How might so much cruelty be reconciled with the prohibition on killing? As he tossed and turned in a fever, not long afterwards, the descendant of Genghis Khan posed himself these and other dilemmas but he did not resolve them, because he was eaten up with smallpox, which filled him with pus and wounds which would not dry, and he died not long afterwards. He was the last khan of the Tunshan to be buried in a cave in the Alatau, beneath a white tent and with supplies of food, but with no horse to accompany him on his journey.

14

URUS OPENED HIS eyes, shut them again, then opened them a second time. A beam of light shone through the hole in the middle of the yurt and divided the space in two halves: Urus lay in the half which was plunged in shadow. The light passed over the bed, over the hearth and settled just above the ground on the wooden lattice of the wall. There it broke into a swirl of dust, like a line of ants milling around in front of an unexpected obstacle, twisted round and then went on in a straight line along the wall until it touched the edge of the embroidered carpet. A ray of sun, herald of a day of blazing sunshine. Urus followed its progress, his eyes sliding along the line of light, down to where it met the opposite wall. A ray of sunlight. And yet it was strange. Urus tried to lift his head, and even attempted to raise himself up on to his elbows and sit up, but gave up immediately and fell back. The sun indicated clearly that the second milking had been over for some time and he, Urus, was still lazing in bed, instead of being outside bringing the horses to pasture and checking to see if the wolf had killed any sheep. But there was something else, and the ray of light, so clearly illuminating part of the yurt, hid it from him and revealed it to him at the same time. Emptiness. There was emptiness around him and a silence which seemed to fill it entirely. Urus made a fresh effort and got his elbows under him, and looked towards the part of the yurt which the sun left in shadow, where the older children usually slept. It was empty and there was no sign to indicate recent occupation of the hides rolled against the walls or the objects neatly stored in the bags hanging from their hooks. To the left of the entrance, as far as the kitchen shelves, the yurt was unusually empty, as though life had come to a halt. Only then did Urus notice Sagatai, crouched at the foot of his bed, looking at him. She sat there so still, and in the shadows, that she seemed a part of the silence; her small, withdrawn presence seemed to offer no obstacle to the emptiness. Only when her husband's gaze lighted on her did Sagatai seem to come alive, sit up and turn her palms to him, as though her words were a gift: 'Praise be to Qormusda,' she said, 'and to the ancestors who protect our hearth. You are better.' Urus lay back on the mattress and gazed at her in astonishment. Was this the face that had been described by a poet on their wedding day 'shining like the moon in her last quarter'? Was this the girl that had once been so plump and so merry? Was this the skin 'soft as the apricots in the valleys of the Alatau'? What insect had carved craters in her cheeks? What needle had furrowed her forehead? Her face, with its two slanted eyes locked on him, was like a clumsily embroidered felt carpet. Urus, as though seized with a sudden doubt, passed his hand over his face and withdrew it with a gesture of disgust: the crusts formed a shell round his nose and mouth, and the back of his hand was covered with them too. A demon had passed over both of them, leaving its terrible tracks behind it. Urus was horrified by himself, and full of sorrow for the face in front of him, anxiously studying his reactions. Her gaze, which burnt through slits in her swollen eyelids, cut him to the core. He was again overwhelmed by a sense of emptiness and his whole body shook with worry. Sagatai feared that the fever had come back, and bent over him, but then she understood. 'Only Timur is left,' she said. 'I had him put in a yurt away from the others; Sigi and Sarkan are watching over him and not letting anybody in. Sojan the shaman is near him to keep the demons away, so that they don't take him too. Your mother is with him. Timur, only Timur is left.' As she said this Sagatai crumpled, her hands gripping the edge of the bed, as her body convulsed with rhythmic sobs like labour pains.

Hold on, Sagatai, and push. The babies slid easily onto the felt blanket and welcoming hands severed them from her with a knife. Sagatai kept six of these knives in the red lacquered chest; six times she had taken the little creatures wrapped in lambskin into her arms; six times she had examined their little bodies, but they were whole and healthy, boys and girls. Now too they had been wrapped in felt blankets and somebody had loaded them onto a horse and let them fall behind him, without turning to look, as a man does when he gets rid of an unwanted thing and pretends he has not noticed losing it. Abandoned in the steppe like *kuraj* bushes forgotten by the wind. Let them not find the road back to the *ayil*, let Sagatai's dead children not return among the living!

Those were the days when one looked at little children as though at beings suspended between earth and heaven, who had not yet decided which place to choose, days when to raise more than one child to adulthood was considered rare good fortune, and even then the stubbornness with which death came back to the yurts and emptied cradles and the children's pallets seemed a challenge to human endurance, an insult to suffering, which the collective tragedy did precious little to ease.

As he looked at his wife, Urus understood that the fever had protected him; it had prevented him from feeling anything beside the burning in his skin, and so shielded him from the tragedy unfolding in his yurt. Pain lay in wait for him now, on the threshold of his convalescence; it leered as it took possession of his fever-racked body, stifling every other emotion and sticking to his temples like an octopus. Urus knew that the pain would leave indelible marks inside him, in the inner recesses where the soul hides, like those which the smallpox had drawn on his face. Now not only did Urus remember the preceding weeks, but they came back to him with a clarity apparently nourished by the fever.

The Great Wind it had been that brought the fever. The demons of sickness had been borne to the yurts of the Tunshan with the first gust of wind, clinging to the grains of dust in the air. They had come into the yurts, even if the smokehole was almost closed in those days, even though heavy felt carpets as well as wooden doors barred entrance. The first to fall ill were old people and children. Urus's father Genghis Khan had dragged his ceremonial saddle out of his yurt in his delirium, and tried to mount his horse. They sent for Urus too because nobody could talk him out of this and the trembling of his limbs seemed to restore something like his former energy to him; they had difficulty persuading him to go back to bed. He shouted that the yurt was on fire and begged them to let him out, but it was his poor body that was on fire with fever; he died eight days later. The children too burned with fever and it was useless for their mothers to press compresses soaked in *kumiss* to their burning foreheads; it was useless for the lamas, who were living with the Tunshan at that time as they did every year, to recite mysterious formulae, taking great care at the same time not to cross the threshold of those yurts infected by the sickness. When the ribbons of black cloth knotted before the entrance were no longer an isolated occurrence, but had spread through all the villages of the Tunshan, and the wind, as if to mock the desolate warning not to enter, reduced them to rags, then the lamas began to give the desperate mothers little printed scrips with strange signs on them, and accompanied the prescriptions with precise instructions: half for each child, a whole one for adults or for more serious cases, chew carefully and swallow. The mothers thanked them, touching their foreheads with their joined hands which clutched the precious scrip. But when the printed scrips had run out and the lamas were obliged to write them out by hand as the queue of women in front of their yurt grew longer every day, then the monks bade farewell to Urus, the new khan, and one breezy morning they set out again for the Talki pass. And still the prescriptions continued to circulate among the Tunshan; out of prudence or merely the hope of gain, some people had laid by a supply and sold them; there were even some prepared to trade in them, buying them from a monastery beyond the Talki and selling them on for a profit to the Tunshan. The women exchanged their wedding earrings for the scraps of printed paper covered in incomprehensible symbols. Urus was compelled to send guards to control movement between the yurts, so that the Tunshan did not lose their possessions as well as their children. But even more than the guards, it was the winter that stopped the sales of prescriptions by blocking the passage over the Talki. Whether it was power of suggestion, or whether the scrips truly worked in curing the sickness, it is a fact that when the first snow whitened the flanks of the Alatau, the epidemic flared up even more violently, as though it had overcome the very last resistance, and fell on the Tunshan with the fury of a river in full flood. Sojan, the shaman, a mere shadow of himself, bent under the weight of his ceremonial dress, continued to burn juniper twigs before the image of a god dancing on a pile of corpses.

This country is hostile to us, thought Urus, and he looked at the banks of cloud headed towards the south-east and low, far away, the whirl of dust and the bushes that the Great Wind was dragging in the same direction. 'This country is hostile to us,' said Urus out loud and immediately started at his own words, because there was nobody near him and it was a bad sign that his thoughts were becoming words without him realising. There was only his horse, tied to a rail, shaking its head and snorting, as though he knew about his illness and had been waiting all this time for him. Urus made ready to mount and immediately realised how weak he was. How strange it was that simply climbing into the saddle could cost him so much effort. Perhaps growing old was like this. You start to think about things which you had previously done without noticing; you gauge where to put your hands and feet and you fear that your muscles will not be able to carry out their intended movements. Urus was on horseback, now, and he could feel the sweat pearling on his forehead and darkening his eyes. He hung onto the animal's neck and raised his head, taking deep breaths. Once more the dazzling blue of the wind-swept sky opened out before him. The horse proceeded at a walk and Urus steered him towards the place where Sagatai had had Timur's yurt pitched to hide him from the demons.

Urus crossed the threshold of the yurt; Timur, who was playing with some lamb's bones, no sooner saw him than he ran to him shouting 'Baba, baba!' Urus swept the light weight up in his arms and lifted him above his head, looking carefully at the laughing child suspended in mid-air. There was no doubt about it, Timur was well.

He put the child down again. Sojan the shaman came into the yurt, ran his hands swiftly over his own chest and forehead, and bowed before Urus. But the latter was in a hurry to speak his thoughts. 'The Great Wind is dragging the clouds and the heaps of *kuraj* bushes to the south-east. The Great Wind brought us the demon who covers the skin with blisters; the Great Wind is clearly a sign from the gods: leave this country! This country is hostile to us, Sojan, it is up to us to leave it before another winter devours our children down to the very last one!' And he looked at Timur who was intent on his game with the bones. Sagatai looked uncomprehending at her husband but this is what Sojan said: 'The Great Wind has always blown to the south-east; the clouds have always rolled across the blue sky and the *kuraj* across the steppe: why are you surprised? And why do you want to set off on a journey just now when the Tunshan are weak and decimated by sickness and have not the strength even to defend their herds from the wolves?' Urus interrupted him with a gesture of his hand: 'It will be you, Sojan, who will say when the most auspicious moment is to depart; you will consult your spirits and propitiate them! As to our journey's end, south of the Kyzylkum and of the great river they call the Oxus there are lands still inhabited by peoples who share our ancestry. These are lands which neither the bear nor the tiger have yet conquered, free lands, where those who live in yurts can travel at will in search of pastures for their animals.'

'Your father Genghis Khan was right to praise you for the sharpness of your mind,' answered the shaman. 'It is true; Kochi, great-grandson of the great Genghis Khan, conquered the land south of the Oxus and made it a Mongol province. They say that before he went to join the rest of the White Horde and the land of seven rivers he left ten thousand soldiers to defend the conquered land. These pitched their camps in the valley of a hundred monasteries that was called Bamian, below the lake bluer than the sky and greener than the steppe in spring. Even if we know nothing of the descendants of these ten thousand, it is possible that they still live in that country. May Qormusda grant you long life, khan of the Tunshan. Forgive me if I ask again, but how do you hope to find a people who have been sundered from us for so many centuries in such a distant and unknown country? How will you convince the Tunshan to follow you, when they are hardly fit to mount their horses? And how do you hope to escape the watchfulness of the Chinese?'

'Sojan, our ancestors conquered countries whose existence they had not even suspected. They travelled much greater distances. Are the Tunshan, despite the sickness afflicting them, so much less than their fathers? If there are still peoples south of the Oxus who are descended from Genghis Khan, we will find them and they will certainly not turn us away: in the name of our common ancestors they will be our allies, if that unknown country is hostile to us. As for the Chinese, we will elude their sentries by skirting the steppe to the south-east, at the edge of the desert. Their fear of contagion has in any case greatly reduced their numbers. And besides we will not all be leaving at once, as the Kalmyks did, but in small groups, one *ayil* at a time, so as not to be spotted by the Chinese, or further south by the sentries of the khanate of Bukhara.'

The real problem was knowing how many of the Tunshan were left and Urus ordered a census, the only one in our history besides those that the Russians carried out when taxing people and livestock. But, while the Tunshan were very careful not to answer truthfully to the latter, the census commanded by Urus Khan revealed a more dramatic truth then expected. The demon of the smallpox had carried away a third of the adults and had attacked the children so fiercely that only a quarter of them were still alive. 'A people without children!' Urus said over and over as he counted the marks drawn by his messengers in every yurt, one for every death, one for every woman, man or child still living. As he counted the black sticks representing the dead and the living, and found that they were massing in great numbers on the side of the dead, he could only shake his head and repeat: 'What people is poorer than the people with no children? What greater misfortune is there than to have no descendants?'

Sojan the shaman consulted the spirits, read the future in the polished bones of a lamb and interpreted the flight of a white hawk which flew over the *ayil* to the right of the yurts. 'Urus Khan,' he said finally, 'when the Great Wind stops blowing and returns to the Eastern steppes, when the first moon of the first month of the new season rises, then we may leave.'

This is what Sojan the shaman said and turning to the earthen altar, sprinkled curdled milk and *kumiss*, and informed the spirits of the earth that the Tunshan were about to leave:

O spirits of the land of seven rivers and a thousand streams!
O Tengri who live high in the white snows of the Alatau!
Be merciful to the Tunshan who are leaving!
Let this parting not offend you!
The Tunshan have left their children in the steppe!
The Great Wind threatens the fire

between the three stones of their hearths.
Let them find damp ground for pastures,
Fill the cradles hanging from the roofs of their yurts!
Make their journey free of dangers,
as this night is free of clouds,
and let the Tunshan find the road at the edge of the desert!
O Tengri who live high in the white snows of the Alatau!
Kuraj! Kuraj! Kuraj!

When the first of the Tunshan left the land of seven rivers the sun had not yet appeared from behind the peaks of the Alatau. A small group said goodbye to them in silence: these were those who still had sick people or convalescents in their yurts. The final arrangements were made. Messengers would travel back and forth between the Tunshan so that they would not lose each other's trail, and they exchanged the last silken scarves. Then Urus, with Timur dozing on the saddle, gave the signal for departure.

The steppe was green and dotted with flowers and the days were getting ever warmer. The Tunshan were now travelling by night in order to avoid the heat and the sentries of the khanate of Bukhara. One day, before sunrise, they had pitched their travelling tents on the banks of the Syrdar'ya, which were a brilliant green in that season. As the light grew brighter, Urus went to inspect the land around. The Tunshan always kept to the left of the desert, far from the villages; they travelled for days at a time without seeing a single settlement. Urus was therefore astonished to find an isolated building a short distance from the riverbank, which he had not noticed in the dark. It was a circular, brick building, with white and blue traces of ancient majolica, although only the upper edge of the old stucco was still there under the dome. Near the mosque, almost touching it, stood a broken minaret. It was impossible to tell whether it had been attacked by enemies or damaged in an earthquake, but it was plainly cut off just where one would have expected to see the topmost part of the building. In place of the dome there was a large nest and two storks stood stiffly in the nest; their red legs seemed like the load-bearing columns of a black and white dome. Birds fluttered all around, inside the crevices and outside, between the corroded bricks, so that it might have seemed like a dovecote if the coloured tiles and traces of writing had not revealed its older, sacred meaning. Urus approached the door of the mosque and opened it. Swallows swirled around nests cemented between the flights of the architraves which, though they had once been elegant, were now encrusted with excrement. The empty space beneath the dome opened in its turn onto a narrow corridor leading to a small room, in the centre of which stood an imposing sarcophagus of carved alabaster. The filtered light coming in through narrow windows with alabaster panes was yellow and dim like the sarcophagus standing with the sunlight falling on it. Urus was so entranced by it that he jumped at the sound of an angry voice addressing him and clapped a hand to his swordbelt. Then he saw an old man behind the sarcophagus who sat up on the pile of carpets he had been sleeping on until a moment ago and adjusted a dirty white turban over his forehead. A threatening finger pointed at Urus's boots, which he hastily removed. The old man immediately calmed down and went on talking to him, but Urus could not understand. Then he signalled to him to wait and bent over in a niche in the wall, removing a wooden cover. He lowered a bucket into the well, brought it up full and offered it to Urus. The water was fresher than any Urus could remember, since all he had drunk for several weeks was the brackish water from the wells they found on the road, water that was the colour of earth and often tasted like it. He thanked the man and in exchange took his tobacco pouch out of the pocket of his *chalat* and held it out to him. The old man emptied its contents into the deep pocket of his caftan, then pulled out a present in turn and held it out to Urus: it was a cube of clay glazed blue on one side and in the middle there was a petal, a single yellow petal. The rest of the flower had ended up in other hands, but that petal ended up in the grateful hands of my ancestor Urus Khan and then his descendants passed it from hand to hand until it reached my grandfather Bairqan.

Urus Khan halted at the Amudar'ya and waited there for the very last of the Tunshan to join him. But not everybody came. Two clans, he was told, preferred to stay in the land round the Ili, while a third had chosen the road east and having crossed the Talki pass, had made for Dzungaria, preferring the return to lands known to them at least by reputation to the risk of a journey into the unknown. By now the Tunshan were reduced to only three clans and three they remained in what became their adoptive country.

Urus Khan hoped that he would be spared the affront that his father Genghis Khan had suffered when he had to bow his head in submission before a Chinese general. He, Urus Khan, had brought his people to a free country, where neither the soldiers of the Tsar nor those of the Chinese emperor would venture. He was unaware that the plain around the Oxus was a land to which not only the Chinese and the Russians aspired, but also other conquerors. How could Urus Khan, how could the Tunshan, coming from a country far from everything, be familiar with the complicated chessboards on the borders of India? And yet for a century and a half history would prove Urus Khan right; neither the Russians, nor the English, still less the Chinese were concerned with these few hundred nomads come to join the many who grazed their animals in the summer on the highlands of the Paropamisus and the Hindu Kush and went down to the valleys and the plain to the south of the Amudar'ya in winter. Nor did the local tribes pay much attention to the new arrivals, since there were so many languages spoken in that region, so many styles of dress and so many peoples. At first the Turkmen and Tajik farmers looked with suspicion on the yurts of the Tunshan, but they were not openly hostile. When Urus sent to the villages to ask if they knew the valley of a hundred monasteries that is called Bamian, the peasants, without wholly understanding and without stirring, would raise an arm to point towards the south, as if to say, beyond those mountains. Perhaps they made the gesture only because they thought it discourteous not to answer, and because a wrong answer was better than no answer at all, or perhaps they had understood and were answering accordingly. In any case, Urus was persuaded that the people he was looking for, a people related to his own, were indeed to be found behind the mountains, in one of the many valleys nestling between them. He looked to the south, studied the entrances to the valleys and continued to enquire in the scattered Uzbek villages and in the huddled villages of the Tajiks. Over there, they all said.

* * *

He finally came to a decision one spring. The yurts of the Tunshan were at that time pitched right behind the ancient walls of the city of Balkh against which the *karaburan* raged, as though it had decided once and for all to raze it to the ground. Urus left the village with a few companions, his son Timur following on horseback, and set off up the valley of the River Balkh. The juniper bushes became trees, the trees became towering cedars; herds of sheep scattered at their approach, while women and girls hurried to cover their faces with their veils. The shepherds, on the other hand, gave no sign of having noticed the newcomers, but watched them with their long narrow eyes, like those of the Tunshan. They followed the valley as far as the place where the Balkh becomes the Band-e-Amir and arrived almost at the river's source. Urus Khan had already begun to think that the long journey had been in vain, when suddenly a stony plateau appeared, spread out before his eyes, with not a tree or a bush, not a tussock of grass, but in the middle a blue-green lake between banks of white limestone, so clear that only the clouds ruffled its surface. The Tunshan stopped and hesitated, afraid that they would offend the spirits of the place if they came any nearer. But Timur was already cantering towards the lowest point on the lakeshore, had already slipped from his horse and taken off his boots and was splashing about on the edge of the lake. Urus Khan was behind him and reached the water too. There was no doubt that it was the lake of which was said:

Transparent dwelling of the Naga
clear pupil of the earth,
the gods have drawn on you
to give streams to the earth.
Let my horse dip his thirsty lips
in your clarity,
let me bend the knee
on your snow-white banks
and let me fill my cupped hands,
my sun-darkened hands, with water
and let me refresh my face with you.

Beyond the lake the Bamian valley widened invitingly; poplars rose at the feet of an enormous Buddha. The rock was honeycombed with monasteries, and yurts like those of the Tunshan were pitched on both banks of the river. The Moghuls wore their heads swathed in turbans and called Allah to witness, but the language they spoke, even though mixed with Persian words, was similar to the language of the Tunshan and they could understand each other.

Timur was the first of the Tunshan to take a Moghul girl to wife; my great-great-great-grandfather Ul'an was the last. Bairqan laughed as he told the story of his grandfather's wedding: when three days after the festivities the bride still couldn't bring herself to take her veil off and show herself to her husband, the latter began to suspect that she was hiding some deformity or dreadful ugliness or that perhaps they had spirited her away, as in the fairy tale, and instead of a girl he had married an old woman or worse still, a jinn. Finally he tired of waiting and took the girl by the shoulders and lifted her veil. 'At last,' she said in her strange Mongol dialect, 'I was afraid I was going to have to look at you forever from behind my *chador!*' She had the broad face and open gaze of the girls from the nomad tribes; she was bright and cheerful too and continued to talk in the language which the Tunshan mimicked and ended up learning. Bairqan remembered a song of his grandmother's and liked to sing it to us; he took a deep breath, closed his eyes, as though the tune came to him from distant depths and he had to concentrate in order to call it to the surface, and intoned in his deep bass voice:

High on the mountain top I sit and play the flute.
I lost my camel and follow the road on foot.
I lost the camel, the king's camel,
so hearken to my song:
Where are you, love?

Bairqan finished on a tremolo and seemed unable to tear himself away from that final 'love'. My grandfather ended the lesson here, with these lines, which linked our most remote past with the more recent past, and with the image of the camel driver sitting on the peaks of the Hindu Kush, as though the history of the Tunshan had run aground there momentarily, like Noah's ark on top of Mount Ararat. It was now up to us to finish the story.

This was our history and we understood that the Tunshan were only a small part of a wider weft that our ancestors had helped to weave, as our women did, when they sat in a row one beside the other and passed the bobbin swiftly along the warp; to look at them you would have said that each was working on her own, while the emerging carpet was the work of everyone. And this was our geography. We repeated the names of the rivers: Ili, Talas, Karatal, Yemba, Volga, and sometimes Bairqan traced an atlas on the carpet. Look, here is the Onon, Genghis Khan's river, and he put a longer bone on the right; here is the Altai, and a small pointed bone stood for the mountain range; here is the Alatau, and here is the Syrdar'ya and the Amudar'ya further down, and here are we. We learnt how to read our own places on the carpet scattered with bones. We knew that these places belonged to us in a way, that we carried them with us as we carried with us the hearthstones and the paper dolls of our ancestors. We Tunshan were few, but the generations at our back peopled our winter camp to the south of the great river and the summer camp to the north. How lonely would the little villages of yurts have been otherwise in the vastness of the steppe! How easily we would have lost our own traces, had we not had at our back that richly embroidered and coloured cloth!

Part Two

THE SOLDIER'S STORY

15

I CAN SEE myself sitting in front of the polished cherrywood table in Dr Wallatz's study, with that gentleman opposite me, scrutinising me, in a place I didn't know. I felt like a creature without a history. What's the good of having a history if nobody else knows it but you? If you don't even know how to communicate it to someone close to you, because, even if you knew the words for it, they wouldn't understand what you were talking about? What did my new mother, Marianne and Dr Wallatz, know about Alcidai, Urus Khan, or even Genghis Khan? I felt like a creature cut off from everything, a marmot dropped by a white hawk in the middle of the desert. Now I was looking for traces that would lead me somewhere. If you find yourself in a place you don't know, they used to say to us, look around you carefully, find a trail, and follow it. In front of me I had the paper with the blue writing that meant my name, Naja. Here was the trail I was looking for, the signs that would lead me to the language I did not yet know. So I took the chalk that Dr Wallatz was holding out to me and I copied the writing onto my slate. I concentrated, following the original with my eyes, and moved the chalk in precise little movements, as though it was an embroidery needle on a black warp. I traced the four letters, compared them with the original, my eyes moving from the blue to the white, rubbed out the tail of the j with my finger and did it again bigger, and then I looked up at Dr Wallatz. 'Good girl!' My hand traced the letters easily, knotted them together to form words, set them out neatly on the lines, and rewrote them with the precision with which my tongue reproduced sounds. My teacher's large hand, which he had put over mine at the beginning to guide it in the bold curves of the writing, had been taken away almost immediately: 'You don't need it.' My fingers weren't those of a clumsy schoolgirl, but were expert at plying a needle, at knotting the most invisible threads, at passing the shuttle swiftly through the warp of the loom, and they had no difficulty in running a pen over the lines of a copy book or in squeezing the four letters of my name between the fences of lines. Naja, Naja, Naja. My hand ran ever more nimbly from the N to the a and then again to the a by way of the loop of the j. Dr Wallatz was pleased with me. 'Now write this: Name.' And I copied: Name, Name. Dr Wallatz touched his finger to his large nose with the tufty hairs sticking out of it that were harder to control than the twigs in his garden, and I pointed to my nose which stuck out slightly between the high cheekbones of my face. 'Nose,' said Dr Wallatz and wrote it, and I dutifully wrote: Nose, Nose, Nose.

'This child is a prodigy!' Dr Wallatz stroked his beard as he talked, while showing my mother to the door. 'Like a sponge, there's not a drop wasted.' My mother looked at me one last time as she left, a look in which a kind of amazement filtered through the usual background of anxiety. A smile flitted across her face, and she disappeared, leaving us in our little *studiolo*.

What impressed Dr Wallatz was my ability to grasp and repeat words and whole phrases without a mistake, retaining them and then pulling them out when they were needed. Dr Wallatz looked at me in admiration, unaware that this ability of mine was nothing exceptional, at home. We were used to listening to and learning words and music by heart in a very short time; some of us excelled at this art. The boy who looked after the sheep was a true marvel in this regard. He was called Nergüj, which means 'no-name'. His parents had given him this name to hoodwink the spirits, so that they would not realise from the name that it belonged to a human being, a boy or a girl, and he would thus be spared the fate of his brothers, who had not reached the age of their first haircut. The name, however, had only been partly successful, as the spirits had found him anyway and Nergüj had hovered for a long time between earth and the beyond before deciding to stay among the living. He still bore the mark of the next world, for his right arm dangled uselessly and 'no-name' had to keep it tied to his neck with a scarf, like a cumbersome charm he could never be rid of. Because of his arm and his precarious health, which made us fear every winter that he would not live to see the spring, Nergüj was put in charge of the smallest animals and spent whole days alone at pasture with his Jew's harp as his only companion. Over time he had learnt to imitate it with his mouth and to produce two sounds at once. Nergüj no longer needed the Jew's harp: he was instrument and voice at once, so much so that we laughed and said that he had swallowed it and now it was playing in his belly. He could also reproduce lines of verse word for word, no matter how long and difficult they were, after hearing them just the once. A Kyrgyz storyteller passed through one day and sang us an episode from the story of Manas in his own language which we did not fully understand, and Nergüj had repeated every line without making a mistake, arousing the admiration of the Kyrgyz who asked him if he wanted to accompany him on his travels. But Nergüj's parents did not want to lose their only male child and 'no-name' stayed with us and sang us the tale of the hero Geser. His voice was strong and he alternated the words with the sounds which came out of his throat, a flute and a violin at the same time. He sang so well that on moonlit nights somebody would always put out pieces of cheese and dried meat on the roof of the yurt, because we thought that the heroes would be summoned by such a voice and would find their way to us, and we could not leave them with nothing to eat. And indeed, when we looked for the food in the morning, there would be nothing there and Ukin my grandmother would look contentedly up at the sky. Who could have competed with that nameless boy who knew how to summon heroes with his voice alone? My ability to remember little childish phrases was a paltry thing by comparison. All languages say the same things and to say them you merely have to train your tongue, press it against your palate or your teeth, make the sounds more or less deeply in your throat and set it vibrating, like the Jew's harp swallowed by the shepherd boy. It was normal to us for things to have several different names: there were things which could not be named, because their name brought bad luck, and we then had to resort to other words. Nobody, for example, would utter the word 'wolf': we used to say 'whiner', 'Erlig's dog', 'sky dog' or 'steppe dog' and there were other ways too of naming it without using its name. The same meaning could be expressed in several ways; the fact that they were different languages was secondary. The need to communicate with the most diverse neighbours obliged us to use their languages; all of us, especially the men, knew a few words of Tajik or Pashto, and Uzbek and Russian were spoken on a daily basis. Ours was a polyglot community. Learning a new language was therefore not too hard for me; but the people around me now, who were unused to speaking languages other than their own, looked with awe at those who could. I very soon understood that this was the way to conquer that alien environment and carve out a place which was not that of the beggars to the left of the entrance door to the yurt. An opportunity soon presented itself. One afternoon, coming back from Dr Wallatz's lessons, and passing in front of the kitchen, I saw the women gathered together. Marianne was sitting with her strong arms crossed, bare as usual, and resting on the table, framing and holding up the weight of her breasts. Kathe was ironing, while Hannah was standing with one fist on her hip and the other arm on the table. They were chattering away and as I passed I caught the word *Morgen* . . . So I went in and taking my cue from that word which was still hanging in the air, I continued the nursery rhyme I had just learnt: *Morgen früh um sechs / kommt die kleine Hex'. / Morgen früh um sieben / kocht sie gelbe Rüben. / Morgen früh um acht / wird Kaffee gemacht*, Every morning at six, / the little witch arrives. / Every morning at seven, she cooks yellow carrots. / Every morning at eight / she makes coffee . . . And so it went on, with the little witch scurrying to and fro all morning between kitchen and byre, hotly pursued by the obsessive hammering of the hours: *Morgen früh um sechs, morgen früh um sieben, morgen früh um acht, um neun, um zehn* . . . It was a trudge round the fireplace and up to the hayloft, an exhausting race to the zenith of midday. In the middle of the kitchen, to the astonishment of the maids who had stopped talking and moving about to listen to me, as though they were hearing the rhyme for the first time, I recited it in a singsong and noticed how my recitation was met with silent admiration: *Feuert dann um elf / kocht dann bis um zwölf. / Spinnen, Krebsebein und Fisch, / hürtig Kinder Kommt zu Tisch!* . . . She lights the fire at eleven / and cooks until twelve. / Spiders, crabs'-legs and fish, / come, children, hurry and eat! . . . The enchanted menu and the summons to table ended the little witch's race through the morning and I stopped suddenly there. There was a moment's silence, then Marianne lifted her bosom from the table, lunged at me, took me in her arms, pressed me to her and said: 'I knew you'd do it, I just knew it!' She was so happy and moved she nearly cried, while the others chimed in with their comments and Kathe narrowly avoided scorching the linen napkin on the ironing board. I had won them over by reciting a children's nursery rhyme. I had grasped that the way to their hearts did not pass through difference, but through similarity. It was not the qualities that differed from theirs that would make them my friends, but my proving that I knew the same things as they knew. What was different in me did not interest them or scared them and I had no choice but to hide it. I thought about this while Marianne, Kathe and Hannah made much of me, and then one of them laughed and said: 'Now we'd better teach her the Cologne dialect too!' And another said, 'Come on, have a try, say *Kirche*.' And she pronounced *Kirche*, church, like *Kirsche*, cherry and like a good girl I repeated the word and I said *Kirsche* for church and I said *Sonntags in der Kirsche*, Sunday in the cherry, and the three women laughed and Marianne hugged me as though I had just awakened from a coma. And they laughed and said *Kirche* and *Kirsche* and through hearing me repeat these words that they knew, little by little they lost their fear of me.

But this fear was liable to flare up again every time the strange creature within me came to light and made its presence felt, although I myself neither wished it nor realised it. One night a violent storm broke over Cologne. Elsewhere, in the old town, the wind blew down the tottering ruins of the houses and knocked down whatever still stubbornly stood, but when it came to our house it only shook the trees in the garden as though it wanted to tear them up by the roots. Thunder and lightning filled the kitchen. Marianne had run to turn off the light 'so that they don't get into the current' and was sitting beside me, her hands in her apron, her eyes half closed, her lips barely moving as she muttered a stream of litanies: 'Jesus, Joseph and Mary, save my soul. Jesus, Joseph and

Mary . . .' She was afraid of the lightning, like me. I had inherited from my ancestors the fear of the spirit who summons the chosen to death with a flash of lightning. For as long as a storm lasted we stayed well hidden inside the yurts and didn't come out until the thunder had faded into the distance and the lightning had died down. Then Ukin, who had seen me being born and whom I remembered as ancient, went round the village sprinkling tea in the direction of the four points of the compass and muttering the spell:

Your summer this way
your bad weather that way,
your colours this way,
your winter that way,
your rain this way,
your whirlwinds that way;
conserving your water,
may your grass be abundant,
may your sound be silence,
may your lightning bolts be weak,
my Qormusda Tengri,
kuraj, kuraj, kuraj.

The invocation came from my lips without my noticing, in the language in which Ukin had intoned it, and as I spoke the final words I raised my voice as the old woman had done: *Kuraj*, *kuraj*, *kuraj*, came from me like a shout. Marianne, who had listened to me as though dazed, sprang to her feet at my final *kuraj*, crossed herself frantically three times and ran out of the kitchen leaving me alone in the gloom.

Every morning at nine I picked up my slate and my exercise books and retraced my steps to Dr Wallatz's villa. My mother did not come with me any more; I walked the route alone, slowly; as I passed in front of Villa Amélie I looked through the gate to see if by chance a window had opened or the house gave any sign of life. Nothing. The gate was the only thing that changed; when the spell of the ice was lifted the metal curves of the tulips dripped with rain, forming an embroidered curtain in front of the garden that loomed out of the mist. I retraced the short stretch of the Schillerstrasse, turned into the avenue of limes and arrived in front of Villa Flavia, where I glanced at the lions to reassure myself that they were still at their posts, pushed open the gate and ventured onto the well-raked gravel of the path, at the end of which Maria was already hovering in the doorway. Every morning was like this. I went back after lunch and often found Dr Wallatz in the garden studying the progress of his plants. He immediately included me in his observations and his gardening worries: 'Look here. Still nothing. The tulips aren't the least bit interested in showing, this year. And the magnolias? Who knows if they survived such a winter as this was! Look here, look, they seem quite dead. And to think that they are usually starting to open by this time of year!' Despite his fears the first buds gradually took on a pink shade on the branches of the magnolias and Dr Wallatz was enchanted by them, as though their appearance was a miracle: 'They're really coming out. How many are there? Count them!' And I would count: one, two, three, four, twenty buds on a branch and twenty-one or twenty-two on another. And how many yew bushes were there on the path in front of the house? How many, if we added the little bay tree? I counted and added up. Suddenly Dr Wallatz would be thirsty for coffee and we would go back in. While he sipped his coffee and I sipped my tea the lesson would continue; I showed him how I had learnt to count, on my fingers, and to multiply, for example: eight times eight. You do it this way: you fold over on each hand as many fingers as there are numbers over five. Three fingers per hand. Every folded finger corresponds to ten. In all six tens, sixty. You multiply the fingers that are still standing: two per hand, four. You add the four to the sixty. Sixty-four. Dr Wallatz tried to copy me: he folded his thick fat fingers, tried and tried again, became confused. 'Ah, I've got it,' he said eventually. 'An intelligent method. And quick.'

Quick. Nine times nine. Who is the first to answer? As always, Malik tries to beat everybody else. Who can solve the riddle of the hundred ducks? A duck meets a flock of ducks in mid-flight. 'Hello, you hundred ducks.' But one answers: 'There are not a hundred of us. If you add our number and half our number, then half of half our number, and then you add yourself, then there are a hundred of us.' How many ducks are there? Malik already knows the answer. He's the first. It's not fair. It's always my cousin Malik who throws his weight around, who wants to be first at all costs. But where is Malik now? And my mare Börte? It's cold in Sinkiang, colder than here, but the steppe down by the Amudar'ya is already turning green. Here the sky is colourless. Colourless is the colour of everything, here. How many ducks are flying? I have forgotten the answer, Malik, and how we worked it out. I wish you were here to remind me, Malik, I wouldn't mind if you were first. But where are you now, Malik?

'What are you thinking about, Naja?' Dr Wallatz was looking at me trying to read my thoughts. 'You're tired. That's enough for today.' And with a pat on the cheek he sent me home.

'What have you got round your neck?' The little girl had two thin blonde plaits and a pale face. I instinctively reached up with my hand to protect my amulet. I never took it off, not even to sleep or to bathe, and it brought bad luck to stare at it. 'There's no point in asking her, you can see from her eyes that she doesn't understand you,' the other girl said, with the authority of a big sister. But the little girl wouldn't give up: 'She does understand me. She's afraid I'll steal it.' They both watched me with a kind of scientific, cold, objective curiosity, but it was my amulet rather than my expression that interested them. 'What's in it?' It was the little girl who asked, stubbornly. 'It looks like the barrel on a St Bernard.' They laughed. The drawing of a big dog with a barrel round its neck had come from the torn page of an old magazine. They had looked at it together the day before. A St Bernard, exactly. Now they transferred the image to me. I didn't understand what they were saying, but I understood that they were laughing at me, even if I was taller and stronger than both of them. I looked contemptuously at them. They were about my age, but they were so childish. What was so funny about my amulet? I clutched it in my hand, to protect it from their prying eyes. Sky-blue eyes in pale little girls. I turned my back on them without deigning to explain.

That evening, however, sitting on my bed, I switched on the lamp on the little bedside table. I slipped the amulet from round my throat and held it up to the light, something I had never done before. It was a little silver box with a relief on it of two snakes entwined, two *naja*, the elegant workmanship of the goldsmiths of Bukhara. The box fastened with a spring lock and I had some difficulty in opening it: the damp-corroded metal no longer responded to the mechanism. It opened all of a sudden and a feather lifted upwards a little. I was almost shaking. I felt as if I was committing an act of sacrilege. I was afraid that the objects enclosed in the box would vanish, that they would turn to dust, like relics when they come in contact with the air. A little tuft of white feathers flecked with brown moved imperceptibly in the hollow of my hand; they were feathers from an owl, the animal which rules the dark. Light and powerful, to challenge the demons of night. There was a claw too. From an eagle, certainly, to defend me from enemies and hold me close to the rock, to fly over the desert, over the peaks of the Hindu Kush, in the always-blue sky I had known. Inside, a paper scrip too. Columns of unknown signs: an invocation, a spell, a prayer. There was nothing else in the box, or just one other thing, perhaps. I bent my head over it. The smell. A smell of smoke came from it, as when the dry dung burns on the hearthstones of the yurt, and of perfume. Above all else, the scent of the lotus.

They were stout little bottles, and the seller filled them according to my grandfather's wishes from great glass containers. The perfume came from India. The merchant held the stopper under Bairqan's nose. He sniffed. Bairqan approved, ordered more. The merchant closed the little bottles with tiny corks. Mai Ling's skin smelt of lotus, and when she bent over me she enveloped me in her scent. You are like a lotus flower, Mai Ling, Om mani padme hum. You, jewel in the lotus flower. The little box contained her scent and now diffused it. The whole room seemed to fill with perfume. Mai

Ling, putting the amulet round my neck. May it protect you. Mai Ling, so slender at the edge of the village. The wind will bear you away! Never fear, my feet are firmly planted on the earth, it won't be able to. Mai Ling, who brought you here? It was your grandfather Bairqan. Tell the story, Mai Ling.

My father spent all day sitting among the rolls of material in his shop. Every now and then I came down to bring him a pot of green tea. In spring he would set out, and would be away for months; he came back from Sinkiang loaded with new silks and each of his five daughters received the gift of a new dress. The Emir himself was among his clients in Bukhara. He lived in the citadel above the old city, had a harem of a hundred women and held his own brothers prisoner in his dungeons. Turco-Mongol states had once dominated the steppes and the oases between the Aral Sea and the Pamir, but only Bukhara had retained its independence, or a semblance of it. The Tsar was master all around, but the Emir and the mullahs ruled in Bukhara. The women of Bukhara wore the horsehair *kimat* which covered them from head to foot, leaving only a slit for the eyes, and was so stiff that the poor women seemed to be carrying their own biers on their heads. They cut off the right hands of thieves, and anybody caught with a woman not his wife was stoned in the Registan, the main square. Criminals, even only suspected criminals, were thrown into a deep well which was said to be full of snakes, and none had ever returned to refute the claim. The narrow, winding streets of Bukhara opened onto many squares with cisterns where people washed themselves and their clothes and drew water for cooking. In these tanks as large as swimming-pools frogs croaked from spring to autumn, and in the evenings they joined in chorus with the muezzins, when they called the faithful to prayer from the many minarets in the city. Even the storks became more numerous every year, thanks to the frogs in the water tanks. Nobody bothered them; they walked beside the tanks as languidly as cats and were left in peace beneath the shade of the old mulberry trees, standing on one leg between the tables where the old men played chess and drank green tea from little china tea bowls.

I was eleven when the first cannon shells breached the walls of the citadel. My father closed the shop and forbade us to go out. He was convinced that 'devils with red stars on their foreheads' would put the city to fire and the sword and would spare no one who owned property. But nothing of the sort happened. The Emir left the city hidden under a woman's *kimat* and took refuge on the farther bank of the Amudar'ya, in Afghanistan; the mullahs suddenly dwindled in number; *kimat* were banned and little by little fell into disuse; the tanks were emptied and frogs and storks disappeared with them. My father became a Soviet citizen, as did we his daughters. Clients were scarce, however, and his daughters had all to be married, not an easy task for a non-Muslim father. One day, when I was twenty-two, as I came into my father's shop to bring him his tea, I saw that client of his with the strong and well-formed limbs and tanned skin, dressed after the fashion of the nomads, but who was not Turkmen. My father was obsequious in the extreme but the stranger had eyes only for me. Subsequently Bairqan would often repeat the proverb to me: the parents choose the first wife, the intellect the second wife, the heart the third wife. I was destined to be his third wife, but it was not easy. Bairqan became an extremely valued client of my father's, bought enough silks to line all his yurts, never tired of inspecting new bales and never said no to the offer of more tea. He himself made the formal request, but my father hesitated. We were a Manchu family, from a venerable line of merchants. We his daughters could read and write, and nomads to us were uncivilised people. But Bairqan did not give up. He pitched his tents on the steppe outside the walls of Bukhara, and every day he came to the shop to repeat firmly and courteously the same request. He was polite but insistent, and my father bowed incessantly and said 'tomorrow' and was already thinking about a midnight flight into Sinkiang with all his belongings and his daughters to be married, but the border was unsafe and he did not take the risk. Bairqan was already khan even in appearance. He had slanting eyes and high cheekbones, like the Manchu, and the polished manners of a nobleman of the steppe. Why not, father? My father put everything off until the following year. My suitor would come back in the spring. And indeed he did come back. I said goodbye to my sisters, hugged the pillars of the house I was leaving, put all my belongings on Bairqan's camels and mounted the white horse he had saddled for me. The caravan seemed like a triumphal procession, the white yurt that had been prepared for me a palace. Ukin and Sarkan, Bairqan's two wives, were obliged to hide their envy under their first wrinkles; when, however, the children expected from our union did not appear, they held their heads high again and made no secret of their disapproval. Bairqan continued to prefer me to the others, but I felt the weight of the women's contempt. A childless wife is a useless creature, an irreparable misfortune. But you two came, the gift of Börte. When your father Ul'an put you in my arms saying 'Mai Ling, you are now their mother' it was as though I had been born again; the two cradles hanging in my yurt transformed it into a palace richer than that of Genghis Khan. I was happy. Then came the disaster. But by then your father Ul'an was already gone.

This was your story, Mai Ling, and it was mine too, and it surged out of the amulet with the lotus perfume and the feathers and the lama's spells. I will wear it round my neck always, Mai Ling, and I will only have to open it to have you back.

16

'KEEP STILL NAJA, how can I cut your nails if you wriggle like that?' Marianne grasped my hand more tightly so that I could not get away. I stared in fear at the pieces of nail falling at my feet. I knew that Marianne would brush them into a heap later; but she would not bury them. She did not know how dangerous they could be! Not even I knew exactly why this was so, but it was so: nail clippings should be buried, if not the cows would eat them and they would go mad. There were no cows around there, at most there was the neighbours' white cat which sneaked into our garden from time to time and for which Kathe put down a bowl in a corner of the kitchen. Cats don't eat nails. But how could you be sure? Cut them short, Marianne. Why? Dead people's nails grow quickly; I don't want to be like them. Marianne didn't understand, for what I had said was muddled and its meaning incomprehensible. In any case I repeated to myself: 'You become a solid white rock, / with supplies of mutton, I will come and go with a couple of horses: do not denounce me to death, / I will not denounce you to the herds.' I felt calmer. But what if these spells had no power in that place? What if there were other spirits who did not understand my language? What did spells sound like in this language I was learning and why did Dr Wallatz not teach me them?

I went home for lunch. That day, however, there were strange comings and goings in the kitchen, murmurings and the sound of sobs. The women's voices, and my mother's with them. The crying could only be Hannah. I slipped my feet into my slippers and went to the kitchen door. Hannah was crying quietly; Marianne had a hand on her shoulder and she was drying her eyes on her apron. My mother had a letter in her hand and did not seem to know where to put it. A letter with a crest and a big stamp and bad news inside. Hannah's husband, who had been reported missing in action, had reappeared only to disappear again, this time for ever. Kathe had a brother at home who was a veteran. Every now and then he came to visit her at work, leaning on two crutches; Kathe brought money home for him too. Marianne's husband was a prisoner somewhere, in Russia. She said in Siberia, but she did not know where. 'If I could just get some warm socks to him!' To compensate she gave me the socks, which I didn't need. 'He doesn't write, they don't let him write, but he'll come home, my heart tells me he'll come home.' I don't know what Hannah's heart had told her, but her husband would not come home. My father Ul'an had come home. My new father, Günther Berger, had come home. I found it hard to understand that we were talking about the same war and that the war was the only thing that really brought us together. The reason Hannah was now crying in the kitchen was the same reason for which I was there in that kitchen. My father Ul'an had perhaps been in the same prison camp from which Hannah's husband wasn't coming back. I found it hard to understand; I looked for a thread which might link the story I knew with the one I didn't know. The beginning had been in Samarkand, no, before, when the news came even to the nomad villages that Germany was at war with Stalin.

'This is the moment to go into Sinkiang. If we don't make up our minds to leave, Stalin will come and take our men for his army. It is said that they are already at Bukhara.' It was Batu, Bairqan's brother, speaking. The Tunshan were once again debating whether to go or stay, once more forced to decide between Russia and China. Now, however, Germany was involved too. 'This Hitler has millions of soldiers and arms that nobody else has. He will force Stalin to surrender. We Tunshan will no longer live in fear that one day they will forbid us to be nomads, take our animals, and force us to work in a kolkhoz. Hitler is against the kolkhoz and promises freedom to the peoples under Stalin.' But who was this Hitler who came to make war in the steppe? And what did he have to do with the Tunshan? Even less than Stalin. The only reasonable solution was to leave before the war took away their sons as the Great Wind had in other times. But Ul'an was insistent: Hitler had more tanks than Genghis Khan had horses!

'Tanks aren't enough to defeat the steppe. The wind and the snow will force them back,' insisted a sceptical Batu.

'Meanwhile the Tunshan will have lost their men; what does it matter what side they fall on? We old men and women will be left. Who will look after the horses and the other animals? Even if this Hitler wins, it will be the end for the Tunshan anyway!' But Ul'an was stubborn; this war was ours too, and our last chance to stay in the land where we were born. Ul'an would not let Stalin conscript him; he had decided to fight for Germany. Bairqan looked at him, angry at such barefaced stubbornness: 'You have two children, Ul'an, who no longer have a mother. Do you want them to lose their father too? Let us rather look to find you another wife, so that you will be happy again and not get foolishnesses like this into your head. What sense is there in the Tunshan fighting for Germany? We don't even know where this country is, or how to pronounce its name!'

But Ul'an was not the only one clamouring to leave; many young men were inclined to follow him, convinced like him that it was their duty to help Germany to defeat Stalin. 'But how are you going to reach this Hitler?' Ulus, another brother of Bairqan, tried to dissuade them by showing how absurd the idea was. 'Will you set out to look for him in the Russian steppe? Will you send messengers to call him to come here in person to sign you up? Can you see this Hitler in the yurts of the Tunshan?' The old men laughed, while the young men could barely conceal their irritation. But Ul'an had thought of this too. The recruitment of the nomads was taking place, he explained, in Samarkand. A murmur went round the gathering. The good cheer, which was feigned in any case, suddenly disappeared. The elders looked at each other and read the same desperation and anger in each other's faces. That day Bairqan, though he was little over forty and was still strong and upright, felt old and impotent. With an angry gesture he cut short the discussion.

The next day, before sunrise, Ul'an and Timur saddled their horses and left. My father was twenty-one at this time, his brother nineteen. At Samarkand they headed straight for the old town, made their way through the winding lanes lined with streams, and asked around for one Mohammed Obermeyer. The Austrian? Yes, that's the one. A door was pointed out to them, in a little alley at the end of which the blue dome of the Gur-e Mir, the mausoleum of Tamerlane, rose up like an enormous melon. Bunches of ripe grapes could be seen behind the mud wall, all carefully wrapped in sheets of paper to protect them from the birds. Ul'an and Timur were not the first. There were already many men in the courtyard, sitting on mats of woven straw or on the ground, sipping tea and talking among themselves in low voices. Every now and then a small group would come out of the house and another little group would get up and go in; from the style of their clothes they could be seen to belong to the different nations, Turkmens with their towering head-dresses, and some Kazakhs, Uzbeks, and Tajiks. The Tunshan squatted in a corner. A teapot was put in front of them; Ul'an poured a bowl of tea, threw it smartly over his shoulder, filled a second. Men continued to arrive; others left. Languages and dialects mingled in the courtyard, but voices were still low and every time the entrance door opened the men inside raised their eyes to the newcomers, then lowered them. Finally it was the turn of the Tunshan. A little boy appeared on the threshold and showed them the way; they went into a larger room, bowed in greeting and sat down on the carpet.

The Austrian was a man in his fifties, not very tall, with fair skin and a little blond beard framing his chin after the fashion of the Mahommedans. On his head he wore the stiff cap of the Uzbeks and his embroidered blue jacket was Uzbek too. He greeted them in Uzbek and looked curiously at the newcomers.

Josef Obermeyer had come to Samarkand more than twenty-five years earlier, on a livestock trailer. He came from the fortress of Przemysl in Poland and still wore the uniform of Austro-Hungary with a lieutenant's stripes. Cavalry Lieutenant Josef Obermeyer was the rank recorded on the military papers he kept somewhere, together with a photograph of himself at twenty and a bundle of letters. It was all he possessed of what he called his first life. His second life had begun in Samarkand, in the barracks which served as an officers' prison, or rather, it had begun with what was the end of prison for his companions and the new beginning for him, because he stayed. Josef Obermeyer had turned his hand to many different things, among them agriculture, having at one time worked for an uncle who had land in Galicia. When the prisoners planted up plots in a corner near the barracks, Josef was keen to see what could be done with the land, on which melons, if watered a little, grew to a gigantic size. He experimented then sold his produce; the Uzbek farmers were amazed when they saw the little piece of steppe transformed into an oasis. The war was not yet over when a wealthy man from the city asked Josef to work for him. Josef accepted. At the end of the conflict, when the surviving prisoners went home, Josef found himself with an Uzbek wife, a new religion and a new name to prove it. His father-in-law, Alischer Navoi, was a man of some influence; even when a kolkhoz was built on his land he managed to hold onto his old authority, and even enhanced it by surrounding himself with former land-owners who had been defrauded of their possessions by the new regime, and with mullahs, who had been deprived of their faith. They didn't plot any concrete rebellion, but they kept alive the memory of the injustices they had suffered, the possessions they had lost and the faith that they felt called to defend. They gathered in the courtyard of Alischer Navoi and between one bowl of tea and the next they toyed with the notion of resistance. Nothing would have come of it had they not read in the newspapers from Tashkent that the Germans had taken the refugees from Uzbekistan under their protection and that Veli-Kajum-Chan, the traitor, as the Soviet press called him, had declared himself head of the Uzbek government in Berlin. It was the signal they had been waiting for; they made contact with the Germans and welcomed agents sent from Berlin. The active resistance against the Soviet enemy was organised in Alischer Navoi's courtyard, just behind Tamerlane's mausoleum. His Austrian son-in-law, whom Alischer Navoi had never set much store by, now became of real use to him, and would translate German newspapers and other relevant materials. Together they studied maps and followed the Wehrmacht's advance. Meanwhile Alischer Navoi had sent trusted men round the villages to say that anybody who wanted to fight against Stalin could sign up for his enemy's army. 'My enemy's enemy is my friend' was a formula everyone understood.

Josef Obermeyer looked curiously at the newcomers. This certainly wasn't the type of ally that the Germans would want. He could not help but smile at the thought that this was the vaunted 'new man' and soldier of the Wehrmacht. But not even he knew exactly, after so many years far from home, what kind of regime had sprung up in Germany and what ideas had spread so rapidly even in his old homeland; it was very probable that they were only a rowdier continuation of the past. The Soviet press certainly exaggerated when it described the Germans as bogeymen. But what did these nomads have to do with the Germans? Sure, sure, they were enemies of Stalin. If they wanted at all costs to join up with the Wehrmacht, by all means let them; it made no difference if they were killed by the Germans or by the Russians.

Josef Obermeyer, called Mohammed the Austrian, former lieutenant of cavalry in the Austro-Hungarian army, unfolded an old

Russian map of central Asia and ran a thin white finger over it as though he were indicating a road.

'You will cross the Amudar'ya at this point. Stay on the Afghan border. When you get to Kushka ask for old Hassan and say that you want to go to Odessa. He will be your guide and will take you as far as the Caspian Sea. It would be quicker to go to Merv and from there to Ashkhabad, but the Soviets control the railway and it must be avoided. The borders to the south have fewer sentries: that is the less dangerous route. Your courier will leave you at Ardabil. You won't pay the agreed sum until that point.' The Tunshan nodded. Those places looked near on the map. 'And now the password. Repeat after me!' The Tunshan clicked their heels, raised their right arms and repeated: Heil Hitler! Josef Obermeyer looked with wonderment at these two would-be soldiers of the Wehrmacht, at their boots with the curled toes, decorated with coloured embroidery, which they snapped to attention, and at their arms clad in the blue *chalat*, which they raised in the Roman salute. Yet their gaze was proud, and there was no doubting their ability as warriors. 'Now repeat the password: *Abwehrunterneh-men Tiger*, defensive action tiger. And now the formula: *Wir sind Freunde. Wir wollen gegen Stalin kämpfen. Heil Hitler!*' The Tunshan repeated. We are friends. We want to fight against Stalin. Heil Hitler! 'Perfect!' With these words Josef Obermeyer dismissed them, but the image of the two nomads clicking their heels and saying Heil Hitler! again brought a smile to his lips.

It was September of 1942. Ul'an my father, his brother Timur, their cousin Alcidai, Borrak's son, and two other young Tunshan, Bayan and Jintai, saddled their horses long before the hour of the first milking and strapped on whatever they were taking with them. Mothers, fathers, brothers, all the members of the *ayil* gathered round them in the dark to see them go. They exchanged the last silk scarves and amulets for the journey. May Qormusda, god of the perpetually blue sky, protect you, sons, brothers!

From that dawn my grandfather Bairqan's humour changed. He said he was beginning to feel old, but it was not the loss of youth that changed his mood, but the loss of his authority. It was not only anxiety for our sons caught up in such an uncertain adventure. As Bairqan reflected on himself in his youth, he recognised in Ul'an his own restlessness and the cool obstinacy he had once had, when the more dangerous a venture seemed, the more it attracted him. He was proud of this resemblance. It was his son's open disobedience which offended his pride as a father and as a khagan and made him fear that his authority was undermined for ever even before the Tunshan. To counter this loss he flaunted his power, shouting his orders to the servants louder than usual and assailing the women with peremptory requests which were difficult to satisfy. When he arrived in the *ayil* he tended now to shout out 'Mai Ling, Mai Ling!', as though she were hiding from him or holding back. In reality he needed her more than ever. She, Mai Ling, was the only person who was capable of calming him down. But Bairqan was not the only Tunshan marked by that gloomy September morning. From that day it was as though a dark cloud had descended on their yurts. There was a sense of dread, as if they were awaiting a catastrophe, which did indeed arrive.

When the tamarind turns pink in June, the slopes along the river take on its colour, and swarm with insects that creep into the little flowers hanging there in clusters. The bright green erianthus looms over the landscape and the riverbanks are swathed in a silvery green veil. All that green draws the children, like insects, round the tamarind. 'Look, the leaves are sweet! Have a taste!' we put the stiff little leaves which stick to hands and palate into our mouths. We ran further down, where the ground was soft and the grass higher than our years. 'Come here, Ginchin, look!' Ginchin appeared among the tamarinds and, like a puppy running to its master's whistle, came bounding towards me, naked, with the amulets around his neck dancing, his shaved head gleaming in the sun and his only tuft of hair, in the middle of his skull, flopping now left, now right, now over his eyes.

Not a lot of time had passed since our first haircut. We had both succeeded in passing the age at which nobody knows if children belong to this kingdom or to the kingdom of the unborn. We were still on earth; the moment had come to sever the very last link with the world beyond and to celebrate our entrance among the living. The grown-ups of the family sat in a circle in the khan's yurt. Bairqan began the ceremony, pronouncing his wishes over Ginchin who sat on the ground in front of him:

May your life be as full
as the bed of the mighty river,
but may it be held by firm, high banks.
May your will be as strong
as the current of the mighty river
but may it yield to the lock
and be tamed by the wind.
May willows and reeds bend over you
and flocks of animals
come down to you to drink.
May you silent reach the sea
and merge with its waters
and may the sea the richer be.

Bairqan lifted a lock of hair from his grandson's bowed head and cut it with a pair of the shears we used for shearing the sheep, which Mai Ling had decorated with a silk ribbon. Then Ginchin passed them to my uncle Batu, who cut a lock of hair in his turn and made a wish, and so on, until only a single lock of hair was left on my brother's head, which bounced now as he ran. Mai Ling had filled a little leather bag with hair and held an empty one ready for me. Bairqan's words settled on my head too, but being a girl child I was left with two locks of hair, one on each side.

We had fallen into the enchantment of spring. Creepers climbed along the rigid stem of the erianthus, their petals spotted with yellow and red. Bent over the orchid, we watched the progress of a hornet going in and out of the pollen sacs of flowers, flowers we had never seen before, which the tall grass of the river concealed like treasure. 'Look, Ginchin, flowers with bags!' The ground yielded easily to our little leather boots. When all of a sudden, directly in front of us, a cobra reared up, and swayed from side to side in a threatening posture. It took only a moment for Ginchin to push me further and deeper into the grass; I scream, the snake grips the little boy's flesh above the knee where the skin isn't protected by the boot, then disappears among the erianthus stems leaving my brother behind it in its blue-pink wake, writhing on the ground. A little above the knee, the red stain is spreading. I run back up the slope, past the tamarind, towards the yurts, waving my arms. Mai Ling is outside with the women: 'Where is he?' and they are already running to the river, already returning. Mai Ling is holding my brother in her arms; he is no longer shouting, or crying. The spot on his leg is bigger now, and redder. They carry him into the yurt and lay him down on the bed. Ginchin gasps for breath, his eyelids closing, weighed down by an invincible sleepiness. Mai Ling raises up his arm but it flops alongside the bed as though it is no longer his. Ügedelegü the shaman arrives; I leave the yurt and squat on my heels, my gaze riveted on the tamarind slope and on the green ribbon along the river; I know that it won't be long before darkness falls from the hills above us. The women's cries reach me from inside the yurt; I recognise the sound of Mai Ling weeping. The green strip along the Amudar'ya is in shadow now and only a narrow band of light still grazes the tamarinds.

Mai Ling came looking for me, pulled me to my feet and took me into the yurt, where she offered me a bowl of *kumiss*. I held it in my hands and ran my fingers over the relief, tracing it all the way round the edge of the cup, as I always did; it was a wavy form, like a *naja* slithering through the grass. I was seized with horror; my fingers shook and loosened their grip; the *kumiss* spilled onto the floor and a white stain gradually spread over the dark red carpet.

The *naja* had taken my brother Ginchin. 'He will be a prince in the kingdom of the *Naga*,' Mai Ling said, to comfort me. But I looked at Ginchin as he lay quite still on the pyre, covered with a white robe, and with cloth slippers on his feet so that he would not make any noise going down to the kingdom of Erlig Khan. His sleeves covered his hands, and only his fingers showed, the small white fingers of a child. His face was hidden under a white cloth and there were two flowers where his eyes should be; now Ginchin saw with flower eyes. The women had gathered flowers on the tamarind slope and beside the river and Ginchin was adorned with all the splendour of June. Nobody spoke as the shaman poured petrol on the wood and the piled thorn-twigs, as the flames enveloped the white robe and the flowers and bore my brother away. But perhaps he was already stepping in his white slippers down the paths of the *Naga* with his eyes shining like petals of fire. The shaman gathered the ashes in a cloth, walked off with the insubstantial bundle and unfolded it higher up, above the village. He urged the wind to blow and scatter it around the steppe. He kept back just a little ash, so that when the lamas arrived they could add their incantations to his own.

The nails of the dead grow quickly. Cut mine short, Marianne, I don't want to be like the dead. 'I will come and go with a pair of horses: don't denounce me to death, I won't denounce you to the herds. *Kuraj, kuraj, kuraj*!'

The death of my brother Ginchin spread panic among the Tunshan. The prophecy! The prophecy had come true! Had our distant ancestor Alcidai not said: 'But when another Tunshan returns to the kingdom of the *Naga*, then they will choose the tiger and will pitch their yurts to the left of the Alatau?' Another Tunshan had gone to the kingdom of the *Naga*; this was the sign from the gods that the Tunshan should choose the tiger, meaning China, and pitch their yurts in Sinkiang. Those who were for leaving put still more pressure on Bairqan. Would you oppose the will of the gods? The prophecy is plain enough! Don't you know the history of the Tunshan? Who didn't know it? The recent history of the Tunshan was one with its past, and went full circle, like a snake eating its own tail. The Tatars had come from the East, their descendants would return towards the East. The *Naga* indicated what their fate should be. Were there not eight *Naga* entwined on the banners of the Tunshan?

Bairqan and the party wishing to wait were driven into a corner. It was Ügedelegü, the shaman, who suggested a compromise: 'You, khan of the Tunshan, and you who have sons in the war in the west, think that they will come home and you wish to wait. You, on the other hand, who do not have sons in the war, think that they will not come back and that it is therefore pointless to waste time waiting for them. If there was a probability that they would come back, it would be the duty of the Tunshan to wait for them. But who can know the future? Who, if not the immortal gods, who are not ignorant of the fate of men? It is them that we must ask: may they be generous in granting us an answer!' His tone was solemn, for it was a solemn moment in the history of the Tunshan. Ügedelegü went on: 'If the gods let us know that our sons will come back, we will stay and wait for them and leave afterwards. But if the gods give us to understand through signs that they will not come back to our yurts, then the Tunshan will leave before the north-east wind blocks our passage into Sinkiang.' The Tunshan welcomed his proposal and also accepted his method of consulting the gods. Following ancient usage, they would use a sheep's shoulder blade. The sacrificial animal was chosen; Ügedelegü took out his books and the Tunshan made ready. Ügedelegü held the cleaned scapula up to the light. It was dazzlingly white and thin, with all the transparency of alabaster. He ran the palm of his hand over it, and found it to be smooth, with no cracks. He ran his fingers along the edge, and it was sharp as a razor. The bone was perfect. Ügedelegü dipped it in a container full of water mixed with milk, added juniper twigs and lit the fire. A dense and scented smoke filled the yurt. Ügedelegü put the scapula still wet with milk in the smoke, then raised it to his mouth, half closing his eyes. The words of the invocation came singsong from his lips, which were nearly touching the bone: 'I address my prayer to the protective deities, the lords of the earth. To Padma Sambhava, lord of prophecies, I address my prayer. Let the signs be clear!' Seven times Ügedelegü recited the formula; at each new beginning he paused to draw breath then spoke the invocation on a single breath. In the end he raised his voice and the words became clearer: 'Deign to show clearly if Ul'an, son of Bairqan, his brother Timur, Alcidai, son of Borrak, Bayan, son of Urus, and Jintai, son of Batu, will come back and if they will come back safe and sound. Deign to show with unmistakable signs if it is right and good that the

Tunshan leave or if they should wait longer!' The fire in front of the shaman burned brightly, and the smoke cleared. Ügedelegü dipped the bone in the fire. Those present kept their eyes and ears peeled. At every crackle Ügedelegü jumped, as though he could see the demons and the spirits in the flames quarrelling over the shoulder blade. An acrid smell of burning spread through the yurt. When the fire had died down the shaman took the scapula, turned it in his hands, raised it up and brought it closer to the fire. Meanwhile he had opened the book and was comparing the drawings with the topography of the scapula, glancing from book to bone and measuring with his fingers and analysing the signs from the gods with the scientific precision of a mathematician studying the trend of a curve. The onlookers did not take their eyes off his hands, but were patient, since they knew that signs from the gods are not easy to interpret. Eventually Ügedelegü turned to Bairqan, saying as he showed him the cracks in the bone bearing witness to his words, 'Khan of the Tunshan and you Tunshan here present: this is the conclusion of my examination. The crack which as you see runs from the Area of the Sky towards the centre and crosses the Eternal Great Way, which cuts the bone in two halves lengthwise, is positive as to direction: indeed it crosses the Area of the Prince. There is no doubt, khan, that this refers to your son Ul'an and indicates that he will come back. However, the rift is black and narrows towards the bottom. This does not bode well: he will come back, but not for long. Look then at this other line, which falls from the Area of the Dragons almost parallel to the first and runs towards the bottom, where the Area of the Slave begins. This says that Ul'an will not come alone. This, khan of the Tunshan, is what I read in the signs. May you forgive me if my interpretation should prove untrue.'

From that day the Tunshan spoke of nothing but the new prophecy. By now everybody knew and could repeat Ügedelegü's words, just as in his time they had been able to repeat those of Alcidai, and there was no child who did not know them. There was speculation as to who would come back with Ul'an, whether it would be one of the four who had gone with him, and if so, which of them. A new light had been lit in our hearts, because every family hoped that it would be their son. But when would Ul'an come back? Why was the line denoting his return black? The Tunshan tormented themselves with gloomy conjectures. And everybody, almost against their own will, turned their eyes to the south-east, where the little group had disappeared into the darkness some time previously; and whenever someone appeared in the distance along the path beaten in that direction, then the person who had seen them rushed to alert the others and together they would squint at the horizon. They looked to the south-east, imagining that Ul'an would come back from that direction. But he arrived from the north and, despite the fact that everybody was expecting him, he arrived unexpectedly. And the unknown man with him was not of the Tunshan.

17

I COULD SEE the glow of light through the frosted glass of the door. I stepped forward and peered through the glass. 'Come in, Naja.' I shyly opened the door. My father, Günther Berger, was sitting in his little armchair at the table, and swivelled round to watch me come in. He was wrapped in an ash-blue smoking jacket, belted with a twisted belt which ended in two tassels. Perhaps it was his clothes, the jacket which was too big for him, its colour, that made him seem older than his thirty-seven years, perhaps it was my still childish gaze. I was nervous of him, all the more so when he was in his study, where even the women were only allowed to enter from time to time to clean. The dark shiny wooden furniture, the heavy curtains, held back with tassels like those on his smoking jacket, but darker, the books on the shelves and on the desk, everything intimidated me. This time, however, as I stood hesitantly on the threshold, my hand on the curved brass of the doorknob, a strange sight caught my attention: there were lots of white squares laid out on the backs of the armchairs and seats and spread out on the table, as though Kathe, instead of hanging the washing between the poles in the garden behind the kitchen, had hung it in my father's study, and instead of using clothes pegs she had simply spread it out, as the Tunshan did. But Kathe had nothing to do with that strange laundry: it was my father who had draped his fine linen handkerchiefs on the armchairs. He suffered, in fact, from a terrible, persistent cold, which lasted from March to the end of June and cost Kathe a great deal of sweat in ironing the necessary handkerchiefs. To avoid wasting time, my father dried them like this, despite the disapproval of Siglinde my mother, who was concerned for the furniture. She seemed to have more feeling for the backs of the chairs than for her husband. The scattered papers and handkerchiefs spread out all around stood out against the furniture, and lent the study an atmosphere of cheerful disarray which reassured me. The house's usual tidiness made me feel not only uncomfortable, but obscurely guilty, as though my presence alone was enough to undermine it.

'Sit down!' my father invited me and I obediently moved a handkerchief from the back of a chair, spread it out carefully beside another and sat down next to him. My father then showed me sheets of paper full of drawings: seats that seemed like open shells, hung on steel wires, interlocking nests of coffee tables, rooms drawn in a few pencil strokes, a triumph of straight lines. I looked around, at the curves of the chair-backs, at the doors of the china cabinet, with two little lacquer pillars on each side, at the green and pale purple striped flock velvet upholstery of the sofa. 'They're prettier!' I said. 'They are furniture of a different design', my father explained to me, looking me in the eye. 'What you're looking at is Biedermeier, a period in the past, over a century ago. Today's needs are different and the furniture is different too.'

Biedermeier, I repeated, but I couldn't explain to myself either the airy lines of my father's drawings or the solid lines of the dark wooden furniture. Why did they need so much furniture here? They seemed to be afraid of space and wanted to fill it at all costs. I wondered why they needed different seats to sit at table or to read, to eat or to talk, different beds to sleep in or just to lie down on, as though every act of daily life needed a different piece of furniture and as though a special prohibition ruled out putting it to any untoward use. And they didn't use their floors at all, perhaps because they thought them impure: they put silk carpets on top of them, with flowers and animals, and then they trampled them with shoes. What use were all those wardrobes, bureaus and chests of drawers? To put things in. What use were all those things? And the armchairs no one sat in, and the chairs that seemed to stand in readiness for meetings that never happened? How long would they take to move house? I thought of the divan that my father called Biedermeier, propped sideways at a slant between a camel's humps. 'What's so funny, Naja? Why are you laughing, Naja?' 'Nothing. I was just thinking.'

'Isn't it too soon to be thinking of new furniture? It's houses we need, houses. Germany is short of nine hundred and twenty million cubic metres of buildings. Nine hundred and twenty million. Three hundred and eighty million cubic metres of public buildings and factories alone, the rest, you do the sums, five hundred and forty million cubic metres, of homes. Today cement's what we need. Style can come later.'

My grandfather Georg Schifferl was casting a sceptical eye over my father's sketches. He was director of the family furniture business, which had survived the Allied bombing raids unscathed, thanks to its proximity to the Glanstoff chemicals factory. Nobody knew exactly what the factory had produced before and during the war, but it was thought to have something to do with the war effort: the factory was surrounded by big cannons which spat fog whenever the air raid sirens sounded. The whole area was then covered with a very dense artificial curtain, which burnt in the eyes and the throat, but made it invisible to enemy pilots. The fog had also enveloped and so protected the German Living furniture emporium, which was renamed as the more up-to-date 'Modern Living', and was one of the few factories in Cologne in working order in 1948. It had been easier, however, to change the name than the style of product, which led to frequent, heated discussion between my father and my grandfather.

'That's just where you're wrong,' my father retorted. 'How can we build for the future, if we don't even have the courage to imagine it? Cement, houses, sure. But what will people put inside them? We need furniture too, but new furniture, right for the new era, made of cheap materials, yes, but which give an impression of lightness and cheerfulness. People have had enough sadness and grey. We need colour, especially in our furniture.'

'People will still want shiny furniture, solid wardrobes, comfortable armchairs with flowered upholstery. People find this comfortable, and they need it more than ever now, after all these years which have been nothing if not uncomfortable . . . Where's the comfort here? How can you feel comfortable in the midst of this kind of furniture, where you feel as though you're sitting in thin air, and with these materials, plastic, metal. The materials alone make you feel cold. People want furniture which makes them feel warm; they're not going to surround themselves with furniture that's so frivolous and . . . chilly.'

'Of course there'll still be a demand for "comfortable" armchairs with flowered upholstery, fake Persian rugs on the floor, dark furniture in walnut veneer. But we'll launch a new line . . .'

'It won't work. You can't change people's taste.'

'We will change tastes ourselves. We will launch a new, beautiful look. We have to convince people that this is in fact their taste, that we're only interpreting. I heard that Knoll International in America want to open a showroom in Stuttgart. If we don't bring ourselves up-to-date, in fact if we don't anticipate and design what is up-to-date ourselves, other people will do it instead and we'll be left behind for good with our nice, antiquated, provincial comfortable style. More petty bourgeois than Mr Biedermeier himself.'

My grandfather shook his head and prophesied the ruin of the factory and of the family. If events were to prove him right, it wasn't my father's designs, nor even the solid traditional stuffed armchairs which we were still producing on my grandfather's orders, which caused that ruin, but the fact that death carried them both off, one soon after the other, and there was nobody left to continue either my father's new, beautiful lines or my grandfather's comfortable ones, and the furniture shop had to close.

However, at the time I was sitting beside my father at the table covered in papers, Modern Living still promised a new beginning, a future. My father unfolded glossy pages which slipped through my fingers, full of photographs which to me were mysteries of light and shade. I learnt the names used to tell the history of furniture, from secretaire, *étagère* and console to Empire and Biedermeier. My father was full of praise. 'Well done, Naja,' he said, 'you're a quick learner.'

That was not the only history I was learning at this time. Whereas my father designed indoor architecture and furniture, Dr Wallatz delighted in his vegetable architecture. 'This,' he said, carrying a large terracotta pot lavishly decorated with reliefs of putti and festoons from its winter quarters in the cellar, 'is *Laurus nobilis*.' The little plant which bore this noble name rose on a thin straight stem on top of which a sphere of leaves opened out like a huge green dandelion clock. 'In order to give it this shape,' and Dr Wallatz looked proudly at his own work, 'whatever you do, you mustn't use scissors! That'd just be asking for trouble! You must use your fingers to pinch off the tip of the growth on every second leaf, like this.' Dr Wallatz nipped off a shoot with his nails and showed it to me between the pads of his fingers: it looked like a louse and yet it was the plant's bid to grow according to its natural inclination.

'Do you want to know the plant's story? One day the sun god fell in love with a beautiful wood nymph called Daphne. But she wasn't interested in the god; she ran away, and he ran after her trying to win her round. And she still wasn't interested; she only wanted to run away. The sun god followed her and was about to catch her when she prayed to her father, who was a river god, to transform her. And suddenly her chest became the trunk of a tree and her arms turned into branches and her hair into leaves and her feet into roots. But even like this Daphne was so beautiful that the god wanted to have her near him for ever. To this day Apollo, who never grows old, wears a wreath of laurel on his head that never loses its leaves.'

I looked at the little plant on its thin stem: how painful it must have been to turn into a tree, suddenly to feel stiff, to be unable to move! Can one be reborn as a tree, a blade of grass, a flower? Men are like trees, I told myself, like this little laurel plant: they stop, they put down roots and only their arms move like branches. And they are transformed, just as you can make a round ball out of the laurel foliage. You don't even need scissors to do it, just two strong, determined fingers. Like Dr Wallatz's, in fact.

But Dr Wallatz was already carrying another vase outside. He had put it out in the sun to see it better, bending over it and talking passionately about it. 'Look, it survived! It survived even this winter! Do you know what it is?' I didn't, of course. 'A cypress. A real cypress. A cypress from the Villa d'Este at Tivoli. And do you know what it grew from? From seed. I picked up the seeds and planted them in this pot, several years ago now. In the beginning, there was nothing to show for it. I said to myself, it's not working, they must have been stale seeds, they're not germinating. For two years I said that. Then the third year I saw a tiny, ever so thin shoot coming up. Perhaps, perhaps not. But it really was a cypress. Just think: a cypress from the Villa d'Este in Cologne!'

After several years of tender care, the little plant had reached about eighty centimetres in height and I found it hard to imagine that it would grow much higher, even above the roof of the villa, as Dr Wallatz assured me it would. When the plant reached three feet and inexplicably withered and died, Dr Wallatz was inconsolable. He spoke of it with a look of such sorrow on his face that one might have thought he was talking about a close relative. The little cypress had been born of his nurturing, brought up, pampered, cared for like a sickly child and encouraged to grow come what may. It missed the light, said Dr Wallatz, but I thought it missed its country. Plants are like people, I thought, you can't force them against their own wishes into a soil that isn't their own. But people are strange plants and sometimes you can't see their roots, yet they carry them along with them as nomads carry the fire from their hearths, and when the time comes, when you're not expecting it, they spread them out on the ground and pitch a yurt over them. And then perhaps they build a history and hand it down to the ones who come after.

* * *

I learnt many things in those months; everybody competed to tell me things and to explain, and I listened. 'Why are you hanging eggs from the branches, Marianne?' Easter was on the way and the house was decorated according to tradition. 'The hare brings the eggs.' 'And hangs them in the tree?' 'No, he hides them.' Marianne seemed to have mixed up two stories. 'But why the hare? Do hares lay eggs here?' For a moment Marianne stopped tying a bow in the ribbon holding up a painted egg, and looked at me, impatient with my pedantry. 'The Easter hare brings the eggs. That's just how it is. Then he hides them in the garden. And the children look for them. That's how it is.' I could look for them too. When? Easter Sunday, of course. And she started to sing a nursery rhyme:

Osterhäschen, Osterhas,
Komm mal her, ich sag dir was,
Laufe nicht an mir vorbei,
Schenk mir doch ein buntes Ei!

Easter hare, little Easter hare, / come here do, don't stay there, / let me tell you this I beg, / bring me a pretty coloured egg!

Every being can change into another: the hare brings the eggs; it actually lays them like a hen. There is nothing that can't be changed and turned into something else. And behind each of these transformations there lies a story, real or imagined, it doesn't matter which. At home, on the steppe, we had stories, and things, plants and animals had them too. What of the people here?

None of the people around me would tell me their story. I noticed that a curtain of silence was hung over the recent past, one I didn't dare to lift. It was like that at home too, for we avoided talking about things which brought bad luck and we didn't call demons by name. A proper name, if spoken by an unworthy person, could bring misfortune to its bearer. But we spoke openly about our recent and distant history. At home, when Ul'an and the others had gone, we spoke of nothing else. And nothing else was spoken of when he came back. The Tunshan were certainly still telling their story even now, in Sinkiang, and they were certainly talking about me too, who was part of it and could rest assured that my name would be on their lips and that they wouldn't look around in fear when someone named the country where I was. When Marianne chanced to say 'Siberia', on the other hand, she would stop instantly, as though she had spoken a forbidden word. Kathe would never say why her brother went about on one leg, where and how this had happened. My father, too, would never talk about his own story, though it was also mine, at least in part. I used often to sit beside him in his study while he explained his designs and the ones in the books to me and sneezed repeatedly and pulled a huge linen handkerchief out of the pocket of his smoking jacket, but I had neither the maturity, nor the words to ask: 'Why did you bring me here?' By the time I finally possessed both, he wasn't there to answer me any more.

18

I LEARNT THE more recent history, the story about my father and me, many years later; I assembled it piece by piece, using the broken words, allusions and mumbled answers my mother gave me, the embarrassed explanations offered by Dr Wallatz, and the meagre information supplied by my grandfather. But it was the cardboard box that I found when my mother died that opened the way for me to understand. It was a big box, one of those that holds the kind of expensive brandy you send as a present, with some of my father's papers inside, a few photographs, a few faded post-cards with greetings, an address, a dozen typewritten pages held together with a paper clip and a packet of letters tied with purple ribbon. My more recent story was contained in those yellowing documents. It was in other people's memories, not my own, that I had to look for the end of the skein that would lead me back to the place I had left.

A kind of shyness, a sort of modesty or shame at the indiscretion I was about to commit made me close the box almost immediately. Was it alright to poke about in somebody else's life without permission? In my own defence I told myself that it was not just someone's personal affairs, but also war documentation, testimony of events that had involved millions of people. How could they be called private? But the silences had convinced me that the protagonists considered them somehow private and that it was therefore their right not to speak of them, and bad manners, or worse, an unwarranted intrusion, to investigate them. This made me hesitate. Then curiosity, and, above all, the need to understand the whole truth, persuaded me.

As I read, I realised it wasn't just my father who sprang back to life in the letters. It was as though the lives which had been linked to his were hidden between the lines. I had released their breath from the envelopes, and it was as though it were a wind, blowing ever harder and pleading to be heard. The voices of strangers echoed around me and as I read I could not silence them. I felt confused and excited, as though it were my task to give them the space they claimed, to help them to emerge from the silence, and to become their voice.

I resolved to be scientific, and laid out the things in the box neatly, with photographs on one side, personal identity cards in the middle, the packet of letters imprisoned in its ribbon, on the left, and the papers and the miscellaneous correspondence in front of me.

I began with the photographs, which were in a tiny format and yellowish-brown with serrated edges. There were landscapes and pictures of my father in uniform, with the caption underneath: *Lieutenant Günther Berger*. Another showed father on horseback, and was labelled *Caucasus, 1942*. One photograph in particular caught my attention. My father was standing with some other officers, in front of a formation of soldiers, and underneath it read *808th Battalion, Turkestan Infantry, Decoration of Legionaries, Caucasus, 1942*. My father Berger is in the foreground, seen in profile, smiling. The decorated soldier is smiling too. The photographer had focused on slanting eyes narrowed in a smile. I looked closer, and at first I didn't recognise him in the uniform of a German soldier, the cap pulled down over his forehead, the embroidered eagle over the breast pocket of his jacket. Was it or wasn't it my father Ul'an? Maybe I was mistaken. I didn't know that face well. It was years since I'd seen it, and then only for a very short time. I had never held a photograph of my father. I looked at it for a long time, and read and reread the caption: *808th Battalion, Turkestan Infantry*. My father Ul'an in German uniform, in the Caucasus. Was it really possible? My other father too, Günther Berger, is in uniform: Lieutenant Berger, a person who is completely strange to me in this guise. The more I looked, the more convinced I was that yes, it could be Ul'an, that the key to my past was hidden there, in that sepia image, that the few words written underneath in ink were simply a coded message whose explanation was perhaps hidden inside the numbered envelopes tied together with the ribbon. I made up my mind, turned to the packet of letters and picked up the first envelope, 1/1939. I took out the sheet of paper. A precise, angular hand, as of somebody sitting at a table, fountain pen in hand.

30 September 1939. Poland. My dear Siglinde, how are you? I have done nothing but think of you for the whole journey. It's the thought of leaving you in these circumstances, still more than the war, which tortures me. I know my departure is like another separation, but while the loss of our Ilse is final, I will not be away for long. They reckon that the campaign will be over by the beginning of winter. Have faith, then, try to distract yourself, if you can, there are many people around you, and they are all keen to help you. I too need to know that you are feeling happier again, you know. Krakow is the saddest city on earth. A pile of ruins, nothing but ruins and people everywhere looking for food. Not one of the houses still has its windows, there is no water, no electric light. God spare our city such a fate! My only consolation in these ruins is knowing that you are safe, in a warm, comfortable house, knowing that you are far away from this desolation . . .

3 October 1939. From the front. Yesterday we crossed the Vistula. An impressive pontoon bridge, 297 metres long. One can well believe that nothing stands in the way of our will to power. Peace is very close, nobody doubts it. We went through a burnt town, only the church in the centre was still standing, like a miracle in a votive picture, all gilded plaster in the middle of the blackened rubble. I understand how my absence must weigh on you, and make you think that fate is against you, against us . . .

The year 1940 is written on an envelope full of letters. Second year of the war, another front. My father wrote:

14 June 1940 . . . Paris! How odd to be back here in uniform! At times I almost forget I'm wearing it, for I feel just like a tourist and I'm amazed when people look at me with mistrust. A strange kind of tourism, but believe me, I would have preferred to come back with you! The speed of our advance makes me hope that it will all be over soon, and that we will soon have peace again.

Does my father really hope that peace is near? Or does he mention it only to reassure my mother, closed off in her impenetrable mourning? My mother's inability to express her sorrow and get over it must have been a perpetual source of distress for him:

30 June 1940. I got your last letter. Thank you. Here we depend on news from home even more than on our rations! I often re-read your letters, but I confess that, if it makes me happy to know you are well, I can't help noticing that you are still torturing yourself, as though Ilse's death was in some way your fault. You are creating phantoms with which to torture yourself to no purpose. Accept fate as it is. You are not guilty, any more than all the other mothers are who have lost sons in this war. Are they more responsible for the death of their sons than you are? Do you really think that to lose a grown-up son is less terrible a sorrow than to lose a child? It is a mistake to make sorrow the centre of one's life . . .

1941. Lieutenant Berger, my father, has to fight on two fronts. There is the actual front, which is still dragging him from one end of Europe to the other, and the 'home' front, where my mother mourns in a trench of her own making. The war increases the distance between the two fronts:

> *25 January 1941. In France, from the front . . . I didn't forget the anniversary, for which you seem to be reproaching me, if I read rightly between the lines. But you must see that we have a real enemy to fight against here, and to defend ourselves against. Pain and suffering are all too tangible here. If you could see the lines of refugees passing in front of us, and if you could grasp how violent and concrete a thing hunger is, and how agonising it is not to be able to alleviate it in any way. If you knew how grateful we are that our country is spared the horror of war . . .*

June 1941. A new front. My father greets every movement of the army with relief, as though the change in itself means the approach of the end of the war:

> *At last we know where we are heading and who our enemy is. The news of the war on the Eastern front has caught us by surprise. How cleverly it's been kept secret until now! I have been assigned to Battalion . . . It's not yet clear what part of the front we are headed to.*

A few days later there is no longer any doubt: *15 July 1941. We are heading south-east.* South-east means the Ukraine and the Caucasus, the Don and the Volga.

> *19 September 1941. The Ukrainian landscape gets more boring by the day. Fields, fields and yet more fields. And every now and then between the fields a dip in the ground and within it, shielded from the harshness of winter, a village consisting of four muddy hovels with thatched roofs. The outside walls are whitewashed, inside, round the chimney, there is just one room for all purposes, sitting room, bedroom and dining room. We are staying in the village school, an almost luxurious billet compared with those of recent weeks. I have made some*

sketches which I am sending with this letter. I think they will give you a clearer idea.

10 October 1941. Today we reached the Sea of Azov. After all the monotony of the yellow-brown fields the blue seems incredibly beautiful. We feel happier, we feel as though we have arrived and reached a specific goal. The days are already cold, but very clear, and the space in front of us seems even vaster, more gigantic. Will we succeed in attaining our objectives before winter? The soldiers talk of nothing but General Winter.

In my father's letters the war seems to be just an unpleasant background, which he prefers not to talk about. Even my mother must have noticed:

3 November 1941. You write that the war does not appear in my letters, that my journey seems more like a pleasure trip or a holiday to you. If you only knew! Yesterday some very low-flying Ratas dropped their bomb loads on us. You see them raining down. Then you say goodbye to yourself, shut your eyes and when you open them again you're amazed to be still alive and you touch your arms and legs, as though to reassure yourself that you are still in one piece. Perhaps it's a 'vacation' in the literal sense of a hole, a vacuum, in this existence which is forced on us, beyond any 'normal' existence . . .

The normality of existence! This is what my father misses above all. The 'normal' life before instead of 'normal' life as it now is.

10 November 1941. Rostov. Marianne's cakes! If you knew how I long for them. But there are no cakes here and even the post is late. It's been raining for days and the ground which started out as dust has now turned to mud. Mud everywhere. One could say that it's a country which is a stranger to variety: everything is yellow, or everything is dust or everything is mud. Or snow, as I fear may soon be the case.

29 December 1941. Rostov. Mariupol'. You know how I like snow, the crunch underfoot, when we go to Midnight Mass. You know how children wait for Christmas and how they always hope it will be white as it is in the Advent calendar. But now I'm beginning to hate the snow. There is nothing romantic about having to cut your bread with a hatchet, or hold it in your arms all night to defrost it. And then there's the dark. It's already pitch dark at half past three in the afternoon. Thank goodness that we officers can allow ourselves the luxury of an oil lamp! I got the parcel with Marianne's cake (thank her for me from the bottom of my heart!) and the books you found for me. You don't know how grateful I am to you. Even if it's hard to read in this light, I prefer it to sitting idly in the dark. But you can get used to anything. Man is really some sort of a chameleon. Put him in a bunker in the middle of the Russian winter, and he'll turn into a caveman! Give him a gun and send him to the front and he'll turn into a soldier! Even these underground quarters can be bearable. Just give me a book and some light, a fountain pen and paper, and I'll even forget the lice.

And again my mother's stubborn, tenacious mourning, her refusal to give in and to take on the role that circumstances have imposed on her: that of the wife who keeps her husband's spirits up while he's away at war, who communicates warmth and hope:

But you, Siglinde, why do you refuse to come to terms with your fate? You are turning your grief into a principle to which you want to stay faithful at all costs; you are making it into the essence of your life. Believe me, this is a mistake, more than that, it is harmful to you and to the people around you. Grief has become a tyrant to whom you submit without resistance, to whom you sacrifice yourself and me too. You're right when you write that the war is keeping me far away from the past: that's how it is, war forces us to live only in the present. It makes us into beings without history. Wars make history only when seen from far away, from books, but for us living them from our point of view in the bunkers, in the boredom of days of waiting, they are long, long moments, spent in places whose names sometimes we are not even told. But if I am forced to live only in the present, you who still hold to the past, it's you who have to remind me of the future, it's you who have to help me to imagine it, even if it must be built on rubble. But you don't know how to take anything from the rubble but dust . . .

In the winter of 1941–42 the letters to my mother become infrequent, brief and terse. Berger finds that he has to fight on two fronts, both of them frozen and motionless. The spring of 1942 seems to bring a thaw. The Russian front begins slowly to move again, my father's letters become more frequent, more affectionate, more communicative:

8 July 1942. The steppe is still in bloom and there seems to be no end to the different kinds of flower: the plain is covered with patches in every possible shade from pink to yellow. And the cherries! We stuff ourselves daily with the most delicious cherries! The trees are groaning with them until they bend under their weight. Every day baskets full of them arrive from the village; every available container is used to pick cherries and our head cook makes us cherry puddings. You see what luxury we live in! But nobody talks of anything any more but leaving; the men are impatient; we expect our new orders from one hour to the next. On a short trip to Rostov I saw that the pontoon bridge is ready and the first armoured divisions are beginning to roll over it. It is no longer a secret: we're headed south-east again and our objective is Baku.

For my father the Caucasus is the fabled South, the unknown land that lives in the imagination as a place of good fortune and unrivalled beauty:

10 August 1942. The steppe is a yellowish-grey expanse extending to the horizon. Every now and then we see a field of sunflowers, then just euphorbia bushes and dry grass under a pitiless sun. You can imagine our delight when the Kuban'

Valley finally comes into view, wide and green with orchards to the west, dug out of the rock to the east and carved into cultivated terraces. We pass through white villages along avenues of acacias . . .

20 August 1942. We have passed through Pyatigorsk, the city of the five mountains, and behind it, at last, there is the Caucasus! The white dome of Mount El'brus appears before us in all its magnificence. I understand how the Russians, a people of the North, were already fascinated in the last century by this landscape, so southern and at the same time so alpine. It is moving to think that we are standing at the borders of Europe, that Asia starts along the slopes of these mountains, and yet the Caucasus is part of our culture: Prometheus was bound by Zeus to one of the very rocks I can now see ahead of me! I couldn't imagine a more fitting place for such torture!

24 August 1942. Caucasus. You will surely have heard on the radio about the exploits of our Gebirgsjäger on the El'brus: the flag of the Reich now flutters on the highest peak in Europe! That has shown the Russians! We have reason to be proud of our troops! But, as I look at the magnificent chain of mountains and I long to be on the other side, I wonder if the task we have set ourselves isn't also a challenge destined to be punished by the gods. The Russians don't seem inclined to give in easily, you could say that it's not just the oilfields of Baku that they're defending, but also the symbolic value of these mountains. I can already see your father shaking his head and reminding me that wars aren't fought to defend symbols. That's as may be, but they're throwing their all into the fight.

28 August 1942. Caucasus. The parcel of books arrived with the post. How did you manage to find them? Give my warmest thanks to Dr Wallatz too. You wonder how I can find time to read. You can't imagine how much dead time there is when you can't do anything except wait for orders. In these nerve-racking hours books are a real godsend, especially if they are small enough to be slipped into a jacket pocket. I have already read Tolstoy's The Prisoner of the Caucasus. *We're prisoners ourselves, shut up here in our bunkers. There are even the local girls as well, who smile and offer us fruit. The people around here are not Russian, but a mixture of every race: Armenians, Circassians, Tartars, Kabardians, all representatives of nations which in the past have made life more than a little difficult for the Russians. It is not for nothing that they used to post awkward characters here as officers, Lermontov, for example.*

1 September 1942. Caucasus. Evening is the prettiest time, when the whole chain of the Caucasus opens up in front of us. 'Kasbek, your regal tent shines with eternal rays.' But these are moments of fleeting calm, because it is in the evening, when darkness falls, that the Russians attack. As soon as the red flares go up the infernal noise of the artillery starts and the aeroplanes play their part by dropping bombs continuously all night. The troops grow more restless by the day, as do I. I have studied on the map all the curves of the military road from Georgia as it crosses the Caucasus from north to south and goes on to Tiflis. I picture the famous Pass of the Cross to myself and the mouths of the Terek river. Everything depends on whether we manage to break through the entrance to the valley. We live in a state of crippling uncertainty . . .

19

LIEUTENANT GÜNTHER BERGER had learnt Russian from his mother, who had stubbornly insisted on teaching it to him regardless of his protests. 'Why are you talking to me in Russian? Aren't you German?' 'Of course,' answered his mother, who had been born and brought up on the Volga. 'But Russian is my language too. The land round the Volga is Russian land. You can't tread the soil without learning its language.' My grandmother Martha had a linguistic theory all her own, and, besides, her love and her tenacity were such that she would not yield to her son's objections. For his part Günther was not by nature inclined to fight to the last ditch; more because of his liking for a quiet life than because he was convinced by his mother's arguments, he had yielded to her wishes and put up with a fairly good grace with the lessons given each afternoon by a Russian exile. Günther often thought back on his mother's words: 'Learn Russian, my son, learn it, one day you'll find a use for it.' She had been right, even though she had certainly not thought that he would use it in war. But what languages were really spoken on the soil now trampled by the German army? There were Circassians, Kabardians, Armenians, Georgians, and Azerbaijanis, peoples of whose very existence Berger had until recently been quite unaware. And beyond the Caspian Sea there were Turkmens, Uzbeks and Kazakhs. In reality, Russian was just a lingua franca used between peoples who habitually spoke other languages, and the sole means of communication between the occupiers and the conquered peoples. That soil, thought Berger, was in no way Russian. A letter dated 11 September 1942 talks of those days:

My dear Siglinde, what surprises war has in store for me! I would never have expected to get to know such interesting people here! Yesterday a group of young Asiatics came up to me. They claimed to be descendants of Genghis Khan! They told me their adventures and I thought I was living in a page of the Thousand and One Nights!

The house had been confiscated from a Kabardian family; it was large, whitewashed and faced south, towards the garden and the Caucasus. Behind the house a terrace planted with vines sloped down to the river, which had carved out a deep gorge directly below the town.

'You get vertigo working up here,' said Major Hartel, looking at the foaming water of the Terek. 'But it's worth it,' Berger answered holding out a bunch of wonderfully sweet little grapes. 'If it weren't for this din,' and Hartel pointed to the bridge over which a line of panzers was approaching slowly, 'you could call it an earthly paradise.' The officer's arm described a wide gesture to include the landscape and the houses with their gardens overflowing with fruit.

'We Germans are really looking for space to the south rather than to the east,' Berger replied, and his eyes lighted on the blue, very sharp-edged mountains to the south of the village. At times the Caucasus was swallowed up in the mist, only to re-emerge straight afterwards, with the fickleness of a fairy appearing at will and each time rekindling the desire to see her. Just then Berger noticed the soldier at the entrance to the vineyard who was looking through the labyrinth of paths for the most direct route to reach him. His trailing rifle brushed the red bunches of grapes. 'Lieutenant Berger sir, there's a group of prisoners, I mean deserters, we don't know, they're civilians. What should we do with them?' And he turned to point to where they stood, in front of the house. Berger nodded to the Major, who was still holding the grapes in his hand, his eyes following the panzers. The line was no longer moving, now; it must have been held up by some obstacle; groups of soldiers were swarming around it as a truck tried to make its way across the bridge. Below them, the Terek glittered in the gorge.

The Tunshan were squatting on the balls of their feet in front of the garden wall, a soldier guarding them with his rifle trained on them. As Berger approached they got up slowly and Ul'an stepped forward. Berger looked at them attentively. 'Where do you come from?' he asked in Russian and peered at the young man's face to check that he had understood. In answer Ul'an raised his chin and jerked it towards the north, the space behind the house. Berger turned involuntarily and saw the line of panzers still at a standstill and the men milling about on the bridge, and beyond that the green-white expanse of the cotton fields, then the steppe, stretching to the horizon. He told Ul'an to follow him and went into the house. He looked for the map and opened it on the table. 'Where do you come from?' he repeated.

'Another map!' thought Ul'an. It was the second time that somebody had opened a map in front of him and, though he could find his way over the steppe without difficulty, he was lost in this pretend landscape. Ul'an knew how to read even the faintest tracks in the desert, but was disconcerted by the signs on the paper. He tried to remember. The map at Samarkand, Mohammed the Austrian tracing their route with his finger. The big blue patch, now that was clearly the Caspian Sea. The curved line coming out of that must be the Amudar'ya. There, now he was sure. He put a finger on the river, and said 'We come from here,' looking Berger in the eye.

Ul'an and his companions rode through the night. The steppe had absorbed the heat of the day and released it in the night hours; the warm air rose from the ground. The temperature fell only after midnight, when the horses breathed more easily and their pace picked up, almost to a trot. They were following animal tracks. The steppe was empty at that season, the animals still on the high pastures of the Paropamisus; the few herds which were still in the valley grazed at night. 'Heat turns life upside down,' said Ul'an to Timur who was riding beside him. 'Sheep go about at night like wolves; the Tunshan ride in the dark like bandits and sleep in the daytime like desert mice.' They were ascending the entrances to the valleys, where the villages of dried mud, nearly invisible in the dark, were almost deserted too. They found only old people, for all the others were up with the animals. They asked for and received cheese and dried meat; the water in the buckets was black and fresh, and slipped deliciously down the throat.

They crossed the border on a moonless night. The Hari Rud was flowing sluggishly; nobody stopped them, neither on the Afghan side nor on the Persian. They skirted Mashhad, the sacred city, and headed into the mountains. They passed through villages which seemed dead, but at the guide's call a door would open and women would bring tea, a bowl of clotted milk and some thin round bread. The boy pointed to the chain of steep mountains to the north-east: 'Turkmenistan is over there. Russians.' He lifted his hand to his throat, flat, like a knife. Beyond the last pass they found the Caspian Sea in front of them. A vast, blue expanse. They had never seen so much water. They were bewildered, terrified. It was as though sky and land had been inverted and the steppe had filled with water. The boy laughed: 'Go down to the water and keep going along the shore, keep to the left.' He was turning back, and wanted to be paid.

As they went down the mountain they felt the air become heavy and begin to stick to their clothes; the dust of so many days' travelling became damp and oppressive. The beach reflected the sun and was boiling hot. They dismounted, took off their clothes and, with all the merriment of small boys, jumped into the water. Out to sea they could see big ships and fishing smacks.

They reached the last village before the border, which was just a cluster of dreary houses, not even whitewashed, smelling of salt and fish, with boats drawn up beyond the water line. They asked for Emirkan. A little boy led them through the narrow streets and disappeared into a house. The man who came out filled the doorway with his bulk. A giant, thought Ul'an, a khan.

Emirkan had fled from Azerbaijan twenty years before, when the Soviets had suppressed the rebellion. Since then hate had smouldered in his breast. 'You are not the only ones,' he said. 'Many cross the border here. Many hide in the mountains of the Little Caucasus and the Great Caucasus and fight a kind of guerrilla war. They carry out acts of sabotage behind the Red Army lines.' But they did not want to be bandits, they wanted to fight as soldiers, to reach the Germans. 'They are over there,' said Emirkan pointing to the north of the Caucasus. 'But it is not easy to reach the front. There are Russians from Baku to Tiflis.'

A boy, not much more than a child, accompanied them along the paths above the sea. The border was somewhere. Further below they could make out houses. 'No, no, the Russians are down there.' In front of them lay the plain furrowed by the meanders of the River Kura, to the right, the sea, opposite them, the Caucasus. The young guide disappeared, but another door opened to offer hospitality to the Tunshan.

The slopes of the Little Caucasus are one large vineyard. In September the carts overflowing with grapes come down to the plain on their way to the markets in the city. Ul'an and his friends sat on two of them. At Baku they mounted horses which were not theirs and rode on, keeping close to the beach. Columns of the Red Army ran along the road, in both directions, towards Tiflis, to the south and towards the front at Terek, to the north. The invisible front cut the steppe in two, with the Red Army on this side, the Wehrmacht on the other. How long was the front? How many men guarded it? What was the least watched place, where they could cross to the other side? They carried on northwards, keeping the sea on their right, looking for the fords and the dry paths at the mouth of the Terek. 'How much further?' asked Timur. The sun set behind the steppe of the Nogai; swarms of insects rose from the reed beds. Only ducks and mosquitoes. Where were the soldiers?

Ul'an and his companions rode by night. No sign of soldiers, only darkness to left and right. Suddenly they heard a drumming sound over them, coming closer, overtaking them; they saw red rockets rising, the sky lit up, an explosion answered from below, it didn't seem far away, but perhaps the steppe made noises sound nearer. They stood and watched, for a long time, until they heard the engines fading into the distance. 'Now we know where the front is,' said Ul'an. There were cotton fields ahead of them; they skirted them, keeping to the dry verges, until they arrived at a cement bank. 'The canal, we're here.' They followed it round to the south as far as the homes of a kolkhoz. They noticed a shed and approached it warily but it was empty. The earthen floor was covered with white powder and with tufts of cotton wool left over from the previous season. They lay down to await the dawn.

The houses of the kolkhoz were still silent; they left the horses and continued on foot, Ul'an held the white silk scarf that Mai Ling had given him. The path carried straight on, following the canal. Nobody in sight. In the distance, however, they could make out the main road between the rows of poplars. They carried on cautiously. There was a truck stopped right at the crossroads and four soldiers standing round it, two busy with a tyre, the other two peacefully smoking, leaning against the vehicle. They were chatting. Ul'an felt his heart leap into his mouth. Germans or Russians? They hid in a clump of acacia. Ul'an wriggled forwards on his belly, nearer to the road. A soldier shouted something to the others from under the mudguard; Ul'an grasped enough to realise that it was not Russian. To judge by their appearance, the soldiers weren't Asiatics. Ul'an went back to his companions, then came out onto the road first, his hands up, gripping his white scarf tightly. The others followed him slowly. The password now, how many times had Ul'an repeated it, how many times, in fear of forgetting, he had made his companions repeat it. Now, Ul'an, now!

The Germans saw him. *Partisanen*! shouted one and pointed his rifle at them. *Abwehrunternehmen Tiger. Wir sind Freunde*, we are friends, Ul'an shouted loudly. *Wollen gegen Stalin kämpfen. Heil Hitler!* The Germans had surrounded the Tunshan; one began to search them, took their pistols and knives. *Wir sind Freunde*, Ul'an repeated. *Schon gut*, said the soldier who had searched them. *Jetzt mitkommen.*

'*Überläufer, was*?' said one of the soldiers. Deserters? *Die schauen eher aus nach Tataren in zivil*, they look more like Tartars in civvies, said another as he nudged the Tunshan onto the truck training his rifle on them. He hadn't lowered it for a single moment; now, in the courtyard of the house on the Terek, it was still pointed straight at Ul'an's chest.

Lieutenant Berger stared at Ul'an in disbelief. They had come all this way to join up and fight as volunteers? And to escape recruitment into the Red Army, of course. The young man wasn't lying, what reason could he have to lie? 'Who are you?' he asked. Ul'an came spontaneously to attention. 'We are the Tunshan-Tatars. We are descendants of Genghis Khan.'

'Genghis Khan . . .' repeated Berger almost to himself, rummaging through dim memories from school to find a solid piece of information. Images of barbarians on horseback, sacking Europe, came to mind. Ancestors to be proud of! He thought, I couldn't name more than three generations of my family, my father, my grandfather, my great-grandfather, and these men are saying they are descended from Genghis Khan! He turned to Ul'an who was watching him with interest: 'Why do you want to fight with us?' Ul'an did not hesitate: 'Stalin wants to take away our livestock and force us into kolkhoz. He wants to make us live in houses. He wants to make Russians of us. This is why we hate him. You are our friends.' He fell silent. He had said all he had to say. These were good enough reasons to justify a journey of more than a thousand kilometres. 'But how did you know where we were?' Ul'an stared at the officer in astonishment. 'News rolls even over the steppe,' he answered. That was the very word he used, rolls, as though news was *kuraj* bushes. 'And how do you know that we are friends?' Berger pressed him, but he immediately regretted the question. 'You are the enemies of Stalin!' said Ul'an and he added in a lower, confidential tone: 'You wear that.' He pointed to Berger's chest and to the spread eagle with the laurel crown and the swastika in its claws. 'It is the knot of friendship that binds us forever.'

Berger felt ill at ease; the rhetorical exaggeration seemed to indicate a lack of respect, and he would even have considered it offensive, if the obvious naivety of the assertion had not been enough to excuse it. But his embarrassment showed no signs of diminishing; on the contrary, he found the excessive sincerity of Ul'an's gaze too much to bear.

He gave orders to the sentry for the newcomers – he purposely avoided the word 'deserters' – to be taken to the volunteer recruitment camp. 'What did you say your names were?' he asked Ul'an again, as he was about to leave. 'Ul'an Tunshan, sir, Tunshan.'

His batman Scholz appeared in the doorway, struggling to hold a big saucepan overflowing with grapes in both arms. He was the son of vineyard owners from the Moselle, who produced, if he were to be believed, the finest Riesling in the region. 'When the war is over, sir, I'll send you a case. You'll be astonished by its bouquet!'

Since the journey had brought the troops within range of the foothills of the Caucasus, Scholz had been eagerly anticipating his first sighting of the vineyards. 'Beyond the Caucasus, you'll see what wine they make!' He was impatient to try that wine, which was apparently a very sweet muscat. To hear him talk you would have said that the whole march into the Caucasus was part of a wine-lovers' excursion and that its goal was the cellars of Tiflis. But however much Scholz trembled with impatience, the Russians did not seem to be prepared to let anybody pass the Georgian road that led to the moscatel vines, on the other side of the Caucasus, not even for the purposes of wine-tasting. Scholz therefore had to settle for the terrace on the Terek where he looked after the vines in his spare time, with a joy and a dedication that made him forget even the war.

'Scholz,' Berger asked him absent-mindedly, 'Why are you here to fight?' His batman turned abruptly, disconcerted, and the saucepan tilted dangerously in his arms, putting the heaped bunches of grapes at risk, but Scholz soon succeeded in righting it again. He cautiously put the container on the ground and seemed to spend a few moments watching the pile of grapes settle, then straightened up, with an expression of ill-defined fear on his face. He was tempted to say: what kind of question is that? Because they sent me. Surely he doesn't think I came of my own free will! but he found that it wouldn't do at all. He began to search, therefore, in the tangle of thoughts he could still draw upon after nearly three years of war, to see if there was a more satisfactory answer, given that the Lieutenant had taken it into his head to ask him, Scholz, political questions. Luckily the Führer's speech on the radio the previous evening came into his head: *Warum wir weiter kämpfen*, why we fight on. Though he had not listened carefully, Scholz ran through a few phrases which he already knew. He came to attention and recited 'To fight Jewish Bolshevism, sir!' By now he felt sure of his ground and went on, with the air of a diligent schoolboy reciting a lesson learnt off by heart: 'The German people needs more space to the east!' As he said this his gaze rested on the grapes and Scholz thought of his vines in the Rhineland and how the grapes would be ripening there too.

Berger caught his eye. 'The grapes here aren't bad, are they?' 'Yessir,' Scholz admitted, hugging the saucepan again. 'They aren't bad, but they can't compare with our Riesling.' He was about to promise the Lieutenant a case of his wine, but thought that he was repeating himself and said instead: 'On the other hand these aren't wine grapes, but the ones beyond the Caucasus are, when we finally get there . . .' And he disappeared with his booty into the next room.

The dispatch must have reached Berger around this time. His orders were to proceed to Pyatigorsk 'for a mission regarding the organisation of volunteers, ex-Soviet prisoners'. The attached circular 'No. 2380/42, 2.6.1942: Instructions for German personnel in reception camps and in the so-called Turkestan Battalions' only gave a vague sense of what it might mean. It began as follows: 'The prisoners of war who have fallen into German hands seem at first to be indifferent and passive. We have, however, learnt by experience that if they are treated fairly and given adequate food and medical care, within two weeks or so their mistrust gives way to the conviction that Soviet propaganda lied when it described the Germans and the treatment they reserve for prisoners. The task of turning these men not only into *lebensbejahend*, persons who affirm life, but also into good soldiers, requires adherence to the following regulations regarding the treatment of Turkestan soldiers . . .' Signed: Count Stauffenberg.

How on earth was one to set about turning Turkestan prisoners, a term which collectively designated Soviet soldiers of a different nationality to the Russians, into men who affirm life, and into effective soldiers too? What had he, Berger, to do with the Turkestans? Just because he knew Russian he had to turn them into men who say yes to life? What kind of absurd assignment was that? In the letter he wrote Siglinde around this time, his doubts can hardly be guessed at:

15 September 1942. Caucasus . . . I am at Pyatigorsk, which used to be a Russian spa. I heard that there are more than forty thermal springs here. The city has a magnificent position, in a bowl between the steppe and the mountains. In the last century it must have been much frequented by high society, by nobles and dandies, and had been a place to take the waters and to meet people. Just think, Pushkin, Tolstoy, Gorky, and I don't know how many others came here to take the waters, which seem to have miraculous properties. Lermontov was at home here, he lived here and died here, in a duel, just a century ago. His house must be somewhere about, but how would I go about finding it? Unfortunately the city was half-destroyed by our artillery. The Russians defended the baths as though they were oil pipelines and apparently holed up in one of the bathhouses, which is naturally now almost razed to the ground. Only a few truncated columns are left (the Russians are crazy about neo-classical architecture too!), and so the rubble looks like the ruins of a Roman forum. I have a new assignment, and I don't yet know exactly what it involves . . .

The organisational section of the General Staff was lodged in the upper part of Pyatigorsk, in a pretty little building which had been a thermal baths before the war and which, situated as it was a little outside the town centre, in a thicket, had suffered no other damage but that which the Russians had caused. The road which passed in front of it carried on over the slopes of Mount Mascuk and led to the Monopteros, the temple situated on the terrace looking out over the city. It must surely have been much visited before the war, but now only panzers and other military vehicles went there. Berger made his way to the entrance, passing between two pillars of white marble and as many sentries in grey-green. Inside he was somewhat startled by the noise of his boots on the marble tiles. I'm really turning into a barbarian, he thought, with all this walking through fields or on beaten earth I've grown unused to proper floors. The room, though degraded by the military use it had seen, revealed something of the building's original decor: the upper part of a fresco or the edge of a floral decoration in pale pastel colours still showed behind the cardboard notices nailed to the walls. The staircase leading to the upper floor, where the offices of the general headquarters were deployed, was elegantly curved, and flanked by graceful marble columns. The red flag of the Reich with the swastika in the middle was hoisted on the last column at the bottom. A masterly piece of scene-setting, or rather a deliberate insult to the aesthetics of the place, thought Berger as he climbed the stairs. A group of officers came towards him. Berger swiftly brought his hand up to his cap and straightened his arm in salute. Perfectly cut uniforms, heavy with gold braid, the Iron Cross attached to one officer's collar: a metal bow tie, thought Berger in soldiers' slang. The only aesthetic that counts now is the military one.

He was admitted to the office of the General Staff. It must have been the office of the director of the baths, as there were still traces of its former elegance, perceptible in a marble bust on the side-board and in massive leather armchairs round a low crystal glass table with porcelain cups on it. Three German officers were sitting round the table, smoking.

'Lieutenant Berger, please, sit down.' Major von Schulenburg, of the organisational section of the Wehrmacht, pointed Berger to a little armchair against the wall. 'Coffee?' He invited him to help himself, holding out a packet of cigarettes as he did so. 'May I introduce the envoy from the Ministry of the East, Professor Breuninger, and Lieutenant-Colonel Schulzt von Neustadt of the Staff Corps. We were just talking about the organisation of the so-called Eastern Legions which, as you will know, are recruited from the Soviet prisoners. Men who of their own free will, I repeat, of their own free will,' he underlined, 'decide to fight in the ranks of the Wehrmacht. I would like to underline once more the principle of free choice. No pressure is exerted. No reprisals of any kind are carried out against those who refuse. The alternative is to be assigned to the work battalions behind the lines. Well, I'd say eighty per cent of the Soviet prisoners who are of other nationalities than Russian agree to go into the legions.'

'They agree, of course they agree!' Schulzt von Neustadt fixed his sky-blue gaze, which had briefly lighted on Berger, on the Major's plump face. 'But that's just the point. How can you turn this mass of primitive men, recalcitrant to any military discipline, into German soldiers?' He was about to say 'Prussian,' but stopped himself in time, remembering that not all those present were Prussian.

'This is where the basic error lies in my opinion,' Major von Schulenburg answered. 'Why do you want to make them at all costs into German soldiers? We need soldiers, so we'll make soldiers of them, sure, equal to German soldiers in the eyes of the law and in terms of the treatment they receive. But we won't make Germans of them, that would be fundamentally mistaken. Indeed, just to show how accommodating we are, we'll focus on their national characteristics. We will offer them what Stalin denied them, namely, the right to be different, and that's how we'll make loyal soldiers of them!'

'Equal to German soldiers, you say? It seems an outrage, an insult, I would almost say, to our soldiers and a waste of time and money. The best we can do is turn them into human material to use in cases where we want to be sparing with German blood. Any other use would be, I repeat, an insult to our uniforms, pure and simple.' Schulzt von Neustadt's sky-blue eyes did not shift a millimetre from their position.

'I don't like to contradict you, Lieutenant-Colonel,' Professor Breuninger interrupted at this point, 'but I don't agree. From the political point of view, political, I stress, the way our army is administering the occupied territories and treating the indigenous populations represents an unforgivable error. We are making enemies of peoples who could potentially be extremely useful to us both from the military point of view and in terms of future collaboration. Let us not forget that we will have to administer these territories when the war is over. . .'

'I don't see what conceivable purpose could be served by giving preferential treatment to the non-Russian peoples, given that the plan after the war is for these territories to become colonies, nothing else. The orders emanating from the Führer and from the Staff Corps strike me as quite clear on this point.' Schulzt von Neustadt did not intend to concede an inch.

'Allow me to inform you that a gradual shift from radical positions of this kind is occurring,' Professor Breuninger commented calmly. 'Even in circles close to the Führer the conviction is gaining ground that a fundamentally different politics of nationality, designed to turn these peoples into our allies, is now needed.'

'This has been my opinion from the beginning.' Major von Schulenburg was clearly glad of the support offered to him by the envoy from the Ministry, and decided to ignore the eyes which seemed to be trying to skewer him. 'The Soviet Union will only be won with the help of the Russians!'

'That's another kettle of fish altogether,' Schulzt von Neustadt commented, with a faint smile. 'We were speaking of non-Russian populations, if I am not mistaken.'

'By Russians I mean Soviets in general.' Major von Schulenburg, caught out in error, barely repressed a snort of impatience. 'But while we attempt to convince these people of our good will, others are carrying out acts of sabotage and pursuing a disastrous propagandist policy. Look here, look!' he grabbed a copy of the *Illustrierter Beobachter* that he kept folded by his cup of coffee, opened it and showed it to everyone present, pointing out a number of photographs. Then, with a vehemence in which was concentrated all the irritation which the conversation had obviously inspired in him, he added: 'Who do you see represented here? Those very Asiatic soldiers, the ones we're trying to organise into legions of volunteers! I'll read the caption: *Widerwärtige Bastarde aus der Steppe*, repulsive bastards from the steppe! *Die Untermenschen des Bolschewismus*! The subhumans of Bolshevism! Do you know how many copies of this are doing the rounds among our soldiers? Thousands! And here we are, trying to convince them that our intentions are honourable!' Major von Schulenburg threw the newspaper onto the glass coffee table and sat back in his armchair.

'These are errors which won't be repeated.' Professor Breuninger looked over his glasses at the others one by one, with the professorial scrutiny with which he intimidated his students back in Berlin. 'And so that they won't be repeated we have organised training for the German personnel of the so-called Turkestan legions. Courses in the culture of the non-Russian populations, that is to say, history, religion, customs and above all psychology. To this end we have brought over highly qualified people from the universities of the Reich.'

'Just so, just so. Know their culture to make them our allies.' Major von Schulenburg looked around him and seemed to remember Berger who was sitting back a little, an empty cup in his hand. 'And you, Lieutenant Berger, what do you make of all this?' His voice had regained the affable, paternalistic tone in which he usually spoke to his subalterns.

Berger started, saw again in his mind's eye the trusting smile of the Tunshan looking at the swastika and talking about the knot of eternal friendship. 'I think these peoples' friendship is sincere,' he said.

'Just so, just so, Lieutenant,' Major von Schulenburg approved. 'They are natural, infantile beings. They need to be looked after, to be given support, security. They are like children. But if you treat them well, they become attached to you and are capable of laying down their lives for you. We have to focus on their friendship!'

'One hundred and sixty cases of desertion, three conspiracies discovered in the nick of time, an entire platoon ambushed, flight in the face of the enemy: I have the details here,' listed Schulzt von Neustadt with the air of one finally laying his cards on the table. 'And you call this friendship?'

Professor Breuninger began in his turn to show signs of losing patience: 'Let us not forget that last year's prisoners were reduced to one quarter, that's one quarter of their numbers, over the winter. They may well feel a little sceptical. We'll remedy this. What we must do now is find the right people . . .'

'Precisely.' Major von Schulenburg straightened up and turned to Berger. 'Competent, trained personnel, who understand how to handle the legionaries. People like you, Lieutenant Berger, cultured people who know their language. Your task will be, after attending the preparatory courses Professor Breuninger was talking about, to inspect the progress of the legions from the cultural, that's the cultural, point of view, and identify any missing elements, and to maintain communication between them, so that we don't miss the moment of integration, both between the legionaries of different nationalities and between them and the German battalions. Captain Brummer will give you the precise details of your transfer. I wish you the best of luck, Lieutenant.'

When Berger left for the Terek next morning, the sun had barely appeared above the steppe. Though it was only September the air was chilly. Berger turned up the collar of his jacket and made himself comfortable in his seat. The private beside him drove in silence. The truck bumped along the road. Berger dozed off from time to time, but woke suddenly as a sense of discomfort spread through his numbed limbs. He felt ill at ease. One can get used to anything, he thought, to war, to sickness, and yet change is what we fear the most. He too had in some way become used to the people around him, to Major Hartel, to his batman, to his men; such an unexpected change, even if the assignment were interesting, frightened him. It occurred to him that there might be something behind it. Perhaps he had annoyed someone, perhaps his reserved manner came across as arrogance. They had resolved to send him away, there was no doubt about it, and the ill-defined 'cultural' mission was simply their excuse. He'd been demoted, that was plainly in some way what it was about; demotion, pure and simple. Berger wholly lacked any military ambition, so much so that on his first leave his brother-in-law had looked him up and down and declared, not without a note of contempt, 'The only military thing about you is your uniform!' Now, however, the conviction that he had been so underhandedly demoted hurt him. War can be learnt too, indeed, it is more easily learnt than one thinks. He too had learnt it, so there was no reason to relegate him to some Turkish or Turkestan battalion or whatever. And yet he remembered the Mongol's ingenuous smile, what had he said he was called?, Tunshan, as he looked at the flashes on his chest and remembered Major von Schulenburg saying that they were natural, childlike creatures. They need to be looked after, to be supported, made to feel safe. It was a new, unexpected task, for which the Wehrmacht was wholly unprepared; for which the excessively crude propaganda used until then was not only no longer adequate, but actually counter-productive. Something else was needed. First and foremost, means of communication, the enemy's language, in fact. The Germans were clearly short of this kind of weapon. Russian. Language too is a weapon, Berger thought. In wartime one takes over not only the enemy's property, his land, his women and his soldiers, but also his language.

* * *

Meanwhile they had arrived at the Terek. Vehicles were rolling slowly over the bridge. A group of sappers was busy around it, on the far bank.

'There must have been an accident,' the driver observed. These were the first words he had spoken since they left Pyatigorsk. 'Or an air raid. You can see they were aiming at the bridge last night. It's lucky that it didn't take a direct hit, or we would have to ford it!'

Underneath the bridge the river roared on, and seemed anything but conducive to easy passage. Berger, however, looked anxiously towards the Kabardian house. He got out of the car and saw the house standing undamaged and white, at the edge of the terrace. He heard someone nearby saying: 'Must have been a hundred and fifty kilos. Only shrapnel got this far.' He felt frozen and was desperate for a coffee. He found this final obstacle in their path hard to bear, and decided to walk the last stretch. He crossed the bridge, felt the cold spray from the river on his face and saw the raging waters underneath the wooden girders. He passed the garden gate, called Scholz. Instead of Scholz, Major Hartel's batman came out of the house and sprang to attention: 'I'm sorry, Lieutenant,' he stated in the neutral tone of a sentry reporting, 'casualty.'

'What do you mean, casualty?' Berger's tone was incredulous, almost resentful.

'The bomb should have hit the bridge. Instead it fell behind there.' The soldier gestured towards the vineyard. 'Usually the bombers come later. Scholz was outside. A piece of shrapnel hit him right in the head.'

Berger set off towards the vineyard. On the left, on the side towards the bridge, among the broken vines, there was still a basket half full of grapes.

Berger had never noticed how narrow his bunk was, until that night. Too narrow to contain the turmoil within him. He continued to toss and turn and every time he thought he would topple off and fall into the Terek. At last he fell asleep and dreamed of a crude cross made of two poles tied together with rope. Bunches of grapes hung from the arms of the cross, like palls from a crucifix on Good Friday. And he, Berger, was walking towards the men and Scholz was among them listening, his head was all red and Berger turned to face him and said in an odd voice as though it were a lullaby, 'I would have liked to bury you in a vineyard, / in a terraced vineyard over the Terek, / when we get to Tiflis I will drink a toast to you / with the sweet muscat of the Caucasus. / When will you send me the wine from your lands, Private Scholz?'

20 September 1942. My dear Siglinde, I can't begin to tell you how saddened I am by the death of my batman Scholz. We had been together since the beginning of the war. I can no longer get used to death.

20

'I DON'T IMAGINE you know the meaning of the word *basmachi.*' Lieutenant Asimov, medic to the 808th Turkestan Battalion, looked upon Berger with the slightly ironic air he always assumed when he talked to Germans. His use of the word 'imagine' rarely failed to confound his interlocutor. Berger confessed that he didn't have the faintest idea what the word meant. 'A *basmachi* is a rebel, a fighter for his people's freedom. I don't imagine you've ever heard the story of Enver Pasha?' Naturally, Berger hadn't. 'One of the Young Turks. He became Minister for War in Turkey during the First World War, at only thirty-two, imagine that. After the war they throw him out of the Cabinet and put him in prison. He flees to Russia. Lenin welcomes him with open arms, for he wields extraordinary influence over the Islamic peoples. A charismatic leader, a genuinely charismatic leader. From Baku he crosses the Caspian Sea and in a few weeks he annihilates the anti-Soviet opposition in Turkmenistan. Wherever he goes, Merv, Bukhara, Samarkand, he is greeted by jubilant crowds; women tear their veils off, men grab their weapons and follow him. Lenin is already dreaming of expanding the proletarian revolution from the Syrdar'ya to the Ganges, with his assistance. Enver Pasha himself dreams of a vast Islamic state, under his own leadership, of course. He gathers together six thousand men, arms them, returns suddenly to Bukhara and shuts the Red Army garrison inside the city. A fantastically bloody battle. The *basmachi* forms an alliance with the ex-Emir of Bukhara, tries to organise his army of rebels along German lines, restores the old Caliphates, succeeds in driving the Red Army from Bukhara and from the Sherafan. Enver Pasha is at the pinnacle of his success, an absolute ruler and the object of a veritable cult. But, alas, he becomes drunk on power, alienates the restored Emir of Bukhara, sows the seeds of hatred all around him and insists on being called "Supreme Commander of All the Armies of Islam", a title which he has printed on a gold seal.'

'The usual story, in other words, of a rebel who is blinded by ambition and who becomes a despot.' Berger poured himself another cup of tea, gestured to Asimov not to forget his own, checked that the samovar was still full of water. The oil lamp lit the Uzbek officer's face and highlighted his thick moustache, jet black like his hair and his eyes. In that light, he too looked like a *basmachi*, thought Berger.

Asimov was one of those people whom others flock to, even without the benefit of a magic flute. It didn't matter so much what he talked about, for his listeners were drawn by the sheer charm of the man. Of course his men adored him. It was said that they had followed him into prison of their own free will and that they would follow him blindly into hell itself. Berger felt an admiration for him that he was scarcely able to explain to himself. He had been impressed not only by the man's intelligence but also by the way his eyes were fixed on you as he spoke, for his eyes seemed to see into your soul; it was the way he moved his long-fingered brown hands, as though he were taking possession of the space around him; it was his self-assurance, the ease with which he took other people's approval for granted. It was his culture too, for he was also a highly cultured man. His culture was different from Berger's but it fascinated the latter precisely for this reason, since it evoked a civilisation of which he had a rather vague idea, but which, naively, he was inclined to consider somehow better than his own. Where he was generally critical of his own countrymen, for Asimov he felt a boundless trust.

'It is and it isn't the usual story,' Asimov retorted, and his eyes became even darker. 'Every story is always a repetition of other stories and at the same time it is different. This one, this time, too . . .'

'What do you mean by this one, this time, too?'

'But of course. The Führer isn't the first to venture into Russian territory on the threshold of winter.' This time his tone was humorous. A comment nonchalantly thrown out. In any case, the comparison was on everybody's lips, even though nobody dared to draw the logical conclusions. Napoleon and Hitler, thought Berger. It would make a fine caricature, the Führer with his hand tucked into the breast of his coat! But he let it go and asked: 'So, the story of the *basmachi*, then?'

'It ended up just as all these stories do. The Emir betrayed him. The Red Army received reinforcements and planted spies everywhere. The *basmachi*'s hiding-place was discovered, not far from Denau, a little way to the north of Termez. The rebels were surrounded and put to the sword. They cut off Enver Pasha's head. On the ground near his body they found a miniature Koran, written in Arabic characters, in letters of gold. He had shown it to his followers before the final battle.'

'A hero of Islam.'

'A model. Veli-Kajum-Chan refers to him constantly in his speeches, in his stance, in the kind of rhetoric he uses. Even his Tiger Defensive Action was only an attempt to repeat the *basmachi*'s deeds, adapted to the circumstances, of course.'

'The Turkestan volunteer battalions stem from this, if I am not mistaken.'

'From the same idea. Everyone who tries to bring the Islamic peoples over to their side, Caliphs, rebel bandits, Stalin or Hitler, invoke the same idea: the independence of the Islamic peoples. But nobody asks: independence from whom?' The question hung in the halo of light round the lamp, though Berger felt no need to answer, nor was Asimov expecting him to. He stubbed out his cigarette, stood up and said goodnight. Before going out he paused on the threshold; the darkness opening out in front of him seemed to want to invade the inside of the house too, where the oil lamp on the table flickered.

10 October 1942. Kalmyk steppe. My dear Siglinde, you can't imagine a more isolated spot. A huddle of houses in the steppe. All around, abandoned, withered cotton fields. A few little plants are still showing a frayed tuft or two. The canals round the fields are silted up and the water in them is stagnant. The desolation gives you a feeling of sadness that is even harder to bear than the desert itself or the steppe. All around there's nothing, not even enemies, or so you would think. One could die of melancholy here. Luckily, I have made friends with an Uzbek officer, a fascinating, extraordinarily intelligent ex-Red Army doctor. We spend whole evenings talking.

Berger considered the sentry who was saluting him, raising his hand to his lambskin cap. Two cartridge belts crossed over his chest and he had a pistol stuck in his belt, from which also hung a knife on the left side. His left hand was firmly clenched on his rifle. If it had not been for the grey-green uniform one would have thought he was a bandit armed to the teeth. A Circassian bandit, thought Berger, and Tolstoy came into his mind, *The Prisoner of the Caucasus*. He smiled to himself. He was about to comment on the sentry's somewhat unmilitary appearance, but Captain Halblaib anticipated him:

'Don't let it bother you,' he said, and when they had taken a few more paces he added, 'these are savages, in a state of nature. Nothing makes them prouder than bearing arms. But the arms have to be well in sight, you understand. If you let them alone they do their duty, well even, but if you force them to observe formal discipline, which they don't understand, they refuse. Like children, just like children.' Captain Halblaib was proud of his experience in the Turkestan battalions, which he himself had helped to found, and above all of his deep knowledge of the psychology of the Turkestani volunteers, as the ex-prisoners were collectively called, even if in reality they belonged to different nations. The 808th Battalion, for example, included Uzbeks, Kazakhs, Tajiks, Kyrgyz, Turkmens and Tartars, who were then sub-divided into their respective national companies, under the command of their own officers. 'It's the only way to respect their national feelings,' Halblaib maintained. For his part he never tired of urging the little group of German soldiers in the battalion to consider the Turkestanis as comrades and to treat them benevolently, as savages, a phrase which he must have relished, as he never failed to repeat it at every opportunity.

Behind the row of little houses, in the large area of beaten earth which must have been used as a warehouse at cotton-picking time, the Turkestanis had spread their field blankets on the ground and were prostrating themselves in the direction of Mecca. The discipline and coordination with which the lines rose to a kneeling position and lowered themselves again to touch their foreheads to the ground was such that a stranger would have thought it was a military exercise. In the front row, an imam was directing the ceremony through a megaphone.

'It's a sight you'll have to get used to,' commented the captain. 'My men are under orders not to be seen about on these occasions, so as not to offend these people's religious sensibilities. And,' he added in a lower voice, 'because there have been cases of soldiers caught making fun of the ritual. A fight broke out once. Coarse people, you know. They're everywhere.'

'Of course, it's an unusual sight.' Berger noticed that he was also talking quietly, as though they were in a mosque. He felt like an intruder, embarrassed to be watching a ceremony from which he was excluded and irritated by what seemed to him a flaunting of religious feeling. Despite his conversion to Catholicism, Berger had remained a protestant, and he continued to see religion as something that belonged to a private, intimate sphere; collective display of any kind was distasteful to him. He had once joked at the wedding of a sister-in-law that he was a protestant Catholic; he must have drunk more than he ought to make such a declaration, and he had never forgotten the look on his mother-in-law's face. This rite in military uniform made him suspicious, even though he couldn't deny that it was very moving. It was a scene fit to turn the most refined propagandist of the regime pale: the lines of soldiers getting up and down in synchrony, the imam's voice echoing as far as the lines of the infidels and perhaps even as far as the Russian atheists, and the steppe like a mosque with a sky-blue dome. A huge blue mosque, where the only intruders were they themselves, the Germans.

Lieutenant Dr Asimov and Obersturmführer Achmadjaer joined Captain Halblaib and Lieutenant Berger. The battalion was ready; they could inspect the men. Every now and then the little group of officers would stop; the Captain would make a remark to one of the men and Achmadjaer would then step forward and praise him: 'Private Sulejmanov, who distinguished himself at the bridgehead on the Kuban. Silver star for valour on the field of battle.' A round silver decoration hung on the soldier's breast. The soldier looked straight ahead, as though these words had nothing to do with him. The officers walked on.

Berger stopped in front of Ul'an. 'We know one another,' he said. 'Yes Sir.' Ul'an did not move, but made as if to smile. His companions were lined up near him. Five Tunshan in grey-green uniforms, with the epaulettes and flashes of the Turkestan Battalion, on their right arms the badge with a mosque on a turquoise ground and the phrase *Tanri biz Menen*. 'What does it mean?' 'God is with us,' Asimov answered promptly and felt bound to add: 'These men have been posted here because of where they come from, but they are a nationality all their own. They are the only non-Muslims in the battalion. Apart from the German personnel, of course,' he added quickly. 'It would be expedient to transfer them to another battalion, to the Kalmyk cavalry corps, for instance.' Berger looked up: behind the lines of soldiers, to the north, he could see the ochre and brown expanse of the Kalmyk steppe.

'You have to give the Soviets credit for one thing,' Asimov took up the theme again eagerly, as though it were up to him to produce a historical summary of the merits and faults of the Soviet Union. 'Which is?' 'That they stamped out diseases which were still common when I was a child. My father used to tell me that in Bukhara after the war there was still an area of the city set aside exclusively for lepers. And heaven help anybody who left it: any citizen had the right to kill them on sight. Entire generations of lepers were born, lived and died in the same miserable shacks on the edge of the holy city. And since all skin diseases were treated as leprosy, there were charlatans going around selling cosmetic mixtures to cover up blemishes. There are several clinics around the city specialising in the treatment of skin diseases, which are still extremely common in the region today. I had many patients of this type at the hospital in Tashkent . . .' Berger realised that he was hanging on Asimov's words again. Of course Asimov seduced women, too, he thought, but in all their conversations they had never talked about it. They never alluded to such things; their friendship, if that was the right word, favoured by the circumstances of the war and by the isolation of the battalion, was limited to themes which did not call for too intimate a discussion. Berger dared not ask direct questions, but he had come to the conclusion that the Turkestans did not talk about women, except to condemn the abolition of the veil by the Soviets. To listen to them become heated on this subject, particularly if there was an imam present, one would have supposed that this was one of the most serious crimes carried out by Lenin and Stalin together. Was it possible, Berger wondered, that Asimov too wanted to revive the custom? He waited for the right moment to ask him directly. What did he think of the veil? Asimov hesitated for a moment, then said: 'No god would stoop so low as to concern himself with women's headcoverings. These precepts are made by men who are too weak to resist their own temptation and so try to eradicate their own weakness in this way.'

That evening Asimov retired to his billet early, but Berger stayed up reading, even though the dim light tired his eyes. Weary though he was, he forced himself to stay awake out of a sense of duty to himself. He considered reading a sort of antidote to the emptiness surrounding him, though it cost him a considerable effort to concentrate on what he was reading. The topics discussed in the book seemed unreal to him, part of a world to which he no longer belonged and from which it seemed to him he would be shut out for ever.

It was midnight when he heard a timid knock. 'Come in,' he said, but remembered instantly that he had bolted the door. He got up and went to open it. In the dark he did not recognise the man in front of him at first. It was Ul'an. Ul'an's salute and indeed his whole attitude, rigidly conforming to protocol, irritated Berger: why would he want to prove his military zeal at that hour! He beckoned to him to come in. A month had gone by since their meeting on the Terek, and those few weeks of training, though they had turned Ul'an into a soldier, had not taken away the natural suppleness of his movements. Ul'an inhabited space as though it were a fluid. He looked behind him and slipped into the room, following the lieutenant to the table. The light was still swinging in the draught through the open door and it lit him obliquely. He was so agitated that he could hardly find the words. 'Calm down, Tunshan, and explain clearly.'

Shortly before, perhaps half an hour ago, Ul'an wasn't sure exactly, he was walking past the wall of the soldiers' block, a few feet from Berger's billet – and here Ul'an gestured to show where – when he heard voices talking quietly, very quietly. But Ul'an has excellent hearing and he knows that men who talk quietly have something to hide. He stops and listens, concealed in the shadow of the block. The voices belong to Lieutenant Asimov and Achmadjaer, talking to each other in Uzbek. But Ul'an understands that language. Asimov is saying: 'Not long now.' And the other man: 'So long as everything goes smoothly.' And Asimov: 'We'll be there in an hour.' And Achmadjaer: 'Let's hope the men follow us.' 'My men always follow me.' Asimov goes back inside and Achmadjaer walks off in the opposite direction. Ul'an stays by the wall a little longer, without moving, afraid they'll notice him. He is in no doubt as to what he has to do. Not only Berger, but the Tunshan too are in danger. Is he not bound to Berger by the knot of eternal friendship? Is he not responsible for all the Tunshan, his companions, whom he has brought this far? Did they not travel all that way to fight for their common cause? It is a sign from heaven that he heard everything, Ul'an is sure.

He stopped talking and looked anxiously at Berger, standing stock still in front of him. But the lieutenant felt incapable of any reaction, as though his brain were refusing to think, his tongue to speak. He felt unable to move a muscle. He saw Ul'an waiting, standing to attention, and he could sense his anxiety. 'Are you sure it was them?' he said at last, but the question betrayed his discomfort. The tone too was wrong. Ul'an refused to be intimidated by the threat concealed in the other man's voice: he was absolutely sure. Fearing that Berger had not fully understood, he repeated that Asimov and Achmadjaer were talking about going over to the other side, to the Russians. Did the lieutenant not understand? What more did he need to make up his mind and to act? Ul'an could no longer conceal his disappointment.

Ul'an was right. The conversation he reported left no room for doubt. Berger looked foolishly at the place by the table, the empty bench where Asimov had been sitting a few hours earlier. He could still hear his voice, and felt again the same admiration he always felt for Asimov. He turned to Ul'an who was waiting, increasingly uncertainly. 'Go,' he said eventually. 'Wake your companions and come here, but don't disturb the others.' Now Berger was nervous too. He went quickly out of the house, made sure that nobody had seen him and headed swiftly for Captain Halblaib's billet.

Asimov was still in his room, alone, when Ul'an appeared before him, saluting: the captain was asking for him, urgently. 'Go ahead, I'll be right there.' Asimov gave no sign of emotion. He looked around one last time, though he knew that there was no way out of the room except by the door. He released the catch on his pistol and stepped over the threshold. He only had time to take one step in the dark before the men were on him; they tied his hands behind his back, clapped a hand over his mouth. Germans. He had been betrayed.

The order was to take the Turkestani soldiers by surprise and disarm them before they had time to leave the barracks. By now it was too late to do this, so the soldiers took up positions at the door. At that moment a white rocket appeared in the sky, high, glowing, a vertical comet which went out almost immediately. There followed an unexpected burst of artillery fire from the Russian side, an infernal noise, but clearly not aimed at enemy lines. The Turkestani soldiers began to leave their billets. The Germans opened fire. Hand grenades flew through the air, the first soldiers ran out and disappeared into the darkness, while gunfire clattered behind their backs. Then, nothing. The wounded, ten all told, German and Turkestani, were carried to the infirmary. Three killed. It was not yet possible to establish how many had deserted. The company Asimov had commanded had all fled, and there was no trace of Achmadjaer. Of the other soldiers, many had spontaneously returned to their dormitory; others, still clearly entirely in the dark, had been asleep, and had not joined the deserters. They put up no resistance when they were disarmed.

Everybody was now waiting for dawn. Captain Halblaib had asked the XVIth Motorised Division, which like the Turkestan Battalion were posted to the Kalmyk steppe to protect the Eastern front, for reinforcements. They would not be long in coming.

When he got back to his billet, Berger couldn't keep still. As soon as a strip of light showed in the east he went back to the captain. He found him sipping tea. It was as though he had shrunk in those hours and the nickname the men had given him – *Halbmann** – seemed more apt than ever. Half a man. His complexion had gone grey and the bags under his eyes were heavier. He acknowledged Berger with the barest nod: '*Unglaublich*,' he said, and repeated it: '*Unglaublich*.' Incredible. He stirred his tea with particular care and precision, as if he could melt the doubts which still assailed him, and made the whole affair appear so incredible to him, in the liquid. After a while, suddenly remembering something, he pushed a notebook across the table towards Berger. He went back to sipping his tea. 'They found it on Asimov. Sewn into the lining of his overcoat. He must have felt very sure of himself, to carry something like that round with him. It's written in Russian. You look at it, your Russian is better than mine. Get an interpreter

* *Halblaib* means literally 'half body'.

to help you if you need one. It's the proof of the conspiracy. *Unglaublich*,' he repeated. He stopped stirring, lifted the cup of tea to his lips, looking over the edge at the same time, into the middle distance. '*Schade*,' he said, finally, putting the teacup down on the table. 'A shame, a downright shame.'

Berger took the notebook, put it in his pocket and went back to his room. He noticed that his hands shook as he opened it. Tiny writing, not easy to decipher. He sent for the interpreter, a boy born and brought up in Russia, but with German parents, who had managed to flee to Germany before the war broke out. The two of them bent over Asimov's writing. Berger wrote the translation down on some loose sheets of paper.

It was the diary of the plot, as Halblaib had said, faithfully documented by Asimov, who declared himself on the first page to be 'Commissioner of the Battalion and President of the Asiatic Communist Bolshevik Party,' whose aim, according to the statutes carefully transcribed into the notebook, was the 'liberation of the battalion', in other words taking it to the other side of the front, 'having liquidated the Fascists', in other words the German personnel. A list of names and their respective functions followed. Achmadjaer: in charge of contact with the Russians. Then the others in alphabetical order. The diary also contained jottings by Asimov, for example: 'Veli-Kajum-Chan, the greatest traitor in Uzbek history. A dog who will meet the same end as Enver Pasha.' Or: 'I have a profound hatred for the old Uzbek customs which oblige girls to hide behind veils. I will never fight to defend them. I will die for a real Turkestan, for a true culture and a true technology.' And further on: 'The Asiatic peoples must also be in a position to achieve miracles like the Russian proletariat and not be eternally their parasites!' There were even pieces of verse, like the one dedicated to the Don: 'O River Don, how I understand your anger! / I understand why you hurl impetuous waves against the bank! / But be serene, Don, calm yourself! Your anger boils over, Don, because today the German invaders are crossing you and bands of Fascists march along your banks. / Moderate your anger, quiet Don of the Cossacks! / Not all is yet lost! / Listen! The Russian thunder is near. / Then your powerful waves will wipe out the enemy filth. / We love you, Don, we will not betray you. / Listen! Justice will descend on the enemies of our native land, on the bloody bands of the Fascists! / They will leave their blood upon your banks in their millions, O Don!'

While he bent over the notebook, puzzling out and translating the pages with the diligence of a schoolboy faced with a Latin primer, Berger almost failed to realise the significance of what Asimov had written. It was later, when the interpreter had gone and he re-read the pages of translation more slowly, that the enormity of the betrayal became clear to him. He felt a burning pain, and it was caused by the humiliation, even more than the tragedy of what had happened. He had been deceived, like a fool he had let himself be hoodwinked by Asimov's words and his appearance; he had fallen unsuspecting into the trap. He thought his offer of friendship had been reciprocated and he discovered that his death had been planned as a pure and simple 'liquidation of the Fascists'. At the same time, however, and despite himself, he continued to admire Asimov, despite the plot, or perhaps also because of it. He felt drained. And alone, terribly alone. Abandoned like an outsider in the middle of the steppe.

The military tribunal did not take long to come to a decision: Asimov, three Uzbek NCOs and seven privates were found guilty of high treason and sentenced to be shot. The Turkestan Battalion was drawn up, disarmed, in the broad space between the houses of the kolkhoz, surrounded by the armed soldiers of the XVIth Armoured Division. The firing squad took up its position. The condemned men were marched out, bareheaded, their uniforms stripped of their badges of rank As they were being lined up in front of the barn wall, Asimov suddenly jumped forward a pace, shouted, 'Long live Stalin!' and took to his heels, running like a lunatic towards the steppe. The others ran after him and were all brought down by gunfire, like pigeons loosed for a shoot.

Berger had tried throughout to look the other way. He only heard the shots and just after, beside him, Captain Halblaib's voice saying '*Unglaublich*!'

* * *

An inquiry was carried out among the volunteers of the 808th Battalion. The suspects were sent back to the prison camps. The others had their weapons restored to them. It was the end of October when Lieutenant Günther Berger walked down the lines of soldiers standing to attention and pinned the silver decoration on Ul'an Tunshan's chest. Somebody took a photograph to commemorate the occasion.

> *28 October 1942. Kalmyk steppe. Dear Siglinde, if I am still alive it is thanks to a young Mongol soldier, who volunteered to fight with us. It is incredible how war mixes and combines people of radically different kinds. Your life depends on chance or on the will of others more than on your own.*

21

> *We are finally leaving this desolation! Of course I don't know if the place we're headed for is any better. But the change in itself seems to me already an improvement, for being stranded in this remote spot has come to seem unbearable to me. I felt like a prisoner, not of the Caucasus, but of the steppe.*

That is what Günther Berger wrote to Siglinde on the first of November 1942.

The Kalmyk steppe seemed to have swallowed up the rain without noticing, like a beach after a downpour. Even the puddles on the valley floors had disappeared in a few days: the cold which had followed the bright days had hardened the ground. Now the steppe was ready to welcome new columns of marching soldiers.

The 808th Turkestan Battalion was moving north. It had to join up with the German XVIth Armoured Division, which was defending the outpost of Khulkhuta and the few villages occupied by the Germans on the Kalmyk steppe. From there it would move on to Stalingrad, where it was expected in early December, to support the German Sixth Army. These were the deployments of the Staff of A Army.

The soldiers crossing the steppe – Turkmens, Kyrgyhz, Kazakhs and Uzbeks – marched trustingly, though they did not know their final destination. Their faith in the invincibility of the Wehrmacht had not yet been much tested by defeats or retreats, and the volunteers in the German army could deceive themselves that the march was bringing them closer to the vague promise of freedom that had been made to them. The Kalmyk steppe opened up in front of the soldiers, and looked to be deserted, but they knew that this appearance of harmless vastness was deceptive and that monotony could well conceal danger. Although they did not know where the enemy – the soldiers of the Red Army and the still more redoubtable partisans – might be hidden, in a landscape which seemed too open to hide a thing, or perhaps for that very reason, their presence could be felt as an obscure threat, though the mounted patrols sent out to reconnoitre came and went signalling that the road was clear.

One of these patrols was led by Lieutenant Berger; the five Tunshan and three Kazakhs belonged to it. Berger rode along contentedly. He liked to feel the animal under him. How long had it been since he had been on a horse? The last time had been in the Ahr valley, in the Eifel, where his father had bought and renovated a farmhouse. They had ridden in the forest together. The ground was soft, the landscape green. He found all that green impossible, unbearable. He had never realised until that day that he had always lived in green places, apart from the brief parenthesis of winter. And in wet damp places. The wood oozed green; the Ahr valley was soaked with the moisture from the river which could be glimpsed at times through the trees when the mist lifted.

Berger looked around for a river: there must be a river or a marsh hidden to the east, where the ground fell away towards the Caspian Sea, or to the north, among the jungle of reed beds. But everything was much further away than expected. Berger had learnt that in the steppe distances are much greater than they appear to the eye; that it was not as flat as it seemed at first; and that in places the ground was riven by deep dells, where the horses scrambled down in a rush only to climb out again panting, dragged by their own momentum up the slope on the other side. The horses stopped suddenly at the edge of one of these hollows. The ground on the other side was rippling strangely. The steppe seemed to be moving imperceptibly, covered by shifting brown and black spots, and filling the air with the same movement. There was bleating, high and piercing or low and mournful, the quivering of young animals, the shuffling of hooves and the crackle of broken bushes, as the herd moved calmly on, filling the horizon; only a few sheep broke ranks and descended the steep sides of the valley, but immediately regretted their temerity and hurried back across the slope to rejoin the herd.

'They're going towards the Volga,' said Berger, turning to Ul'an who was patting his horse on the neck to calm him. 'Do you reckon it's the season for changing pastures?' 'Changing pastures? I don't think so. They're going to feed the Russians!' replied Ul'an. 'That's what I think too. The Russians are surely waiting at the Volga to ferry the beasts over to the other side.' Berger remembered hearing that a huge number of heads of livestock had been removed by the Russians from the Kalmyk kolkhoz and taken to the other side of the front unbeknownst to the Germans, who, for their part, were trying to hold onto the animals and bring them behind their own lines. The flocks heading for the Volga so late must have escaped the vigilance of the occupying forces.

'What do you say, Lieutenant, shall we spoil their meal?' An expression of great cunning had appeared on Ul'an's face. Berger nodded: 'Find the herdsmen and bring them back here!'

Tunshan and Kazakhs spurred their horses down the valley and climbed the other side, where they split into two groups. Their arrival frightened the sheep, which scattered, but recovered immediately and carried on. The Tunshan reappeared, escorting two horsemen; the Kazakhs brought a third. All three were very young and they now looked at the officer nervously. 'And the others?' 'They ran away. Perhaps they hid. They are Kalmyks; they will come back.'

They were Kalmyks, the herdsmen confirmed, friendly to the

Germans. They had been forced to move the sheep: it was the livestock of the kolkhoz, all their capital, which was destined to end up in the mouths of the Russians. They had nothing against keeping it. In that case, they were to take it back to the kolkhoz, ordered Berger. The boys lost no time in obeying. They whistled up their dogs, reached the front of the herd and began to drive it round in a curve, so that the change of direction was not too abrupt. Tunshan and Kazakhs helped on their flanks, while the missing herdsmen had appeared on the other side. Faced with the dogs' threats and the barrier of horses, the sheep began to slow down, but with difficulty, because they were pushed by those behind them. Many sheep in the front rows, however, turned right around in fright in too rapid an about-face: the sheep following, unable to imitate them, found themselves in this way squashed between two masses of animals, one following the path they were already on and one trying to turn about, and their hooves went from under them. In order to avoid being squashed several lifted their front hooves onto their neighbours' backs, while others, exhausted, were no longer able to hold their necks above the throng, so that from the outside the herd seemed nothing but a swarming of wool, bobbing tails and heads, from which every now and then legs and feet protruded. For a few moments it seemed as though panic had seized the animals, then order returned to the front ranks and they began to trot in the direction urged by the herdsmen; picking up speed, their trot became a run. The sheep behind followed the ones in front: the whole herd was running now, a moving carpet in light and shade, which traced a large *U* in the steppe and retreated westwards in good order, leaving bleating and dung in their wake.

Tunshan and Kazakhs rode happily back to Berger. 'We took some prisoners, sir,' laughed Ul'an when the herd were some distance away, and he pointed to two sheep tied by the feet, who were trying in vain to stand up and swinging their heads about, their eyes rolling in fear.

'I could have you arrested for unlawful appropriation of civilian property,' said Berger, but he himself did not believe his own words. 'You would have no proof, sir, for by tomorrow not even the skin of our prisoners will be left.'

By now it was evening, and the patrol looked for a safe place to spend the night. Timur slit the breast of one of the sheep with a quick stroke of the knife, put his hand inside, felt for the main artery with his fingers and cut it. The animal did not have time to let out so much as a moan; its eyes just clouded over; the head tried to rise one last time and then it fell limply to the ground. 'That way no blood is lost and the animal doesn't suffer,' Timur explained. No trace remained at the place of the sacrifice. The fire too was soon doused and was only used to heat some large stones which were placed in the stomachs of the animals to cook the meat. They sat in a circle, Berger in the middle, as Ul'an carved the sheep and offered him the best bits, as though he were his guest. And in a way he was.

They were not far from Yashkul by now, on the beaten track that leads to Elista, capital of the Kalmyk Republic, when the patrol found themselves facing a band of horsemen. They were in German uniforms, but without tabs, and their only badge was a yellow cord worn around the right arm. 'First squadron, Kalmyk cavalry,' said the soldier when they were near. 'Stay alert. The road is swarming with bandits,' and he meant the partisans, employing the same term the Russians used to designate the Kalmyks. He turned his horse and they saw him ride to a large copse lower down. Soldiers, horses and vehicles were milling round it, but from a distance you could not tell why. Gradually as they came closer, what seemed like disorder was revealed instead to be military strategy. The copse had been surrounded by Kalmyks on horseback. A group of them, on foot, disappeared into the thicket, and shots and bursts of machine-gun fire were heard; suddenly, a man ran out from the other side of the thicket. He had time to take several steps. A second followed, running like the first one, and fell immediately. Like shooting pheasants, thought Berger, you flush them out and then you bring them down. Finally a group of men appeared. They wore no uniforms, but clothes such as the peasants in the area wore. They had their hands up and walked slowly, in silence. The Kalmyk cavalry let them advance a few yards and when the signal was given they fired. The men fell in a heap.

5 November 1942. Elista, the capital of the Kalmyk Republic, is a terribly sad place. You can tell that it was built as a Soviet centre. It is lifeless. The Kalmyks were forced to abandon their tents, and live in square little houses made of mud. The whole city is an expanse of little cubes round the cement cubes of the government buildings, which are ugly but pompous. Tangles of electric wires hang from the pylons with their festoons of filth; everything gives an impression of poverty . . .

'The bond of friendship between the Kalmyk and German peoples is of ancient date. It was already firmly established when the city of Elista was still only empty steppe.' Here the orator, Professor Breuninger, envoy from the Ministry of the East, paused. His backdrop was Elista city hall, grey and pock-marked with bullet-holes, and two crossed flags framed him on the podium, the yellow flag of the Kalmyks and the red flag with the swastika. The crowd of Kalmyks sat on the ground behind the red line of lamas. 'Did the great captain Sserep Schan Tjumanj, glorious son of the Kalmyk people, not fight in the ranks of the Prussian army? Was he not decorated by Frederick-William III, King of Prussia? And did the great painter and sculptor Fyodor Ivanovic Kalmyk not produce some of his masterpieces at the court of King Ludwig of Baden? He too chose distant Germany as his second fatherland; there he lived in honour and praise and his bones rest in German soil. Well, the ancient friendship between our peoples is strengthened today by historical events: today, when the German army has definitively liberated the greater part of Kalmyk territory from violent Bolshevik rule, today our ancient bond is reinforced by the blood of our soldiers who fight shoulder to shoulder against our common enemy!'

Applause from the crowd interrupted his speech; children began to wave little yellow flags up and down and to shout '*uukai, uukai*', until the orator gestured for silence and went on: 'The German people is deeply indignant at the countless insults and the deep suffering undergone by the Kalmyk people at the hands of the Soviet tyrants, but it is proud to be able to guarantee them a better future. Kalmyks! You are free to decide your own fate! Go back, if you wish, to the nomad life of your ancestors, the lords of the steppe!'

The crowd had leapt to its feet shouting; the women waved pieces of yellow cloth, the children their little flags. The orator was surrounded and had difficulty in shaking all the hands which were held out to him. When the press of people had thinned a little, the lamas came up to him and, enclosing him in a red circle, began to speak animatedly, then brought their joined hands to their foreheads and moved away.

Berger, who had stood to one side, seized the opportunity to come forward. He saluted.

'Oh, lieutenant, it's a pleasure to see you again.' Professor Breuninger maintained a kind of civilian cordiality even in this military environment. 'As you can see, their enthusiasm is a little overwhelming. The lamas have just told me that they plan to send a messenger to the Dalai Lama, to inform him of the support they are giving us.'

'In Tibet?' Berger gazed at him in disbelief. 'Distances are relative,' winked Professor Breuninger. 'It's a short walk for people used to living on the steppe!' 'But the front is in between!' 'The front is a very coarse net. Especially to the south-east.' 'But where does this front lie?' Berger pressed him. 'Roughly speaking, at the Volga, but, as you know, we have allies on both sides, the Kalmyks to be precise. There is talk of organising a rebellion among the Kalmyks in Soviet territory,' added Breuninger in a lower voice, as though he was afraid there were Soviet spies about. 'We have already sent out agents. We will turn the Kalmyk Republic into the Vendée of the Soviet Union.'

Berger looked at the Kalmyks who were still lingering in small groups in the square. They were old people, women and ragged children, their faces often marked by smallpox and by chronic poverty. The only ones with any dignity were the horsemen in the Kalmyk squadrons, who were even now riding round the square; they wore their Wehrmacht uniforms with pride and held their yellow flag high, as though it were the banner of a victorious army. The Kalmyks were no more than a hundred thousand in all, many of whom had been conscripted into the Red Army and were fighting on the other side of the front. The villages contained people like the ones in the square. Was Professor Breuninger serious? The Vendée on the Kalmyk steppe!

The Professor regained his cordial tone of voice and asked more loudly: 'Tell me about your work in the Turkestan Battalion . . .'

10 November 1942. Kalmyk steppe. Dear Siglinde, I am in the most remote place on the steppe, far from everything. Here the war has become as primordial as can be: we are fighting for water!

The village of Khulkhuta was the easternmost point on the entire Russian front. 'It's a wretched place,' Major Schneider, who had recently occupied that extreme bridgehead with his men of the XVIth division, had said to Berger. Not only was the village, a handful of tumbledown houses clustered in a hollow, the same colour as the steppe, but you would have said that it stuck to it, like an iguana waiting motionlessly for an insect to pass, legs extended and stomach flush with the ground.

'The Russians can watch our movements in perfect comfort.' Major Schneider had the reputation of being a *Nörgler*, a grumbler. Indeed, he made no secret of his dissatisfaction with the progress of military operations. In his view, if a thing was worth doing, it was worth doing well, and finishing well too. This playing for time on an unreliable front, justifying plans that could not be implemented, was not only contrary to his nature and to his principles, but, to listen to him, contrary to reason itself, or to military reason at any rate. 'How can we hold out with our supply lines so far away?' More than once, indeed, the division had run the risk of being surrounded and had only just managed to evade an enemy attack. 'In addition water is scarce and brackish and they have captured the wells.' Since the Major had the reputation of being a *Nörgler*, nobody paid much heed to his objections. The orders were clear; to hold the bridgehead to the east at all costs. Operation Heron was at stake, and with it the conquest of Astrakhan and of the shores of the Caspian Sea. Major Schneider had something to say about that too: 'Before we get to go fishing in the Caspian Sea,' he commented ironically, 'the Russians will be coming to fish for us. If, that is, we don't die of thirst here in this desert.'

Schneider also looked mistrustfully at the Turkestan battalion which had just been placed under his command: 'We need soldiers, not the scrapings from prison camps!' he said. 'As if you could strengthen the front with deserters! Anyway, before sending battalions to certain defeat at the front, you have to test the soldiers, see what they're capable of.' For once, we agreed with him and this was how the Turkestanis were sent to capture the Komintern.

The Komintern kolkhoz had been a major livestock breeding centre, but the livestock had been removed some time earlier together with the civilian population. Houses, offices, schools and stables now sheltered Soviet soldiers, who defended the village fiercely, though they had been cut off from the rest of the Red Army. 'It's not as if it was the Kremlin, either,' Schneider had said sarcastically. Even if it wasn't the Kremlin, the kolkhoz possessed a resource more sought-after on the steppe than the domes of a cathedral: a well, one of the few between Khulkhuta and the Volga. It was defended by a mixed unit of Russians, Kalmyks and Kazakhs, of whom Nazarov, a Kazakh officer in the Turkestan Battalion, had said: 'We're the real representatives of international communism! Proletariat of the same nations on both sides!'

He is right, thought Berger, the geographical front can be drawn more or less accurately on a map, but the human front? How can you divide it into two distinct parts? Soldiers of the same nations on both sides. It's not like wars used to be, where the fronts were clearcut: black on one side and white on the other, like chess. Here it's all a mixture of nations, the same people over here and over there. In the end you even forget who is attacking and who is attacked.

In the case of the Komintern, however, the two roles were clearly defined, for the Germans and their allies were attacking the kolkhoz, while the soldiers of the Red Army were defending it, from inside. The Soviets had turned the Komintern into a heavily fortified stronghold, with a brick wall all around it and mortars and machine-guns behind it. Because the kolkhoz stood on a bluff and dominated the steppe, seen from below it looked like a castle under siege, over which fluttered the red flag rather than the arms of the chatelain. This red could be seen from far away, so much so that the Turkestani soldiers and the German soldiers had already laid bets on who would be the first to tear down that rag and put an end to what was in their eyes unheard-of provocation.

The Turkestan Battalion attacked the Komintern while it was still dark. Covered by their artillery, the soldiers slithered along the slope towards the outer wall of the village. It was a baptism of fire for the Tunshan.

'You will feel more comfortable among the Kalmyks. Aren't they more like you?' Berger looked from the Kalmyks to the Tunshan. The similarities were obvious enough. But, while the Kalmyks were extremely proud of their patched uniforms and were at ease on horseback, the Tunshan, weighed down with the heavy equipment of the infantryman, looked awkward even in ordinary uniform, like sailors forced to fight on dry land. Ul'an thought for a moment before answering, then looked at his younger brother Timur, at Alcidai, Bayan and Jintai, as though to remember a decision they had already taken, and eventually said: 'You're right, we have a past in common with the Kalmyks. But our present is here now, with you.'

The Tunshan slithered behind Berger through the scrub, artillery fire behind them, the enemy dug in behind the wall of the kolkhoz in front of them. The night had lightened when the attackers passed the first line of defence and reached the Komintern buildings. Many had been left lying very still on the slope, but the others had already occupied the first houses and were advancing towards the centre of the village, taking cover behind the courtyard walls and fences. The Soviets had barricaded themselves inside the buildings and a group was doggedly defending the well, among the long low stable blocks.

The Tunshan went into what had been the administrative centre of the kolkhoz; the shelves were crammed with dusty yellow documents, tied with ribbons which barely contained the overflowing papers. On a table there were stamps of different sizes hung by the neck, in an elegant display; piles of forms covered every available surface. As the soldiers burst in, their attention was drawn to the punctilious bureaucracy of the kolkhoz, now quite at their mercy, and to year upon year of ordered lists, painstakingly written out by rural administrators but now swept aside, reduced to chaos and heedlessly trampled underfoot. There was not even a wall to defend that little enclave of culture; the outside of the building had been hit by a mortar shell and laid the ridiculous vulnerability of the paper out for all to see. The Tunshan took cover among the shelves and aimed their weapons at the enemy outside.

Suddenly a hand grenade whistles through the breach into the building. Ul'an is in time to get down and avoid it, Timur behind him is not. Ul'an hears the scream, turns, sees his brother crumple and collapse onto a shelf, dragging a heap of files with him as he falls; he sees the red stains on the paper. But he has no time to help Timur; at a sign from the lieutenant he advances with the others at a run across the space separating him from the door of the building opposite, which is hanging at an angle in the doorway. Ul'an stoops and makes his way into the stable. It seems deserted. The ground is still covered with a layer of straw mixed with dry dung and wisps of wool. Ul'an advances warily, then thinks he sees something moving in the straw, aims and fires. The wounded man stretches an arm up towards the manger looking for a handhold, arches his body and falls back head first among the remains of the feed.

The defenders have barricaded themselves in the barn with the farm machinery, the last stronghold of the Komintern. It is not clear how many there are inside, but they must have plenty of ammunition, and are unsparing in their use of it. Nobody dares to go any nearer before the artillery arrives, but someone throws a grenade which reaches a window in the barn, and falls in. They hear a louder explosion, a crackle of small mortars, then tongues of flame appear at the windows and lick outwards, reaching the roof, devouring it, enveloping the door, demolishing it and spreading into the street. Men come out waving their arms like flaming *garuda*, and some even run to the well and throw themselves in. Germans and Turkestanis retreat before the fire. Now Ul'an runs back to the kolkhoz office, grabs Timur, hoists him over his shoulder and rejoins his companions on the slope in front of the burning Komintern.

Berger assembles his men. The nurses collect the wounded; Germans and Turkestanis pull out. It is evening. When the flames finally die down, the soldiers make their way through the blackened ruins collecting the dead, shrunk by the fire like the remains of dwarves. The well is full of debris and corpses. 'In the end,' the victors observe bitterly, 'who won the bet? It was the fire that pulled down the red rag from the roof. And the well? All that effort and not even a mouthful of water to drink.'

Timur lies in the infirmary. His eyes are clouded and he is staring straight ahead, but he can't see anybody. There are no last words, no goodbyes, nothing. 'I'm sorry,' says Berger. Ul'an's eyes are wet. 'For what?' he answers. 'You know what the horse said to Geser Khan? It said to him: what use are tears in the eyes, what good is sadness in the breast? That's what the horse said to Geser Khan. You die if you are destined to die. Timur my brother was; now his soul is with the lotus flowers.'

The Tunshan planted a stick over the grave, tied yellow ribbons to it and piled a little cairn of stones around it. The body of Bairqan's son Timur was left in the Kalmyk steppe.

22

THE TRUCK BUMPED over the frozen steppe, searching out a track among the ruts worn in the road surface by heavier vehicles. Berger was hunched up, deep in thought. He was thinking about the little Kalmyk boy. He might have been ten years old, but the seriousness of his demeanour and his awareness of danger made him look older. He had dismounted with the ease of one used to riding from earliest childhood. He wore a yellow ribbon round his right arm. He asked for the 'commander' and his voice, which was still that of a child, was determined. They brought him to Berger. 'Commander,' the boy began with no sign of timidity, 'the Russians are bringing reinforcements into our village. Panzers and motorised units. They are preparing for an attack.' He stopped talking. Only then did his round face take on a timid expression, the expression of a child in a new place, in front of strangers. He had Kalmyk eyes and he narrowed them like a cat as he looked around. Berger thanked him, gave orders for him to be fed. The boy asked for water for his horse and left immediately.

So this was the Kalmyk rebellion, the Soviet Vendée, as Professor Breuninger had called it. They send children over the steppe to act as messengers. They attract less notice than an adult, but the Russians take no account of age when shooting collaborators. The little Kalmyk boy knew it, as he knew that he too was at war. War leaves nobody out, thought Berger.

It was still dark around him. It was already mid-November and the days were so short by now that it was impossible to set out and to get to their destination in daylight. They set out in the dark and they arrived in the dark. Their headlights barely lit the road, and they might as well aspire to light up the night with a swarm of fireflies. They could barely make out the edges of the track; sky and ground fused together. What use was it to wander over the frozen steppe like this, and what use was the little Kalmyk boy's journey or the danger he had faced? Berger thought back to what Major Schneider had said: 'We are ill prepared for an attack. We won't be able to hold Khulkhuta for long. They've left us on our own to defend hundreds of kilometres of steppe. They only care about Stalingrad. Because of the name, that's all. I'm sure there are other, better places to cross the Volga, but they refuse to give up on Stalingrad.' The Major's tone was disillusioned, bitter even. He was not only offended, as a good officer, by the outrage to military logic. From what he said it was clear that he was particularly attached to the stretch of sandy ground that he had been doggedly defending for weeks and he did not relish leaving it, although it was hardly his fatherland.

Berger, on the other hand, didn't in the least mind leaving

Khulkhuta, any more than he minded being posted to Elista. On the fifteenth of November 1942, he wrote to Siglinde:

> *I am once again wandering over the Kalmyk steppe. I feel like the battalion outrunner: I get pitched here and there in the steppe, constantly under new orders, though the landscape is always the same, particularly now, in winter. But sometimes it can spring a surprise on you, and how! I don't know whether to be more surprised by my discovery or by my perplexity with regard to it. I will tell you all when I get home, and you will understand.*

They were about halfway there when an oath from the driver and a particularly violent jolt interrupted Berger's soliloquy. A cloud of black smoke was rising from the truck's motor, clear, calm, unequivocal. Hammer the driver got down, lifted the bonnet, looked into it, fiddled, poured a canteen of water into it, climbed back into the driver's seat and switched the engine on again. The cloud remained, as ineffable and stubborn as a spirit of the air. They needed water. Ul'an and Alcidai grabbed the buckets and filled them with snow; Hammer filled a sack too, put it to thaw on the bonnet, and poured the resulting liquid into the radiator. The engine calmed down for a bit, but then the steam began to puff through the grille again, apparently making fun of the travellers. However much the driver wore himself out trying to mend the fault and took out his exasperation in curses, failure was staring them all in the face, as visible as the cloud of steam. The sack on the bonnet of the truck, which the Tunshan were energetically filling with snow, resembled an inflated sheepskin, of the kind the Mongols used to use to cross rivers, but this one was collapsing little by little and it in no way promised to bring the vehicle which had been entrusted to it into port.

Berger grew ever more anxious as darkness fell. At every jolt of the truck on the beaten earth track, at every hiccup of the engine and at every curse from the driver he peered into the darkness to either side of the track and began to see partisans in the looming shadows of the bushes. The closer they got to the point where the engine would finally cease to turn, the more the shadows took on a definite and threatening shape and jumped out at them waving and pointing their weapons. Berger's imagination had taken such a hold of him that he felt his hands turning to ice inside his woollen gloves as he clutched the butt of his pistol nervously. The moon itself could not dispel the phantasms but instead made the shadows between the bushes still more mysterious, while the truck lurching down the moonlit track became even more of a target, as thought it had been put there on purpose to attract the partisans.

Berger turned to Ul'an and Alcidai who were sitting on the back seat, showing no sign of fear or nervousness. It looked at first sight as though the breakdown didn't concern them, but their faces were alert and they were following events with a kind of detached curiosity. Could it be that they were able to shut themselves off from events and observe them from outside? Is this true? wondered Berger. Perhaps they have other things on their mind. But what? Berger could make out their features, Ul'an's prominent nose, his almost oval face, in which only his slightly slanting eyes revealed his Mongol ancestry, and beside it, Alcidai's rounder face with its high cheekbones and small, narrow nose. What were they saying to each other, under their breath? Berger could only hear the more guttural sounds; the meaning was closed to him. It was impossible to guess the emotions they felt either from the few words they said to him, or from the expressions on their faces. At times this impenetrability exasperated him, or perhaps it was only the acute and embarrassing feeling of alienation which vexed him. Often, seeing Ul'an so distracted, he wondered just what he was thinking about. But it struck him as indiscreet to ask. Probably, their thoughts were no different from those of the other soldiers, of whatever nationality. They will be thinking about their land, their women, their families, about food. War strips us of the superficial layer where our differences lie, and reduces us to a primordial core; it makes us all alike. We are all prisoners of the same thoughts, even of the same dreams, thought Berger. Even the impenetrability of the Tunshan was only an illusion. There were times, though, when their intent calm reassured him. Rightly or wrongly he thought that the Tunshan would not lose their heads in the event of danger and that they could be counted on more than the other soldiers. For this reason he liked to have them with him and had chosen them for this mission.

Elista probably wasn't more than thirty kilometres away when the truck gave a last shudder and the engine snorted, emitted a final, particularly dense cloud of steam and stopped dead. The driver cursed one last time, then also fell silent. Around them there was nothing but the grey-white of the steppe, but they could make out the shapes of houses not far off, a Kalmyk village. They headed for it and knocked at the first house.

An elderly Kalmyk opened the door and beckoned them into the smoky little room. The strangers' unexpected visit, and the cold blast of air they brought in with them, caused a flurry of agitation inside. A big tousled dog got up, whined and sniffed at the newcomers; a sheep which had been lying by the door got to its feet and flattened itself against the wall bleating, imitated by two lambs. A cluster of hens scattered into the corners of the room, while three children busied themselves straight away with clearing the table. A young woman disappeared into the next room. The smell of the house was an unbearable mixture of human and animal stink, and affected the men violently. Berger felt his head swim, and had half a mind to go out again, but it had become bitingly cold outside. He gave up and took his place at the table. The room's warmth enveloped him, and the tea the woman set before him with millet bread and a plate of cheese banished any remaining thoughts of seeking another shelter.

As he drank the tea eagerly, Berger sensed the gazes of the children and the woman, who did not miss a movement from where they were, half-hidden in the shadows of the next room. Although he had often found himself studied in silence by the local people, it always embarrassed Berger. There was no malice in the eyes observing him, nor was there mockery, but only curiosity. It was simply an innocent, open curiosity, and yet Berger found it difficult to eat all the same. He envied with all his heart the driver who was concentrating on the food and did not seem to care who else was there, while the Tunshan, entirely at their ease in the smelly little room, exchanged a few words with the old Kalmyk.

Suddenly the oldest of the little girls got up from the bed she was sitting on, came over to Berger and began to tug at his arm. She was plump and clumsy in her movements; there was a vacant smile on her face. Her mother called her back immediately, in a sharp but fond voice. Another, smaller girl got up, took her sister by the hand and led her back into the shadows. The little girl followed her meekly, but not long afterwards, there she was again tugging at Berger's arm, like a dog trying to persuade its master to take it for a walk, and all the while she smiled her stupid smile and said: 'Bang! bang!' 'Don't mind her,' said the old Kalmyk, 'as you can see, the child is not normal.' 'But what does she want?' asked Berger, annoyed. 'She wants to take you outside,' said the old man. 'But why?' 'Because of what happened in September . . .' began the old man and then stopped. 'What happened? Explain,' ordered Berger. 'It happened in the valley behind the house. They rounded them all up and shot them.' 'All who?' 'The Jews, they were the Jews of Elista, maybe a hundred families.' 'Who shot them?' asked Berger again, in disbelief. '*Nemieskiy*,' answered the Kalmyk and he shrugged, as if to say: that's all I know. Then he went on: 'Since then my granddaughter is forever wanting to go back to the place. She saw your uniform and . . .'

Berger felt his cheeks blush bright red. The word *nemieskiy* struck his ears like an insult. The little girl's plump hand was still tugging at the sleeve of his uniform jacket. 'Take me there!' ordered Berger. He suddenly found the overheated room unbearable.

The old man looked as though he wanted to object, but said nothing; he put a cloak on the little girl, put her boots on. Then he took her by the hand. Berger and Ul'an followed them.

The moon was now high; the sharply defined shadows of bushes cut the snow. They went perhaps a hundred metres and came to where the flat ground extended in a terrace over a deep valley, half lit by the moon. The little girl was all excited; she was pointing to the bottom of the hollow and repeating her stupid 'bang, bang'.

'It happened down there,' said the Kalmyk. 'They brought them from the city, all the Jews in Elista. The men and women dug a ditch. Then they fired. First the children, then the women, the men last. After they threw earth over them.'

The bottom of the hollow was covered with a layer of snow which shone with a sinister glow. They went back. The Kalmyk had to drag the little girl after him, and she went on twisting and trying to escape from the old man's grasp.

He's lying, Berger told himself, he has made all this up. But what reason could the Kalmyk have for lying? And the little girl? Idiots can't lie. He turned to Ul'an to confirm his doubts: 'Tunshan, do you think the old man is lying?' 'No, sir, he is not lying,' answered Ul'an. 'Why should he lie?' And he added after a pause: 'I'm sorry, Lieutenant, but I don't understand. Why did they kill them?' 'I don't understand either, Ul'an,' answered Berger. He immediately regretted saying this. What is there to understand here? I'm not used to thinking things through deeply. Am I afraid of my own thoughts? Four terms of philosophy, an apprenticeship in thought, interrupted. But do you need philosophy to judge what can be understood at a single human glance? A glance. And who is preventing me from seeing? And from understanding? Me, myself. But others must have seen too. What do the others think?

Berger was later to talk about this in Stalingrad with Major Mahnkopf, a highly cultured man, who in peacetime was a secondary school teacher in Nuremberg, able even in the midst of war to lose himself for hours in philosophical discussion. Berger told him about the valley near Elista, and the Major first looked at him with the expression of an examiner scrutinising a candidate who is straying from the track during a viva, then said: 'War is a job like any other. Some tasks are more or less pleasant than others. And somebody's got to do them. You may go, Lieutenant.' Berger never spoke of this again with anyone. There is a phrase in a letter from this time, however, which struck me particularly: 'The heightened violence we observe and enact each day annihilates every human emotion in us.' Perhaps my father was referring to that episode and horror made him forget to be prudent. Certainly the letter did not pass through the hands of any censor, because no matter how obtuse, he would certainly have grasped how little such a phrase conformed to wartime propaganda!

The next day, Berger and his little group arrived in Elista on a cart lent to them by the Kalmyks. In the diffused light of morning the city was even sadder, the grey pallor of the buildings more sordid. The only people about were soldiers, and they too were silent and grey.

Professor Breuninger was no longer so cordial either. His words were curt and clipped, as was his whole manner. What did Berger think of the 808th Turkestan Battalion? Had any new cases of insubordination come to light? How had they coped with front line action? Berger had precise instructions. He sang the battalion's praises and approved their deployment at the front. Professor Breuninger seemed pleased. He then explained his new assignment to him. The Turkestan Battalion was due in Stalingrad a week later; Berger would be in charge of the preparations. Breuninger spoke in the tone of a notary quoting a law that he knows by heart, with no full stops or commas. At one point, however, he stopped, looked at Berger out of his sharp little black eyes, took a deep breath and said: 'All a waste of effort. What they want is soldiers to send to the slaughter. Stalingrad must be taken at all costs. These peoples are our allies now but nobody cares what happens to them afterwards. They won't become soldiers with the same rights as German soldiers.'

Berger went back to the truck. In the meantime the driver had found a spare part for the engine. 'Are you sure we'll make it to Stalingrad?' 'Yessir,' answered Hammer. Over his years of military service he had learnt that it was better to assert something baldly, even if it had no basis in fact, than to voice a well-founded doubt.

The road to Stalingrad, which cut the Kalmyk steppe from north to south, ran parallel to the bleak Jergen mountain range. The front was interrupted at several points, and there battalions of Germans and Romanians defended it.

Berger and his little group had left Elista. A layer of low mist covered the plain and the road, so that the travellers in the truck felt as though they were sailing on a white sea. All of a sudden, however, a white cloud of steam issued from the bonnet. Before Berger had time to think 'here we go again', the vehicle had ground to a halt in the middle of the swirling sea of mist. Once again the jute sack of snow on the bonnet got them back to Elista.

Berger was appalled at the thought of having to stay in Elista; he wanted to leave immediately, at whatever cost. When the driver told him that there was an armoured column about to leave for Stalingrad, he didn't think twice, but distributed his small escort about the vehicles and took his place in the lorry leading the column as it set off slowly.

The trucks were covered with green canvas; a chorus of tightly packed animals came from below, bleating to be freed. 'Sheep for Stalingrad,' the driver had said. He was a jovial Rhinelander and not sorry to have company. 'In peacetime,' he added, 'if they had given me mutton to eat, I would have said *pfui Teufel*, what do you take me for, a Turk?' To express his disgust, he pretended to vomit. 'But now I'd eat a camel!' 'Let's hope that there are at least camels at Stalingrad to feed the troops!' said Berger. The Rhinelander laughed, but Berger too was in strangely high spirits. He was not sorry to be departing for the city on the Volga, perhaps because the departure seemed to him to be a return. A return to the Volga.

His mother's words were gradually taking hold of Berger's mind, and he heard them as though she were sitting beside him talking to him and they were both headed for the German colony on the Volga and for Bauer, the village of farmers and artisans from the Rhineland, where Martha Berger had been born and raised. Six hundred and sixty-six farms there were, exactly six hundred and sixty-six, a diabolical number, but this was how many farms there were round Bauer, neither more nor less. As a child Berger had found it hard to grasp the idea of all those houses, lined up along the two roads which met in the middle of the village: the Milchstrasse, Milk Street, and the Kirchstrasse, Church Street. The church was large and built of wood, as were the farmhouses. Like the colonists, the pastor spoke in the dialect of the Rhineland and he preached and intoned the psalms in dialect to the community assembled at the foot of the pulpit: 'We thank you for the land you have given us, Lord!' For the rich black earth of the Volga, a land where everything you sow grows, his mother had told him, so that the barges left the village overloaded with corn, a small cabin in the middle for the boatman, and all around, nothing but corn. They glided over the water to the Volga and then to Saratov, Volgograd, which was not yet called Stalingrad, and Astrakhan. All this took place in a pre-revolutionary limbo, when it was not yet a sin to be rich. Some of the families who lived along the milk street and along the church street had full granaries and others provided them with maids and labourers but there were neither Whites nor Reds with the star on their caps. There were only the rich, the less rich and the poor along the milk street and the church street. That's how things stood in the happy time when there was still a Tsar. Berger's mother waved her small hands as she talked as though stroking her memories. But when she got this far she would break off to look for a handkerchief, overcome by emotion which welled up again as she talked and always caught her unawares. It was not just nostalgia for her lost country. It was her way of participating in a collective tragedy which she only knew from other people's stories: the people who died of starvation in '22 brought to light by the spring thaw, the ruined church, the pastor singing his psalm, the last: 'We thank you, Lord, for the land you have given us' in front of families forced to leave that land. His mother had heard all this from somebody who had made it back to Germany and she had found out from that same somebody that the two streets of the village were no longer called the milk street and the church street, but bore the names of the two collectives Red Star and New Life. Who knows what happened to the six hundred and sixty-six farms, thought Berger, smiling to himself as he remembered his mother's words; who knows if they were divided equally, three hundred and thirty-three to the Red Star collective, three hundred and thirty-three to the New Life, who knows if the barges still glided down the Volga with their cargoes of grain. The more Berger thought about it, the more natural it seemed to him to come back to the Volga and the more sure he was that he would find the road to the colony without difficulty, up as far as Saratov, along the right bank of the stream, then up to his mother's village by the river.

Ul'an was travelling in the second lorry; he sat quietly between the driver and his companion listening to a conversation he didn't understand. The two men for their part had immediately abandoned any attempt to talk to Ul'an. 'Can't you see he's a Mongol?' the soldier sitting on his right had observed. Ul'an gazed at the road ahead, swathed in mist, and thought of the story of the Tunshan. For him too the journey to the Volga was a return. Had his ancestors not got as far as that river? Not only the first of the Mongol hordes, but the Oirats and two Tunshan tribes had reached the Volga after leaving the land of seven rivers. Ul'an knew the story. The Kalmyks had reached the river from the east; his ancestor Mongotai had been the first to pitch his yurts on the banks of the Volga, and from there his descendants had departed a century later to return to the land at the foot of the Alatau. Now he, Ul'an, son of Bairqan and future khan of the Tunshan, if ever it was granted to him to go back to the Amudar'ya, was approaching the Volga from the south, in the company of foreign soldiers going to take the city on the river. But this time the inhabitants of Caricyn would not come with boats and rafts to help the newcomers across. This time there were panzers and Katyushas waiting for them and the frozen river was the front.

As Berger traced pleasant paths through his daydreams and Ul'an went over his people's history in his mind, the column of trucks crawled along, took hazardous bends, was left at times poised on the edges of particularly deep ruts, or came to a sudden halt. Sometimes these pauses lasted a long time; the men got out, hung around the vehicles, exchanging comments and smoking as they waited for the convoy to set off again. Then the bleating got louder under the canvas, as though the animals too wondered why they had come to a halt. The fog was a wall on the horizon. Wherever you looked, there was only the grey of the snow on the ground and the grey of the fog above it. Nothing else. And no other sound, except the bleating of sheep bound for Stalingrad.

23

> *19 November 1942. My dear Siglinde, I arrived in Stalingrad in the company of . . . sheep! Real sheep: they are going to swell the livestock at Stalingrad and to fill our soldiers' mess-tins. In the end the sheep are luckier than us: they are not responsible for their own fate . . .*

This is one of Lieutenant Berger's last letters. He cannot yet have suspected that he too had fallen into the trap of Stalingrad, as the tone of the letter seems openly humorous and gives no hint of any undue worry. Or does it? What exactly does he mean when he says, a little mysteriously, that 'the sheep are not responsible for their own fate'? Perhaps it is a way of getting a message across without saying too much, and thereby outwitting the highly efficient military censor. Perhaps Berger wants to convey his state of mind or a premonition he has and is using the comparison to get that across to Siglinde. But by now the packet of letters has become much thinner, and the correspondence will soon cease. The next few letters give little real information about the situation my father had to face and offer a very fragmentary picture of the furnace of Stalingrad. There is no trace of the horror to which the soldiers trapped inside the city are subjected, almost as though there aren't in fact any soldiers. To judge by my father's letters one might suppose that he was alone in the city, or at most with Ul'an and another two or three men, in what was in fact a battlefield with almost three hundred thousand soldiers. My father's letters allow him to carry on a sort of conversation with himself; he writes more to try to distance himself from the reality surrounding him than to communicate it to other people. It is not the collective tragedy he is interested in describing, but his own intellectual, rather than emotional, re-working of it, to which only a few characters have access. Descriptions are few and far between, and the setting is blurred.

Two days after writing that first letter from Stalingrad, my father could already clearly see the enormity of the trap into which he had fallen. Now he knows he is shut in with the others: *And now*? he writes to Siglinde on the twenty-first of November. *I should have made preparations for the arrival of the Turkestan Battalion but instead I only prepared for my own and for the two Mongol soldiers and the driver that I brought with me. We came to swell the human flock shut in here and already rather thinned by the latest events of the war. I write this and hope for an answer from you, even though I doubt they will be able to track me down in the middle of this boiling cauldron, where it seems that nothing and nobody stays in the same place for long. The whole army seems to ebb and flow, in the grip of a whirlpool, which brings men together and then drags them apart forever in its endless spin. There is a bit of everything in here: infantry of the Sixth Army, Romanians, Croats, Russian volunteers, prisoners, Italians delivering winter kit for the Germans, soldiers who simply got lost. Chance has brought us together, chance and the generals' orders!*

The armoured column coming from Elista and loaded with livestock went a little further along the tracks, passing alongside tents and low huts surrounded by barbed wire, stopping every now and then at a sentry's 'Halt, who goes there?' Then the driver got down to show his papers; the soldier checked them by the light of a torch and waved them on. The byres for the animals destined to serve as provisions for the winter were near the powder magazine. The trucks stopped in front of them, one beside the other: then a procession of sheep came out of the trailers, trotting first uncertainly, then ever quicker, down the ramp, propelled by the soldiers' shouts and by the animals pressing behind them, funnelled towards the pens. Berger waited with his little group, because the livestock trucks were the only way to get to Stalingrad. There wasn't a soul about. The evening was quiet and still shrouded in mist. The war seemed very far away.

* * *

Another column of trucks, longer than the first, rumbled towards the vehicles unloading sheep and stopped. The German sentry walked towards them shouting: two soldiers leant out of the first truck, tried to explain, got out. There is an excited waving of arms, the sentry points north with hand and gun, repeats, 'Gumrak.' Now the other drivers also lean out of their cabs: 'Where are we going?' they shout in Italian. 'We seem to be on the wrong road,' the soldier who got out first shouts in answer: 'Live sheep here, the warehouse for sheepskins is further north.' He climbed back into his cab and the column disappeared into the fog in the direction of Gumrak. Silence fell around the livestock trucks; the bleating had been swallowed up by the pens. Berger and his men set off again towards the city and the Volga, travelling east.

A little way behind them, an Italian army truck was also lurching along the frozen track. It was full of wood intended for the bunkers of the Alpini on the Don, but was heading by mistake into the brazier that was Stalingrad. Sergeant Aiazza and Privates Sabaudi and Bonino were sitting inside, chilled to the bone and famished. The snowstorm had driven them off course and they had been wandering for two days, not knowing what side of the line they were on. When a sign appeared at a crossroads, encrusted with snow, but still without a doubt a road sign, on a wooden post, Bonino could have hugged it for sheer joy. And indeed the sign, which was written by hand but still legible, said twenty kilometres to Stalingrad, and Stalingrad, even if it was not on the Don, still promised shelter and hot rations for the Italian soldiers. The truck with its load of wood and its last reserves of petrol – and it's just as well, said Sergeant Aiazza, that we brought a considerable supply – was now heading east to the Volga, along the road which led to Stalingrad.

'Yet more Italians!' the sentry exclaimed, stamping his feet against the chill and checking the papers of the soldiers in the truck. He said it as though they were surplus to requirements, as though the city hidden in the darkness was crowded with Italians and there was no space for the newcomers. In reality they were just three lost soldiers who would be lost with the others, more lost than the others, if you like, because nobody knew they were there, on the road to Stalingrad, although they were expected on the Don. That was the last that was heard of them. They were reported missing on the Russian front: whether on the Don or the Volga, who cared? Anyway they were in the wrong place. But on this evening of the nineteenth of November 1942, wrapped in their overcoats, on their way to bring wood to burn in Stalingrad, Sabaudi, Aiazza and Bonino of the Alpini were not yet thinking of the label 'missing in action' which would soon be attached to their names and surnames. If they were thinking about anything, it was simply whether the Germans would give them a hot meal, something to ease the hunger they carried inside, and where this might occur, given that they could see nothing but the high white banks to the side of the road. The evening was peaceful and quiet, as though the enemy was very far away or was playing silently at hide-and-seek.

'It's infantry we need!' Captain Hetzenecker saluted Lieutenant Berger coolly when Berger went to join the Second Battalion, Eighth Corps. The battalion had been formed in a hurry with men from companies which no longer existed, because they had been disbanded or destroyed by the enemy, with scattered men and men who had come there by mistake, like the Alpini from Cuneo. Among them were men of the most diverse origins and specialisations, but by now, as Captain Hetzenecker had said, only the infantry was of any use. It wasn't clear from his expression whether it was the ethnic diversity of the new soldiers or the sheer variety of their uniforms that most disturbed him. Finally he said to Berger, 'You can make yourself understood, Lieutenant, so you'd better take charge of them.' And in a single gesture he lumped together Mongols, Italians and Croats, who looked at him with a mixture of unease and curiosity, trying to guess what awaited them. 'They'll have to be trained,' he concluded.

I'm obviously destined to work with foreign soldiers, thought Berger. He looked in his turn at the scruffy and poorly equipped men facing him. Train them, just like that? With this in mind, they were to spend a brief period of time at Dubinin, right in the middle of the circle that the Red Army had drawn around the Sixth Army. To make that herd of men, brought together more out of a love of order, he thought, than because they were expected to be of any use, into useful infantry. What use were specialists anyway, if there were no more specialisations, and what use were drivers if there was no more petrol left for the vehicles? The last journey of the Italian trucks had been the journey to Dubinin, to the training camp; and they had squeezed out the last drops of diesel to get there. Now the big vehicles lay abandoned along the last stretch of road, useless and unwieldy, while the men had had to complete the journey to their assigned position on foot. Their destination was Baburkin, on the banks of the Rossoshka, which unwound like a frozen ribbon behind the bunker. The sentries looked west. A few kilometres further on was the front line, the perimeter of the furnace of Stalingrad, which was vaguely round in form, with a bulge to the west. The men did not have a lot to do, in those days, except follow the same order: hold the line. In order to carry out this one order Lieutenant Berger and Captain Hetzenecker had to maintain a semblance of discipline among the men. No easy task, thought Berger, what with weapons and ammunition running short and inadequate or non-existent rations. And what happens when we finish the last of the horse soup? Were there camels to butcher at Stalingrad?

So here I am underground, wrote Günther to Siglinde on the twenty-fourth of November. *We didn't even have to build the bunker ourselves, but found it ready made and comfortable enough, the officers' quarters at any rate. They have posted us to a hamlet about thirty kilometres west of Stalingrad. I am writing this not in the hope that my letter reaches you, but because it is possible to survive in this hole we are living in only by thinking that there is still normal life somewhere and people living it in our place. I say 'normal' even though I know that it is no longer so even where you are, because you too are under enemy fire day and night. But I, dear Siglinde, continue to think of you as you were before, in your everyday life. You are normality, for me.*

Here everybody is writing, even those who are entirely unused to writing, so great is our desperation at not receiving post; it is a further torment to add to our hunger and makes it appear even more unjust to us. We feel far away from everything, as though we were already actually underground. Writing has become our life. And yet yesterday I witnessed an event where a letter itself gave rise to a tragedy.

Among the Italians assigned to the Second Battalion, Infantry, there was a curly-haired Sicilian by the name of Salvatore Calì who had volunteered for the blackshirts 'because', he said, 'I couldn't take it any more at home'. Calì had eleven children and in-laws who bossed him around and, as his companions maliciously suspected, even beat him. They said too that the blackshirts had transferred Calì to the transport division as an unloader in order to get rid of him. His companions laughed at this story every time they heard it as though they were hearing it for the first time. And there was always somebody who asked him: 'And the letter, Calì, where did you put the letter? You haven't read it for a while.' Then Calì would go red as a beetroot, frown, and curls and eyebrows would come together to form a single thick and bristly bush. The letter which Calì asked someone to read to him from time to time contained the following: 'My son, you've been cuckolded time and time again; your wife's having it off with Antonio Lentini the deserter. And while you're off defending Italy's honour, who's defending yours?' And every time Calì heard these words he would begin to punch himself in the head, then he would take a run up and bash his head against the dividing beams of the bunker, as though he wanted to break them into pieces. The others laughed or ignored him or made comments, like Sergeant Mazzoni, who usually wrote his letters for him: 'If he's crying about his honour it means he hasn't anything worse to complain about!' And he would add: 'The next time we'll write to your parish priest and ask him not to pass on all the tripe your mother tells him!'

There was a week to go before Christmas when they heard from outside that Calì, who was on guard duty, was stretched out in the communications trench. They carried him inside. Mazzoni took off his helmet and freed the mass of his hair: his forehead was smooth and slack, but his mouth was a well of blood. Calì didn't move, even when the sergeant bawled in his ear: 'You miserable sod, it's your wife you should have shot, not yourself!'

It's an act of insubordination, thought Berger; but to kill oneself is a free choice and a way of affirming one's own existence. By killing oneself? Sure. That soldier's death had arisen through a sense of honour all his own, which he had not been ordered to feel. So-called heroism only served to tie black ribbons on the necrophilia of the regime. Calì had not given the regime that pleasure. He had died for himself. These were Berger's thoughts as he looked at the thick head of hair of a soldier whom until then nobody had taken seriously.

Sometimes Berger was amazed at how that motley group of soldiers had somehow gelled. There was no greater lack of discipline in the battalion than elsewhere; guard duty was carried out without complaint; orders were followed and everybody got by somehow; they even understood each other. For this purpose they used a kind of lingua franca, a mixture of German and Russian, flavoured with a few words of Italian. The soldiers cherished no linguistic ambitions, needing only a few words in a language put together at random for everyday living. Though it was obvious that the real conversations took place in the different languages spoken by the soldiers and Berger was not always able to understand them.

The Alpini Bonino and Sabaudi were sitting in front of the stove trying to dry their boots without burning them. 'I never thought I'd miss our bunker on the Don,' said Bonino. He spoke of it as though it was a villa on the Ligurian Riviera.

'The Russians may already have moved in,' Sabaudi answered him. The pair were distant cousins and friends too in civilian life, both handsome, tall, with glossy hair combed back. They resembled each other. The girls who walked under the old arcades arm in arm and gathered in groups in the big square in Cuneo used to cast sideways glances at them and giggle. But all that had happened hundreds of years ago. Now Bonino and Sabaudi regretted the bunkers on the Don and their companions of the Cuneese and didn't give a thought to the girls under the old arcades, to Teresa, Carla and Maria. Bonino had even forgotten Pia, who had a tiny waist and black hair and every time he passed her he whispered 'Creole' and she smiled. Bonino and Sabaudi missed other very different things about Cuneo.

'I can't tell you what I'd do for a handful of chestnuts,' Bonino began, 'those big fat ones, like this: you cut them across,' and Bonino mimed cutting into the husk of an imaginary chestnut, 'then you put them to roast on the stove. Maybe my wife will send me some.' 'That's likely,' Sabaudi answered sarcastically, 'and why not some marrons glacés? From Arione, of course.' The old Arione pastry-shop under the arcades of the main square in Cuneo was known for making the biggest marrons glacés in Piedmont. Even the packaging was famous: elegantly shiny boxes in dark green or bordeaux, with a photograph of the piazza with the snow-covered Bisalta in the background, and the chestnuts inside perfectly wrapped in their sugar mantles, arranged in pretty paper like pearls in their shell.

'Carlo,' said Sabaudi after a short silence, 'what on earth are we poor souls doing at Stalingrad?' 'And what were we Italians doing on the Don?' Sabaudi asked in turn. 'This seems to me to be more of a German party!' retorted Bonino. 'There's nothing in this war which has to do with one more than the other. We're all involved always. On the Don or the Volga, it's all the same. The same shit everywhere.' 'Do you think Hitler will really get us out of this frying-pan?' Bonino still had the mirage of the roast chestnuts in his head. 'The Duce certainly won't lift a finger to help us out of here. But if you want me to tell you what I think, I think that the pan we've landed in is already full of holes.'

On the twentieth of December Berger writes: *My dear Siglinde, it has been ages since I received your last letter. I've had no more news of you. I dreamt about you last night, not for the first time, you know, but this time you weren't holding Ilse in your arms and you were still a girl. We were both young in fact.*

Berger was thirty-one in 1942, and the time when they were young must have seemed very far away, a phase of their life left behind forever. When they had met at the celebration of their final school exams, Günther was a student and Siglinde had just got her diploma from the 'English' misses' school. He was twenty-three, she was nineteen. As they danced, and Siglinde's mass of wavy chestnut hair floated under his nose, Günther felt a strong urge to plunge his hands into it. 'What beautiful hair you have, Fräulein.' Siglinde had then told him what the perfume was that he smelt as he held her by the waist and they celebrated the diplomas obtained by the eighty-five young 'English' misses, who had just completed nine years of convent education. Marianne put vinegar compresses on her hair to make it shinier, and rosewater to perfume it, and that was the source of the mingled scents that Günther could smell as they danced and which made him want to plunge his hands into it and run them over her throat, her shoulders and her breasts. In his dreams too he could see her waving hair and he would have liked to plunge a hand into it and run it down Siglinde's throat, over her shoulders, her skin, as she shook her head and shrugged off the nine years of convent education. In his sleep Günther stretched out his hand, but a bulky figure intruded between the hand and the floating, gleaming mass of hair. It was a figure with a stiff felt hat, an overcoat with padded shoulders, a badge on the lapel of his jacket. The owner of the furniture concern German Living was saying to him: '*Sie studieren also Philosophie*?' and sneering at him: '*So, so*.' 'And why, may I ask, did you not study medicine, like your father?' Herr Schifferl, Siglinde's father, had asked him. 'I can't bear the sight of blood,' Berger had replied. Herr Schifferl had looked at him first with amazement, then with irony, and then burst out laughing. In the dream too he looked at him with a mixture of amazement and irony, and laughed: '*Sie studieren also Philosophie? So, so*,' and the owner of the furniture company German Living went on laughing, in the dream too. But then Siglinde was there with her mass of chestnut hair and her round perfect breasts, and she didn't care about philosophy, or about the badge her father wore on the lapel of his jacket, or about the furniture makers, and she didn't even care that Günther couldn't bear the sight of blood. The only thing that mattered to her was that he plunge his hands into her hair and run them down her shoulders and over her breasts; not a great deal else mattered to her. Berger woke, and fell asleep again. Siglinde is wearing a peach-coloured crêpe de Chine dress and they are in the garden of the Schifferls' villa in Cologne. It is August 1936. Günther and Siglinde are celebrating their engagement, but the guests are talking about the famous singer from the carnival who died very recently and it looks as though the Cologne carnival will die with him. Siglinde's mother grimaces; she finds the carnival vulgar and anyway it is her daughter's engagement party, what has the carnival got to do with it? It is getting late, but there are still a few guests in the garden and they have clearly drunk too much and they sing the last song by this singer, in dialect, swaying with their glasses in their hands: '*Ich möchte zu Fuss nach Köln gehen*,' I want to go on foot to Cologne. And they say *Kölle*, instead of *Köln*, and Siglinde's mother purses her lips and shakes her head, but Siglinde doesn't care about the carnival and perhaps not even about Cologne, and she and Günther embrace behind the villa, outside the kitchen, among the bushes of unripe blackcurrants. The voices sound louder and coarser from the other side of the garden, in front of the house: I want to go on foot to Cologne, *Kölle*, *Kölle*. In his dream Berger can hear the carnival tune again and the words of the song seem to him to have a deep meaning and to merge with the waving chestnut mass of hair, smelling faintly of vinegar.

Berger woke up again, this time for good; there was a bitter taste in his mouth and a burning in his stomach. The air in the bunker was cold and damp, still full of cigarette smoke and smoke from the stove which didn't draw properly. Suddenly the dark weighed on him. After three years of war? Rubbish! And yet he felt the need to go out into the fresh air. He got up quietly. Beside him he could hear Captain Hetzenecker breathing heavily, every now and then smacking his lips and turning over, muttering something, but Berger couldn't make out what. He put on his boots and his fur hat, threw his overcoat round his shoulders, opened the door of the bunker carefully and went out. The sky was overcast, a dirty white colour. Bad weather on the way, thought Berger, it might snow. The changes of weather were frequent and swift on the steppe; it could go from freeze to thaw overnight and then the layer of fresh snow would become an impassable bog. It might snow tonight, Berger repeated, walking towards the sentry, standing in the trench. He recognised Ul'an, who stood to attention and saluted.

'At ease, Ul'an,' Berger immediately said; military formalities irritated him, all the more because as the days passed it was becoming obvious that they were only a pathetic attempt to keep an army together which was now no more than a parody of itself. He offered Ul'an a cigarette and they smoked for a little while in silence.

'It's not cold, is it?' said Berger.

'No, in this season it is colder at home,' answered Ul'an. It occurred to Berger that Ul'an's home wasn't much closer than his own; even if Stalingrad was not exactly half-way between them, it was enough to make one feel equally far away. Suddenly he asked: 'Do you regret it, Ul'an?' The question which he had wanted to ask for so long came out as though by itself. Ul'an seemed amazed:

'Regret what?'

'Coming to fight with us!'

Ul'an searched for the words, then said: 'I could make no other decision at that time.'

'Why, Ul'an?'

'Because I was not the man I am now.'

'And now you no longer believe?' Berger interrupted.

'Now I know that neither you nor I can help us.' Ul'an paused, then added in a quieter voice: 'Our Genghis Khan knew how to take cities!' Berger was stunned. 'Are you saying that as a war leader the Führer is not the equal of Genghis Khan?' 'He is not worth the sole of his boot,' Ul'an stated firmly.

Berger was taken aback. In all the weeks they had been prisoners of this lost battle, despite the discomfort and the hunger, he had always sensed that there was in his men a spark of optimism and faith in the Führer. Nobody criticised him openly, not out of fear, but because that faith was linked to their last hope of getting out of there alive. This descendant of a Mongol tribe from the most remote part of Asia was now standing smoking quietly in front of him and daring, without batting an eyelid, to express this judgement about Hitler. However absurd the comparison seemed, Berger decided to continue along the track suggested by Ul'an. 'And why is he worth so little?' he asked.

'He doesn't know how to take cities, but neither does he know how to let them go. A great khan has to know how to let go and save the lives of his men. And anyway where is your khan?'

'The front is long, Ul'an, and the Führer cannot be everywhere.' Ul'an shook his head.

'When a khan is worthless, his men choose another. But why do you keep this khan who does not know how to win?'

'The war is not yet lost, Ul'an!' Berger retorted forcefully. Ul'an shook his head again.

'But it is lost, all lost! Are we the winners, perhaps, in here?' Berger was at a loss for an answer and Ul'an went on, following the thread of a thought which he had often brooded over; 'Genghis Khan made the Mongols, nomads and shepherds of the steppes, into a great people. Your khan has made a great people into a people of slaves!' 'A people of slaves! You exaggerate, Ul'an!' 'Slaves do not dare to rebel against the khan when he makes a mistake. They do not even notice that he makes a mistake.' Berger was finding it difficult to refute Ul'an's logic. Where did all this arrogance come from? Didn't he know that Genghis Khan was a myth? He didn't know and it would be useless to explain it to him. He tried to invoke history: 'More than seven hundred years have passed, Ul'an, since your Genghis Khan came here with his archers. Seven hundred years! How can you compare two such different things?' 'Seven hundred years are a lot for a man, not for a people,' answered Ul'an. Berger thought he saw an expression of triumph on Ul'an's face as he carried a cigarette to his lips that was no more than a tiny point of light.

24

BERGER'S LAST LETTER bore the date 5th of January 1943. Again it was the casual encounters that interested him the most, perhaps because they could be said to reflect the impact of chance on individual destinies: *Yesterday I made the acquaintance of an Italian officer, who also ended up by mistake in Stalingrad. You should have seen us conversing, first in French and then I risked some Italian and he tried out his German. We had a fine old time!*

They met in Gumrak, at General Staff headquarters. Colonel Fuchs was in his underground office, standing in front of a table that was too large and too grand for the place, and had been brought there from God knows where. Audiences were in public, since there was no door between the office and the corridor in which officers waited their turn. Captain Di Bella had only just come into the office when Berger too entered the bunker. He saw from behind the tall, relaxed figure of the Italian, who was wearing the grey-blue uniform of the airforce, and he heard his calm, deep voice, which was barely audible, whereas Colonel Fuchs, who was seated at the table, spoke too loudly, as if he wanted to show those waiting outside just how well he spoke French. Di Bella had come once again to request air transport for his unit, which had ended up by mistake in Stalingrad, and the colonel assured him in an exaggeratedly nasal tone: *'Je vous ai dit plusieurs fois –'*. He seemed to be losing patience. 'If you came here by mistake, take it up with your army headquarters. We are not responsible for orders given by your command. We never asked you to build an airport in Stalingrad. Even if,' he added in German, turning to a third person, whom Berger from outside could not see, 'another airfield would come in handy, Ziller, wouldn't it?' Then he turned back to the Italian: 'I've told you more than once that I'll do what I can to evacuate officers but, as for the men, there's nothing to be done!'

Captain Di Bella said something. At this point the colonel seemed to lose all patience and his tone became hectoring: 'Don't you realise that we lack the means to transport the wounded? Why don't you go to Pitomnik and see how many gravely, very gravely wounded men are waiting to be flown out? And you come here and ask me to send away thirty men, all healthy into the bargain!' 'They are not all healthy,' objected Captain Di Bella, who was now also speaking more loudly, 'and there are no longer thirty of them.'

'Even if they were twenty-five or twenty, dammit! Why does the Duce not send out one of his fighters to take all of you away, and some of us too while he's about it!' Di Bella made a gesture of impatience: 'I didn't get to speak with the Duce.' 'Then have a word with General Messe, or with anyone you like, but stop pestering me! I have two hundred thousand men to consider, and you harass me about twenty Italians!' Di Bella raised his hand to his cap, clicked his heels and went out. Berger saw that his face was pale and drawn, and that he was clenching his teeth. A line ran from his mouth to his cheekbones.

Colonel Fuchs was drumming nervously with his fingers on his imposing desk, and when Berger, whose regiment was so far away from the centre, mentioned the situation as regards supplies, he merely said 'sorry', extended his arms and gestured to him to leave.

Outside the bunker the snow was gleaming still more brightly, and the sun seemed determined to melt it all in a single day. Captain Di Bella was still there with the motor-cycle rider, and together they were trying to get the bike started again.

My father's correspondence from the front stopped here. Berger may well have written again to Siglinde, but his letters ended up somewhere on the steppe, brought down with the aeroplane that was carrying them. Or perhaps a last cruel jest was played on the men trapped on the Volga, and the letters never left Stalingrad but remained in mail bags which no one even thought to load onto an aeroplane. Among the other letters jumbled up in the box I found one which was linked to the last one sent by my father. At first I didn't understand, and only gradually, as I read on, did I realise. The envelope was edged in black, and at the top, in a hand I did not recognise, was the address, Mr Günther Berger, Schillerstrasse. The handwriting was large and clear, and belonged to a person who was still young, and who was not German. The letter in fact came from Italy. When I opened it, a small card fell out, and with it a photograph of a thin young man smiling from beneath an officer's peaked cap. The letter was written on a folded sheet of paper:

> *Ragusa, 30th April 1948. Dear Mr Berger, You will surely understand just how painful the news conveyed through you to me not long ago must have been, and yet it is with deepest gratitude that I am writing to you today. Thank you for carrying with you, and thus saving, the last lines written by my husband. It is not easy for me to express what I felt when reading them, but it was as if he had written them to me just a short time before. You cannot imagine how many times I have re-read them. I keep that torn scrap of newsprint with his writing on it as if it were a relic. I sense what you must have suffered together, and just why you were a witness to my husband's sufferings. Although I have never met you, I feel very close to you and count myself a friend. I congratulate you on having rejoined your family and homeland and I extend my most heartfelt good wishes to you and yours. If you ever chance to pass through distant Sicily, please rest assured that there is one house here in which you would be received as a most welcome guest. With my deepest gratitude, Rosa Di Bella.*

The Sicilian officer's fate had thus remained in some way intertwined with that of Berger. The two letters, the last from my father in Stalingrad and the one sent by the widow from Sicily, suggested to me a trail which, though interrupted on 5th January 1943, reappeared like a river that ran underground on 15th May of the same year, the date of the Italian officer's death.

Among my father's documents there was a bundle of typewritten pages. I recognised the letters from the old Adler which he occasionally used, a pre-war typewriter with keys that protruded from the metallic frame like tentacles. The keys were very stiff, and the pressure of my father's fingers when striking them was uneven, so some words were firmly imprinted on the page, others much less so. The chiaroscuro effect, and the wayward nature of the typing in no way detracted from the value of the pages which I had before me, since they had been written by my father, certainly some time after his return but before I had arrived in his house. It was a manuscript, then, and one that filled the silences and gaps in the story I was trying to piece together. There were ten pages in all, which were written, by contrast with the letters, in the dry style used in official reports, and without description or comment. When I released the pages from the paper clip holding them together, I saw that it had left a small *u* of rust in the top corner. Here, I told myself, was an ancient manuscript. It may seem to be scarcely credible, and yet the manuscript is real enough. I even know the typewriter roller the pages were fed through, and I once knew the fingers that pressed the keys, although even I find it a little hard to believe that it is not a fabrication. Perhaps my story is one of those cases which, when told, would make anyone shake their head and say it was an invention, so very unreal does it seem. Yet it is reality that invents the most absurd stories, I said to myself as I read the terse sentences of my father's report, which begins with a place and a date, Rossoshka, 9th January 1943.

Hold the line, hold the line! The line held by Berger and his battalion ran along the valley of the Rossoshka. The soldiers had the Rossoshka behind them and their eyes on the Don. Stalingrad was a strange fortress, and no mistake. There was no wall round it and no loopholes through which to spy on the enemy's movements and, strangest of all, the defenders were on the outside and the attackers on the inside. Yet inside or outside, the landscape was the same, with fresh deep snow and a cold white sky. On the night of 10th January, Ul'an said to Alcidai when he came to relieve him on sentry duty: 'Be alert. They've been moving around for hours. They are up to something!' Alcidai's eyes were smarting from sleep and his empty stomach hurt him. His arms and legs seemed not to want to obey him any more, as if a *naja* had bitten them. Alcidai was strong, and it was not by chance that he bore his mighty ancestor's name, but hunger had consumed his muscles and if he put a hand on his chest, beneath the jacket of his uniform, he felt his ribs sticking out like the dry branches of a bush bound together with a crude leather strap. He felt that he was carrying a skeleton on his back, and that it was not even his own. How had the ancestors managed to hold out when they rode across the steppe for days on end? Did they not feel hunger and thirst? Alcidai knew that they carried a bag of *kumiss* tied to the saddle and little pieces of dried meat, and that in emergencies their own horse could serve as a source of nourishment. A little cut under the throat, and the rider would swiftly apply his lips to the wound and suck. A few sips of blood lasted for days; the horses didn't suffer at all and soon revived. But Alcidai didn't have a flask of *kumiss*, or dried meat, or even a horse to take blood from, and he felt oh so weak as he kept watch and as the noise of engines from the west grew ever louder.

'Men soon revive,' Hitler had said around this time to the general who spoke to him of the hunger suffered by the soldiers within the circle of Stalingrad, and he had ruled out surrender. It was because of this sentence, uttered far away from the furnace in which the soldiers were dying, at Stalingrad, that Alcidai, standing in the trench, could now hear an airplane engine coming closer and moving away again in the expanse of white sky between the front and the river. Ul'an was right, thought Alcidai, the Russians are up to something.

Two hours later, the plain in front of Alcidai gradually began to light up, as artillery shells, seeming to skim over the hard, icy terrain, pounded them from the front line, while high-pitched whistles, gliding over the snow, reached even the rearguard. Officers and men ran from their bunkers in panic. 'In a matter of days, perhaps hours even,' said Berger, 'they'll be on the Rossoshka.' The noose was being drawn tight, but the order was still to hold the line. Berger and Captain Hetzenecker drew up their men. By midday the Russians had reached the Rossoshka. In the afternoon there was fighting in Baburkin, on the right bank of the river. It was evening when the first outlines of the panzers emerged out of the shadows in the west, five hundred, three hundred or two hundred metres from where Ul'an and Alcidai crouched in their trench. They still had very few shells for the mortars. Alcidai took aim, fired and missed, fired again and the first panzer in the line stopped; the second drew closer, then also halted in front of the trench, like a giant made of snow. The other armoured cars withdrew. 'General, the line is still in our hands!' Captain Hetzenecker communicated by radio.

On 11th of January at dawn the snow swirled in front of the soldiers' eyes, blinded and confused them, encrusted eyelashes and moustaches, formed crystals on their helmets and covered the grey-green of their threadbare uniforms in a white mantle. When it encountered an obstacle, it piled up, like the desert sand forming dunes, but here the dunes were the bodies of the dead abandoned in the steppe like heaps of frozen *kuraj*. The Eighth Army Corps managed to drive the enemy back to the west of the Rossoshka. But on the 12th of January at midday the whole army retreated; the Russians regrouped and pushed on to the river, while the defenders of the fortress shifted to the eastern bank of the Rossoshka. On 13th of January, before daybreak, Russian panzers advanced beyond the valley of the Rossoshka, while in Baburkin the men held the line until evening. On 15th of January, when it was still dark, the order came by radio to retreat. The new front line, which lay further to the east, would be reached on foot. There were no trucks, horses or mules, so as much as possible was loaded onto sledges pulled by the men.

During the night of the 16th January, the Rossoshka was abandoned. Alcidai is with the others, in front; four of them are dragging a sledge loaded with munitions. Ul'an too is loaded down and sinks into the snow. Suddenly he sees that one of those ahead of him pulling the sledge has fallen down. Alcidai! Ul'an runs to him. There are two of them, in fact, for Berger too comes to Alcidai's aid. They support him beneath his armpits and drag him forward through the snow. How light Alcidai's body beneath his military jacket had become! But the feet inside his boots are heavy and no longer respond to orders. Ul'an, Berger and Alcidai are left behind as the others disappear into the haze. On either side of the road lie the bodies of soldiers, some of whom are still alive, able to speak and to beg for help that never comes. Come on Alcidai, be brave, we're with you. But Alcidai weeps and raves: 'The *ayil* is not far off, I'll get there by myself, I can already see the yurts and the smoke coming out of the hole in the roof, there ahead of me, I can see it. It's not far, let me go alone, Bairqan, I'll rest a while and catch up with you later.' They let him rest on a heap of snow. 'Hurry up, Ul'an, the Russians are catching up!' Berger drapes Alcidai's arm round his shoulders, while Ul'an carries the rifles. Alcidai's body is light enough beneath his overcoat but a strange rigidity makes it heavier. They sink into the snow. Berger cannot go on with a load like that. They rest again. Alcidai is finding it hard to breathe. 'I can no longer feel my legs, Bairqan! Bring me my horse, help me to mount! But where is my horse? The Russians have eaten my horse!' Alcidai weeps and raves, and is as white as those lying by the road. Then the cold in its mercy gradually takes hold of his thin body in its military overcoat, starting with the legs and climbing up to the vital core. Alcidai is no longer cold and no longer has a voice either, for he has become the same as the countless others who lie by the edge of the road leading to the new front line. Ul'an rummages in the pockets of Alcidai's overcoat, recovers a hunk of bread and a document, slips the silver amulet from around his neck and takes the engraved dagger from his belt. In an inside pocket he finds the little carved bones they used to play dice each evening in the bunker, and he puts them in his pocket. Then he lays his cousin's body out on the ground, fully extended and facing south-east, in the direction of home. There are no yellow ribbons or cairns for Alcidai, and not even a grave, unless you count the faint hollow impressed in the snow by his body.

Meanwhile in Pitomnik, where the airstrip was, Captain Di Bella had managed to transmit a message to the Italian army headquarters on the Don. 'We will do everything in our power to evacuate Italian airfield staff,' was the reply. Every day Di Bella waited for confirmation, although he knew that planes were scarce and the Italian airfield a long way off. Yet he kept on transmitting his message, which never varied: 'We await evacuation of Italian airfield staff.' He and his men were billeted in a bunker, not far from the landing strip. They got by as best they could, in the midst of crates full of supplies and instruments, the radio station and the camouflage nets still tightly tied up in bales like straw, on which the men sat.

On 15th of January the Germans made ready to evacuate the airfield. The wounded had been waiting for days in the open, but when they saw the planes leave with the specialised personnel aboard, they realised that their turn would never come.

Berger and Ul'an reached the new front line, which the General Staff had traced in red on the map and which ran from north to south, dividing the circle of the siege into two unequal parts. This was now the front to be held, at any rate by those who still heeded orders. The order was to close ranks and to resist, but Berger could not find his own battalion or Captain Hetzenecker or the Italians. He could not find anyone at all, and so stayed on his own with Ul'an.

By now the Russians were pressing forward from north, south and west, and slicing through our lines of defence as they advanced in their groaning monsters. The men were retreating towards Stalingrad in small groups, in companies or on their own, scattered or in military formation, as if their last hopes of finding refuge lay in the pile of wreckage on the Volga.

Berger and Ul'an joined forces with a close-knit group of German gunners and, on reaching the outskirts of the city, they slipped into the ruins of a destroyed factory. By now the front had broken up into a myriad different strong points, where, in underground shelters or beneath shattered walls, soldiers roamed around, some wounded and some in good shape, some in bands that were fighting while others had given up all thought of resisting. Everywhere there were corpses piled on top of each other like sand bags arranged to dam a breach in a dike. The defenders used those human walls to steady their aim.

Berger noticed that Ul'an was still bothering to look through a gap in the wall. 'Ul'an', he said to him, 'why do you go on fighting?' 'I have no choice', Ul'an answered, 'for if they take me prisoner, they'll kill me.' Berger remembered Asimov, the Uzbek traitor, who'd said: 'We are risking more than you Germans. If they capture us, we haven't a hope in Hell.' He looked more closely at Ul'an. He was as filthy as the rest of them and hunger had imparted a senile gauntness to his face. His cheeks were so caved in that he looked as if he had lost all his teeth, and his eye-sockets were so swollen by tiredness that his eyes seemed to have disappeared. Berger was gripped by a sudden anxiety and looked around at the faces of others. He recognised in them the same senile features, the same blankness in the middle of the face, the same protruding edges and the same dirty, colourless skin. Suffering had made them all the same, and by cancelling out all differences between them had turned them into a homogeneous crowd of old men. As Berger surveyed the blank faces and the bodies which now bore no resemblance to the young soldiers who had been sent out to the front a few months before, his gaze fell upon the badge still very visible on Ul'an's right arm, depicting the blue mosque and above its domes a text reading *Tanri biz Menen*, God is with us. The sight worried him, for the badge disclosed Ul'an's origins, and so made him more vulnerable than the others. Like the double-S tattooed in the armpits of special forces, which marked them out as members of the Nazi elite, Ul'an's badge showed that he was part of the Turkestan battalion, and therefore in Russian eyes a deserter. Berger was now beside himself with worry. Ul'an was the only person left from before, and this 'before' was an undefined time, although certainly prior to Stalingrad. He felt more clearly than ever how necessary Ul'an's presence was to him. 'Now we are with you. You are our present,' Ul'an had said to him in Khulkhuta, and now Berger could well have said the same, since his own existence depended on having Ul'an at his side. By now they knew each other well, and Berger knew how a yurt was made, how colts were raised and when in the *ayil* the new *kumiss* was celebrated. Ul'an had seen the photos Berger kept in his wallet, in the inside pocket of his jacket, and in the light of the kerosene lamp had peered at the chubby baby girl in her mother's arms, and had asked if the house that could be seen behind Siglinde was their own. Berger knew that on the very same day on which Siglinde had brought the little girl into the world, in Cologne, Ul'an's wife gave birth in a yurt to twins. Ul'an noted the coincidence and pondered it. 'It is not chance,' he had said, 'nothing happens by chance.'

When Berger saw the faded but still recognisable mosque on the sleeve of Ul'an's uniform, he almost screamed, 'Ul'an, the badge!' Ul'an was startled and did not really understand at first but Berger was looking round frantically, as if the Russians were already in front of them with their rifles pointed at them. They took a jacket from a soldier who had just died. 'Put it on, Ul'an!' 'But it's a non-commissioned officer,' said Ul'an. 'What's that to you?' Berger looked for the soldier's pocket-book, opened it and read out his first name and surname: Andreas Tillmann, Liliengasse 2, Kronberg. 'Take the name too,' he said to Ul'an. 'Learn it by heart: Andreas Tillmann, corporal in the artillery, Kronberg.' Ul'an repeated the name obediently, like a small boy learning a lesson off by heart.

How absurd it all is, thought Berger, as he carefully corrected Ul'an, and who do we hope to deceive with the false name and the uniform? The Russians? Fate? But where the whole thing is absurd, he said to himself, individual actions are bound to be too. Whatever we do, nothing makes any sense here.

20th, 21st, 22nd of January. Berger and Ul'an go in search of food and share out what little they manage to find. They are still in the basement, and the wall of corpses grows higher by the day. 23rd of January. Berger and Ul'an decide to flee, to escape from the furnace on their own and to get out. They do not really know what is outside, where the front has shifted to, where the German army is and where the allies are, but they are determined to try. They leave under cover of darkness from the northern part of the built-up area, and shielded by the rubble they cross the street and reach the nearest block of houses. Everywhere they encounter throngs of famished soldiers, wounded and groaning men, and armed men still fighting fiercely. Berger and Ul'an want to reach the river, and hope that the mesh of the net now drawn so tightly around Stalingrad will be looser there. The plan is mad but no madder than everything else.

Captain Di Bella could not readily have reconstructed the route taken by the little group of Italians from Pitomnik airport to the tractor factory to the north of Stalingrad. Yet he had managed to keep his men together, despite their zig-zag path through the snow, by urging them on, by rebuking them and by supporting those who did not want to, or simply could not walk any further. The tractor factory no longer had a roof and was now a white, open space lying between ruined walls that resembled the façades of non-existent houses overlooking a square. 'A fine landing strip!' observed Biagini, the telegraph operator, ironically. 'Just right for grazing sheep!' retorted Cossu.

In Sardinia Salvatore Cossu was a shepherd and had a sheepfold near to Ottana, but only in the winter for in the summer he took his flock up into the mountains. Morning and evening, from January to June, Cossu would milk his three hundred ewes and after the first milking he would make Sardinian *fiore sardo* cheese in the sheepfold. According to Cossu, the sea was to blame for his being at Stalingrad. If he had not been so scared of the sea – even the sight of water lapping against the ferry jetty brought on sea sickness – Cossu would never have thought of becoming an airman, for he really only felt safe with the rocks under his shoes. Had it been up to him, he'd never have gone on the sea or in the air, and still less on the mainland, given that there was sea in between. In the years before the war Captain Di Bella had been in Sardinia; whenever possible he used to travel around studying the *Nuraghes* and from time to time he would call in at Cossu's house in Mamoiada and buy a whole cheese from him. When his call-up papers came, Cossu got it into his head that he was to be dispatched to the navy, he of all people. He told Di Bella as he was wrapping a whole *fiore sardo* in newspaper. 'Why not join my unit?', Di Bella had asked him. 'Me, fly?' 'Not all airmen fly', Di Bella replied; he didn't have to fly, and if he wanted to, he could be his batman. So it was that Cossu had gone off to be Di Bella's batman. Di Bella had been right. Apart from the journey by boat to the mainland, Cossu had got as far as Stalingrad using trains, and in his all too brief career as an airman he had never had the chance to discover if it were true that, as people had told him, you get seasick on planes too.

In those weeks at Stalingrad, Cossu had grown a thick black beard just as he used to do when he was with his sheep in the countryside, far from his own village, and when he returned home his mother would say: '*Esu santissimu, pares unu sirvone essiu da sa tuppa*,' you look like a wild boar dragged through a bush. His friends for their part said that he resembled a Barbary pirate, if only because of the bearskin hat he wore on his head.

On 24th January, the remains of the two disbanded companies assembled in the tractor factory. The order was to *einigeln*, to roll up like porcupines and hide their vulnerable parts from the enemy. The tractor factory, with its shattered walls and twisted metal girders, also seemed like a gigantic porcupine with its quills pointing up into the sky.

On 25th January, a plane, a *Storke*, flew over Stalingrad by night, came down lower, dropped food parcels to the besieged soldiers, regained height and turned away to the west, managing by some miracle to avoid anti-aircraft fire from the ground. It was a bright, majestic night, and the moon, high above the ruins of the city, lit up the glorious dome of the sky. Far below, a bedraggled throng watched the rash stork distribute its gifts. One packet was dropped directly onto the tractor factory; hundreds of eyes watched it fall through the air and from a hundred mouths there issued an oh of disappointment when it snagged on a metal girder which protruded from the wall like a monstrous gargoyle, its forked tongue sticking out into the void. The sack rocked for a while in the air and then stopped still. Furious hands gesticulated from below, and reached up towards the shape that dangled mockingly above them, like a ham on the tree of Cockayne, and was too high for them to reach. Cossu was there with the others and, no sooner had he seen the parcel snared on the girder than he turned to Biagini and said: 'That one's ours. You stay down here and I'll climb up.' Without waiting for a reply, he ran to the wall and looked for holes to grip, slipped in his hands and feet and began slowly and surely to climb. His body slid up the wall like a lizard and came out into the light. He was now clearly visible and an easy target for a sniper. But no one fired. Cossu soon reached the point at which the girder protruded from the wall, wrapped one arm round it, then the other, draped his legs over the metal, hugged it tight, and then slid forwards. When he got to the end, he leant out and gave the parcel a push, but it merely rocked and did not fall from the hook. Cossu then plunged a knife into it, once, twice, the gifts from the gods hidden inside began to fall through the gash in the side, and all that remained of the parcel was an envelope, hanging from the hook like a lamb's stomach left to dry in the sheepfold.

The courtyard of the tractor factory now became a fish bowl in which swarming heads tossed, dived down and re-emerged like a shoal of trout around little pieces of bread. The soldiers shoved, trampled and lashed out, and all for a packet of biscuits or a square of chocolate. In the middle, Biagini and the others defended their loot, hid it beneath their jackets and, faced with a swarm of angry disappointed and hungry men, laid about them with their fists and elbows.

Only Di Bella was waiting for Cossu down below, and the captain watched him as he slid back along the girder, blindly sought out footholds, felt his way down the wall and, finally, with one jump made it back onto the ground. He then said to him in all seriousness: 'You ought to get eight days for that.' But Cossu looked at his bleeding hands, spat into them and made no reply.

Di Bella confiscated what he could from the soldiers and then handed out a little to everyone, and to Cossu an extra half packet of cigarettes. If anyone had seen the airmen, in the cellar beneath the tractor factory, they'd surely have taken them for bandits sharing out their booty. But just then, on 25th January, none of them, not even telegraph operator Biagini, had it in mind to joke.

* * *

On 29th January, Berger and Ul'an took refuge in the tractor factory. The Volga was only a little further on but it was impossible to reach it.

On 30th January, the tenth anniversary of the regime, Field Marshal Paulus sent his congratulations to the Führer. The national anthem boomed out from loudspeakers and even reached those living underground in the factory.

That evening Berger remembered the date: 'My Ilse would have been five years old now, like your children.' Ul'an pondered for a while and then said: 'It's not by chance that our children were born on the same day.' 'What does "it's not by chance" mean, Ul'an?' 'It means that no one is born by chance, just as no one dies by chance. If two souls are reborn at the same time, though in different and even distant places and though different mothers have given birth to them, they are sisters. There is an understanding between them. Your daughter is dead, and I have a son and a daughter, both of whom are living. It was destined to be. If we get out alive, and if I am destined to return to my village on the Amudar'ya I want my daughter to become yours. Please accept the blood of my blood as a pledge of friendship and of obedience to fate.'

Ul'an was talking in a calm but solemn voice, and his gaze was serious. The consecration of friendship with blood was an ancient ritual, and it was not uncommon for the Tunshan to give children to be adopted by couples who did not have any. As far as Ul'an was concerned, there was nothing absurd about such an exchange or, rather, gift. Had it been another time, and had Berger been in another place, not shut in with just twenty bullets in their magazines and two biscuits each to survive on, he would have refused and sought gently to dissuade Ul'an. Berger would perhaps have explained how different their customs were, how different his house in Cologne was from a yurt, and how difficult an adoption between such different families would be. But since just then they were, like beggars, dividing up cigarette ends, the notion of dividing up children seemed no more absurd to him than anything else. Normality seemed so distant a thing that consecrating a friendship with the gift of a daughter appeared to be a normal episode, indeed, one which augured well and which was somehow a challenge to fate. Only by coming out of the furnace alive could the pact be fulfilled, and how could anyone have thought that possible, on 30th January 1943, in Stalingrad? 'OK,' said Berger. They shook hands and embraced. I was the pledge of their friendship.

On 31st January Field Marshal Paulus surrendered, to the south of Stalingrad. But in the tractor factory the General of the XIth Army still refused to yield. On the night of 2nd February, in the cellar beneath the factory, a rumour spread that negotiations with the Soviets were under way. 'This is it,' Berger then said to Ul'an, and unstrapped his wristwatch with the gold strap. It was a present from Siglinde. On the back, an engraved dedication in longhand read 'To Günther, Siglinde. 10th October 1937.' Berger held it for a while in his hand, re-read the inscription, turned it over again, took out his fountain pen from the inside pocket of his jacket, and removed the letters and photographs from his wallet. He looked around, saw a fissure in the ground, bent down, slipped the watch and pen in, turned the wallet over in his hands, then, thinking better of it, put it back in his jacket pocket. As he stood up again he saw that Ul'an had been watching him. 'Be brave, Ul'an,' he said, 'now it's your turn.' Ul'an took the little silver box from around his neck, opened it, tipped its contents into a pocket, removed his knife, and Alcidai's, from his belt, took his snuff-box and slipped the lot into the fissure. Berger plugged it with a stone. Let whoever rebuilds these walls have the treasure, he thought. They threw down whatever weapons they still had and together moved towards the basement's exit, through which a line of disarmed soldiers was already leaving.

Just a few metres further on, Captain Di Bella removed his watch from his trouser pocket, looked at its cover with its engraved floral decoration, and opened it. The name of his grandfather, Tommaso Di Bella, was on the inside. The hands of the watch were gold. Di Bella was looking intently at the time. It was ten minutes to seven and a faint light came in through an opening barricaded with sacks. Di Bella closed the watch and then with a sudden, enraged gesture hurled it to the ground, trampled on it and crushed it with his heel as if it were a loathsome insect. As he did this he pressed his lips so tightly together that two deep furrows, a compound of rage and sorrow, appeared on his cheeks. His fountain pen met the same end.

Cossu then took out his knife, the one he had used in the sheepfold to carve wood, to split cheeses, to cut lambs' throats and, more recently, to rip open the sack full of provisions. It had a mouflon horn shaft and a broad blade, which became thinner towards the tip. 'What should I do with this?' he asked doubtfully. 'Stick it in the Duce's guts!' Biagini replied. Cossu cast him an angry glance and hurled it away, as if it were a stone.

On 2nd February, at the basement exit from the tractor factory, soldiers in white overalls with slanting eyes pointed their rifles and searched those who emerged from the gloom with their hands up like a throng of disorientated ghosts.

25

BERGER RECOGNISED Di Bella by his voice. He turned around. The captain was giving orders to his men: stick together, don't get lost in the throng of prisoners, support the weakest. The little group of Italians crowded around him, hoping to draw from the presence of others the strength to withstand the emptiness that threatened to engulf them. Di Bella was therefore deliberately standing very straight, and his demeanour and thinness made him seem even taller. He recognised Berger, made as if to raise his hand to his cap but then extended it to him in a gesture of friendship.

The men emerged from their hiding places, assembled in the square and joined those already waiting. The place was oddly silent. It was not a real silence, for the throng was moving, orders and shouts were flying back and forth and the soldiers' boots were echoing on the hardened snow of the square. But the noise of gunfire, which for weeks had provided a backdrop for the soldiers confined to the cellars of Stalingrad, and which had shredded their nerves, had suddenly disappeared, leaving them with the apprehension that it might start up again at any moment.

The uncertainty was almost more painful than the state of clearly defined danger in which he had lived during the previous days and which he preferred to the present emptiness, Berger thought, as he waited and as the sky lightened above the square. Even the fact of being in the open air, of having the sky above you rather than a cellar ceiling, and of standing still and waiting, seemed strange. If it were not for the fact that he was continuously shifting from one foot to the other, and moving his fingers around in his threadbare gloves, Berger would have believed that he no longer even had a body and had dissolved as he waited into that emptiness.

At first he did not realise that the throng of prisoners had begun to move. A column had formed somewhere, and the men assembled in the square had been drawn towards it. Gradually, as the movement reached them, the prisoners bestirred themselves, glad of a change, and lined up. Berger cast a glance to his right to check that Ul'an was nearby, and heard Di Bella's order: 'Stick together'. He was heartened to see that comrades were near at hand.

They marched for hours but neither Berger nor Ul'an nor Di Bella nor, indeed, any of the others, had the slightest notion of time or of space. The first places they passed through were known to them, for scattered along the road were the residues of what just a few weeks before had been an army, but now the dead were Russian, as were the burnt-out vehicles and the armoured cars half-buried in the snow. The prisoners did not know what time it was, but they knew that they were heading north and that it was evening. Berger watched Ul'an as, without stopping, he bent down, scooped up some trampled snow and put it in his mouth. After a moment's hesitation, Berger did the same and began to suck slowly on a filthy ball. He glanced at Di Bella, who was marching beside him. He had managed to preserve the rudiments of military discipline but Berger noticed that his shoulders had become more stooped. Berger turned to look back at the column, which was lost in the evening gloom. He saw faces rendered blank by the strain of marching and by the cold, and feet that were dragged ever more painfully through the snow. Every now and then a dull thud could be heard, and the line would break up. Then the bent bodies straightened again and their legs sought a steadier rhythm. The death of a comrade imparted new life to the others.

It was dark by the time the column reached a temporary camp, a deserted kolkhoz. Berger, Ul'an and the group of Italians were driven into a roofless building which had once been a school, the only trace of which was part of a torn alphabet still stuck to a wall. Only four letters were still intact, together with drawings illustrating them for children: a *g* with little red-capped mushrooms behind it, an *sc* with a tree, a *z* with a star above it, and opposite it an *n* with a teddy bear and a ball behind it. The drawings were supposed to call to mind familiar objects but they must have seemed exotic and strange to the children in the school, because there were no trees, still less mushrooms on the steppe, nor were there toys in the hovels between the Don and the Volga. Stars though, there were, and in great numbers, glittering like those on the alphabet beside the letter *z*, for *zvezd*, star. The prisoners, crowded together inside the school walls, only had eyes for the open sky above them. They were too cramped to sit down, let alone to stretch out. They had to shelter one another from the cold, and could find no rest. It was then that a surge of rage began to pass through them. They shook off their lethargy, their tongues loosened and at first in whispers and then more loudly they unleashed a chorus of insults against the regime and against Hitler. Their excited voices rose to a crescendo of yelling and shouting, as if everyone wanted to outdo the insult uttered by the man next to him, and so give vent to his own feelings of powerlessness. It was as though the prisoners, exhausted as they were by the long siege, the weeks of hunger, their dismay at being imprisoned, their weariness from marching and their fear at what was in store, were coming for the first time to understand the deception that had been practised on them. It was as though they were discovering all of a sudden what up until then they had not even wished to think, and in howling it, with clenched fists, to the heavens, they were calling upon God to bear witness, making him share in their rage and imploring him to intervene.

Lazzaro Manoli had fallen behind. He had been taken prisoner near to Valuyki, beyond the Don. The captain of the flame-throwers' company had said to the little group of soldiers: 'Come on, lads, let's take out the machine-guns!' The Russians were higher up, and were firing on the column of retreating Italians, and the group had surprised them from behind. Lazzaro had removed the magazine from the machine-gun, then had turned round and run down through the valley. But the Russians were now where the Turin division had been, and they cried out '*Vainaplenniy*!', prisoner, and Lazzaro put his hands up. As he walked towards them, he thought about the magazine in his jacket pocket. There had been no time to throw it away and he said to himself, now they'll search me and kill me. They did not search him, however, but lined him up with the others in a column advancing westwards and leaving the Don behind. Lazzaro could think of nothing else but the Russian machine-gun magazine weighing down his inside pocket, and every now and then he would run his hand over it to check that it was still there, as if he hoped that a guardian angel had made it disappear. It had not disappeared. Lazzaro felt the metal protruding from his inside pocket and said to himself, sooner or later they'll realise and then they'll shoot me on the spot. Lazzaro Manoli, he said to himself as if composing his own obituary, born in Genoa 15th March 1923, died in Russia 20th January 1943. Twenty years old, and it was all the fault of the magazine in the inside pocket of his jacket. He had to get rid of it. Lazzaro could think of nothing else and looked furtively around, but the Russian soldier was always there, alongside him, he was still pointing the rifle at his back and Lazzaro was convinced that he never took his eyes off him. The weight of the magazine distressed him more than hunger or his left big toe, which was frozen, or the march in the snow. In the evening, when the column began to slow down, Lazzaro thought, now I'm for it. They'll search me, and it'll be curtains! His fear, however, lent him fresh courage. He saw a pile of snow a few paces from the column, kept the magazine hidden up his sleeve and, when the soldier went a little way ahead, leapt to one side of the line, plunged his arm into a pile of snow and buried the magazine in it. Lazzaro at last felt lighter, like a man who has cast his ballast into the sea and trusts to a favourable wind. Fortune had not deserted him, of that he was certain.

All this had happened the day before, somewhere around Valuyki. Now, however, Lazzaro had fallen behind. The fault lay with his big toe, which was hurting him. He heard the shots that killed those of his comrades who were too tired to continue, and he pressed on. But it was no use. His legs could no longer carry him, and that was why he lagged behind, one hundred, two hundred metres, no matter how hard he tried to catch up with the column, he could not manage it. This time the game's up, he thought, and was quite calm. He felt someone grab him by the shoulders and he turned round. *'Davai, davai'*, the Russian sergeant said to him and pointed at the column. But Lazzaro didn't move. He was a blonde lad, with pale eyes and a skin that never went brown, even in summer, so much so that his schoolfellows taunted him by calling him *'gianchetto'*, tidler or even *'Kraut'*, which really riled him. Now, at the front, Lazzaro was often mistaken for a German, and he realised how dangerous that might be. Even now the sergeant asked him: '*Nemiesky*?', and Lazzaro quickly said '*Nyet, nyet. Italiansky*.' The Russian pointed behind him, there's a village back there, off you go.

So it was that Lazzaro began to wander from village to village, knock at doors, say '*italiansky*', and smile gently. The women would give him a baked potato, a mug of soup or a bowl of curdled milk. Lazzaro would thank them and be on his way. He was heading east. He went back to Rossoshka, found the bunkers built by the Alpini, and knew them to be empty and undamaged though still defended by rings of mines. He reached the Don. Before him lay the bend of the river which the Alpini had dubbed 'the hat'. It was in this very stretch of river, in September, that the Russians had sunk a large number of wooden piles which, once compressed by the ice, formed a bridge sturdy enough to take armoured cars. From above Lazzaro could make out the dark line of wood in the middle of the ice, and beyond the river he saw huts and smoke, and without thinking twice made his way down to the riverbank. He ventured onto the pile bridge but stopped in the middle of the river. He was alone. The river was a mirror of ice, gleaming in the sun, and the banks were high and white. There was no one about. Just to be in the midst of so much light and silence gave Lazzaro an absurd feeling of omnipotence. He'd have liked to yell, to leap around on the pile bridge and to slide on the ice. He did none of these things but instead got to the other bank and headed for the village. He no longer hesitated when he came to an *izba* but knocked straightaway and walked in without being asked, politely, as if he had been invited to dinner and was doing his duty as a guest. Come on in, *Italiansky*, sing us a song! Lazzaro had a thin but tuneful voice and when he did not know the words he made them up. '*Va' pensiero*,' he sang, and the Russians listened in silence, clapped and offered him some bread or an egg, even though they too had very little. He would stay for two or three days then slip away because he didn't want to trouble them any further. He was still headed east, for he thought that the further away he got from the war, the better chances of survival he'd have. When peace comes, I'll go back, he said to himself, and it seemed to him that peace was no further away than the next village and just as easy to reach. In one hamlet he found another disbanded soldier, who shared his shelter with him, a large room which had been a theatre before the war. It was infested with rats but still had a scrap of curtain which hung down like a forgotten carnival festoon. The German used what was left of the cloth which, despite the holes and the filthiness still retained a little of its original purple colour, to make a blanket and he said jokingly that to be a bed fit for a king all he needed was a baldachin. A Russian patrol surprised them there. They were escorting a group of German soldiers, and lumped in Lazzaro and his comrade with the others. But Lazzaro kept on saying '*Ya Italiansky*', 'I'm Italian', as if that were a safe-conduct, and he gestured at his flashes, pointing his index finger at his chest, above the pocket, look, there's no eagle with the swastika in his claws, this is an Italian uniform. 'If you're Italian,' a Russian said to him putting a rifle into his hand, 'take this and shoot.' He pointed at the little group of Germans who stood with their hands behind their necks and watched him with a kind of curiosity in their gaze, as if to say, I wonder what he'll do. Lazzaro did fire, but into the air. In a fury the Russian snatched back the gun and pointed it at the prisoners. None were left standing. Lazzaro was taken to Frolovo. It was the beginning of February; a column of prisoners from Stalingrad milled around the entrance to the clearing camp and was slowly engulfed.

Frolovo clearing camp was nothing more than a vast open space fenced in by barbed wire, with three parallel lines of hastily built huts in the middle. Everything was temporary and already run-down. The arrival of so many thousands of prisoners had not been anticipated, and no one knew where to put them. There was not enough room or wood to heat the overcrowded huts, water was scarce and the kitchens were too far off. It was wartime and food was scarce for the soldiers too.

That evening a soldier entered the hut, pointed at random at a group of prisoners and gestured to them to follow him. Lazzaro thought, here we go, now they really are going to kill me. Cossu followed, cursing inside that it was his turn, and Ul'an followed Berger without saying a word and joined the others. Each man was given a spade and shown where they were to dig a trench, a few metres behind the hut. Here we go then, thought Lazzaro, now they are making us dig our own graves and afterwards they'll shoot us. He knew the ritual because he'd been present at an execution of that kind. It had been a group of partisans taken prisoner by the Italians, and this time they hadn't handed them over to the Germans and it had been they themselves, the Italians, who had ordered the trench to be dug, right behind the village. They had been little more than boys, and some of them were women too, as Lazzaro remembered all too well, because he had been one of those who aimed the rifles. The partisans dug in silence, and the only sound had been made by their spades striking the hard ground and the earth piled up along the edge of the trench. When the trench was deep enough, the order was given to fire. Lazzaro had shut his eyes in order not to see. Now it was his turn to dig, his feet in the earth. Shovelling was difficult, for the ground was hard, the spade would not go in, and Lazzaro had blistered hands. I wish they'd hurry up, he thought, surely they're not going to make us shovel all night.

The ravine in the Kalmyk steppe, Berger thought, this is how it must have been. And he saw again in his mind's eye the Kalmyk child pointing towards the sliver of moonlight at the bottom of the hollow in which the Jews of Elista had been buried. Theirs was to be the grave behind the huts in Frolovo camp.

They dug until evening, when they were sent back inside, and the following day others were called upon to shovel. By this time they'd all understood that they were building latrines for the camp. Frolovo really did have nothing at all.

Ul'an managed to count to three hundred and then wearied of it. Three hundred lice taken prisoner, one after the other. If he picked them off, held them tightly between thumb and index finger, squeezed them with his nail pressing with precision on the most vulnerable part of the insect, between the thorax and the abdomen, he could then use the same finger as a shovel to rid the other of the small ball that was smeared across it. He repeated the procedure three hundred times before admitting defeat. No matter how many times he slid his fingers under the collar of his shirt and fished for them, the number of lice remained the same. He carried an inexhaustible army on his back, and not just on his skin either. He merely had to turn up the lapels of his jacket to observe whole battalions of new-born lice about to march on the warm reserves of blood that he, Ul'an, unresistingly offered.

There are black lice, yellow lice and red lice. Ul'an remembered his great-uncle Mongotai, who used to visit Bairqan's yurt and had a lambskin beret which he never removed and which, on closer inspection, proved to be crawling with lice. Mongotai maintained that lice take their colour from the soul on which they feed, sucking its blood, because there are black, red and yellow souls, or even colourless souls, like the insect Ul'an held at that moment between thumb and index finger. That means that my soul is transparent, thought Ul'an as he squashed the insect with his nail. The idea that lice had something to do with the soul of the person on whom and off whom they lived, seemed wholly plausible to Ul'an. He had in fact several times observed what happened on soldiers who had just died, as all of a sudden the community of lice which had resided there was thrown into turmoil, left the seams, folds and turn-ups in which it had lived and abandoned the corpse before it was quite cold. To look at the swarming mass, one would have said that it was the tangible form assumed by the soul as it abandoned the dead person in search of another body from which to suck the colour.

Ul'an was pondering these questions when a sudden uproar attracted his attention and distracted him from the lice. He stood up and slowly approached a group of prisoners who were making a tremendous din. They were fighting over the soup yet again. The two men detailed to carry the soup-can were trying to fend off attacks from the prisoners, who were bearing down on it from all sides. To prevent the assailants from dipping their mess-tins in or, failing that, their hands, they whirled their free arms round as if they were clubs, dealing out slaps and punches at random. The attackers would not leave off, however, and in their turn drove back the prisoners pressing from behind, until those carrying the can ended up losing their balance. The receptacle slipped from their hands and overturned, drenching shoes, boots and foot-cloths, along with a sizeable patch of snow, in brown liquid. A chorus of outraged oaths went up, and then the prisoners who shortly before had come to blows threw themselves on the ground as if obeying an order, trying to recover the lentils, which ordinarily stayed submerged at the bottom of the can, from the trampled snow and the mud. The quickest got hold of the container and brought handfuls of lentils to their mouths, while the unlucky ones scooped up and ate muddy snow mixed with soup. Ul'an noticed some Italians in the group, and saw Captain Di Bella recognise his men, stride over and immediately begin to yell: 'Wretches! Do you all want to fall ill and croak?' In the meantime he seized them by the shoulders and pulled them up. They reluctantly got to their feet, without really understanding and obeying simply out of habit. Ul'an saw Biagini wiping his mouth, smeared with lentils and mud, with his left hand. Before letting the handful of snow fall from his right hand, he studied it at length with a look full of sorrow.

Cossu looked with a critical eye at the piece of bread to which he was entitled, his daily portion of five hundred grams, and weighed it in his hand. Did it really weigh that? '*Tuttu abba*,' he then said to Di Bella. '*Abba*, nothing but water.' He bit off a corner and then hid the rest in his pocket, in order to eat it later in the hut, sitting on his bed. 'You'd best do as the sheep do,' said the captain, 'eat it all at once and then bring it up later and chew it at your leisure.' 'I already do that, Captain, but in my opinion not even a goat would manage to digest this bread, and you know what a goat is capable of digesting. The truth is this bread affects me like *armulanza*, a giant chicory that sheep are crazy about, but when they eat it they swell up so much that they may even die.'

It was to avoid this effect that Cossu hid the bread in his pocket and ate it later in small mouthfuls, chewing it with rapt attention. He was convinced that 'ruminating', as he called it, like sheep, leaving the bolus as long as possible in the mouth and bringing it back to the palate, served to reduce hunger, given that the simple fact of lengthy chewing deceived the stomach as to the quantity of food it had been given. This is what Cossu had always done when spending whole weeks in the mountains with his animals, when he would spread the ricotta onto the dry bread and eat it slowly, following a train of thought now quite lost to him. Now his thoughts went straight to the ricotta and cheese which he melted over the fire in order to eat it in strands over his bread, and to the slices of sausage which accompanied it. If it had not been for Captain Di Bella, who had taken him with him, at that very moment Cossu might have been in Barbagia milking sheep. Thinking about it now, the cold of dawn when he was up milking, the pain in his hands, the filth and mud of the autumn rains, the wolves and the rustlers, the months living far from home like a hermit, all seemed the life of a lord. The hut was gloomy, the air thick and damp. Most of the prisoners were already asleep but even in the middle of the night there was never real silence, for many stirred and talked in their sleep. Cossu could hear Di Bella above him toss and turn, making the planks over his head creak. Next to him slept the German, Berger, and every now and then he stretched out an arm in his sleep and more than once Cossu had thrown it back like a rag. In fact the Germans slept on the other side of the hut, and between them and the Italians were the Romanians and the Hungarians, for, as Di Bella had noticed, the lay-out of the dormitory reflected the disposition of troops on the Don. Yet this Berger preferred the Italians and was always with them, and especially with the captain, together with his Mongol whom he'd come across somewhere or other. As he lay there thinking, Cossu felt a slight movement of the air close to his face and in the darkness could just make out a hand about to pounce on his bread. Without even pausing to reflect, he felt his own hand bunched into a fist fly through the air, sensed the violence of the blow, and heard someone make off groaning. 'Who was it, Cossu?', asked Biagini, on his right. 'I don't know,' Cossu answered, calmly chewing a little piece of bread and rolling it against his palate. If he could have seen himself in the mirror, he'd have recognised on his face the same expression of thoughtful satisfaction that he'd so often observed in sheep, when they stood next to one another ruminating. In the summer, when the sheep were put out to graze at night, the shepherds would entrust them to the dogs and withdraw to the sheepfold for a few hours to sleep, until dawn called them back for milking.

Cossu and Ul'an often wondered how it was that Captain Di Bella and Lieutenant Berger had so much to talk about.

'There's no better cure for hunger than not thinking about it, at any rate for as long as hunger allows you to think.' Berger concentrated on finding the Italian words to explain the paradox. Di Bella nodded: 'At home people have always been used to hunger. The diet of the popular classes in the south is a poor one, just greens, tomatoes and little or no meat. Yet there are carob beans and prickly pears . . .'

Berger had never eaten prickly pears, and had in fact to confess that he didn't know what they were like. Di Bella then bent down, picked up a small stick and drew a prickly pear bush in a layer of snow. 'And this is the fruit', he said as he finished the illustration. 'You need to know how to hold it with all due care, then you cut it into three parts without wholly separating them: two horizontal cuts to the shell and a vertical cut down the middle. Then the fruit, if well cut, comes out of the shell without a mark on it. The flesh is juicy and rich in seeds; the best in my opinion are the red prickly pears. We have a hedge of them close to the house in Sicily, and in September the bailiff brings us whole baskets of fruit.'

Even if Berger did not grasp all the details, or perhaps for that very reason, he listened intently, trying not to miss any of the words which Di Bella pronounced very clearly, in the Sicilian manner. The things he failed to understand were not, however, wasted, since they added a further element of mystery to the myth of Italy which Berger had shared with many of his fellow countrymen since he was a child. The myth, born in a classroom, reinforced by his father and refined through conversations with Dr Wallatz, was now dusted off by the emaciated officer, who was busy drawing a prickly pear bush in the snow and talking about his island, as they paced up and down the prison camp and tried to forget their hunger. Although Berger could not quite imagine the flavour of such a thorny fruit, behind Di Bella's words he saw Sicily, in the shape of solid Doric columns and the tympanums of temples against a perpetually blue sky.

Captain Di Bella, for his part, was unstinting in his admiration for the Germans, whereas he felt only contempt for the Italian government and army: 'The simple fact that we airmen are here provides irrefutable proof of the incompetence of our leaders, military and civilian. Sheer recklessness led to our fighting in Russia, without the least preparation, and it will prove disastrous for Italy. Proof of this is supplied by the shameful, and I mean shameful,' Di Bella uttered this word with his mouth twisted in disgust, 'lack of proper organisation at every level. I must confess with shame, as an officer and as an Italian, that we are no match for our allies.' Di Bella's features stiffened, and it was evident that, as a military man, this judgement was wounding to his pride. He pursed his lips and the furrows on either side of his mouth grew deeper. His face was a chalky white, and his grey eyes seemed to have shrunk back into his dark eye-sockets.

'Hold on a minute,' retorted Berger, as he struggled to find the right words. 'Do all these prisoners around us now not prove the incompetence of our commanders?' He laid particular stress on the 'our', which referred to the Germans, but in his heart of hearts he meant a generalised incompetence, to which he, Di Bella and all the others had fallen victim in much the same way. But Di Bella was not prepared to yield. The Germans had made a military error, and an unforgivable one at that, in that they had not attempted to fight their way out of the furnace of Stalingrad while it had still been possible to do so, but it was an error nonetheless. By contrast, the Italian case was one of 'chronic organisational incompetence'. Di Bella pronounced each syllable with care as he reiterated his favourite argument concerning the inefficiency of the Italian high command: 'It's an inefficiency that has become a modus vivendi at every level of our civilian and military hierarchies. From the lowliest soldier to the general at staff headquarters, there is just one rule everyone zealously follows: everything's fine just so long as it works.' This was the formula Di Bella used to summarise the improvisation, neglect and culpable negligence which in his opinion afflicted the army. 'Its enough that something works there and then, or appears to work. No one gives a fuck what happens next.'

The captain had a reputation for being an awkward customer, who would not connive at the usual underhand deals, and who did not form close ties with his fellow officers. A stubborn Sicilian, it was said, who was a stickler for honesty and for precision. 'That one's more German than a Prussian!' said his men, who took for granted their German allies' reputation for precision. With Di Bella, if someone muddled through his work any old how or, worse still, deceived him, he would not get off lightly. The withering looks he gave were worth a thousand rebukes. Di Bella rarely raised his voice, would never insult a soldier, and his strictness was due to his integrity. He did not say much but what he did say was fair and always in line with what he thought. His men understood him, sensed that the captain was harder on himself than he was on them, and took him seriously. They may not have loved him but they certainly respected him. Where his colleagues were concerned, some secretly admired the courage with which Di Bella paraded his opinions, without worrying about treading on anyone's toes, but for this very reason they thought it advisable not to be seen with him and tended to avoid him. Others considered his moralising an irksome affectation. Di Bella was a notorious spoilsport, a man who, when others were 'shifting for themselves', would talk about 'stealing public property', and when someone boasted of the ruses he used to get by, even in Russia, judged them to be disgraceful rackets harming civilian populations and soldiers alike. He was now explaining as much to Berger, who for his part tried to object that things were much the same in the Wehrmacht: 'I've heard tell that at Stalingrad someone in the officers' bunkers had a whole cellar of French wines, not to mention gastronomic delicacies . . .' Di Bella paid no heed to his objections, indeed, seemed to be thoroughly irritated by them: 'It may well be true, but it's certainly an isolated case. At least with you there is some awareness that it is not lawful. We, on the other hand, steal in broad daylight, and the man who does not steal is regarded as a blockhead. Believe me, where public administration is concerned, the Italians have everything to learn from the Germans.' He fell silent and turned to look at some untoward movement among the prisoners around the huts, but he was clearly still pursuing the same line of argument: 'You will perhaps have had occasion to note, Lieutenant, the condition our men were in when they set out to wage war. The Alpini were going to march on the plain but had spikes on the bottom of their shoes, while the infantry had to face a Russian winter with windcheaters. It's not that the clothes weren't bought, indeed, untold millions were spent, and some made a fortune selling them to the army, but when they arrived, those that did arrive, they were stolen from the warehouses in our supply-lines. There was a veritable trade in such clothing. It was a scandal. I saw it with my own eyes at Stalingrad and I even denounced it to the authorities.' The men whispered among themselves that the sudden transfer to Stalingrad, to build an airstrip that was of no use to anyone, had been due to that denunciation, which everyone knew about. But Di Bella was not one for confidences, and said nothing about all that to Berger. However, seeing him together with the German officer, noting how he leant towards him when he spoke, with his long fingers opening out into a fan-shape or coming together, with the fingertips joining like an artichoke, it was plain that he was deeply involved in that conversation, and that he was unloading onto the lieutenant, who did not even fully understand him, the weight of thoughts that had been tormenting him for some time. 'I chose a military career because I was convinced that my duty lay in defending the fatherland, that this was my profession . . .'

Defending the fatherland? Berger felt a sense of embarrassment. Surely there was no fatherland thereabouts to defend. To come and be butchered on the steppe, was that the duty of an officer and a soldier? He, Berger, like the overwhelming majority of those sharing hunger and prison with them, had not chosen military service of his own free will. It was therefore not easy for him to follow the argument expounded by the captain, who was letting himself be carried away by his own train of thought: 'The worst thing is that the man who does his duty renders himself, for that selfsame reason, guilty. It is, how should I put it, the reversal of all values. For an individual there's no other way out but to put a bullet in his skull.'

'Many of my colleagues took that path, but for other reasons,' said Berger, trying to get a word in edgeways, 'they did not consider it honourable to be taken prisoner.'

'That's a heroic vision of war and of the military profession which today is wholly anachronistic. The true scandal is not being taken prisoner but the paradox that doing one's duty is an act which undermines one's honour.' Di Bella was looking straight ahead. That confession must have been deeply painful to him. 'It's no use removing oneself physically, given that it is not a question of individual guilt.' He paused, and then continued, as if speaking to himself: 'I've always striven to act according to my own principles, freely. I was deceiving myself.'

Guilt, a word that often recurred in their dialogues, as if finding the guilty parties would settle everything, render imprisonment less harsh and hunger easier to bear. Who was guilty? Berger too had often asked himself this, but the more he looked back, to the time when he'd still been free, the more he became convinced that the word was inappropriate. We were prisoners before becoming such, he thought, and it is pointless looking for a scapegoat, since all of us, from the general down to the lowliest soldier, are guilty of our own imprisonment. And we will bear this guilt all our lives, no matter how many absolutions we seek to give ourselves, even when peace comes and no one wants to know any longer about responsibility and guilt.

If the other prisoners had taken any interest in what was going on around them, aside from the doling out of rations, they would perhaps have noticed the pair of officers, an Italian and a German, who paced up and down between the huts and only left off talking when they were queuing with the others for their portion of bread. Sometimes they did not speak but simply strode along together, and it was the Italian, the taller of the two, who set the pace. Perhaps only Cossu and Ul'an noticed that friendship, which imprisonment rendered all the deeper, but if they had managed to hear snatches of those conversations they would have been completely stumped. As were Berger and Di Bella, for all their striding up and down between the huts, seeking for a way out of the tangled skein of guilt and responsibility, and above all for some rational explanation as to why they'd ended up in that accursed prison camp.

26

COSSU OPENED HIS eyes and jumped down from the bunk. This was what he had done when he was a batman and had got up to make the captain's coffee. Even now he still felt himself to be the captain's batman, although he no longer had any duties to justify the role. He kept to the routine of getting up first and wishing Di Bella good morning, because he felt that keeping the old relationships intact would help to preserve a semblance of normal life even in prison. Cossu was therefore alarmed when no one answered his greeting. He climbed up with his feet on the bunk and leant over Di Bella, who was sleeping in the tier above his. The captain was fully stretched out and seemed even taller than when standing. He was quite still, although his teeth, which were chattering violently, appeared to be shaking his entire body. When he saw Cossu's face framed in his black beard appear at the side of his bed, Di Bella turned to him and said to him in Sicilian dialect: '*Chi fai 'ncapo 'u muro, Giova'? Ti vinisti a arrubbare i ficu?*', What are you doing on the wall, John? Have you come to steal the prickly pears? Cossu was so shocked that he nearly fell over backwards. 'For god's sake, Captain, since when did you talk to me in Sicilian?' But Di Bella had already turned his eyes to the front wall, where a bright, rainbow-hued light was pouring into the hut through a little window closed somehow or other by an old photographic plate.

A bright light came in through the door of their house in the country. The interior was in shadow and the child could barely make out his mother, who was dressed entirely in black up to the lace around her white neck, and saw from behind the bun of light honey-coloured hair which when untied fell lustrously halfway down her back. She was holding a broom in her hands and was busy chasing away the chickens, but they kept on coming into the courtyard. The child seated at the kitchen table saw them appear and look around warily, standing upright on one leg, the other raised and extended, as they took the decision to press on. His mother then sent them packing with cries that sounded like shoo-shoo-shoo, and threatened them with the broom. Every now and then, however, she would turn round to the child and say to him: 'Eat up, darling!' The child was about to pick up the long, dry biscuits and dip them like sponges into the milk when suddenly the chickens all jumped up onto the table, ruffling their feathers, clucking around the bowl of milk, pecking one another and soiling the floor with excrement. In the uproar, the child could see the yellow, scaly skin of the chicken just a short distance away from his face, as it raised its claw and immersed it in the bowl of milk. Then he burst out sobbing, while the milk mixed with biscuit crumbs spread across the table and the chickens dived in and began pecking.

Di Bella tossed and turned in his bunk and tried to drive off the chickens, but they were all over him and pecked up all the biscuits down to the last crumb. He became still more agitated, used his flailing arms to drive them away and could hear them clucking in terror and feel their feathers full in his face. In fact, Cossu and Berger were trying to calm him down, and the clucking he heard was their voices speaking to him, as they decided to move him to the lower bunk, so that he would not have so far to fall. 'He's got typhoid,' Cossu suggested, 'lousy typhoid.' Di Bella was not the first to fall sick, indeed many in the hut were feverish and delirious. Di Bella seemed to calm down a little as Cossu, Berger and Ul'an laid him on the lower bunk. The light that had seeped through the photographic plate had gone, and now it was the noises that intensified and roared in his ears. There are bells, like those you hear when carts approach from a long way off, and a cart does now stop right in front of the gate. The child runs down the path and as he runs he smells the scent of the jasmine which accompanies the sound for a while. The sharecropper and his wife climb down from the cart with a large basket. His mother has come to the door, and she lingers in the shade beneath the pergola, wholly black in front of the jasmine flowers. The sharecropper's wife makes a half bow, greets Signora Di Bella, and says, '*ci purtai i guastedduni e 'a picuridda*.' Saying this, she puts the basket on the bench, lifts up the napkin to reveal the golden shapes of bread, decorated with plants and foliage made of dough, and in the middle there is the marzipan Easter lamb holding the two-pointed banner between its feet. The child reaches out a hand to touch the basket; the bread is still warm from the oven and smells again of jasmine, but a small, white hand falls on his and knocks it. The child withdraws his hand and turns round abruptly, but in so doing the basket falls, the loaves roll across the terrace, are scattered over the stone, and the smell of the bread is stronger than the jasmine and fills the whole garden. The child sees the marzipan lamb on the ground, squashed flat, and the banner pressed into a pinkish, shapeless mass. He makes off, across the garden, climbs the boundary wall and his mother and the share-cropper's wife cry 'Carmelo!', but he keeps on running, across the field where the grass is already high, climbs another little wall, and runs and runs, and still he hears 'Carmelo!' Di Bella can hear that they are calling him, but it is a masculine voice, it's Berger who is calling him, the fair hair is his and there are no little walls around nor fields with grass growing.

They take it in turns to nurse Di Bella but the others also fall sick one by one. They become delirious and ask for something to drink. Cossu, Berger and Ul'an bring water and soup for all of them.

In the middle of the prison camp there was a low well, with no parapet around it, and with a swingle tree contraption for raising up the bucket. There was always a huddle of prisoners around it and someone ready and willing to come to blows over questions of precedence. Cossu saw the bucket emerging full of glistening water and the hands outstretched to grasp it; he saw a prisoner, a Hungarian, who was grabbing hold of it and already held it firmly, when someone pushed him from behind and he fell into the well. A splash was heard; a cry of dismay arose from the prisoners, then they all ran back to the huts. Cossu withdrew too. He went back to the well a few hours later; there was the same throng as always, just quieter than before. He awaited his turn and when he laid his hands on the bucket he glanced downwards, where he felt that he could just make out the shape of a khaki military overcoat floating at the edge.

After three or four days of delirium, Di Bella suddenly sat up in bed, looked around, pointed a bony hand at Berger and said: 'Make them stop, make them stop! The bombs are piercing my brain!' He had broken out into a sweat, and was very agitated. 'Paper, bring me paper.' Ul'an and Berger looked around, and were at a loss as to what to do, when Ul'an unrolled the newspaper cigarette he'd kept to smoke outside and offered it to him. 'Take down what I say!', the captain ordered, speaking in the same commanding tone he'd used when fit and well. Berger and Ul'an looked about them; Cossu had gone to fetch the soup, the others were in bed with the fever and in the throng of prisoners passing in and out of the hut there was no one who gave the impression of having a pen or of being willing to lend it, even if only for a moment or two. But there was in fact one person, and that was Lazzaro Manoli, who was sitting on his bed a few metres away. He looked at them in turn and then took out a tiny, tiny object from his inside pocket and offered it to Berger. It was a pencil stub. Berger gratefully took charge of it and passed it on to the captain. Ul'an had procured a plank of wood and put it on his knees. Di Bella gripped the stub between his fingers, although they could barely guide it. Berger held the little piece of paper firmly so that it wouldn't roll up again and Di Bella wrote an address and the following words 'With all my love, your Carmelo'. Then he handed the piece of paper to Berger and, dripping with sweat, said: 'If you make it, this is for my wife.' That was all he said, then he fell back and that same night he died.

Berger read the note and slipped it into a cartridge case which could be shut at the end with a pebble and sewed it into his jacket pocket with wire. From then on he ceaselessly checked to see if it was in its place and nothing terrified him more than the thought of losing it. It was as if the task with which he in particular had been entrusted, as a final pledge of friendship, provided him with a valid reason for attempting to survive and return home.

Berger was not among those who bore the captain to the mass grave beyond the barbed wire. For the next day he too fell ill. He tried to reach the latrines, stumbled on the entrance steps and lay across the threshold, unable to get up. He spent hours in the cold before anyone realised and carried him back to his bed. He didn't stir for ten whole days. Ul'an brought him water and a little soup, helped him to drink and nursed him. Berger felt that his head was exploding and his body hurt so much that the wooden slats seemed like nails. On the tenth day the fever lifted, just as the order to get ready to leave was given. Cossu and Ul'an stood on either side of Berger, who was in the middle, with his arms around them, like a

Christ taken down from the cross; Biagini joined them; they fell in with the others and marched off to the railway station.

Lazzaro was the last to get up into the wagon; they pushed him bodily inside before closing the door on the outside. The prisoners were so thin that the soldiers escorting them were inclined to think that they had no substance and that they could squeeze them in at will. The wagon was so crowded that Lazzaro, who had got in last, had to remain standing, with his shoulders against the door. His position allowed him a full view of the inside of the wagon, in which the cramped men were huddled together, propping one another up. When the train began to move, the heads that Lazzaro could see beneath him were driven violently forwards, and then began to sway rhythmically. Lazzaro made no attempt to shift, until he heard a voice from the back of the wagon calling to him and saying, 'Come and sit down here, in the front!' He recognised Cossu, made his way forward, accompanied by a volley of curses, and crouched down beside Cossu, Berger, Ul'an and Biagini, who was feeling ill and was lying stretched out across the others.

The train first swung round to the east, and then headed north along the Volga, but the men shut up in the wagon saw only platforms covered in rubbish as they passed through the stations. Berger, who was able to lean against Ul'an's back, did not even realise that the station at which they halted for more than a day was Engelstadt. However, he heard some Germans catch the name and repeat it to themselves, with all the delight of children when they discover something important that adults have tried to keep from them.

His mother used to speak of Engelstadt as though it were 'our' capital. 'Just like Berlin here,' she used to say, and Günther called to mind the triumphal arch with horses on top, as on the postcard. But in Martha's day the city had a different name, the capital was somewhere else, and the monument in the main square was of the person who for Martha was 'our' Tsarina, Catherine II. Everything around her was German: school, the language and the pupils. 'You didn't even have to know Russian, but you breathe a language as you do the land in which you live. Above all,' and at this point Martha's face took on a sly expression, 'if someone teaches you when they are courting you.' The child found it hard to understand the events that his mother was alluding to, for he had never lived in a German colony in Russian territory; he did not know what it meant to speak of 'the days in which there were still Tsars', and he could not understand why his mother lowered her voice when speaking of the young Russian who had been in love with her, an officer or so it was implied, although she seemed to be afraid that her husband, Günther's father, would learn of it. 'Why didn't you marry the Russian officer?' 'My father didn't wish it; we Germans only married one another. One day he asked me to elope with him, but my father got to hear of it. It was my sister that betrayed me. This may have partly been why my father brought our departure forward. Our family was amongst the first to leave the country.' Every time Günther heard the story of the betrayal, he felt a deep hatred for this aunt, his mother's sister, whom he had never known.

What on earth would my mother say if she knew that I was here, Berger wondered, and pushed his way up to the door to see if he could catch a glimpse of Engelstadt, or at any rate of the station. All he could see was a patch of dirty snow between the platforms. He would willingly have sucked a little of that snow, and wouldn't have minded how dirty it was. Berger was thirsty. Ever since the dried herrings had been handed round and he had eaten the head that had been his due, without spitting out anything, he felt that his mouth no longer had any saliva in it and his throat was burning. His cracked lips hurt him. Then it was that Ul'an slipped a pebble into his hand. Berger looked uncomprehendingly at the flat, smooth, pink-veined stone, which seemed to him to be just like any other stone. 'Put it in your mouth, it is from the Amudar'ya. It quenches the thirst.'

Only stones fished out from the bottom of the Amudar'ya have this quality. The Turkmens, who know what thirst means, come once a year from the Caspian Sea to lay in a fresh supply from the

Amudar'ya. But the right stones can only be found on a stretch of river on the border between the Soviet Union and Afghanistan. The caravans stop at Termez in order to buy them, in exchange for salt, and the merchants, in clinching the deal, would say 'stones that combat thirst in return for stones that produce thirst', because the salt too was sold in the form of crystals.

Berger put the pebble in his mouth and began to suck; the overwhelming feeling of thirst really did subside, and his mouth began to produce saliva again. The others looked enviously at him but did not speak and did not ask for anything. Words had dried up, just like the mouths that would have uttered them. Ul'an rummaged in his pocket, gathered two pink stones in his hand, showed them around as if they were pieces of gold and then offered them to Cossu and Lazzaro. They shifted the stone around from one corner of the mouth to the other, and sucked on it, while the other prisoners licked in turn on nails and bolts covered with a thin layer of steam. Thirst was their greatest torment inside the wagon. Berger and Ul'an were to suffer yet more from thirst, for that was just the beginning.

Biagini died during the journey. It was the dysentery that finished him off. In the last few days he could no longer even manage to reach the hole in the middle of the wagon; it was then that he decided to die, and by the time they realised he was already cold. 'What's to be done with him?', Cossu asked. In a little while they'd come and open up the wagon and ask how many deaths there had been. 'Let's hold onto him,' Lazzaro proposed. 'He's not disturbing us and we'll nab his bread.'

They laid him out along the wall and he really was no trouble to them, just as he'd been no trouble when alive, so much so that many had never even noticed him. He was a quiet, gentle man and when he was seated at his table behind piles of papers that had to be checked, no one knew precisely what he was doing and no one took the trouble to ask him. They simply hadn't noticed him, just as they didn't notice that he was dead. But his comrades shared out his ration of bread and were grateful to him.

* * *

When the train arrived at Volks, the prisoners inside the wagons now had enough space to be comfortable and could even sleep, but when they were brought out many could not move their legs and walk. The prison camp was better equipped than the previous one; first of all the prisoners were lined up in front of the disinfection hut.

Berger found it difficult to take off his clothes, which were so encrusted with sweat and dirt that they stuck to his back. The warm, damp air of the baths made them stick even more tightly to his skin. He was already naked when he remembered Di Bella's message sewn into his jacket pocket with wire. He was seized with panic. The boiling water in which his clothes had just been plunged could well ruin the message, and he felt that he could not leave it where it was. His turn was coming up soon, and the warm air, weakness and anxiety brought Berger out in a sweat. He let Cossu go first and took his jacket from the bundle of clothes, unthreaded the wire, found the cartridge case and, after a moment's thought, put it in his mouth. Then he shoved the clothes back into the pile, and hurriedly caught up with Cossu, who in the meantime had advanced a few paces.

Each man was given a bucket of hot water and a square centimetre of soap. It was the kind used by the women in Cologne when they did the washing, but this soap did not produce any suds and turned into lye in your hands. Berger soaped himself and tipped the bucket of water over himself; suddenly a pleasurable sensation overwhelmed him such as he did not remember ever having felt before, and all thanks to a piece of slimy soap and a bucket of water. You need so little to feel good, thought Berger, and he could not even remember what use the luxury of 'normal' life had been to him, and whether it had really been luxury or merely seemed such to him from his present perspective, when the simple fact of being alive was a luxury.

His turn for depilation came. His hair fell onto his shoulders in clumps, and the Russian girls wielded the razor with such skill that his skin was left completely bare. They worked in pairs on each prisoner, and chatted with each other and laughed all the while. They're laughing at me, Berger thought, and the fact of being completely naked in the midst of the little group of girls made him feel ashamed. He felt ashamed to be so thin, and bowed his head when the girl ordered him to, so that the nape of his neck could be shaved too, raised first one arm and then the other, and the halo of hair on the ground around him grew ever larger. Finally a girl, who was blonde and plump, bent down and casually began to shave his pubic hair and in so doing moved his penis aside. And Berger, on seeing it so small and tame in a girl's hands felt more ashamed than ever before in his whole life.

They were lined up again. The worst punishment suffered by a prisoner, Berger thought, was having to wait in line and never knowing until the last minute whether, when your own turn comes, you'll get through unscathed or not. This queue was anyway more worrying than the previous ones, in that for the first time since their capture the prisoners were being asked for their particulars. For this reason the line was moving more slowly than usual and the beginning could not be seen, because it wound into the hut being used as an office, where each man's name, surname, date of birth, rank, regiment and place of residence was being taken down. It seemed that the Russians, after having done nothing else for months but arrange for the dead to be taken away, without being concerned overmuch with the living, wanted all of a sudden to know everything about the latter. They were counting the prisoners, cataloguing them, interrogating them as if they were the repositories of military secrets, and moving them back and forth across the vast chessboard of prison camps scattered over the whole territory of the Soviet Union, according to criteria that few, and certainly not the prisoners, really understood. You could not foretell what the consequences might be of revealing your name and rank held in time of war, and whether concealing it would benefit or harm you. This was a particular dilemma for officers, and therefore for Berger too, since he, like most of the others, had opted to conceal his rank. In the throng of waiting prisoners, almost no one was still wearing epaulettes, emblems or flashes; by now there were only ordinary soldiers. Officers, especially the German ones, had melted away, and the hierarchies had disappeared along with the eagles and the gold braid. The men in the queue, shaved and grown thin through hunger, differed only in height, given that their uniforms, already barely recognisable, so discoloured and worn were they, had long since been exchanged and combined at random. Many soldiers wore a mixture of garbs from all the armies, whether allied or no. Lazzaro, for example – whom Berger could readily observe because he was just in front of him, next to Cossu and Ul'an – had Hungarian leather ankle-boots, Italian Zouave trousers which hung down round his calves, a Russian shirt and a German officer's jacket. Just to round it off, he wore an alpine cap which rendered the whole masquerade still more ridiculous. But there was no one to laugh or to find anything whatsoever to say about that fancy dress, although they may well have envied the leather ankle-boots, wondered how he had got hold of them, and whether they were the fruit of some racket.

Ul'an was still wearing the military jacket they had taken off the dead soldier, at Stalingrad, but now Berger realised more than ever that the uniform meant nothing. As the queue slowly approached the entrance to the wooden hut which was swallowing up those at its head, Berger would now and then tap Ul'an on the shoulder and say softly to him: 'Have you got it?' Ul'an nodded, turned round and repeated in a low voice: 'Andreas Tillmann, Liliengasse 2, Kronberg, artillery.' Berger nodded and tried to calm down.

Ul'an had not forgotten the name which he had borrowed, just as seven months before he had not forgotten the formula which had enabled him to enter the ranks of the Wehrmacht. It was because he had uttered that formula, and because he was now in the midst of soldiers who had fought against Stalin, that he, a Soviet citizen, was now in danger of losing his life. There was no uniform that could protect him, and no name that could hide his origin. He wore it stamped on his face, and while his nose could pass muster, the eyes would fool nobody, and least of all the Soviet soldiers who might perhaps have eyes just like his and would laugh in his face when he came to blurt out his lie. Nonetheless Ul'an went on repeating under his breath, while trying to imitate Berger's accent, 'Andreas Tillmann, Liliengasse 2, Kronberg, artillery', until his turn came. There were five officers seated at the table, with as many interpreters standing behind them. The officer seated in front of Ul'an had grey hair and only one arm, the right one, with which he had just written a note below the previous name. Then he asked, as if reciting a prayer, 'your name?' Ul'an gave name and surname without faltering. 'Address', his interlocutor went on. At that moment the officer raised his eyes and looked Ul'an full in the face. They were narrow eyes, the eyes of an Asiatic, for he was in fact a Kyrghyz. Ul'an lowered his gaze, for the officer was older than he was and it was not seemly to look directly at him. He expected that he would speak to him in Russian, and if he does, Ul'an said to himself, I won't reply, I'll pretend not to understand. A single question from the interpreter would have unmasked the deception and would have got him arrested on the spot. The officer looked down again at the piece of paper, asked 'Which service?', and wrote it all down diligently. Then he gestured to Ul'an to go.

'They will call for me later,' said Ul'an to Berger, and each time a Russian approached he thought, 'Here we go', and cast a terrified glance, which was at the same time a goodbye, at Berger. Even in the night the slightest noise woke him, so sure was he that they would come to find him. Many prisoners were in fact removed under cover of night and never returned to their beds. But no one came looking for Ul'an. Berger, partly as a joke but partly out of extreme wariness, took to calling him Andreas Tillmann. Ul'an would answer to the name and the other prisoners at first looked at him in amazement but then shrugged their shoulders. What did a name matter, and who cared if it was true or not? Even those who answered to their real name had long since ceased to be what they once were. The only true thing about them now was their name. Ul'an on the other hand was the same as before, but had a false name.

In the meantime May had come, but the grass had not had enough time to grow behind the huts and along the path between the camp and the open ground in front of the wood, where the logs to be sawed up were heaped, before it was uprooted, hidden in pockets, and cooked up in the evenings in makeshift pots. Cossu had got hold of a can and used to cook greens soup, as he called it.

'We just need olive oil,' he said, 'and then it'd be perfect.' Lazzaro got him some, although it was not really made of olives.

Lazzaro worked in the kitchen, because he had been classified as too weak for other kinds of work, and the Russian doctor had taken pity on him. As he was cleaning, he came across a tin of sunflower oil in the corner. It was in fact already rancid and no longer fit for cooking, and it should perhaps have been used in some other way, but Lazzaro was convinced that they had forgotten about it and that it was just what the soup needed. One evening, at the end of his shift, he put the tin down just outside the door; Cossu passed by and picked it up later on. The greens soup with the oil in it was a dish fit for a king, Cossu declared as he dipped the dry bread in it, and with every spoonful he said, 'It's so good, so good!', as if he had never eaten anything better.

Lazzaro was sure that it was that bastard of a cook who'd denounced him. They searched the hut and found Cossu's little cooking pot. They made all the prisoners go outside. The Russian captain in overall charge of the prison camp appeared, turned towards Lazzaro and Cossu, who were standing in front of the others, and asked them: 'Why did you steal the oil?' The interpreter translated. 'We were hungry,' Lazzaro replied. The captain looked them up and down with contempt: 'Really?' and addressed the throng of prisoners. 'If any of you are hungry, step forward,' he ordered. No one moved. Lazzaro and Cossu were sentenced to seven days in the bunker, with just bread and water.

The bunker was a dug-out which was half below ground, and there was nothing at all in it. It had a floor of beaten earth, walls of beaten earth and a porthole with a grille and hinges, nailed down so as to let in a little light. Time was the thing that tormented them the most, for in there one lost all sense of its passing. 'Tell me something, Salvatore!' 'What should I tell you? How one makes cheese?' 'Tell me!' And Salvatore would tell him. Lazzaro for his part invented stories, recounted books that he had read and films that he had seen. Cossu listened to him.

On the third day, towards evening, they heard someone knocking very softly on the porthole. A tube appeared in a crack between the hinges. They heard Berger's voice saying: 'Here's some soup. Get underneath it.' Lazzaro understood, squeezed the opening of the tube between his lips, as if it were a tap, and the soup, which was still warm, slid into his mouth.

Once Cossu had got out of the bunker, he could think of nothing else but escape. 'We're all going to croak here,' he said. 'We might as well have a go.' 'Where do you want to go?', Lazzaro asked. 'You can't escape from here. And even if you did, where'd you go?' 'It'd be better to be devoured by the wild animals in the forest than to be devoured by hunger in here.' He could clearly think of nothing else. 'Do you know where we are?', Berger asked him. 'Sardinia's far away from here.' Cossu shrugged: 'Sardinia's far away from everywhere. Rather than croak like a rabbit in a cage I'd prefer to meet my end like a wild boar.' 'They'll chase you like a hare,' Lazzaro warned, but Cossu was unable to turn his mind to anything else: 'If I stay here, before I realise it I'll not even have the strength to stand up. When the war is over, I'll be an invalid.' The others did not really pay any heed or at most, if they were in the mood for joking, would say to him in the evening when they came back from work, 'Salvatore, are you still here?' But Cossu was a stubborn fellow and thought only of flight. He made himself a knife by patiently filing a little metal rod, which he had slipped inside a stick. In the daytime it was hidden in a crack in the floor, in the hut, and then in the evening he secretly filed away at it. One day he hid it in his boot, wrapping the laces tightly round it to mask the metal. He managed to get through the checks and this emboldened him. He worked with his comrades stripping the logs and cutting them up into pieces, all by hand, but that evening he did not return to the camp. Cossu had faith in the forest. Didn't his mother say that he was like a wild boar coming out of a thicket? *Pares unu sirvone essiu da sa tuppa*. A wild boar is not afraid of the forest. He waited until the column had moved some distance away, then he plunged deeper into the trees, followed the stream for a while and headed west.

They got him while it was still pitch dark. He heard the barking of the dogs and the cries of the men, saw the torches and the soldiers drawing ever nearer. The dogs surrounded him; Cossu could see their white teeth in the dark. It was a shooting party and he was the wild boar. He put his hands up and let himself be taken. He did not return to the hut but was transferred to a special prison. A fifteen-year sentence which became ten for good behaviour.

Strange to tell, Cossu was the only one from that little group of Italians in Volks to return home. His mother, when she set eyes on him, ran her hands through her hair, which by now was grey, and was so terrified at seeing him that she could not even bring herself to say to him *pares unu sirvone essiu da sa tuppa*. Later on in the village bar, once their initial curiosity was satisfied, everyone avoided him, for they could see how gloomy and unfriendly he always was. Cossu went back to his sheep. At least in the sheepfold there was no one to ask him questions.

One night, the wind was up and the animals were restless. A fox must be prowling, Cossu thought. He grabbed his rifle and went out of the sheepfold to have a look. The dogs were barking wildly, and the sheep were pressing up against one other. Cossu did the rounds, but did not see anything suspicious. Meanwhile the wind was blowing more strongly and the dogs had not stopped barking. Suddenly the big bitch, a shepherd dog from the Maremma, leapt into the middle of the meadow, as white as a ghost; perhaps she had been badly tied up and had got loose but it seemed to Cossu that she was out to attack him. He saw in the gloom the white ring of her teeth, and her long canines, which were as sharp as knives, and he took aim and fired. The dogs began to bark louder, and Cossu, in a highly agitated state, pointed the barrel of his rifle at them and fired again, until they fell quiet. Then, as if he could no longer stop, he turned towards the fold where the sheep were thronging in terror and fired the whole magazine at them. He went back into the sheepfold, reloaded the rifle in a state of feverish anxiety, as if he feared that he would not manage it in time, and went out again. He reached the pen where the panic-stricken sheep were leaping from side to side and trampling the wounded animals beneath their hooves. Cossu fired until all was still. Then he threw aside the rifle and opened the door of the little room in which every morning he heated up the milk, prepared the cheese and set it up to drip; he went in, took a rope off the wall and headed towards the boundary of the meadow, where the wind was shaking the leaves of the oak trees. The sky was full of bright streaks as if the mistral had carried away the night too soon. Cossu worked with quick precise movements, as though he were following a carefully conceived plan. He looped the rope round a branch of the oak tree, tied it, made a noose, placed his head inside it and finally kicked away the block which had served him as a stool.

27

IT WAS RARE for it to rain on the hills of Kazakhstan. At the beginning of October, however, thick clouds gathered above Karaganda and covered the steppe with a violet light, as far as the mountains which on a clear day stood out in the east. When the rain then fell, in a sudden and heavy downpour, a strange spectacle might be seen in prison camp no. 7099/2, for down the electric cables, along the pylons in the steppe and in the power station just beyond the mine there flashed sparks, like magical stars on a Christmas tree, as if a festoon of lights had been suspended above the steppe. It was a natural firework display which lasted as long as the rain lasted, and even a little longer, because the drops of water dried up immediately. The prisoners watched the spectacle, but did not therefore stop or slow down, maintaining the same very slow, measured pace. With the image of that electrical arabesque still in their pupils, they queued at the entrance to the mine. Rivulets of black mud fanned out in all directions, and at times flowed into huge puddles of stagnant water. Right in front of the gate where the prisoners lined up to be checked, there was a pool which seemed to have been dug out precisely to add one further affliction on those rare days when the rain fell on the hills of Kazakhstan.

Berger could feel his damp trousers clinging to his legs. This unpleasant sensation would be with him the whole day long. It was lucky that the tunnel was dry and that they did not have to stand with their feet in the water, as was the case in other mines. Ul'an had already put a helmet on his head and had grabbed an oil lamp; Berger did the same and went down the corridor of beaten earth. It was midday and their gang was on the second shift. They would come up to the surface again for the four o'clock break, when it was already dark outside, and they'd only get back to the huts at eight. That'd be eight hours of darkness and dust.

The gang arrived at the point they had reached the day before, where the corridor curved and ended abruptly at an apparently untouched wall. In fact the ground around them was covered in already partly piled up coal, ready to be loaded up. That day Berger and Ul'an had been deputed to shovel; the coal was tipped onto a conveyor belt which took it to the entrance of the main corridor, and loaded into wagons which another member of the gang had to count. Other prisoners would push the wagons up to the surface, where they would be emptied. The slag heaps, the mine scaffolding, the electricity pylons and the watchtowers were the highest points around camp 7099/2 in Karaganda; even the hills which rose in the south seemed lower, while the height and distance of the mountain chain to the east were impossible to guess, because depending on the wind and the light it seemed either within grasp or unreachable. Berger and Ul'an only saw the mountains during their short journey from the prison camp to the mine, or when it was their turn to unload the wagon and they had to climb up on the wooden scaffolding. Once the cloud of coal dust had dissolved in a veil darkening the air, the entire steppe was revealed to their reddened eyes. The camp in the middle of it, with its triple enclosure of palisades, barbed wire and lines of bunkers, was so isolated that it made you think that enclosure and sentries served to ward off dangers coming from outside, for standing on the scaffolding it seemed wholly absurd to fear threats from inside.

Once Berger and Ul'an saw bushes rolling on the distant horizon, like mill wheels driven by the wind. Berger was amazed. 'It's the wind that makes the bushes run,' said Ul'an. 'We call them *kuraj*. Look, it's driving them towards the south-east. That's the direction we'll take.' Berger looked at him without fully understanding, and Ul'an explained: 'The village of yurts on the Amu-dar'ya lies south-east of here. Once the season for leaving is upon us, we'll be off.' He said it quite naturally, as if they were free to leave whenever they wished, as if the triple enclosure and watch-towers did not exist, as if the steppe, which unfolded before them in all its immensity, was but a meadow. It was as though they too were *kuraj*, and simply had to expose themselves to the wind. But Ul'an was quite serious, and had hatched his plans. 'I'm at home here,' he said, as if that explained everything. Ul'an spoke with great confidence, settled on dates and on places, as if he had an appointment on the steppe or with the steppe, in the spring.

Berger looked at his flayed hands, felt the damp in his bones and reflected that the winter had not really set in yet. How were they to hold out for all those months? 'Do as the grass on the steppe does. When the wind passes over us, we must bend and rise up again when it has gone. Don't resist it, bend before it, until the season for leaving comes. Anyone who fails to bend is torn out by the roots, like the *kuraj*, and the wind drags him where it likes. The *kuraj* never returns to the place it was torn from, but we, you and I, will return. We will not let ourselves be dragged hither and thither. The winter is but a season, and the others come after it.'

They hauled the empty wagon back into the tunnel and Berger felt the pain in his knees and the damp soaking deep into him. Could one really get used to this? 'One gets used to everything,' Ul'an said. But his face too grew thinner by the day, and his shoulders more stooped. 'I am used to the steppe,' he said as if justifying himself, 'but the steppe above ground, not the one below.'

Yet it was indeed below the steppe that they went during the day and also at night, depending upon the shift, and they would cover the stretch of road between the camp and the mine at four in the morning, at midday or at eight in the evening. The night shift was not in fact the worst. Beneath the steppe it was always night, and it was only when they went outside to push the wagons that they realised that it was dark outside too. Sometimes they chanced to leave the tunnel just when the sun was rising above the steppe; then they would race to see if they could get up onto the scaffolding before the sun rose in the sky.

One morning in December Berger looked to the east and saw a double sun. He looked again, and found that he was not mistaken. There were two red, superimposed circles just touching the horizon. Ul'an too was looking intently and in silence. 'A double sun, what does it mean, Ul'an?' 'It means a snowstorm is on the way.' The Russians called it *buràn*. No sooner was it known that a snowstorm was approaching than word spread around the mine; the prisoners whispered '*buràn*, *buràn*' to one another and, when they had got back to the surface, could not take their eyes off the sky. The *buràn*, when it came, took over the steppe and everything else, so that the sun, the camp and even the slag heaps were swallowed up by the whirlwind of snow. Indeed, anyone caught below ground might not be able to get out again.

Ul'an was not the only one who had a method for resisting. Many of the prisoners seemed to have an innate instinct for getting by, others strove to learn it, and still others forged one for the purpose, adapting it to suit themselves or imitating the others, but there was no one who was entirely lacking in such a resource. Often the method used was collective, as in the matter of evading the 'quota'.

The daily quota for each gang was sixty wagon loads of coal, which amounted to a ton of coal per wagon and two tons of coal per head. The men had to work hard, one scooping up the coal with a shovel, another with a spade, and this was the toughest work of all, because one worked bent double in the lowest shafts, and yet another pushing the wagons. A gang leader allotted the jobs and decided the shifts. The man in charge of Berger and Ul'an's gang was a German by the name of Fleischhacker, who was from Bremen, and had been a captain at Stalingrad, but he'd torn his stripes off his uniform before being taken prisoner. At the front, when the men had seemed reluctant to volunteer for a *Himmelfahrtskommando*, in other words, a military mission that took you directly to the beyond, he began to holler: 'You're just out to save your skins.' He shouted so loudly than he was known even to the Russians who, punning on his name, kept on yelling through their megaphones: 'Fleischhacker, Fleischhacker, we're going to make mincemeat of you!' This was when they were still on the Don and the enemy lines were near. At Stalingrad Captain Fleischhacker had readily sent his men off in *Himmelfahrtskommandos* of every kind. At Karaganda he no longer had his officer's stripes, but they still called him captain and he still shouted, at the prisoners, needless to say, because he had formed close friendships with the Russians, and especially with the *natschalik*, the officer in command of the camp. It was not uncommon to come across them of an evening arm in arm and completely plastered. There were days when the commandant stank of vodka even in the morning, and then tasks were allotted to the men at random, without regard for the regular shifts. The unlucky ones would find themselves having to scoop up coal with a spade for an extra day, while the more fortunate might go out with the wagons for a further, unscheduled round. But there were also occasions when the gang took advantage of the captain's drunkenness to lighten their load. One day Ul'an was responsible for counting the wagons. He had barely finished writing the number thirty in chalk when Mirlach, whose job it was to transport the coal outside, said to him: 'Write thirty-five!' Ul'an looked at him in astonishment. At the exit there was a perforated blackboard, and the girl stationed there would move the stick into the appropriate hole each time that five more wagons had gone through. The stick was fixed at twenty-five, as Ul'an knew perfectly well. But Mirlach had seen how tipsy the girl was and how the captain was all over her, and how he was playing with the plaits that hung down over her chest, and as soon as he got outside he moved the stick on to thirty. As the wagons went through, the girl reluctantly freed herself from the captain's embrace and moved the marker on to thirty-five. That evening the gang was granted an extra ration of soup for each man as a reward for exceeding the 'quota'.

There was never enough food. Inside the threefold circle of barbed wire, in the earthen bunkers grouped within camp 7099/2, at Karaganda, the prisoners used to think about food, to talk about it, to dream up strategies for getting hold of it, and to compose the most bizarre and fantastical cook books. Berger and Ul'an's bunker was divided about halfway across by an invisible line, with Germans on the right of it and Italians on the left. On both sides of the boundary bed-bugs fell from the ceiling with the same frequency, so that Italians and Germans alike called it 'rain', but the culinary barrier was rigid. On the left of the entrance they spoke of shin of pork with its skin crisped up with beer, and in imaginary ovens they cooked plum tarts and *Bienenstich* covered with a lattice of almonds, just as their mothers had done in Upper Bavaria or in the Palatinate. On the right-hand side they prepared *agnolotti* filled with meat and flavoured with gravy, or lamb stuffed with cloves, and put rich timbales in the oven. But on both the right and the left of the boundary the cooking remained entirely imaginary. Lazzaro was the only one who sought to put into practice the fantastical gastronomic fantasies prompted by hunger, in order to fill not only the brain but the stomach also, although the results were much inferior to the recipe.

Chance had brought Lazzaro, along with Berger and Ul'an, to Karaganda, for like them he had survived the train journey in those wagons that the sun had turned into ovens. Unlike the other two, however, Lazzaro had been classified as suffering from dystrophy in the third degree, and therefore as unfit to work. 'It's a damned nuisance,' commented Lazzaro, who had become all but transparent in the course of those months and more than ever merited the nickname 'tiddler'. 'So I'm entitled to a smaller ration than you and will end up below ground before you.' But Lazzaro was too stubborn to let himself be dispatched to the beyond without putting up a fight.

The idea of boiled crow came to him one afternoon as he did his stint peeling potatoes and observed through the kitchen door a flock of crows that were bustling about like chickens on the refuse heap. The more he looked at them the more he was persuaded that they must be as fat and, indeed, as tasty as chickens. He began to study their behaviour, and to note how they hurled themselves at the refuse, how they rummaged with their beaks, and how the stronger chased away the weaker, who fluttered away and then returned straightaway to the same place. 'You can't eat crows,' said Ul'an. 'You can't catch crows,' said Berger in turn. But

Lazzaro had already worked out how to do it, for hanging on the wall of the kitchen was a heavy plywood table which had been used for heavens knows what and still had from its previous use a series of holes along its edges. Lazzaro used it as a drawbridge, which he tied with a rope and set up alongside the pile of rubbish. When the crows returned to their meal, Lazzaro slackened the rope and the table came down with a thud. There was a stampede of birds, a terrified croaking, and a flurry of feathers in the air. Under the table there lay a squashed crow, just the one, but Lazzaro was triumphant. He plucked it, cleaned it and began to cook it in the 'pressure cooker' he had built with some cans; every now and then he tested the flesh with a fork and tried it, but the crow showed no signs of boiling. 'It's like cooking a stone,' said Ul'an, 'you can't eat crows.' Lazzaro ate it all the same. He tore off the flesh with his teeth, rolled his eyes and looked just like one of those terrifying devils who devour the damned in medieval frescoes.

It was Lazzaro who said 'Once upon a time we used to talk about girls . . .' The others looked at him, disconcerted. 'Girls? We no longer even know how they're made!' He had no difficulty remembering his last girl, whom he'd known at Stalingrad. She was working in one of the Allied armies' brothels, in a little room so small it could barely hold a cot, divided from the next one by a simple cardboard screen covered with cloth. When Lazzaro went in, he marvelled at the sight of that pink girl with her babyish blue eyes. She seemed like a *babiuska*, who, as she emerged from ever smaller containers, had from time to time shed some garment until she ended up with none at all. Yet she still preserved her initial bewilderment, as if she had been caught naked in her child's bed and transported by magic or by force to that place of ill-repute. The cot really did look too small to hold her: her breasts alone seemed about to overflow it on either side. It can readily be imagined what happened when you added a soldier, not all of whom were as light as Lazzaro was. As for him, the girl laughed and said that she didn't even realise he was on top of her. Lazzaro himself felt as if he were reclining on cushions of the softest pink velvet. In the end he got a taste for it and looked her up as often as he could. She was called Nadezhda and Lazzaro, who by then had already learnt a little Russian, said to her, punning on her name, 'You are my rose-coloured hope', and Nadezhda smiled with her wretched pink lips and blew a blonde curl away from her mouth. She seemed to have come straight out of a Rubens or a Tintoretto, but she was not a courtesan. Just a few months before she had been working with the girls in the kolkhoz, but while the others had been taken away to Germany, she, when asked if she preferred working in that way, said that she did. Now she worked in her wretched child's bed rather than in a German factory and became fatter each day by dint of not moving around, but she managed to slip something to brothers and sisters waiting for her at home. She preserved her air of innocent bewilderment, which the Germans found *entzückend*, and which their allies did not despise either. Before returning to the front, Lazzaro presented her with a medallion of the Virgin Mary. Nadezhda kissed it fervently and hung it round her neck. The small oval of metal, once slipped into the deep valley between her breasts, gave her still more the abashed air of a virgin surprised in her bed by wanton eyes.

Christmas Eve was a day like any other, in Karaganda. Lazzaro leapt down from his bunk and said: 'You'll see, they'll give us star dust to eat today!' This was what the prisoners called the supplement they were given every now and then, for the vitamins, or so it was said. It was pulp from soya, after the oil had been extracted, a kind of hard brown paste which had to be cooked for a long time to be chewed at all and which left one's mouth feeling dry. 'Today it'll be comet dust!', added Lazzaro, whose wit had not deserted him, even in the camp. 'Baby Jesus might at least bring me a little tobacco dust!', he ended up saying. For all their jesting, none of them found the prospect of Christmas down the mine easy to bear.

On Christmas night Berger and Ul'an's gang were on the third shift. They had been granted permission to hold a brief party, though without leaving the mine. Towards midnight they all gathered near to the end of the tunnel, where there was a temporary prop, a wooden pole with hinges nailed into it, which stuck out like the branches of a withered and undecorated Christmas tree. The men unhooked the lamps from the hooks along the corridor and hung them on the pole in the shape of a pyramid. When all around was dark and in the middle there was just the light coming from what to them was a Christmas tree, Werner Huber, who had been a choirmaster, sang 'Silent Night' in a loud voice, conducting the choir with his thin hands, just as he used to do in the apse of Ratisbon Cathedral. When he raised his hands, the men sang the first verse at the top of their voices. When, however, the choirmaster intoned the second verse, the voices following him had begun to waver and not all of them got to the end. Although in the dark they could not be seen, the only man with dry eyes was Ul'an.

Werner Huber possessed a remarkable musical talent. At home, in his room behind the cathedral, he used to play piano, flute and 'cello, and he sang too, with a voice that seemed not to come from him, for it was robust and he was tiny. When he was not playing, you would hardly notice him at all, since he was often flustered and a slave to a domineering wife. Yet his choir represented his self multiplied by the voices which, at a sign from his nervous hands, would rise or fall, bend or sing out in broad and solemn passages. Huber it was who had composed the music to '*gute Nacht, mein liebes Mädchen*', a song that all the prisoners in the camp learnt. Some were content just to whistle the tune, while others, if they were German, sang all four verses right through. No one knew who had written the words, whether it was a collective composition or whether among the prisoners there was a poet going incognito. The lines were grouped in couplets and between one verse and the next came the refrain with its haunting *gute Nacht*. Berger tried to transcribe the song, once he was home, but he could not get past the first verse, whether because he had forgotten what followed, or because remembering it caused him embarrassment or pain. The opening could still be found among his papers: *Abends wenn der Mond am Himmel steht, / mein Mädel gern mit mir spazieren geht, / durch die Wälder uns'rer schönen Heimat.* In the evening when the moon sails high in the heavens / I go walking with my girl / in the woods by my beautiful home town. In

Karaganda they just had the moon, which certainly inspired the choirmaster of Ratisbon's music and the unknown poet's words. As for the rest, the home town, the girl and the woods, only the really lucky would get to see them again.

28

THOMAS ARBINGER ALWAYS needed paper but, unlike the other prisoners, he did not use it for roll-ups, because he did not smoke, but to write on. He had in fact decided to learn Russian and since you need to know the words to speak a language, and the more of them you know the better you speak it, in order to be sure of not overlooking any Arbinger had decided to learn them all. All 9,424 words in the 'brand new Russian-German dictionary', a pocket edition and the only one available in the cultural centre of camp 7099/2. Even as a prisoner Arbinger was still as precise and meticulous as he had been when working as a clerk in the Huber furrier's shop in Munich. Arbinger had nothing directly to do with the furs that Mr Huber showed to the ladies and their husbands, and stroked, before helping his clients to slip them on. His work simply consisted of transcribing prices in the bound cash register, the spotless pages of which he would first cover with blotting paper and then smooth out with his hand, almost as though they were beaver hides. For years Arbinger had stroked the pages of cash registers filled with figures and admired the totals, more for their aesthetic perfection than for the round sums they represented, of which he, Arbinger received only the tiniest part. Yet he was happy all the same and every morning, when he took off his loden coat and put on oversleeves to protect his shirt, he felt as if he were slipping into one of the furs that he would never have been able to give to his wife. Arbinger was an aesthete, and he would never have resigned himself to recording the profit and loss on potatoes or barrels of beer because they were indubitably less refined products than those sold in the Huber department store, in the Weinstrasse, in Munich. Precisely because he was an aesthete and furthermore an accountant, Arbinger was particularly vexed by the disorder, unpredictability and lack of clarity in war. As a good accountant, he looked for debits on the one side and credits on the other, in straight columns ending in the reckoning at the foot of the page, but he soon realised that all the display of order and discipline served only as a smokescreen and that behind a semblance of perfectionism there was really no long-term plan. 'The accounting of the war will be done after the event,' he used to say, 'and then we'll be in the red, with investments such-and-such, soldiers such-and-such, losses such-and-such and deaths such-and-such. And here's your declaration of bankruptcy.' The war was not run by businessmen, as was proven by the prisoners in Karaganda camp, because they were clearly added to the figures on the right-hand side, in the losses column.

Arbinger had decided to learn Russian because a bi-lingual dictionary was the nearest thing to an accounts book that there was to hand, with the difference that the two columns side by side represented equivalences. Copying out the Cyrillic characters in block letters, since he knew no other script, gave him huge satisfaction, and made him feel like a monk and scribe tackling an ancient text. The size of the Russian-German dictionary held no fears for Arbinger, who was a born planner, and used to far more complicated calculations. Reckoning so many words per page, and so many pages, and calculating a period of imprisonment of three hundred and sixty-five days meant twenty-five point eight words a day to transcribe and to learn by heart. The problem lay not so much in writing down and learning the words, for Arbinger was endowed with an excellent memory and could reel off debits and credits with only occasional errors after the decimal point, but in finding enough paper. This was why Arbinger, though he wrote like a miniaturist, always needed paper, and white paper of course, not paper which had already been written on. This, then, was how Berger set about getting hold of some for him.

Berger was detailed to the library in the cultural centre. He was responsible for books and newspapers, and he it was who handed out copies to the handful of readers who had requested them, who re-shelved them, and who would be held responsible if any were missing. He had volunteered for the work because he felt that he ought to do something for his head apart from putting a helmet on it, for fear that working in the mine might cloud his brain too. Who knows, he would say to himself, it might be of use to him in the future.

Ever since he had got it into his head to learn Russian, Arbinger had become a habitué of the cultural centre. Berger had watched him while he was copying out the words of the dictionary onto the white edges cut from *L'Alba*, a newspaper which he used to buy from the Italian prisoners and which he preferred to the *Freies Deutschland* because the white margins were wider. They were both newspapers produced by exiles and distributed for free among the prisoners, but the latter, of course, charged for them, even if they were only reselling the margin. Berger, when he saw the meticulous fashion in which Arbinger was writing, had pity on him. The library had around three hundred books, including the standard texts of Marxism-Leninism, together with various classics, Russian and otherwise, which took up a number of shelves, and which might perhaps be dusted once a year but which otherwise were left to turn yellow in peace. The books were bound in red and blue cloth covers, and were produced in the pre-war style, when paper was still in plentiful supply. Indeed, the publishers had often been lavish and in many volumes there were two blank pages before the real start of the book. What was the use of those pages on which nothing was written? They were an unimaginable luxury for prisoners who had to write on the margins of newspapers. Berger pondered for a while. His natural respect for books made him loath to mistreat them in any way, even by tearing out a blank page, but Arbinger's despair at seeing letters smudge as soon as they were written on cheap and shoddy paper from *L'Alba* persuaded him to put into action a plan which had real commercial advantages too. Berger would supply paper in return for tobacco, for which Arbinger had no use. Berger set to with a razor-blade and cut out the pages at the beginning and end of the books, then folded them several times so as to make little notebooks about the size of a prayerbook.

Arbinger, however, needed ink too, and this was supplied to him by Ul'an, who got it from a Kazakh girl, with whom he had made friends, and it came from pieces of indelible pencil. Arbinger bought them from him, dissolved them in a little water and dipped a filed nail into it as if it were a nib. With these tools he copied out the Russian-German dictionary, twenty-three point four words a day on average, thirty-five on holidays, twenty on days when he was on the night shift, twenty-five when he was on the early morning shift and emerged at midday, with the whole afternoon stretching out before him in which to write. As soon as he had seen to his other commitments – working as a barber, mending clothes or making exchanges with the other prisoners – Arbinger took refuge in the library, where Berger would set out the dictionary on the table ready for him.

'Which word have you got to?', his comrades asked when he returned to the hut. *Buch*, Arbinger would reply, or *Danke*. He made good progress, kept up with his schedule and did not waste time. Then they'd ask him: 'What's the last word?' 'You'll find that it's "peace", and then we'll all be able to go back home.'

Arbinger wasn't entirely sure himself quite where such optimism sprang from, but the fact was that he too began to believe in the end-point that he had set himself, as if 'peace' were a magical word and as though simply uttering it would make it come true. However, when he got to the *f* of *Frieden*, peace was not even on the horizon. His comrades laughed: 'You started at the wrong end. What's "peace" in Russian?' '*Mir*', Arbinger answered promptly, for he prided himself on his ability to pronounce the words. 'Do you see?', Mirlach pointed out to him, 'it begins with *m*. If you had begun with Russian, instead of German, you'd have realised that peace in Russian comes after peace in German. It also comes after *Krieg*, or war, as is only logical. You've got the words the wrong way round, and so we'll have to wait a little longer.' Mirlach was right, peace was a long time coming and when at last it did arrive, they did not send them home straightaway, so perhaps no one really trusted that word.

Arbinger reached *z* and peace was not on the cards at all; he had time to transcribe the whole dictionary from Russian into German, and to repeat the whole exercise, one word at a time. In the meantime, the steppe had turned brown, then white, and then green and yellow again, and Arbinger's supplies of paper and of ink had long since dried up. He therefore amused himself by running through the words again so as not to forget them, but he was not as disciplined as he had once been. Sometimes his mind even wandered. When he said the word *Garten*, for example, although he murmured *sad*, *sad* to himself, he could not imagine a garden in Russian but continued to think of what he had left on the outskirts of Munich, where, before he had been called up, he had spent his happiest hours. That was the month when he would usually check to see if the snowdrops were coming through, and every day he would count the crocus corollae that had already germinated, as if he were holding a roll-call. Then it was the turn of the tulips, then the dahlias, and in the summer there was the corner with the giant strawberries as big as plums. At the beginning, when he had first had the garden, his wife used to help him, but then she had declared that all that counting and measuring, even the height of the grass, as if there were a law, can you imagine, covering that, got on her nerves and she took to staying inside the house. When all was said and done, Arbinger was happy with the situation; he had the garden to himself and could amuse himself counting, measuring and checking his flowers. Even in Karaganda he often thought about it. Goodness knows if his wife had thought to pick the gooseberries in time, or if she had made a batch of marmalade in the right way. He did not know that his wife had already planted potatoes there the previous year, that she had put tobacco in the strawberry patch, and now sold it to the neighbours, who had no land to cultivate except their window-sills. Arbinger never dreamed that for the last year or so, when the weather was fine, his wife had gone every day to his allotment to check the seedlings, to count them to make sure that none were missing, and that on some July nights, when the beans were almost ripe and the courgettes were fat, she'd been so afraid of her vegetables being stolen that she had slept in the potting-shed. Arbinger knew none of all this, and his garden was so far from camp 7099/2 at Karaganda that he found it difficult even to recall that there was a home front too.

* * *

Arbinger really was the only one to use paper to write on. The other prisoners, without exception, used it just for cigarettes. 'What's the use of paper?', they would ask, rolling what they called 'a national' with a scrap from *L'Alba*. 'To write on,' Lazzaro replied. 'And what's the use of paper that's written on?', they asked again. 'To read, of course.' 'And once it's been read?' Lazzaro lit his cigarette cupping it with his hand, as if a great wind blew through the hut and threatened to blow it out, a necessary precaution this, because no one could afford to waste a match. 'To smoke,' Lazzaro replied, 'but if we insist on smoking Robotti's editorials in the presence of Bellotti, sooner or later he'll denounce us and then there'll be no more cigarettes, my friends!'

Robotti was the editor of *L'Alba* and Bellotti the political exile whose job it was to look after the little group of Italians who happened to be in Karaganda. He was a little set in his ways, the prisoners said, but they let him have his say.

'Paper is patient', Lazzaro said expelling a little cloud of smoke, 'for it never complains about what is written on it.'

Bellotti, too, was patient with those Italians who just didn't get it, and took their side when the Russians criticised them: 'After twenty years of fascism, how do you expect them to think rationally? What do you expect them to understand?' Yet the Italians were forever being rebuked: 'Why have you come to wage war on Russia? What did the Russians ever do to you? Did they occupy your country, invade your fields or grab your women?' Bellotti was a Venetian and, although he had been out of Italy for many years, he had not lost his fine accent, so much so that, according to Lazzaro, from his way of speaking and moving you'd take him for a Harlequin. Out of prudence the prisoners answered: 'We went to Russia because they sent us there.' 'What are you, sheep, that you just go where you're sent? Why didn't you desert?' 'If we hadn't gone, they'd have put us up against a wall,' Lazzaro replied, speaking for all of them. 'And who exactly was putting you up against a wall?' 'Who? Military police, police, the army. . . .' 'And who gives orders to the military police, the policemen, the army?' 'The Duce,' said Lazzaro, who had got Bellotti's drift and didn't want to needle him too much. 'And who put the Duce up to it?' asked Bellotti, who showed no sign of relenting. Lazzaro, to put an end to it, then said: 'In any case, it's nothing to do with us.'

Answers of this sort made Bellotti go red in the face, look as if he were about to explode, but then conclude: 'It's just as well that you're in here!'

Behind Bellotti's back the prisoners would say the crudest things, even though at bottom they all believed him to be a decent sort and knew that he took their side against the Russians. One day, however, they came within a whisker of making him really lose his rag, when a prank very nearly ended in tragedy.

It was a Sunday in mid-April, and the sun had clearly sent winter on its way. The Italian prisoners were all in a good humour, had just had their turn in the baths and felt as good as new. 'If this was the sea, it'd be like the riviera!', Lazzaro said cheerfully. At that moment he caught sight of Casanova. Ever since he had been taken prisoner, Vittorio Casanova seemed to have been struck dumb. No one knew what he was thinking about or if he was thinking at all, or even if he was capable of understanding what others were saying. He did what he was told and that was it. Now Casanova was standing out in the yard, in the sun, at attention and with a broom held stiffly in his left hand. When Lazzaro saw him, he burst out laughing and said: 'At ease!' Casanova obeyed without batting an eyelid. 'Forward march!', Lazzaro yelled and Casanova began to march with the goose-step, holding the broom to his shoulder as if it were a musket. Everyone in the courtyard stopped to watch, Italians, Russians, Germans and Romanians alike, they all stood there laughing as Vittorio Casanova went up and down with the broom on his shoulder. Then the Italians, just to take the piss, began to march behind him as if they were parading in front of the podestà, and pretended to have rifles against their shoulders. It was Lazzaro who struck up '*Faccetta nera*', and the others joined in. '*Faccetta nera, bella abissina*,' the Italians sang at the tops of their voices, marching up and down the camp courtyard in front of an audience bent double with laughter and applauding their every step. 'Wait and hope that the time is soon approaching . . .'. The yard was bathed in sunshine; outside of the triple enclosure the steppe was like a green sea and the prisoners were like drunken sailors. Then Bellotti emerged, and made them stop. 'Wretches,' he screamed, 'are you out of your minds? If the Russians realise what you are singing, they'll send you to a forced labour camp!' They scattered in the twinkling of an eye, and Vittorio Casanova was left on his own in the courtyard, bemused by the empty space which had suddenly cleared around him, and with the broom still on his shoulder.

The following day he disappeared. Some said it was Bellotti who had him sent away, while others suspected the commandant of the camp: word of the episode must have got back to him and he'd picked on the weakest, as usual.

The commandant of the camp had a Russian name which was exceptionally difficult to pronounce, and none of the prisoners even tried to remember it, since there was never any need to call him by his name. If they wanted to name him, all they had to do was to call him 'iron Ivan', which was their nickname for him. He had been invalided out after a grenade had blown his leg clean off and had replaced the missing limb with a wooden one. The epithet 'iron' did not refer to the pretend leg but to his third limb, an iron baton which he used both as a prop for his legs and as an extension for his arms. Despite being an invalid, Ivan was often on the move, and at times he might be seen even in the morning striding across the yard, like Captain Ahab on the bridge of his ship. Ivan had various things in common with that more famous character for, like Ahab, the dull sound of his wooden prosthesis on the hard ground warned of his approach, and like him he had a permanently scowling expression, as if he had it in for the whole world. Unlike Ahab, however, he did not have whales to pursue across the oceans, and iron Ivan therefore avenged himself on those who, like him, sailed over the more limited surface of the camp, and whom he held to blame for his misfortune. No sooner did he get wind of the tiniest hint of an infraction than he would whirl the iron baton around as if it were a golf club. If that baton had actually struck all those who were threatened by it, there would probably have been no one left to work in the mines. But the prisoners had healthy legs.

Iron Ivan could not reach his victims with his spear, and therefore harpooned them with punishments, which never failed. Days in prison or additional hours of work rained down on the poor unfortunates, many of whom were led to wonder whether the blows from the baton might have been less painful.

It was probably iron Ivan who had Casanova sent away because, even though he was no trouble to anyone and did his share of work, marching in a prison camp yard with a broom on one's shoulder was assuredly against regulations. For their part, the prisoners who had marched behind him were so grateful to have got away with it that they failed even to feel any pity for the poor wretch. People said that he ended up in the special lazar-house for the mentally ill, and never mentioned him again. Vittorio Casanova disappeared from Karaganda much as he had first arrived there, without so much as a word.

29

EVERY TIME THEY left the tunnel to empty the coal out of the wagon, Ul'an would look very carefully at the terrain around the mine, as if he were trying to imprint every bush on his mind. 'What are you looking at, Ul'an?,' Berger asked him. 'I'm studying the route we'll take,' Ul'an answered, and looked southwards, where the now green hills rose languorously above the steppe. Behind the hills flowed the Scerubaj-Nura, which appeared suddenly further to the right, like a viper rearing up from the sand with its head pointing straight ahead, and went and joined the Nura. From that quarter, on a clear day, something blue could be seen: it was the point at which the river was imprisoned by a lock and gave rise to an oblong lake. Gazing out from the scaffolding in summer, the lake seemed like a mirage. To the right of the mine, where the karagàn bushes, the acacias which had given Karaganda its name, were dense and yellow, the railway, a black ribbon unreeling across the plain, could clearly be seen. Twice a week, at dawn, a goods train went along the tracks heading south; that same day, in the evening, a passenger train went south, while the same number of trains came from the opposite direction, on alternate days. Neither Ul'an nor Berger knew exactly where the trains which went south were headed. 'They'll go left,' Ul'an said, 'trains go where the rivers are.' The rivers lay to the east, where the mountains rose up and where, behind the hills, Lake Balkhash was, whereas on the other side there was nothing but desert. Sometimes, when they were unloading the wagons at daybreak, they chanced to hear a whistle and to see the lights of a locomotive, a fleeting vision which swiftly faded. 'That's the train we'll take,' Ul'an then said. Berger nodded, and both of them spoke as if it were a sure thing, and they had their tickets in their pockets. Ul'an had quickly begun to work out a strategy. While the other prisoners' priority was to resist what would be a lengthy bout of imprisonment, Ul'an's plans were designed to shorten its duration, and to resist in order to escape.

The girl whose task it was move the stick in the relevant hole for each gang's wagons was fed up. Captain Fleischhacker was all over her when he was drunk, but when he was sober he looked down on her, because he despised all women, especially if they had Asiatic features. Ul'an on the other hand smiled at her whenever he came in or went out of the tunnel and sometimes gave her some tobacco. Ul'an spoke a little Kazakh and a little Russian and they understood one another. She was called Gulnar Iskatova, lived in the village on the other side of the railway and with her sisters looked after the cows in the kolkhoz. In summer they would take them to graze on the Scerubaj-Nura, beside the lake, but in winter there was not much to do, which is why they had sent her to work in the mine. Her family, however, came from Balkhash. Her father had been transferred to Karaganda when they had built it, ten years before. The city was in fact younger than she was, for she was about to turn seventeen. 'It is the youngest city in the world,' Gulnar said, and added, as if to apologise for its youth, 'all the cities are young here, for once upon a time there was just steppe, then the Russians built a prison on the steppe and turned it into a city.' She liked to really explain things, Gulnar did. Ul'an had no difficulty believing that cities were born from prisons. Camp 7099/2 already resembled a city of prisoners. 'The same was true of Balkhash. Before the Russians built it, there was no city there, but just nomads who pitched their yurts around it. My grandfather was one of them. They had many cattle, far more than the kolkhoz has today.' Where did her grandfather live? Had Gulnar ever been there? 'My grandfather used to pitch his yurt close to Balkhash, sometimes to the right and sometimes to the left of the lake.' When the Russians came, they told him that he'd have to give up moving around with his cattle and that he'd have to build himself a house. But my grandfather just couldn't stay in a house, so he pitched his yurt in the place allocated to him and went on living there until he died.' And when had Gulnar's grandfather died? 'He died a year ago and then the whole family, I mean my sisters and my younger brother, because the two older ones are away at the war, we all went away. That's to say, not all of us, no, my sister-in-law did not come because she was expecting a baby, and her mother didn't come either, because she had to attend the birth, but the rest of us went to Balkhash to bury my grandfather.' And how had they got there? 'By train of course!' Gulnar laughed. 'Did you think we went there by camel?' She had small, white teeth and looked pretty when she laughed. 'We got onto the train for Balkhash, the one that leaves in the evening and arrives the following evening, and we took up very nearly the whole train.' Did the trains go as far as Balkhash then? The girl pondered for a while. 'I think they probably do', she said, 'because the line ends at Balkhash. Unless they go on to Dzhezkazgan'.

Dzherkezgan. This was the first time Ul'an had heard the name. And where's Dzherkezgan? The girl looked at him with a schoolteacherly air: 'You don't know much,' she said. 'It's after the junction, on the right.' Ul'an persisted: 'Which trains go to Dzherkezgan, and which to Balkhash?' The girl shrugged her shoulders. 'And where do the two lines divide?' 'I know that: at Zarik station, which is not far from here.' And what's Balkhash like? 'There's a lake which is so big it's like a sea, with boats on it, but only little ones because it's not very deep. My grandmother still lives close to its banks; even after my grandfather's death she did not want to leave her yurt and go and live with her daughter-in-law. They leave her in peace because she's old and stubborn, and her yurt is the only one left in Balkhash.' 'And what would happen if I went there and took her your greetings?' The girl looked suspiciously at him: 'You can't go there because you are locked up in here, and if you escaped they'd catch you straightaway and send you to a special prison.' 'That was just a manner of speaking,' said Ul'an, correcting himself. 'But if I were to go there, what'd your grandmother say?' 'My grandmother would offer you tea and *kumiss*,' answered Gulnar, laughing. 'My grandmother would not look askance at anyone. Whoever enters her yurt is her guest.'

This conversation did not happen all at once but over the whole winter, and piece by piece Ul'an collected the information he wanted. He failed, however, to learn anything further about Dzherkezgan and about the trains that went there. Which of the trains they used to hear passing in the morning, and which of those they sometimes managed to see in the evening went to Dzherkezgan, and which to Balkhash? The junction after Zarik station, which settled the fate of the trains, with some plunging ever deeper into the steppe, until they reached the mines of Dzherkezgan, and others going east, towards the hills and the lake, as far as Balkhash, where the line ended, was therefore still the key to their plans of escape. Ul'an gave tobacco and received in return information and sometimes a clove of garlic or an onion which Gulnar, acting all mysterious, produced from the pocket of her smock and Ul'an hid between his legs. In the evening he and Berger would rub the garlic or onion on dry bread, and in low voices, crying, they would finalise their plans. Yet no matter how much onion they applied to their bread, they could not untie the knot of Zarik.

On the evening of 2nd May, Berger and Ul'an entered the mine and took with them their ration of bread and a clove of garlic each. They had decided to try their luck, given that all the circumstances seemed to be favourable. The sentries had not yet slept off the previous night, there was a new moon and besides it was a Tuesday. Furthermore, the morning after, at dawn, the southbound goods train would be passing through. Berger and Ul'an were on the shift with the shovels and others were pushing the wagons. Finally, the slag heap outside the mine was so high that only a few metres now separated it from the scaffolding. Berger and Ul'an had been waiting for weeks for the right night.

About halfway through the night shift there was always a tea break; the prisoners then gathered in the kitchen hut and dunked bread saved from supper into the warm bowls. That night Berger and Ul'an hastily drank up, crept away from the hut one after the other and went back into the tunnel before the others. At the end of the corridor there were still two wagons waiting to be transported, for Mirlach and Arbinger had interrupted their work and would shortly resume. The time was ripe to carry out the plan. Berger and Ul'an made a hollow in the middle of the coal. Berger jumped into the first wagon and crouched down; Ul'an draped rags over his face, and then himself jumped into the second. They heard Mirach and Arbinger's voices; the first wagon started moving and Berger felt the lumps of coal slipping over him. He feared that he might still be visible, but the weight on his back did not lessen. He found it hard to breathe, although he had made a kind of screen around his face with his arms. The wagon stopped, and Berger heard the supervisor's voice saying 'twenty-five', then the wagon started up again, uphill first of all, then on the flat, then it stopped again. It must have reached the edge of the scaffolding. Berger could hardly breathe; his heart was pounding. There was a lurch; the wagon was put in the vertical position and Berger slid down towards the bottom. He stretched his arms out in front of him, like a frog about to leap into the water, and found himself falling on the heap of coal. He rolled forward a bit, buffeted and overwhelmed by the black lumps of coal, then came to a stop. The heap was less steep than it had seemed from above. He did not fear being seen, for he knew that the prisoners never turned round to look at where the coal ended up, and even if they had done so, they'd have seen nothing but dust. He judged it prudent to wait a while, then began to climb down, metre by metre, waiting with each step for the cascade of coal accompanying his movements to stop. Finally he reached the bottom; beneath his feet and all around him there was just coal. His first instinct was to run, but he checked himself, waited a little longer, and crouched down low before crossing the slippery terrain, which was covered with bits of coal. It was very unlikely that anyone could see him from above, not only because that part of the mine was not watched, but also because in the darkness and on a moonless night only a bat would have been capable of perceiving the presence of a man. Berger reached a clump of bushes which grew on the edge of the mining zone. They were acacias, which had survived, although it was hard to understand how, in the midst of the coal. From the top of the scaffolding they had simply seemed to be black bushes but Berger now realised that there were little yellow flowers, although the branches were still black, like everything else that grew around the mine. They had agreed to meet there. Berger crouched down and waited.

How long did he and Ul'an usually take to unload the coal, take the empty wagon back down and push it against another? It had always seemed to them that they were fairly quick, and yet, thinking about it now, it took quite a time. But did it really take so long? How long were Mirlach and Arbinger taking? Could they really be so slow? Perhaps something had happened; they had discovered Ul'an and were already looking for him. Even though he could now breathe freely, Berger felt short of breath. His mouth and throat were full of coal dust; he could taste it, and his stomach and lungs must be full of it too. He was huddled behind by the acacia bush, and did not even dare to lift up his head and look. There was darkness all around; a light breeze blew above his head and ruffled the little yellow flowers of the acacia, but to Berger the wind seemed to smell of coal too.

30

FINALLY BERGER HEARD a scuffling nearby and Ul'an crouched down on the ground beside him, still panting a little. Berger placed a hand on his back. He could have hugged him for sheer joy. Ul'an stood up almost immediately, bent down and crossed the open ground, until he reached a clump of bushes further off. Berger followed him. They continued for a while, keeping close in order not to lose one another, and stooped, as if the roof of the mine at its very lowest point were just above them. Only when the slag heap had sunk back into the darkness did they straighten up and begin to walk faster, at a marching pace, one behind the other. They didn't speak. Their plans had been settled long before, and discussed a hundred times. Their direction was the one Ul'an took to be the surest, to the south, and towards the hills. Further on was the Scerubaj-Nura.

When they'd looked from the top of the scaffolding, the hills had seemed to be laid out in a straight line, shielding the river. When they climbed them, however, they realised it had been an optical illusion. It was not a line but a kind of terrace between plain and river, from which hills rose up like domes in a covered bazaar. To follow a route through the middle of them was to discover endless ups and downs and twists and turns in a labyrinth of bushes. Berger was already thinking that they were lost when suddenly the terrace came to an end in a steep slope that descended to the river. Then they broke into a run, and in their excitement did not stop until they felt the ground give way a little beneath their feet. They took off their boots and jackets and paddled in the river, sinking deep into the sand, filled their mouths with water and splashed their face and arms, in the grip of a strange joy, as if they were drunk on water.

They continued along the bank at a brisk pace. It was still dark when they caught sight of the dim outline of the railway bridge suspended above the water. They climbed up onto it but could hear no noise from either direction. They crossed the bridge quickly, for once out of the protective shadow of the hills they felt vulnerable. Their earlier joy had gone, and now both of them looked anxiously to the left, fearing that the sun might reach them at any moment. Their chances of escape hung on their outstripping the sun, and on reaching Zarik before the first train of the morning. They could think of nothing else.

The sky was beginning to brighten when they heard the whistle behind them getting closer. They threw themselves onto the ground, saw the lights of the locomotive and the snake of the train, and could smell the gust of smoke rising into the air above them. No sooner had the sound faded into the distance than they began to run along the tracks, almost as if they hoped to catch up with the train. Berger had begun to feel his heart bursting in his chest when Ul'an, who was ahead of him, slowed down, turned round and gestured to him. Now Berger too saw something white, a house, the station, and the train, directly in front of them and at a standstill. The sky to the left had become a little lighter, but not yet enough to dispel the shadows around the houses. The train was dark, and there was no one around. It had been hurled across the steppe and then left, to wait in that deserted place, which, in the uncertain light of dawn, appeared to be uninhabited. Berger and Ul'an approached it warily, and reached the end wagon, which was bolted. Further on, however, there was another, open one. Berger clambered up and looked inside. The wagon was half full of planks of rough wood stacked sideways, but in no apparent order. They jumped in and made a nest among the planks, arranging them into a roof over themselves, and settled down to wait. Berger felt his eyelids growing heavy through sheer tiredness, but whenever his head lolled, he woke again with a start. Gradually the wagon was lit up by a bright light. They heard voices, orders given in Russian and shouts, and then someone went down the track checking the wheels of the wagons. The train slowly began to move. Suddenly the planks inside the wagon began to move too, slipping like chopsticks in the hands of a clumsy practitioner and endangering the two fugitives, who struggled to get them under control. They were so busy trying to steady the planks that they quite forgot all their doubts as to whether the train would veer right at the junction, and head for Dzhezkazgan, or left, towards Balkhash. Berger suddenly remembered, and in his excitement almost shouted, as if the direction taken by the train depended on him: 'Ul'an, the junction! We'll be there shortly!' Yet they did not dare to lean out and look, and their uncertainty was agonising.

Make it go to the left, Berger was thinking, although he did not really know by whose good offices the train was to be diverted. To calm his nerves, he ran over in his mind the plan they would fall back on if the train were to go in the opposite direction. But it was a makeshift solution which would have placed the whole venture in jeopardy, as they both knew perfectly well. In the camp's cultural centre Berger had found a map of the Soviet Union, but it was very old, and the zone they were now in was marked as unexplored. There was no trace of a railway. It was clear from the map that, if they had gone to the right, for miles there'd have been nothing but desert. They'd have had to get off, but where would they have gone? Back in Karaganda their gang would long since have reached the camp, and the alarm would have been raised; they were certainly searching for them already and the order would have been given to check the trains. Make it go left, left! What was the good of even thinking about it? It was not they who chose which direction to take, it was already decided, the driver was in the know, the stoker too, they alone did not know it. It seemed to him deeply unjust that they were kept in ignorance and could do nothing but wait. Their fate would be decided at the junction, when the train would go left or right.

When, later on, in Cologne, Berger thought back on his escape or, as was more often the case, relived the detail of it in his dreams, the same scene always came up. He would be crouched down in the wagon; the junction just refused to come and he was filled with the anxiety of not knowing which way the train would take them. Every now and then he would wake up drenched in sweat, because in the dream the train never managed to reach the junction and he could therefore never free himself from his anxiety except by waking up. Whenever he happened to travel by train, which he rarely did, because he sought to avoid trains as much as he could, he would be gripped by a similar anxiety; he would begin to think that the direction was still in doubt, that he had caught the wrong train, or that by means of some bizarre manoeuvre the locomotive must have suddenly skidded onto another set of tracks on the right. As if it had happened just the day before, he remembered the precise moment at which the train had suddenly begun to slow down almost to a halt, how there was then a judder and the wagons had begun to move off again towards the left. There was no doubt about it, they were going eastwards. Shortly afterwards, the sun, which had already attained a reasonable height, was straight ahead of them and lit up the wagon, but the sensation of waiting had been so intense that even the relief seemed painful to him.

If Berger had had to choose, not a particular episode, but rather a state that characterised the whole affair, he would probably have spoken about their thirst. The most agonising thing about thirst is the fact that it does not leave you with enough strength to feel or think about anything else, and the fact that it is not just a sensation but something which wholly absorbs you and becomes a veritable state of mind. 'If only we'd brought a little water!', Berger said, and thought of all the water they had left in the river. 'You must be camels to resist thirst, wolves to resist hunger and men to resist temptation,' answered Ul'an, who, despite his thirst, still had enough strength to speak sententiously. 'What's to be done against thirst, Ul'an?' Berger asked, although he could barely speak. 'Don't think about it,' replied Ul'an. 'How can I not think about it? Am I the master of my own thoughts?' 'Who then, if not you?'

Berger was too thirsty to verify whether Ul'an had a formula for remaining master of one's own thoughts, or to ascertain what the devil he meant by it. He withdrew still further into himself and tried desperately to think about something else. He started to think about trains, and how crazy he'd been about them when he was a child. Take me to see the train! His mother used to go with him to Cologne station, which, with its metal rosettes and its glass roof, seemed like a drawing room for trains. The locomotives filled the vault with black smoke, puffing away like impatient guests. And what a delight it was to travel in them! To see from the railway bridge the Rhine running underneath, so slowly, to watch the raindrops forming on the window, and to eat a snack and cover the striped velvet seats with crumbs. Those trains differed so much from the ones he had travelled on in recent years, first as a soldier and then as a prisoner, and from the one he found himself travelling on now, as a fugitive, sitting on a rickety floor, among wooden planks which threatened to fall on top of him, and with that thirst inside him too.

Thirst would cause Berger and Ul'an a deal more suffering yet, in the course of their flight southwards, nor was there anything surprising about that, given that to reach the Amudar'ya they still had to cross a fair number of steppes and deserts. After the Kyrgyz steppe there was the steppe of the bears and the steppe of hunger, and the Kyzylkum desert, which lay between the Syrdar'ya and the Amudar'ya. Ul'an was well aware of this, more so even than Berger, who had studied the map. When he saw for the first time the outline of the Alatau behind Lake Balkhash, Ul'an pointed eastwards and said confidently: 'Behind there is the Talki pass, and after that it's China!' He spoke as if that were their goal but he meant to say that they were not far from the border, that the vast state which still held them prisoner ended at that point, and that everything with a border, precisely because it is finite, can be overcome. This is what Ul'an had meant when pointing to the eastern borders of the Soviet Union, but to reach the village of the Tunshan they would have to reach its far more distant southern borders.

These places were not alien to Ul'an. War, imprisonment, the mines and his escape had taken him far away from his own history, and yet he had not forgotten it. He did not need to consult maps to know the names of places, of the rivers they were crossing and of the mountains they were gazing at. He knew that on the other side of Lake Balkhash lay the land of seven rivers, where the Tunshan used once to live, and that the Karatal and the Ili flowed into the lake. He likewise knew that the rivers were swollen with snow at this time of year, which was why the reeds visible on the surface were so short. He may not have been familiar with the names of the cities, which were too young to be known to the Tunshan, but he remembered the names of the peoples who used to live in those places. He knew that they were related to the Tunshan, that, like them, they preferred yurts to houses, that they raised animals and knew the steppe and that, even if the borders had been changed, they for their part, though the state might frown upon it, certainly clung to their old ways. What were twenty years of Soviet citizenship compared to the centuries they had behind them? You'd need a deal more than that, said Ul'an, to transform nomads and to make them forget the laws of civilisation of the steppe. Those laws had not changed, and they were certainly the same as his father and his ancestors, all the way back to Alcidai, had known and honoured. Ul'an was therefore not surprised when, not far from the cabins of a kolkhoz, on the shores of Lake Balkhash, they saw a cluster of yurts; in front of the central one sat an old and wrinkled Kazakh woman with a pipe in her mouth and a handkerchief on her head. When they approached her, she did not stir, but as soon as Ul'an spoke she invited them into the yurt. The rest happened of its own accord. Some fishermen cleared a space for them in the midst of their nets, on a flat-hulled, high-sided boat which they then rowed out towards the open sea. They conveyed them from one cove to the next until they reached the southernmost point of Lake Balkhash. At that point the lake, before it gave way to the steppe, again opened out into a pool which it seemed to be pushing with its nose, like a dolphin playing with a ball. The last branches of the Ili reached as far as there, and the land was a long succession of ponds and marshes and a shrieking of birds, which grew louder when the boat approached the bank. A cluster of yurts was visible in a raised position, not far from the tip of the lake. Aluminium pipes protruded from the roofs, and from the pipes there issued plumes of smoke; the women bustled about the yurts, because at that hour the men and the children were sleeping and it was up to them to prepare the tea. This was all quite normal to Ul'an, whereas Berger felt overwhelmed, not by any fear, but by the magnificence of it all.

Such a big lake. And to think that I did not even know of its existence, reflected Berger, as he looked out across its vast expanse. The lakes I have seen up until now are paltry by comparison. He tried to imagine how many times Lake Geneva would go into it, and whether even Switzerland would fit comfortably, but he had no standard of measurement to help him with the comparison. His ignorance vexed him. As a boy he had spent many hours poring over his father's atlas, a monumental book, whose pages seemed to have been covered in wax, and the world in it seemed a succession of light greens, ochres, dark or very dark browns, to represent height, and light and dark blues, to represent depth. Yet the child Günther, who used to follow roads with his finger, if there were any, or to invent them, if there weren't any, had missed both the yellow ochre of the Kyrghyz steppe and the light blue of Lake Balkhash.

There were many things Berger did not know about that part of the earth. He did not know that the mountains he could see to the east would put the Alps to shame, that the land at their feet was crossed by seven rivers and studded with a thousand springs, and that there were tribes living there which knew nothing of any orders from a central authority and continued to be nomads, like the Kazakh tribe on the heights near to Lake Balkhash, towards whose yurts he and Ul'an were now headed.

The khan received the fugitives as if they had been relatives, fed and clothed them, welcomed them into his yurt and gave them his pipe to smoke, in exchange for which he wished only to have detailed accounts of the war and of their imprisonment. When sufficient time had passed and they had regained their strength, he supplied them with provisions and horses, and for the first stage of the journey, with a guide too.

In order not to arouse suspicion, they decided to transform Berger, who, even when dressed as a Kazakh, had an irremediably Western appearance. He was therefore entrusted to the women, and when he re-emerged, his beard and hair had lost their treacherous blonde colour. Berger was amused: 'What do you reckon, Ul'an? I look like a real Kazakh, don't I?' Ul'an looked at him critically: 'You could pass as a cross between a Kazakh and a Russian. If it weren't for the fact that you don't move like a Kazakh or a Russian!' Berger was offended. He didn't know where the difference referred to by Ul'an lay, and for his part he tried his best to imitate him in all respects. He had even learnt how to remain crouched down as Ul'an did, with the whole ball of his foot planted flat on the ground, whereas before, he used to keep his balance using his toes, a position at once unstable and uncomfortable. His efforts did not escape the sharp eyes of Ul'an, who tried to reassure him: 'You don't need to deceive the Kazakhs but just the Russians, and you've done enough to fool them.' I don't know if Berger felt genuinely relieved upon hearing these words; despite his faith in Ul'an, the journey to the Amudar'ya still worried him. When he reflected that he did not have a clear idea of where they were going, that he did not know the roads, that he had no instruments to ascertain which direction they were headed, that he did not speak the local languages, that he had no money, and that he was wholly dependent on Ul'an, he felt very far from calm. Then there were other sources of suffering, not just the saddle, which was very hard, but also the style of riding, whereby the horse knew just the one pace, midway between a walk and a trot, which for Berger was tiring in the extreme. Furthermore they travelled by night, so that Berger, being unable to detect subsidence in the terrain, had to entrust himself wholly to his horse, to endure frequent, painful jolts, and even to risk losing his balance. His state of mind was none too joyful either. He felt very different from what he had been two years before, when he used to ride across the Kalmyk steppe in command of a patrol of soldiers. Then he had been an officer in the Wehrmacht, well-equipped, able to get his bearings in the steppe and, even if the enemy were nearby and lying in wait, he knew that he had a powerful army behind him and he was still convinced of victory. Now, however, he was one of the defeated. He had to flee under cover of night, like a smuggler, to skirt villages and cities, and to suspect all figures in the far distance of being Soviet sentries. He was merely a fugitive reliant upon the goodwill of nomadic shepherds, who by himself would have lost his way in the course of a single night. There was cause enough to feel humiliated and depressed, Berger said to himself. In a sense, however, his had been a freely chosen adventure, whereas two years before he'd been carrying out orders and that was all. Was he freer now than when he was wearing a uniform? The very idea was preposterous and yet he had escaped of his own free will from a prison camp where even to imagine escaping seemed absurd, with Ul'an's help, admittedly, and with a fair amount of luck, but it had still been his own choice. What sort of choice was it, though, when the alternative was to croak in a mine? Berger just could not put his thoughts into any kind of order; he therefore tried to cut short the conversation going on inside him and distressing him more than it ought to have done, and to concentrate on the journey and on the movements of the horse carrying him, neither at a walk nor at a trot, up and down on the steppe. Whether free or no, what mattered to him was reaching the Amudar'ya, on the southern border of the Soviet Union, where Ul'an counted on meeting up with his own people.

As they got nearer to the border, Ul'an gradually stepped up the pace, so that Berger found it hard to keep up with him and begged him to stop, for fear that he'd not be able to follow him. Ul'an slowed down, but was clearly impatient. They had reached places which he knew well and even at night he had no difficulty in getting his bearings. They had left Samarkand behind them, and, much to Berger's disappointment, had not even entered the city, because too many Russians lived there and they couldn't risk it; then they had cut across the mountains and reached the plain of Termez from above. They reckoned on reaching the *ayil* that same night, and waited until it was dark before pushing into the cotton fields and on towards the site of the summer camp, a little way beyond the point at which the Kahungàn flows into the Amudar'ya.

The destinies of Berger and of Ul'an will in a short while also divide for ever, but for now they are still closely tied one to the other, and Berger looks on with mounting concern as Ul'an moves anxiously from one height to the next, looks for recent traces of the yurts on the ground and discovers the stones which had served as a hearth not very long before. 'They went away earlier, this year.' And he looks straight ahead, where he knows that he'll find them. 'Did something happen?' Ul'an says little and doesn't explain to Berger what it could be but keeps on searching and looking down at the point where the tributary flows into the larger river. 'The ford, the one we usually take, is further north, because it is easier to cross with loads and animals. The bank is steep here but the two of us will manage. There are no sentries, so far as I know. At any rate, we'll wait until dark, just to be sure.'

In crossing the river, Berger realised that the current was less placid and innocuous than it had seemed from above. His horse made slow progress, for the water stung its hocks and drove it back. They had covered around a hundred yards and were just at the deepest point, where the river seemed in full spate, when they heard the shots. Berger could not say for sure whether they had been preceded by warning cries or the other way round, but they came suddenly from the bank they had only just left. The horse started, made as if to bolt, tried to jump, then, as if it had seen reason, fought more vigorously against the current, until it reached shallower water, where it could increase its speed. At last it gained the Afghan side. As soon as it had left the water it broke into a gallop, although the shots had ceased some time before. Berger sought to calm the frightened, agitated horse, and then turned round to wait for Ul'an. He soon made out the shape crouched over the horse, and saw that Ul'an was clutching it tightly for fear of falling. Berger understood in a flash that the plan agreed upon in Karaganda, which had worked perfectly up until this point, had fallen apart at the last moment. The Amudar'ya was the last obstacle and Ul'an had got entangled in it.

31

THAT YEAR THE Tunshan had crossed the Amudar'ya early. Whether it was due to the war, and to the rumour that Stalin was planning to reinforce the Afghan border, or to the weather, and a very hot summer in which the pastures had dried up too soon, I cannot say. I do remember, though, that it seemed strange to us children to be returning to Birbesc, south of the river, in summer. It is true that the green had long since been swallowed up by the sun, and that the plain was as yellow as it was in autumn, and yet the wind was calm and the air was still warm, even at night. The calamity was in some way caused by the change of plan, which was so much at odds with Tunshan custom, even if no one in particular could be, I wouldn't say blamed, but even held responsible.

Once Ügedelegü, the shaman, had foretold the arrival of Ul'an, the Tunshan simply awaited him and scanned the horizon to see when he might arrive, but no one expected him to come from the north. The prophecy had not spoken about directions, but said that he would not return on his own and that he would not stay long, but the Tunshan persisted in thinking that he would come back from where he had left. This perhaps was why that year Bairqan had given orders to return to Birbesc at the end of the summer. He wanted to go some way towards meeting his son, to make at least the closing stages of his journey a little less arduous, and to enable him to avoid crossing the river, a thing that in time of war could be dangerous, especially for a young man who looked like a deserter. It was his father's solicitude that had caused the tragedy, but how could Bairqan have foreseen it, and how could the Tunshan ever have imagined that those they were expecting would come from the place they had just left?

I was the first to spot the horsemen. We were playing with coloured stones not far from the yurt when I looked up and saw them. I leapt to my feet and said, in an entirely matter-of-fact tone, 'It's my father,' as if he were expected that very morning. I then ran to Mai Ling, who was working with the women mending the yurt roof, taking off the felt to be repaired, and said, in the same tone as I'd used with the children, 'Mai Ling. My father's coming.' Mai Ling put down her work for a moment and looked in the direction I was pointing, northwards, but the horsemen, the two of them, there was no doubt about that, were still too far off. Now the other women had left the yurt roof too and were squinting at the horizon. Despite the calmness of my tone, they were very agitated. 'They're certainly not coming from there,' said Ukin. But they continued to look in the direction of the river, where the two horsemen now loomed larger. Once they were fairly near, a throng of children left the village, like a flock of sparrows suddenly rising up from a bush, and began to run towards them. I stayed beside Mai Ling and the women waiting in silence. When the horsemen could be seen more clearly from where we were, the women also started to move, gathered round the wounded horseman and helped him to dismount; as they did this they recognised that he was Ul'an, my father.

Ul'an was set down on the bed on which, just a few years before, my mother Börte had lain in a fever. It was now Ul'an's turn to fix his gaze on the hole in the middle of the yurt and wonder how many more times he would see the sun appear and indicate its passage within. Ügedelegü was bent over him, with a remorseful look on his face. The bullet was lodged too deep, just under the armpit, in the lung. Ügedelegü knew that it was not the wound in itself that threatened Ul'an's life but the fact that the membrane lining the lung had been grazed. The right lung had stiffened and was no longer absorbing air, the heart was pounding, and Ul'an was flailing around and gasping for breath. Bairqan seemed to have turned to stone and looked fixedly at his son. The prophecy had proved to be only too true. Ul'an was not to stay long with the Tunshan.

Outside the yurt the mothers of the young men who had left with Ul'an for the front were waiting. 'I just wish he'd tell us where our sons died!' Mai Ling tried to persuade them: 'What's the use of knowing where they died? You don't even know where the land in question is. And even if you did know, would you really ever go there yourselves to pay your respects to your sons?' Alcidai's mother answered for all of them: 'What I want is to be able to attach a name to the land where my son is buried, so that every time I think of him I can imagine him in that place; wherever we happen to be, that place, simply through having a name, will be nearer.' When they learnt that their sons had remained on the Kalmyk steppe, they went away in some degree consoled, for it was a familiar name and their sons had not been left there in a wholly unknown land.

The following day Ul'an sent for me, patted my head, gestured towards the central pole, with the two branches diverging at the top, where he had cut two notches six years earlier, one on the right and one on the left, one for me and one for my brother. One of the branches had become superfluous: it had not been possible to keep Ginchin's death from Ul'an. I looked at the father I did not really know with a degree of fear, and in a confused fashion I linked the two affairs, the death of my brother, and the death, which I understood to be imminent, of my father. Admittedly Ul'an had not been killed by the *naja*, and yet he had been struck quite close to the place in which Ginchin had been bitten. Perhaps Ul'an had trodden on the boundary between the riverbank and the river, which was as sacred as the threshold between the inside and the outside of the yurt. Perhaps the sentry who had fired had not been a soldier but a demon posted to defend that place, or even the *naja* itself, which, as I knew, could assume any form it wished. The idea that my father too had something to do with the *naja* caused me to tremble with horror; I could not stop thinking about it, and the more I thought about it the more plausible it seemed as an explanation. But how had the stranger with the white skin and the blue eyes of a jinn managed to elude the *naja*? This fact made me suspicious of him. Just a few weeks before, we had been on the other side of the river and I had encountered a jinn. I'd ridden with Malik as far as the cotton fields, beside the villages with white houses in which the Russians and Uzbeks lived. All of a sudden a fair-skinned creature had loomed up from amidst the plants and had stood stock still looking at me, much like a boy although he was in fact a jinn. In a state of great terror I checked my horse, and lashed out with all the force I could muster at the creature that was trying to bewitch me, until I saw it dash back among the cotton plants and disappear. Only then did I spur on my horse and rejoin Malik. Might the stranger be a jinn too? Yet Bairqan held him in great esteem, Mai Ling bowed to him and Ügedelegü spoke to him with respect. Berger never stirred from the sick man's side, as if it had been his task to gather up and preserve his very last breath. Ul'an was not long in entrusting it to him. A few days later, after a final desperate attempt to drive some air into his lungs, he died.

Berger stayed with us the whole of that winter, as my grandfather Bairqan's guest. The Tunshan never tired of hearing his story.

Again, again, they said, tell us about the war, the imprisonment, the escape, right up until the last stage, and they hung on his every word. Berger did his best to make himself understood, as did his audience to understand. I was as always just behind my grandfather, but of the tale I understood only the anguished silences and the comments of those present, together with the expressions that came and went on Bairqan's face, which I saw express disapproval or crumple in sorrow.

Berger was gracious and in the end the Tunshan forgave him for having come instead of their long-awaited brothers and sons. He was also very curious and was forever asking something; everyone, especially the women, would laugh at his questions. Do you want to learn how to make felt too? Do you want to make *kumiss*? That's women's work. Yet they explained it to him all the same, as best they knew how, and he tried as best he could to understand. Sometimes he called me, but I would run away and he would put it down to shyness and would try to draw me back with the few words of our language that he had learnt. He certainly cannot have had any notion of the occult powers I ascribed to him. When spring came, a little group of Tunshan accompanied the stranger along the same road Ul'an and his companions had taken, years before. We children followed them for a while on horseback. I saw him wave to me before disappearing behind the hills to the west.

32

IT STRIKES ME, as I tell the story of Berger and Ul'an, that of the two of them I knew the former best, and not only because I lived longer with him, Ul'an, my real father, having been snatched too soon from my life, but also because I only know Berger's version of all their adventures. Of the two of them the unknown one is Ul'an, who remains blurred, because I can only see him through Berger's eyes. Ul'an did not leave me any letters to interpret or manuscripts to read, and there was not even time enough for him to recount to me the episodes of which he too, as much as Berger, had been the protagonist. Ul'an did not bequeath me any written words, but the weight of a promise that no one could declare null and void, given that he, the only person who could have done so, was no longer there to take it back. Indeed, after Berger's departure, the Tunshan were forever talking about that promise. Some of them, the women in particular, held that no heed should be paid to it: you don't send a girl to live with parents on the other side of the world. Distance alone made the promise null and void. But Bairqan did not see it like that, and many of the men agreed with him: 'Ul'an made me solemnly promise to abide by his wishes. How could I, his own father, betray such a promise, made on his deathbed, and on my honour!' 'But what about your granddaughter! And the living are more important than the dead!' Bairqan looked askance at Mai Ling, for her assertion was, to put it mildly, irreverent. Had it not been the case that behind these seemingly sacrilegious words one could discern the fondness which she felt for me, her granddaughter, and which he shared, Bairqan would have fallen into a rage. But in this affair he felt far from firm in what he proposed, and he feared that one day he would yield to Mai Ling's entreaties. He then sought out other arguments, which would have at any rate a distant relationship to reason: 'Don't forget that in a year or two we too will go away. What do we know about Sinkiang? You can rest assured that a desolate land awaits us, where it will be still harder to find a suitable husband for our granddaughter. This German, this Berger, will look after Naja as if she were his own daughter. It is likely that a better fate is in store for her than for us.' He spoke like this but not even he was wholly convinced. The promise, however, still stood. Forced to choose between the certainty of a word that had been given and the uncertainty of the fate to which he would be consigning me in Sinkiang, Bairqan opted for the former, and for what he believed to be his honour.

I still had two more years to spend with the Tunshan, for it had been agreed with Berger that I should leave in the autumn of 1947, before the onset of winter. Mai Ling had insisted that I should remain in the *ayil* long enough to become a woman. 'You can't leave the yurt in which you were born,' she said, 'before you have completed the first cycle of nine! Naja is still a child; would you send her out into the world all on her own?' Besides, Berger too thought it ill-advised to take me away with him immediately, and Bairqan agreed with him. There was the war to consider too, whether it was really finished and Germany defeated, as they were saying in Samarkand. Stalin's propaganda was swifter than the messengers of Genghis Khan but more deceitful too, the Tunshan said.

I still knew nothing and enjoyed privileges and freedoms which the other children did not have, and which were due, I thought, to my being the khan's daughter. In fact they were the means by which the adults sought to assuage their own remorse and to beg my forgiveness, though without telling me anything, for the injustice they were about to do me.

On the day of Berger's departure my life changed. I was sitting at the loom with the other girls. The shuttle was flying swiftly along the warp; the pattern was unfolding before my eyes and I was eager to see it completed. Yet as soon as Malik came looking for me, 'Are you coming too, Naja?', I set down thread and shuttle and joined the little boys. The girls seated at their work, with their legs crossed and their backs straight, cast reproachful and envious glances, but I was already pursuing other wefts and was setting my thread running along the warp of the mountains and valleys around the yurts of the Tunshan.

Once Malik and I went further up the valley. We had never ventured so far; up there, along the flank of tufa, caves like open windows in the rock could be seen. 'Are you scared to climb up there?' Malik had turned nine that year, and I, being eight years old, did not want to be outdone. Of course I wasn't scared, and so we began to clamber up worn steps, clinging onto the rock face, which luckily offered an abundance of handholds for our still small hands. Once we reached the top we saw that behind what had seemed a window there opened out a great room, and behind that there were many other smaller interconnecting rooms, which led ever deeper into the mountain, until the light which was filtering through from the outside gave way to pitch darkness.

We turned back in terror to the outermost room, which was delightfully light and cool, and we went on from there to a second room, which opened out onto a terrace overlooking the valley. On the side wall, flooded by the sunlight which entered at an angle into the cave, I spotted the figure. A seated, cross-legged Buddha, bigger than a normal person, but not gigantic, protruded from the rock with his smooth, round forms, his eyelids half-closed over his almond eyes, his body uncoiling in elegant curves down from his ears, his shoulders, the arms bent in his lap, to the folds of the garment gathered between his legs. I ran my finger over it. 'What on earth what are you doing?', Malik reproached me. 'You mustn't touch. Can't you see it's a god?' 'It's precisely because it's a god that you need to put your hands on it. Because touching it gives me its godhood.'

Godhood, or some such word, was precisely what I said, although I didn't know what it meant either, unless I meant by godhood the smile that I was stroking. My cousin did not understand and for once he did not insist. We climbed down. We were almost back on the ground again when Malik, who was behind me, suddenly said: 'What have you done to your arm? You have a black mark below your elbow.' My arm was extended across the rock face searching for handholds and I could not answer him straightaway. Once on the ground, however, I looked carefully at it and made as if to dismiss what Malik had said: 'I've always had that mark,' although I actually wasn't so sure. I had not yet begun to explore my body and I did not yet know its gradations in skin colour, if indeed there were any. My cousin was not convinced by my all too hesitant explanation and retorted triumphantly: 'That's your famous godhood, that's your reward for laying your hands on a god!'

We might well have come to blows, but I remembered just in time that he was a year older, and a palm taller than me, so I preferred to run back to the *ayil* and ask Mai Ling to confirm what I had said.

Mai Ling let me know what was expected of me. Of course I did not understand what my father's promise meant and why I had to go away and become the daughter of a stranger I barely remembered. Since I didn't understand, I was not frightened, but simply asked why, and the answers did not convince me. They seemed to boil down to just the one: because we promised your father, and that was all. Once we were talking about it, and I was insisting as ever on asking why, Sarkan said to me, turning at the same time towards my cousin Haysce, who was three years older than me: 'Haysce will soon leave the *ayil* too. As women it's not our fate to grow old before the threshold where we were born.' Haysce would go away as bride, I as daughter, so what was the difference? Both of us were going to live in places that we did not know. They were trying to reconcile me to my fate. But Haysce was not happy with her fate either: 'But I still want to stay here. I don't want to marry someone I don't know.' The older women laughed: 'You'll do as we all do. What's the good of resisting your own fate?'

But Haysce saw things differently, for the simple reason that she was different from the others. Her mother came from a Tajik family, one of those which had kept their Indo-European features, their fair skin, blue eyes and long nose, which they said they had inherited from the Greeks. We didn't know if it were true, but it was certainly the case that Haysce had inherited all three features from her mother, and she used to walk proudly round the village, as if she were a direct descendant of Alexander the Great. Her stiff and haughty demeanour suggested that she was born to be a queen, and not to follow the normal fate of girls. When she turned twelve, every single one of the boys was more or less secretly in love with her, but above all Batu, who, at fourteen, was all the more smitten at finding her so beautiful and mature beyond her years. To win her heart, Batu resorted to rhymes, which he would also sing, as was our custom. 'Your irises are blue like the steppe in spring,' he rhapsodised, for the sake of the rhyme confusing blue with green. Haysce laughed at the bombastic nature of the verse: 'The steppe's green, not blue. If anything, my eyes are like the sky.' The poet blushed, but did not give in. Once, when they were at close quarters, he hummed in her ear a verse he had learnt from one of the storytellers who every now and then stayed with us, and whose declarations of love were on the direct side: 'I long to put my hand between your white thighs.' This time Haysce took offence. It was she who told me what happened next.

'Idiot,' she rebuked her clumsy admirer. 'Bet you don't dare!' Batu felt that his honour was at stake. 'Come on then, follow me if you dare to!' Saying this, Haysce broke into a run, drew away from the *ayil*, went down the hill and reached the valley, where during that season a stream still flowed. Batu was close behind, without understanding what the race meant, and caught up with her among the bushes on the riverbank. Haysce stopped and, to the boy's astonishment, slowly began to take off her clothes. She unlaced her *chalat* and slipped it off, revealing her already well-formed breasts; the necklaces strung with precious stones and amulets hanging round her neck made them appear whiter and still more shapely. But Haysce did not stop; as if Batu were not even there, she untied the straps of her big leather boots and stood naked gazing defiantly at him. Batu did not know where to look and wondered if the apparition before him, utterly white save for the black patch of pubic hair, were the lady swan. Youthful desire prompted him to act, but fear prompted him to flee. Fear got the upper hand, and he fled, with Haysce, quite naked, and as lovely and as white as the lady swan who bewitches men, mocking him as he ran.

My cousin laughed as she recounted this episode but, to judge by her hints, she had not waited long before finding among her many admirers one who was less fearful than Batu. At home we were very tolerant about matters to do with sex. Even when a girl happened to get pregnant, there was no great drama, indeed, far from it. A cradle would be hung from the roof of the yurt, and the young mother would also bring her future husband a baby as a part of her dowry. But when my cousin Haysce left the yurts of the Tunshan, her stomach was as flat as when she'd shown it to Batu. When she went away she seemed a queen, but a queen who had been defeated, wrapped in the mantle of her offended pride.

'Lucky you,' she said to me before she left, 'at least you'll get to choose your own husband.' 'How do you know?' 'I feel that it will be so.' It didn't seem to me that I was luckier than her, but I did not dare to contradict her, all the more so given that her irises, be they green or blue, like the steppe in spring or like the sky above it, were veiled with tears. A woman is not destined to grow old before the threshold where she was born, and this turned out to be true for me too.

The time came to gather together my finest clothes. Mai Ling took from the case the jewels that were kept there, necklaces, earrings, a diadem, turquoises and carnelians mounted in silver, a dowry worthy of a khan's daughter such as I. She wrapped them in silk scarves, placed each in a little bag, drew the strings tight and stuffed them all in a large leather bag together with the clothes, bits and pieces of fur, my tea bowl and whatever else might be needed on the journey and afterwards, in the place I was going to, which not even Mai Ling could imagine. They rebraided my plaits. Up until the very last moment I continued to hope that something would happen to prevent me from going away, but I did not know what. I simply could not bring myself to believe that my departure was inevitable. Finally the bag was ready, as was I. I crossed the threshold of the yurt and once again, just as I had done throughout all those years, I lengthened my stride more than was absolutely necessary for fear of inadvertently touching the little wooden plank which marked the boundary between the outside and the inside. I did not really need to exercise such care, for I was big enough to adjust my step, but I continued to make it longer out of habit and to amuse myself. Ever since I had been a small child I had been afraid to offend the spirit living beneath the threshold. At times, before going outside, I'd find myself looking at it anxiously, wondering how it managed to stay all the time huddled beneath the wooden plank and what it would do to me if, by some mishap, I had put my foot on it. I imagined a pain of the kind Haysce felt that time she had put her bare foot on a scorpion, which luckily was not a poisonous one, and yet her foot had swelled up terribly. I turned around now, once outside, to look at the yurt which I was leaving for ever, and with exaggerated care I shut the little door of coloured wood behind me.

Mai Ling said farewell to me: 'Be a credit to your own people,' she repeated, 'Behave as we have taught you to.' She went straight back into the yurt. She was not to accompany me. Bairqan, my uncle Borrak and Malik, together with some other Tunshan, formed a retinue, and brought reserve horses, provisions and tents for the journey. The road was for a while the same as that taken first by my father Ul'an and later by Berger, but while Ul'an and his companions had headed for the Caspian Sea we would reach the Syrian border. I was so excited by the journey that up until Izmir I almost forgot the destination.

Malik and the others left us where the railway began. Only Bairqan and Borrak, his younger son, climbed onto the train with me. For the most part my memories of the train journey consist of their lolling heads; the journey on horseback had been long, and all three of us were tired. At Smyrna I smelt the sea for the first time; I clung to my uncle, while Bairqan whispered with the ship's captain and a sailor, a Kazakh, was summoned and I understood that they were talking about me, and that they were agreeing rewards and routes. Then, I don't quite know how, I was on the boat; I saw the jetty moving further away and my grandfather and my uncle becoming smaller, until they completely disappeared. From that moment I didn't see anything at all. There was a darkness round about me and within me. Someone may have looked after me, perhaps the Kazakh to whom my father had entrusted me; perhaps there was someone who gave me something to eat, and to drink, but no matter how hard I try to remember all I see is darkness. I only know that when I again became aware of what was around me, another port was in sight. We had reached Genoa. The Kazakh helped me to carry my luggage, for my bag seemed huge to me. He put it on his back and took me by the hand. We crossed roads together and went into a station; I saw that he was speaking with the station-master, and there I was on a train once more, with my leather bag stuffed in the net baggage-rack, which touched the roof. I was alone, and all I had to explain where I was headed was a little pouch round my neck, inside of which was a folded piece of paper written by Berger, with his name and address, and perhaps a few lines in case I got lost. I gripped the pouch tightly as if it were an amulet, but I don't remember if I ever took out the little piece of paper, if anyone asked me for anything, the train ticket at any rate, did I have it? I believe that I changed trains at Basel, and I remember that someone else took me by the hand and carried my luggage on his back. I am sure that I did not sleep during the whole journey, but the terror I felt has obliterated all memory of it. When the train drew in beneath the roofless vault of the station, at Cologne, a man came, perhaps it was the ticket inspector, and accompanied me; someone took my baggage down from the netting, and someone accompanied me to the *Bahnhofmission.* I crept into a corner, my head between my knees, and I did not look around, for I did not want to see anyone. I felt a knot in my throat, as if I were suffocating and could not breathe. The roof was falling on top of me, and crushing me. I felt like an animal in a cage. Someone spoke to me, there were women's voices, but I did not raise my head until I heard a voice that I knew, which was calling me, Naja, Naja. It was the voice of my father, Günther Berger.

Part Three

NAJA

33

I REMEMBER HARDLY anything of those early days. I must have been living in a kind of fog. I remember the perpetual knot in my throat, the feeling of suffocation and the fear that the roof was falling in on my head. Why did these people live in houses with no holes in the roof? Why did they shut themselves of their own free will between brick walls? Why did they enclose space with hedges or garden fences? I was afraid of enclosed spaces; I was afraid of everything. I would only drink out of my own cup, the one I brought with me in the bag, with the carving around it. I ran my fingers over it and felt the carved relief; it was the *naja*, I knew, I could feel it come to life again under my touch. I wasn't afraid of the *naja*. My bulky leather bag had been spirited away to the back of the wardrobe. Marianne had suggested emptying it. 'It smells so!', she had said in disgust, but I realised what she was up to and swiftly drew it towards me like a toddler clutching a toy; this is mine, don't touch it. I was ashamed of what I'd done. What would they think? I was too old to act like that! But I held on tightly to my bag, so as to keep it from Marianne's grasp; she gave up, and left it to me, as one does with a snotty-nosed, stubborn child. Every now and then I opened it and put my face inside it to smell the smell I knew and which was still inside it. The smell. I mustn't let it escape. It was the only thing left to me. What use would even the objects stuffed inside it be without their smell?

A few weeks after I arrived I woke one morning feeling damp. I pushed the eiderdown aside; the sheet was red with blood and there was congealed blood between my legs. Mai Ling had warned me, and I knew what to expect; at home we didn't make such a mystery out of what was after all the normal course of things. But in a house I didn't know, lying between white sheets that resembled the sheets the dead are wound in, the blood dismayed me. Right then I thought I was wounded, maybe dead already. I wished

I could hide or even disappear. Little by little I calmed down, but I felt I didn't have any choice but to hide what had happened. But how do you go about hiding a secret in a place you don't know? I knew that the maids' eyes followed me everywhere, that they told my mother everything, and that they would tell her this too. I felt guilty and ashamed. What was I to do with the sheets which so shamelessly revealed my guilt? I took them off the eiderdown, removed the undersheet, rolled them all up together and stuffed them into the back of the wardrobe, together with my nightdress. I took a towel, which was also white and had embroidered initials on it, from the bathroom, cleaned myself with it and folded it like a nappy. I didn't come downstairs until they called me. Marianne found out anyway. They whispered in the kitchen for a long time. God knows what they taught her where she comes from.

Mai Ling, how can I do credit to myself? What constitutes good behaviour in this place? Mai Ling had taught me, always be honest, and do your duty as a daughter. Bairqan had taught me, keep your word. Ügedelegü had counselled, respect the gods. Hey, Naja, will there be caves to explore there too? Malik was ablaze with curiosity. Will you choose your own husband?, my cousin Haysce had said to me before she left. Perhaps Haysce was already expecting a baby. She too was far from her people, but she knew what she had to do and what her duty was as a wife and mother. She had learnt it, despite her queenly airs and graces. But what about me? What did it mean to be a good daughter in that house? Where were the gods to respect and the caves to explore? Where were the boys from whom I would shortly be able to choose a husband, now that I had become a woman? At the *ayil* we held a party when a girl became a woman; the other women would bring her a gift, a scarf or a sweet. I just hid. The women whispered in the kitchen, while my mother looked more scared than ever. Maybe this too was different in this country, and had to be hidden like guilt. In the evening I found some white cloths on the bed which still held a faint smell of chlorine. Marianne had put some big safety pins beside them, like the ones holding up the doll's nappy. Nothing else. Nobody explained a thing to me; nobody said a word. I could feel them watching me and that was all.

Lots of people came to the house, although they were nearly all women. Every now and then one of my mother's sisters would show up, sweep along the corridor like a scented phantom, disappear into the sitting room and then reappear almost immediately with my mother in tow. More rarely Frau Schifferl, my grandmother, would make an appearance, and look blankly at me before turning her attention to weightier matters. My other grandmother, Martha, my Volga grandmother, as I called her, always came with her husband, because they lived in the country; we would hear the car stop in front of the gate and my grandmother come bustling in. She was small and just couldn't keep still. Coming up the path she was already enthusing: 'Look at the crocuses, how beautiful, look how well they're doing. They aren't out at home yet but look, and the primroses, how lovely!' As the season wore on, she was delighted by the lilac and the border of peonies. She greeted flowers even before people, but as soon as she saw me she poured her joy all over me: how you've grown, she would say, as though I were a flower too, and she kissed my cheeks with the same fervour with which she bent over the clusters of lilac blooms to smell their scent. Her greeting was still *ach ty bednyi rebyonok*, but it had shed the tone of commiseration it had had at the beginning and now expressed a kind of secret alliance between us. 'We understand each other,' my Volga grandmother would say, as if we were fellow conspirators, and she meant that we both still saw the vastness of the steppe before us: it was our need for space which made us alike. She had come away from the steppe several decades earlier, but to listen to her you would have thought it were only yesterday; she sighed so much at the memory. What are years?, she would ask. The air that children breathe stays in their lungs all their lives, as does the country which is ours when we are young. My grandmother Martha's view of life was essentially tactile, and though somewhat naïve, perhaps, was generous through and through. She tucked her arm in mine; I was a head taller than her, for she was tiny, and I could feel her thin arm, wrapped in sweaters and coats even in the summer, which seemed to radiate energy just by touching: 'Tell me. Good girl, your German is really coming on!' And turning to my grandfather following a few steps behind: 'I tell you in a little while this one will speak better than us, and proper German too, not this dreadful dialect.' My grandfather smiled and looked at me with a critical eye: 'Good girl, you've put on weight. That means you're beginning to like the food.' We were arriving three abreast and my father who was already standing in the doorway came to meet his parents while my mother finished laying the table for coffee along with Marianne.

My Volga grandmother was always restless; she would jump up and go on a wander through the house on the slenderest of pretexts. 'That woman can never keep still,' my grandfather would smile indulgently, as if he felt he had always to be making excuses for her. In reality he too felt embarrassed by his daughter-in-law's perpetual silence and stiffness of manner, and he cheered up perceptibly when the coffee ceremony drew to a close and it was time to withdraw to his son's study for a smoke. It was the only room in the house where one could smoke and my father often took refuge there, so much so that in my memory when I look back I can still see him with a cigarette between his fingers, or a handkerchief, depending upon the time of year. For her part, Marianne maintained that she had to hold her nose so as not to choke every time she came into the study and that even the legs of the chairs smoked.

I was never happier than when my grandparents took me away with them for a few days. Then Marianne would pack me a little suitcase which my grandfather put on the roof-rack. During the journey my grandmother never stopped talking, telling me stories of past and present, of people who were already dead or still alive, places she had never seen again and which were perhaps no longer there. I looked out of the car window and was amazed at how green everything was and how many trees there were. Then we would arrive at the lake. It was really a volcano, my grandfather explained, we live on the slopes of a volcano and if we go up there, and he pointed to a higher hill, from there you can see that it's not a lake, but the eye of a volcano. The soil was special too because of the volcano underneath; junipers grew there and the entire slope was covered with low, bushy trees; in summer the ground was purple with berries. But I looked most intently at the wide open spaces, rather than the volcano, at the rolling hills, green as far as the eye could see, and at the river at the bottom. And then there was Lucifer, my grandfather's dog, who always made a great fuss of me. Why didn't I end up in a family like this, I wondered, why didn't I live here? This was a land I could understand, a place I could be in. My grandfather used to take me with him when he went to visit a patient, and on these occasions Lucifer and I would share the back seat; the dog would put his paws in my lap, his tongue would loll out of his mouth, and we would wait patiently to be let out. Sometimes my grandfather would put his rod on the roof-rack too, then we would leave the car on the road and walk down a track as far as the Liessbach. My grandfather would unfold his director's chair, as he called it, and sit there for hours, his two rods side by side in the ground. 'You don't fish,' I would tell him, 'your rods fish by themselves.' 'That's not true,' he would answer laughing, 'you have to understand fish, or you won't catch them.' 'But aren't you bored?', I would press him. 'You must be joking! With all the things you can learn from the river?'

The Liessbach flowed in great curves and from his director's chair my grandfather couldn't see beyond the nearest bend. But what matter, perhaps he felt like the director of riverside scenes, with the blue dragonflies alighting on the water lilies, the wagtail landing on a rock in the middle of the stream, the trout at long last biting. Meanwhile Lucifer and I had climbed up the slope; there were caves to discover there too, some deep and winding. But however hard I looked, I never managed to find a single carved relief, and nothing to bear witness to the purposes of artisan monks able to sculpt a god's smile in the rock.

When I went back to Cologne, I would feel like a prisoner for a few days; the knot in my throat tightened again, and I couldn't swallow a thing. 'Who knows what's the matter with her,'

Marianne would remark, 'the Eifel seems to do her more harm than good.'

What with Dr Wallatz's lessons and my homework I didn't have a lot of time. When I came home from lessons my mother would sometimes call me. She did her embroidery in the morning-room. My mother was always embroidering, always in the same cross-stitch, but in different colours, and always tablecloths, but in different shapes. I couldn't imagine what she did with so many tablecloths, also because except on special occasions, Kathe always laid the table with the same damask cloth, already worn from many washings. The tablecloths my mother embroidered, whether they were never finished or were too beautiful for our everyday use, never made an appearance. Nobody except my mother and Marianne was allowed to look inside the wedding chest, where the women put the carefully ironed and starched linen before closing the lid on it as on a tomb.

'What do you do with all these tablecloths,' grandma Martha had once asked on seeing my mother embroidering the umpteenth printed linen cloth. 'Are you preparing a dowry for your daughter?'

She had laughed as she said it, but my mother gave a start. She would never have thought to give me a dowry, not only that, but the idea had never even occurred to her that I might one day need one, that I might one day get married like all the other girls. The very fact of having a daughter was wholly alien to her, and especially at the outset. You might say that she embroidered because she needed to move at least her fingers, because the rest of her didn't move much at all. She embroidered in order not to have to think about anything, as she said to me once, because all her attention was focused on the stitches, which were all alike, all stretched in the same way, the knots perfect on the other side of the material. My mother trapped the thoughts which tormented her in linen, pinned them down, drained them of all content and turned them into crosses which changed only in colour; in some way hers was an act of exorcism, like that performed by the women at home, when they sew seed pearl eyes on the cloth dolls who bear present and future misfortunes. My mother used little coloured crosses to exorcise the demons which assailed her from within, and knew no other way of getting rid of them.

Every now and then when she heard me come in she would call out to me from her sitting room, not even raising her face from the cross she was sewing, and say to me, in a tone which was meant to be affectionate: 'Come and read me something.'

I would obediently pick up a book, even though I would have preferred after so many hours of lessons to walk in the garden or throw myself onto my bed and stare at the ceiling, thinking of nothing. But I didn't dare to answer back to my mother, so I would sit beside her, concentrate, read. My mother seemed entirely absorbed in the thread she was cutting with a pair of little scissors, and heaven help us if they got lost between the skeins of thread or elsewhere and couldn't be found. Then she would get upset and I would help to look, happy to break off the reading. My mother never praised me, though sometimes she corrected me; at heart I didn't mind reading to her. She liked fairy tales: 'Read me this,' she would say, handing me a heavy book. I would look at the illustrations, one of which always caught my eye. It was a kind of dragon, but if you looked closely it was only a snake with its head held high in the air. *Undine* was the title of the story. I read it to my mother, but stopped at every line, because the tale reminded me of another story: 'Little brother and little sister played by a well, until they fell in. In the well there was an undine who said to them: "I have caught you and from now on you will work for me." She set the little girl to weaving and filling a bucket of water. The little brother had to cut a tree down with a blunt axe. And they had nothing but stale bread to eat. Sunday came, and when the undine went to Mass the two siblings ran away. But the undine noticed and went jumping and bouncing after them. Then the little girl threw a hairbrush over her shoulder, and the hairbrush grew and became a mountain with a thousand thorns. The undine found it very tiring to climb up it. Then the little boy threw a comb over his shoulder, and the comb became a mountain with thousands of sharp spikes. But the undine managed to cross it. Then the little girl threw a mirror over her shoulder. The mountain of mirrors was so smooth that the undine couldn't climb it.' There was no doubt that that undine was a *naja* and snakes can't climb mirrors. So they have snakes in the water or near it here too, I thought, and they are really witches or undines, or spirits. The little girl threw a mirror over her shoulder so that the *naja* couldn't catch her. We too had little mirrors to chase away the spirits, looking-glass eyes that the women sewed on our clothes; that's what the mountain of mirrors in the fairy tale must be. I looked at the childish drawing and read on, trying to grasp the meaning of the story, or its meaning for me. Because without any doubt the story referred to my brother and me. Except that in the fairy tale of the brothers Grimm the little brother managed to escape. In mine he was left on the banks of the Amudar'ya and the *naja* had borne him away.

'What is it Naja, is there something you don't understand?' 'No, no,' I hurried to reassure my mother. However could I convince her that the fairy tale in the book I was holding open on my lap referred to me and to my brother, that it had been written specifically for me, so that I would read it that day?

'It's too long!' Marianne was talking about my hair. She was running a comb through it and it hung in the air in the shape of a dark upside-down arch. Too long, she repeated, shaking her head, as though there was something unseemly or at least reprehensible in that, to her, excessive length. *Too* long, the emphasis was always on the little word *zu*, too, which Marianne dropped on me at other times as well like the blade of a guillotine. 'You look like Rapunzel letting down her plait from the tower right down to the ground. You could do the same. Except that her hair was blonde.' To Marianne, the blondeness of the hair of the girl in the tower seemed to be an extenuating circumstance, which served to redeem the disgraceful, too-long hair. But my hair had no redeeming feature, being not only *too* long but also *too* dark. From the way she offered her judgement it seemed that there was a limit for black hair beyond which its blackness itself became *too* much. Marianne wasn't the only one to include *zu* in all her opinions, particularly if they had to do with me. In that house there were fixed measures for everything, and anything which had the misfortune to fall on one side or the other was only too deserving of the epithet *zu*. Everything was always too expensive or too cheap, too hot or too cold, too short, like some girls' skirts, or too long, like my hair. With respect to me, though, the word took on a threatening emphasis, so much so that when Marianne said it she accompanied it with a gesture of the fingers that clearly indicated what she meant by *too* and what needed to be done to reduce it to reasonable dimensions. The duly formulated judgement was laid before my mother with a gesture traced in the air, which practically sliced through the upside-down arch of my hair: 'Don't you agree that it's too long, Frau Berger?' My mother nodded and Marianne laid it on even thicker: 'Girls don't wear their hair long these days.' The assertion was peremptory: this was the new law and it must be adhered to come what may.

My grandfather Berger had a theory about women's hair. Their haircuts were, he thought, a kind of self-castration, though of course he didn't use the word, to which women subjected themselves voluntarily, taking the wrongs of a war and above all a lost war upon themselves in an act amounting to expiation. 'Women cut their hair at the end of a war, I mean a lost war. They cut their hair after the First World War too. That too was a lost war, actually. This didn't happen in earlier wars because in those days war was a purely masculine affair, in which women were only involved as prisoners or as the mothers and wives of soldiers. But women were directly involved in the last two wars. That's why they cut their hair at the war's end.' My grandfather had not only arguments but also tangible proofs in favour of his thesis: 'The Greeks represented Victory with long hair, loose in the wind. Can you imagine her with a fringe and gamine style?' Nobody could imagine Victory like that and so they agreed with him. I didn't understand what they were on about, but I couldn't imagine myself with short hair and a fringe, all the more because the plait which hung to my knees was, in the opinion of everybody who had felt the weight of it at home on the Amudar'ya, a magnificent plait, thick and shiny from the nape of my neck to my knees. I was proud of my plait, which wrapped around me like a cloak when I undid it, and inside which I could have hidden myself like Muslim women in their *chadors*. I was attached to my plait, and Marianne's *zu*, and still more, the scissorlike motion of her fingers, filled me with dread.

If they had asked my grandfather's opinion, he would certainly have answered that my hair wasn't too long for him, but of course it didn't occur to anybody to consult him or my father over such a feminine matter. The women of the house resolved it in their own way, with all the cruelty of which only a person convinced they are acting for the good of others is capable.

One day Marianne said to me, 'Look at yourself in the mirror, don't you think you look ridiculous with this Rapunzel's plait of yours? Apart from anything else it's a real nuisance now that it's summer and you go swimming. And when you go to school, goodness knows, your classmates will laugh at you!' These were the same arguments she had been directing at me for weeks, only now my progress in German meant that I understood every word. It was hot in the bathroom; my grandparents were coming to pick me up that afternoon and I didn't want to keep them waiting; I wanted to get out and I thought of Lucifer whom I would be seeing shortly. And Marianne chose that precise moment to have another go at me about my hair; in addition, as though on purpose, my mother had come into the bathroom too and was gazing distractedly at the black mantle which covered my back. 'Come on, be brave, one snip of the scissors and it'll all be over.' Marianne wouldn't leave me in peace, she was determined to elicit my consent. 'Come on, do it for your mother.'

For my mother? Might it please my mother if I let them cut my hair? This was a new argument and my mother seemed at first to be caught on the hop. 'Yes, yes, wouldn't you be happier to have a daughter with hair like all the other girls? Isn't that true, Frau Berger? Tell her, tell your daughter.' My mother nodded wearily, but I blushed. I was beginning to understand; my mother was ashamed of me, also because of my hair. That was why she never went out with me, because of my hair. Marianne was trying to make me understand this; this was what she had been trying to make me understand all this time, and I was only now beginning to get it. I couldn't decide. Time was passing; I was becoming more and more anxious to get out of the bathroom, when would my grandparents arrive, had they already set out, would they bring Lucifer? Marianne was already brandishing the big scissors: 'So, shall we do it?' She was no longer threatening me with her fingers, but with that sharp pointed instrument. It was my mother who took the initiative, and who said: 'Plait her hair again, Marianne, then we'll knot it at the top and at the bottom, so the plait won't unravel and she can keep it all in a piece.'

Marianne was keen to go ahead. She went to look for a ribbon, came back with a red velvet one, cut it in two, made two bows, one level with my shoulders and one at the end, then lifted the plait in her left hand and cut cleanly with her right. One cut was not enough. The plait was thick, the smooth strong hair slipped from the blades, but eventually the plait was left dangling in Marianne's hand. I followed the ceremony in the mirror, saw Marianne behind me with the scissors in one hand and that stump of hair in the other, saw my mother looking blankly at me and myself with an expression of horror on my face and my hair clear of my shoulders and I fled. I ran and shut myself in my room, hid under my eiderdown and didn't want to see or hear anything. I did not even cry but just felt a deep emptiness inside. I felt lost. I felt that I was the stump that Marianne held in her left hand, lifeless, severed, useless, and held together by two absurd red ribbons.

A little later Marianne handed me a long, shiny red box. 'Open it,' she said with a mysterious air. Inside was my plait arranged on a red velvet cloth. They had had to coil it to get it all in and that made it look like a poisonous snake, black and shiny. I shut the box in horror and threw it into the wardrobe. I never opened it again.

There had been something definitive about the act of cutting my hair, and never again would I wear a plait like the one that had been stuffed into the red box. On the other hand, the bid to rid my hair of its other defect, that of being too black, could be reversed without doing too much damage. It was a more spontaneous operation, undertaken almost as a game: 'I wonder how you'd look with blonde hair!' Another of Marianne's ideas; the women laughed but took it seriously. 'Hey, maybe you wouldn't look bad at all.' 'Do you want a blonde daughter, Frau Berger?'

Did she want one? My mother couldn't imagine a daughter who wasn't blonde. Blonde like the little girl in the portrait on the chest of drawers in her room. Blonde like the little girl in the painting on the wall of Dr Wallatz's study. Like the girls who played in the garden, Marianne's nieces. Girls were supposed to be blonde. At any rate the girls in the portraits and in the garden plainly were. I had nothing in common with the portraits and with the girls in the garden.

'Let's have a go, and if it doesn't turn out well the original colour will soon return.' I found myself sitting in the bathroom with a towel over my shoulders, Marianne busying herself putting a pomade on my hair, lock by lock, which made my eyes burn. The procedure was called 'peroxiding'; I could feel my eyes burning and Marianne telling me, 'Patience, my girl, you have to be a little bit patient and keep still or it'll get in your eyes.' The cutting of my hair had been horrible, but the outcome this time was even worse. I burst into tears when I looked in the mirror and saw the havoc that had been wreaked on my head. Marianne tried to console me and didn't dare contradict me. My mother shook her head. I don't know if it was because the result was so plainly a disaster or because she regarded the attempt to turn me into the little girl in the picture as an utter failure. I would never become little Ilse, however hard Marianne tried, however hard I myself tried to become her.

My mother never directly reproached me. It wasn't my fault if I was in her house, just as it wasn't her fault if she couldn't accept me as a daughter. The fault, if fault it was, rested entirely with one person, and that was my father.

When I think about them, my father and my mother, I barely recall ever having seen them talk to each other or stand near to each other, just arm in arm, say, let alone in a real embrace. I remember them together once or twice, when they were going to a party. Then my mother would put on a long, black dress with a cinched-in waist, a wide flaring skirt and a décolletage which opened softly onto her breasts. A diamond necklace stood out against her honey-coloured skin. 'We can wear them again now,' my mother said as if to justify herself, while the women gathered round admiring her and said: 'But how lovely you look, Madame, you should go to parties more often; they would cheer you up.' My father, also dressed in black, in a double-breasted suit, with silk socks and diamond cufflinks at his wrists, patted me gently on the cheek. They went out arm in arm, leaving a scent of cologne and lily of the valley in their wake; the women lingered in the doorway, as though bewitched by the now vanished apparition, repeating to themselves: 'The Bergers make such a lovely couple.'

But such occasions were few and far between, and I don't know if perfume, necklace and silk ever lifted the curtain of incomprehension which hung between them, and above all overcame the bitterness which my mother felt towards my father. It is probable that they never spoke of it; but once I caught a snatch of conversation and I was the subject. I think it was after one of those parties. They were in their room and the house was quite silent. I had gone to the toilet, quietly, barefoot, perhaps still half asleep, but awake enough to understand the words which seeped through with the light from the side lamps into the darkness of the corridor where I crouched.

'How could you think to substitute one person for another?' My mother's tone was unusually aggressive. 'That's not what I was thinking. But I did hope to distract you, to give you a new motivation, given that we can't have any more children.' My mother must have been cut to the quick: 'It wasn't my fault. And I don't need distracting.' She was almost shouting. 'Quiet or they'll hear. You do need it. You can't spend your whole life thinking about a dead daughter when you have one right here in flesh and blood who needs you, whom you should be looking after.' 'I didn't ask you to bring her to me. You didn't even ask. I know, I know you couldn't, I know the story, please don't tell it again, I know the circumstances, but I am not responsible for your history.' 'You can't seem to manage to step outside your own shadow. She's here now, you must understand that; you can't send her back. You could look after her, be a mother to her. Instead of which you reject her.' 'She can never be like a daughter, like the children we could have had if . . .'

I heard my mother sobbing and slipped along the corridor back to my room. I hid under the eiderdown, as I did when fear caught me by the throat. I tried to curl up and think of other things. But I wasn't just afraid. Words were no longer unknown phantasms whose sense I couldn't grasp; they had now taken on a clear and precise form which was not easily denied. It was that meaning, in all its bluntness, which wounded me, so deeply in fact that streams of water seemed to be trickling down the walls of my cave. It was my tears which dampened them, though I didn't even know I was crying.

34

THERE WERE TWO pale little girls in the garden again, Marianne's nieces. It was August and they often came to play. Sometimes as I came back from Dr Wallatz's house I found them in the yard behind the kitchen eating two large slices of thickly buttered bread spread with jam; they devoured them as though they were prey to be dispatched as quickly as possible, before somebody noticed and tried to take it away from them.

Once I stopped to watch them while they were skipping. 'Fifty, fifty-one . . .' the bigger girl was counting, as the smaller girl took little jumps, now forwards, now back, over the rope that she was twirling. They went on for a bit, one jumping and the other counting, without paying any attention to me as I watched, until the little one tripped and stopped, panting and protesting, 'That doesn't count!' 'Do you want to play?' the big girl asked me then. Her name was Heidi and she wore her plaits rolled over her ears. She was smaller than me, though we were the same age, but she looked me straight in the eye with an air of defiance, as if to say, don't think to lord it over me because you're at home and you're taller than me, I know what's what. The invitation to play was clearly a gracious concession, not a sociable act between equals.

Anyway it was more fun with three. Two held the rope and swung it, accompanying it with a rhyme which I couldn't catch; the third jumped, then we swapped around. The smaller girl, Ingrid, was so tiny and light that she seemed to fly over the rope like a bird. I could have lifted her easily. And yet she too looked defiantly at me with those blue eyes, copying her big sister. What strange girls, I thought, did they know anything apart from skipping games and writing on slates, as my tutor was teaching me to do. From their thinness and pallor you would have said they never went out in the sun and they ate too little. Like at home, when provisions ran short towards the end of the winter and the youngest children's abdomens swelled up, although nothing else did. Perhaps food was scarce here too, though I didn't notice. There seemed always to be meat and potatoes on the linen tablecloths, and Marianne always made me a slice of bread and jam, like the ones she gave, surreptitiously, to her nieces. Strange girls. And yet they were the first young things I had met in that country and I was curious about them. I could hardly understand them; their language was different from the one that Dr Wallatz was teaching me, but we didn't need a lot of words to understand each other. They played with dolls that they brought from home. Ingrid had one made of old stockings, and Heidi's doll had a wooden body, and a head and legs sticking stiffly out of a clumsily stitched dress. They were like the dolls in the yurts, except that ours were decorated with small stones and had feathers on their heads. We gave them food, sprinkled them with *kumiss* and tea and hung them over the threshold, for they were the tangible representatives of immaterial beings and it would not have occurred to any of us to play with them. These little girls played at being mothers to their dolls, rocked them, dressed them, gave them food and drink and above all played a game I didn't understand at first. They abandoned them on a branch or hid them in a bush and went away. Then as they ran they remembered their children, desperately searched for them, called them, looked everywhere, until finally they found them where they had left them and then there were hugs and a joy which seemed wholly sincere and the flight began again, between the forsythia bushes and the magnolia tree, among imaginary, eagle-eyed enemies. Once, seeing them play like that, I ran into my room and took the pink doll from the chest of drawers where she had sat since my birthday. I showed her to the girls. Ingrid opened her blue eyes wide as though hardly able to credit such a miracle; Heidi took her from me and cradled her, made her open and close her eyes, then gave her back to me. 'Take it,' I said to her, 'you can play with it.' Heidi shook her head: 'She's too beautiful to play with. What if she got dirty, what would your mum say.' They went on playing with their rag dolls and the pink doll was put down on the stone bench under the Japanese cherry tree and sat watching with her glass eyes, like a good child who isn't allowed to play.

One Saturday afternoon Heidi came to the garden alone. 'Where's Ingrid then?' 'Sick.' That time Heidi had come on her own to play with me. I was suddenly seized with curiosity. Ingrid had stayed at home, but where was the girls' home? And what was it like? They came and went, but I didn't know where. They belonged to a world which was entirely unknown to me and which they referred to vaguely every now and then in their conversations. Over there, they said, on the other side. Where was that other side? I only realised then what a recluse I was. I only knew the two streets I took, the corner of the Schillerstrasse, then the Goethestrasse, or the avenue of limes down to the Rhine. When my grandparents came to pick me up, we went by car and I didn't see anything of the city. It was a forbidden area. I wanted to see it. 'Let's go and visit Ingrid,' I said. 'We can't.' 'Why not?' 'Because it's too far.' 'But you come here.' 'Yes, but you can't come to our house.' So there were laws which applied just to me. They could and I couldn't. I rebelled. 'Of course I can. We'll go tomorrow. And don't you dare not come.' Heidi looked at me a bit surprised. It was the first time she had heard me talk like that, commanding and threatening at one and the same time.

The next day was a Sunday. Heidi did come. My mother was at her sister's house; it was Marianne's day off and Kathe and Hannah were in their rooms in the attic and paying no attention to me. I had got everything ready. I took the wicker basket, the one Kathe used for the shopping and then hung on a nail in the kitchen. 'Let's go!'

Heidi led me quickly, quietly, and every so often looked around as though she was afraid to be caught doing something unlawful. We went on like that until we got to a street called Bayenthal, which was where Marienburg ended. The city started on the other side, the zone that had been out of bounds to me until then. It stretched out there before me and I entered it for the first time on foot. It was like a fortress in ruins, but they were recent remains, on which the grass had not yet had time to grow. There were half-collapsed walls which now shamelessly revealed the floral patterns in a sitting room, the yellow stripes in a dining room or the faded blue of a bathroom. There were no steps leading from one floor to the next, but sometimes ladders placed on floors which were still stable offered a tenuous link between above and below. If you looked more closely, you saw that many of these floors were inhabited, and where a fragment of roof remained there would be mattresses and people around them, as though nobody had noticed that the walls protecting them from the gaze of passers-by had gone. The houses without façades or rear walls looked like roofless anthills in which the ants continued to move and run about without realising they were being watched. The swarming amidst the ruins was very much the same. Women were hanging washing on ropes strung from one hook to another in what used to be a shop, or so the surviving tiled floor and the signs on the walls indicated; women were handing bricks along a line to rebuild the walls; children were playing tag and people were looking for scrap and loading it into wooden-wheeled wheelbarrows. We had beasts of burden, in the *ayil*, oxen, horses and camels to carry heavy loads, but here the pulling was done with bare hands, arms fully extended and backs bent double. Every so often Heidi greeted someone and that person would look curiously at me. One or two little girls came over and asked who I was. Heidi answered quickly. They went away again. We arrived in a courtyard, with demolished houses around it, which had broadened out into a square in utter disregard for any urban planning; in the middle a half-burnt-out tank stood as a monument, with children all over it.

A group of little boys had taken possession of the tank. Arms and heads poked from the blackened gun turret; legs swung on either side of the barrel, and children of various ages balanced unsteadily on the treads. They had raised a rag of a blue flag over the tank and were shouting, mocking other children crouched behind the remains of a wall, over which flew a cloth of an indefinable colour. 'The ones in the panzer are the Catholics and the ones on the other side are the Protestants. The Catholics generally win.' Heidi's explanation was concise, objective; anyone could have confirmed the superiority of the Catholics at a glance. Of course I didn't understand what the terms meant, but I was used to not asking about everything I didn't understand. It was clear what game the children were playing, and the fact that the Catholics were inside the panzer and the Protestants were outside was secondary. Children's gangs have names, that's normal, and they are playing at war, which is also normal. I could understand that. But I didn't understand why there was a blackened tank left in the middle of the square. Who had owned such a huge object, and why was it there?, I asked Heidi, who looked at me pityingly, as though to say, where on earth does this one come from?, and didn't see fit to answer my question. Rather she continued in the same tone of voice as before, telling a story rather than explaining: 'Last week the Protestants found a hand grenade and Joseph from the Catholics lost his legs. But they didn't know it was live.' It was clearly a tragedy that Joseph had lost his legs, but Heidi must consider it to be a fairly normal tragedy, which didn't merit further commentary: 'You can find loads of that kind of thing round here,' she concluded. The cleverer children took the powder out of the cartridges and exploded it. There'd be a terrific bang, but the adults would come out and start shouting and call them delinquents and roar at them for hours. Sometimes the children exploded that kind of bomb under someone's nose on purpose, for example in front of Herr Gerz's house; he was an old Nazi, as everybody knew, and now he lived at the back of a shop. As soon as the children found a cartridge they would explode it against his door and he would come out; he was old and he would wave his stick at them and say that he would make them pay for it, that's what he said, but the children took no notice and shouted: *Nazi-Kopf*, *Nazi-Kopf*, Nazi head, Nazi head, behind him in the street.

There were still a great many Nazi heads around in Cologne in those days, some hidden among the ruins, some who had entirely respectable professions now and didn't remember the old badge that they had worn on the lapel of their overcoat and their brown uniform, reduced to rags by now or dyed a different colour. Heidi knew these things because her mother told her, when she went to collect her husband's pension and came back home in a rage, weeping in her anger and despair.

Ingrid and Heidi's father had been a railway inspector and hence a state employee and a member of the Party. Just like everyone else, said Heidi's mother, like everyone else. Then when the war came they sent him to the front, in Russia. But when the city began to be bombarded from morning till night, they, mama and the two girls, had been sent to Lower Saxony. The school there was held in the open air, Heidi said, and it was the most beautiful thing, that school in the garden, under the trees. But in the winter they had to bring the coal themselves to heat the classrooms. Not books, exercise books or pencil cases, but sacks of coal. But then the Russians came there too. From the way she talked about it Heidi seemed still to be afraid of the Russians, because children were told all kinds of stories about the wickednesses the Russians were capable of. When they arrived, the family had had to escape on foot, with their grandmother with them too. Once the Russians stopped them on the road, but mama succeeded in bribing them with one of her few remaining possessions, and they had let them go. Her mother pushed a wheelbarrow with Ingrid inside and every now and then Heidi changed places with her. They had come the whole way on foot and they slept wherever they could find shelter, once even in a cinema, and grandmother kept on saying: 'There's no point in going to Cologne, we won't find anything there anyway.' The city was destroyed, that was for sure. Where should they go, then?, mama would ask. To Bavaria, the grandmother would reply, because she had relations there. But mama wouldn't hear reason, she had Cologne fixed in her mind and destroyed or not it was the only place worth living in. So they went on walking, but always with the idea at the back of their minds that they would find nothing but ruins. They hadn't taken the shortest route, because mama was convinced it wasn't safe, but had made a wide detour round the city. Finally one day, it was in May of '45, they found themselves right above the city, in Benzberg. Heidi remembered clearly, because Benzberg is on a height and from there you can see the whole of Cologne rising from its bowl and they had got there in the afternoon. Heidi remembered how they were all, girls, mama, grandmother, standing looking down, at the bowl of Cologne, lit by the sun, with the cathedral in the centre, whole among the ruins. When she saw that the cathedral still stood her mother burst out crying and then grandmother cried too and the girls, though they didn't understand why mama was crying and they thought it was because there were so many ruins and their house too was surely destroyed. But mama was crying for joy and her joy was in seeing the cathedral still standing, just the cathedral, while the rest had all been flattened and grandmother had been right. Then they had gone down into the city and the Americans had sprayed them all over with something to get rid of the fleas and had given them a pass to go across a pontoon bridge. When they got to their house their mother cried again, but this time not for joy, because all they could see of their house was a bit of wall on the second storey, and it must have been the girls' room, because it was all pink but the rest of the house was gone and everything they possessed in the world was inside the barrow their mother was pushing, with Ingrid in it too because she couldn't walk very far. Later they had found the flat they were in now and their mother had made the glass in the windows herself, collecting pieces of glass and putting them together with flour glue and wire. Their mother was very proud of her handiwork and when she wanted to joke she said they were like the stained glass of a cathedral. But their mother was rarely in any mood to joke, on the contrary, she often cried since they had written to her that Papa had been taken prisoner by the Russians and then she hadn't heard anything more. Now Mama was trying to wrest a pension out of them but there was nothing doing. It turned out that Heidi's papa had been a member of the Party, so it was out of the question. Their mother traipsed from office to office and behind the counters she recognised the same people from before the war, and they'd all been members of the Party. Don't you recognise me?, she would ask. She would give her husband's name, surname, occupation. Can you believe it? Nobody recognised her. Mama wept with rage, but there was no pension.

'And where is your mama now?' 'She went to the Eifel. To *Hamstern*.' *Hamstern*, that's what Heidi said, to do what hamsters do. 'You know what a hamster is, don't you?' Of course I knew: they go round looking for food and they put what they find, a berry, a nut, in their mouths and when they go back to their burrow their cheeks are full of provisions. People in Cologne acted like hamsters. They filled shopping bags, bags, wheelbarrows, prams, hand-carts and pockets with everything they could find and carried it back to the city and went home loaded with bundles, their laps full of provisions and supplies of food under their shirts. 'I usually go too. But because my sister is sick, my mother didn't want to leave her alone.' Heidi was good at being a hamster too, her sister Ingrid less so, for she was too small and frail and she was often sick. Heidi, however, was great at it. She knew how to glean ears of corn in the fields or to find the odd potato or beet, depending upon the time of year, which the farmers had missed, and she knew how to steal lumps of coal. Sometimes she brought whole kilos of them home and piled them up carefully, as though they were building blocks, in the entrance hall which was also the kitchen.

That wall of black coal was the first thing that surprised me on the way into Heidi's house. The second thing was the hole in the ceiling, under which someone had put a zinc tub, like the ones you do laundry in, although here it was used to collect rainwater. It was easy to understand that the hole in the ceiling had not been made to let smoke out or sunshine in. Light came in from the roofless upper floors, but cold air and water must also have come in, as the tub testified. The second room, where the whole family slept, was undamaged though, and there were even some traces of stucco left in the middle of the ceiling. Three mattresses had been put on the ground along the walls, one for the girls, one for their mama and one for Mama's friend who was a policeman, Heidi told me, and slept with them when he wasn't on duty. Their grandmother though, really had managed to get to Bavaria.

Ingrid lay in a corner of the big room, wrapped in an old blanket, playing with her rag doll. She was paler than usual and her blue eyes had dark blue circles round them. She was amazed to see us and broke into a smile. Immediately, with the air of a conjuror pulling a rabbit out of a hat, I took the present I had brought her out of the basket and held it out to her. It was the pink doll, prettier than ever and dazzlingly elegant in her lace-trimmed tulle dress. Ingrid opened her eyes wide as she had done the first time, took her in her arms, held her to her chest and began to rock her. I saw a shadow of envy pass over Heidi's face, but I was happy. I didn't know what dramas my present would cause, nor did I learn about them until many years later. By that time Heidi and I were young women sitting side by side in front of the telephone switchboard and Ingrid was building towers with boxes of chocolates in the window of a Bonbonnière, and not even she played with dolls any more. What happened was logical enough, but I could never have predicted it.

Their mother returned from her exhausting, dusty and back-breaking work, and approached Ingrid's bed. The latter had hidden the pink doll under her blanket, but her mother noticed straight away in any case. What have you got under there? Nothing. Show me. And whose is this, who gave you it? She had to tell the truth. Her mother was inexorable. They might pay anything for a toy like that on the black market; there were always people looking for luxury goods. The doll was instantly confiscated; Ingrid wasn't even given a stay of execution of one day, for fear that she would spoil the doll and they would no longer be able to sell it. Ingrid cried all night. I didn't find out and didn't see her for more than a year. Heidi said to me that they had sent her to Bad Godesberg, where there was a children's clinic, and that they gave her fish with melted butter over it to eat there. She spoke with some envy, for in her heart of hearts she plainly believed that melted butter on fish more than made up for the loss of the doll. Heidi didn't bring me to the house with the wall of coal in the kitchen and the hole in the middle of the ceiling again; her mother must have forbidden it and maybe Marianne had something to do with it too. The latter, if she noticed the disappearance of the famous doll, was careful to say nothing. In reality there was nobody to miss it, because nobody had ever loved that doll who was so pointlessly and shamelessly luxurious.

35

WHEN SCHOOL STARTED, Heidi was around less often. But I was very busy too, for Dr Wallatz had got it into his head that I should start school with children my own age. 'You can't put her in with the little ones, given that she's tall,' he said, and he was quite right. I would have been still more embarrassed. Therefore I studied, did page after page of exercises, read aloud and compiled lists of words. I became as eager as he was to start in the appropriate class for my age, and to show what I could do. There was a kind of undeclared bet between us and the world, a wager in which Dr Wallatz had invested all his skills as a pedagogue. I was the horse on which he had staked everything.

'You'll see,' he said to my father. 'We'll cover six years of work in the space of two. I have always maintained that children waste a good deal of time at school, or at any rate in schools as they are nowadays, where everybody goes. The better ones get bored and make no progress, while the others make a nuisance of themselves and waste precious time too.' Dr Wallatz was an avowed follower of Rousseau, and held that the school should adapt to the ability of the pupil, not the pupil to the school. But how was this to be done, with so many people to teach? Dr Wallatz shook his head. I was in some sense the proof that his theories were correct, and I was a virgin terrain on which to apply them. He therefore paraded the whole of human knowledge before me, or rather the small part of it that was covered in school syllabuses. But as time went by his ambitions extended further still. One day he made the following proposal to my father and to myself: 'This girl is so intelligent and is so keen to learn that it would be a shame not to send her to the grammar school. I am convinced she could handle it.' 'But you'd have to set her studying Latin too!', my father objected. 'I am convinced she could handle Latin too.' The two men turned to look enquiringly at me. Up until that point I'd said yes to everything and had diligently learnt everything they wished me to learn. I would strive to pronounce in a single breath, without faltering, the composite words in German and to breathe through my teeth the English *th* sound, but I baulked at the proposal to teach me Latin, said that I did not want to learn it and that I would not go to grammar school. I could see the disappointment on Dr Wallatz's face. It had been his favourite subject, he had taught it to grammar school students for thirty years running, and would willingly have taught me too, but I was implacable and said a firm no to Latin. My father understood, but my mother was plainly disappointed, although not for the same reasons as Dr Wallatz. In the milieu in which we lived it was normal for children to go to grammer school. It was the most natural thing in the world for them to study Latin, for it was simply what was expected of an educated person destined to hold down a responsible job in the future, as fathers did, or to marry men with responsible jobs, as mothers did. For my mother, my refusal to take that path served as yet another proof that, as a daughter, I was not living up to her expectations. She must certainly have thought that Ilse, if she had lived to be my age, would have studied Latin and furthermore played the piano and perhaps, who knows, learnt how to sketch too, as a girl of good family was expected to do. The war may have wrecked everything, but those ideals remained intact, at any rate in my mother's head. I was to go to the junior secondary school which, furthermore, was still further away from our house, because all the boys and girls in Marienburg went to the grammar school. The junior secondary school was located on the other side, beyond the boundary between Marienburg and Bayenthal, and girls and boys living 'over there' tended to go to it. They enrolled me in the second class.

My father had no doubt had a word with the headmaster, and Dr Wallatz may also have gone to present me. Everything seemed in order when the secretary, in copying out my personal details, asked in an absent-minded fashion what my religion was. My father felt the ground give way beneath his feet. He hurriedly replied 'Catholic' but said it with so little conviction that the secretary looked up and hesitated for a moment before writing above the dotted line '*römisch katholisch*', Roman Catholic.

For a couple of days it was the sole topic of conversation in our house. Marianne said that she had been the only one to point out that I had never been baptised, and it was quite true. They had been so preoccupied with the good of my intellect that they had forgotten my spiritual salvation. The women in the kitchen agreed with her and shot disapproving glances at me. But their disapproval was directed less at me than at my parents, who had been guilty of leaving me in a state of unwitting paganism.

'How ever could you have forgotten it!', said grandma Schifferl, my mother's mother, who fixed her daughter with an inquisitorial stare. 'You have an idolater in your house and you didn't even realise. Don't you know that it's a Christian's first duty to convert those without a faith?'

My mother bowed her head, like a little girl caught doing wrong. The truth was that all that business to do with church and religion was not very important to her, and hadn't even mattered very much to her when she used to go and kneel down each morning with the other girls in the chapel, and never once had she really managed to concentrate on her praying. Even then my mother had had no other space within herself save that defined by her own desires and the thoughts connected with them. She had not the slightest aptitude for abstract concerns, such as matters having to do with faith, and she therefore found it hard to devote even a fraction of a second to them. If she went to Mass on Sundays, at midday, in the parish of Saint Mary the Virgin, it was because everybody went and one couldn't miss it.

Faced with his mother-in-law's severity, my father, who had never troubled to conceal his own neglect of his religious duties, felt more embarrassed than ever. Frau Schifferl was forever reminding him of his Protestant origins and telling him that she, for her part, had never really believed in his conversion, given that it had occurred shortly before his marriage, out of love for the daughter and not for God. There was some truth in what she said, for conversion to Catholicism had been the sole means by which Günther Berger could lead the beautiful Siglinde to the altar, given that in the Schifferl household a mixed marriage was not something you could even mention. My own case was in a sense more easily resolved, because it was not a question of shifting from heresy to the Roman faith, but from a condition of paganism to Christianity. Theological disputes or disquisitions would have been out of place, for what I required was a baptism and an accelerated course of catechism designed to bring me up to the level of spiritual education appropriate to my age.

'I know the reverend father very well,' my grandmother concluded, cradling her coffee cup which she had held in her hand throughout her preaching, and which she had waved to right and left in her rhetorical ardour, as if it were a thurible, 'I'll make sure to speak to him tomorrow.' No one dared to contradict her, and so the following Sunday I found myself in a room on the ground floor of the reverend father's house, at the end of Schillerstrasse. My grandmother accompanied me. This was the sole occasion upon which we went out anywhere together and so far as I can remember she did not speak to me as we walked along. I understood that she was doing me a great honour by taking such an intense interest in the state of my soul, and that she probably felt embarrassed by my presence alongside her. As luck would have it, the parish priest's house was not very far away and my grandmother disappeared almost immediately, although not until she had whispered something into the priest's ear, as if it were the grille of the confessional.

The priest was no longer in the first flush of youth, and had glasses, a chubby face and a crown of grizzled hair. He moved and spoke in a mannered way, with gestures ill-suited to his build, which was not tall but stout. He stared at me through his glasses and sat me in front of a booklet containing a great number of coloured pictures. Look! Meanwhile he looked at me, with his elbows leaning on the table and his fingers interlaced, as if they were praying, and this posture too had something forced and unnatural about it. I concentrated on the booklet, leafed through it page by page and with astonishment recognised in the naïve drawings, which were meant for much younger children, images which I already knew. I'd seen so many devils like that in our religious icons, for the monks who used to visit us always brought painted or printed sheets depicting red and blue devils tormenting the souls of the damned. Things were much the same in the book of catechism I was holding, in which the damned were depicted in meticulous detail languishing in the flames, with angels flying above their heads, naughty children pulling faces with little devils laughing behind them, and devout children praying on their knees with rosaries in their hands. They were exactly like the monks and the worshippers at home. I was so surprised and so happy at finding so many similarities that I said to the priest, who was still looking at me: 'I know all this very well. People pray like that at home too.' Instead of congratulating me on my perspicacity, the priest very nearly swept aside prayerbooks and crucifix, so vigorously did he pull his interlaced fingers apart and drum them against the table. 'This is blasphemy! How dare you compare pagan customs with our faith and our worship?'

I quailed in terror, more because of the sudden transformation than because of the words. In the heat of the moment I thought that he was one of the winged spirits, with sword in hand and with a threatening air, that was massacring sinners in the book. I would not have been at all surprised if all of a sudden he had begun to fly around the room. But no, he once more leant his elbows on the table, interlaced his fingers yet again, resumed his unctuous tone and set about trying to convert me.

I resolved to say only what was necessary, for I simply wished the lesson to end as soon as possible. For the rest, it didn't matter to me if I had to pray to our own god or to the one to whom they prayed. Where religion is concerned, we Tunshan were tolerant and ready to welcome saints or gods from anywhere, just so long as there was something miraculous about them. To tell the truth, the image of the mistreated Christ on the cross, enduring the pains of hell, inspired me with pity rather than devotion. I did not understand why in that country they chose to pray to one who suffered so much, and in such a human way, or so it seemed to me. The gods which I knew, even the more terrifying ones, were gods in a guise which in no way could be judged human. It was not for nothing, for good and for ill, that they were gods. I thought about a god suffering and dying and wondered how it was that a god could die. It was true that the one hanging in the corner of the parish priest's house nailed to his cross did later rise from the dead, but the fact of being dead remained, and that was not worthy of a god, or so I thought. Take the Buddha, for example, did the Buddha die? I recalled the one I'd seen in the cave with Malik, sitting on his lotus flower throne, and smiling with a happiness unknown to men. I felt pity for this god with his head lolling against his shoulder and his bleeding side, just as I would for any dying man. It would never have occurred to me to run my hand across his thin, bleeding body, in order that he might give me a little of his 'godhood'. This one, who was, from what the priest said, the son, was too human, while the other, the father, was too abstract. I was not much convinced by the new religion, but I obediently learnt by heart all the formulae of the catechism and the prayers, so that in a short time I was able to say, without even having to think, what the difference was between venial and mortal sins, and to recite the Ten Commandments, even when the parish priest asked me them out of order. What does the fifth commandment say? The fifth commandment says: Honour thy father and mother. And the seventh commandment? The seventh commandment ordains: thou shalt not commit adultery. I didn't have the faintest idea what adultery meant, but I was careful not to ask for an explanation, nor did the priest venture to explain, for he was clearly satisfied with the proofs of my faith. A fortnight before school began, he gave me absolution without laying too much emphasis upon my sins. One doesn't ask a child about to be baptised if it has sinned. The reverend father generously took my innocence for granted.

A private ceremony was held. I wore a veil of white lace on my head and carried a beribboned candle in my hand. My mother slipped into my hands a prayerbook which had once been hers, with a mother-of-pearl cover which could be shut with a little button, and my grandmother gave me a Lives of the Saints. The parish priest uncovered the baptismal font and sprinkled my head with holy water; we then moved over to a side chapel of the parish church, in front of a plaster Madonna who held her son's martyred body in her arms, and it was there that the parish priest celebrated Mass and put the host in my mouth. From that moment the 'Roman Catholic' written by the secretary on my form became a reality.

I don't know which of us was happier when we came out of the church in the September sunshine, whether it was the parish priest grateful for the generous donation given to his church by my father, my grandmother because she had saved my soul, my mother because she had been spared her own mother's zeal, Marianne and the other women because they all had the day off, or my father, who always felt a little guilty towards me, and who out of sheer relief gave me a watch with a white leather strap and with an inscription on the back which read 'From your father, 10th September 1949'. For my own part, I never again knelt before the wooden grille of the confessional, for the very idea of an ear in the darkness ready, like a funnel, to gather up my sins filled me with terror, and I also avoided going to communion, for fear of the fingers which offered me the host, and which had so swiftly shifted from praying to accusing me of blasphemy. I set foot in Saint Mary the Virgin only for special occasions, at Christmas and Easter. My mother, for her part, forgot to remind me of my duties as a Christian.

My secondary school was in Hölderlinstrasse. While the houses on either side of the building bore all too visible traces of the war, the school itself had hardly been damaged at all. It had a grand staircase and huge classrooms, which not even forty-five little girls managed to warm up, despite breathing next to each other for five hours in a row. The benches bore the marks of generations of carvers who had attacked them doggedly, and had holes for the dried-up ink-wells. The walls of our classroom were quite bare, and nothing was left of the posters which had previously hung there, and which someone had torn down, save for the drawing-pin holes, and here and there a few shining heads of brass, which just would not come out. It seemed that in the whole school there was nothing to hang on the walls to cover up the old holes and the more recent dirt, or simply to cheer up the forty-five little girls who sat within them, poorly clothed and with feet which were always cold. Sometimes their fingers were cold too, as they gripped their pens and dipped their nibs in an ink-well which seemed always to need re-filling. Forty-five frozen little girls. But however could one hope to heat such a large classroom in the winter of 1949–1950?

The teacher of German was a tall, wiry woman, with a large mole right on her lip, on the left-hand side. A single black hair sprouted from the mole. When Fräulein Jung spoke, the mole moved with her lips, and the hair shook like a small antenna. The class's attention was always drawn to the mole and to the hair that danced like a ballerina. They hung on her every word, indeed they could not help it, for her dry lips seemed to hold them under a spell. Fräulein Jung knew how to attract their attention, and then how to hold it, and furthermore was able to use her own ugliness as a sort of provocation. Her grey hair was tied in a bun and scraped away from her temples so tightly that her skin seemed to be pulled back too. She persisted in wearing a black smock, until one day the headmaster ordered her to take it off, because uniforms were banned from German schools. Fräulein Jung pursed her lips, so much so that the hair on her mole stood up more impudently than usual, and took off the smock without saying a word. When she came into the hall in the morning she made us stand up and sing a prayer, but it was not an ordinary prayer but a hymn to the sun: *Die güldene Sonne / voll Freude und Wonne / trägt uns an Grenzen / mit ihrem Glänzen / ein herzerquickendes liebliches Licht*, Full of joy and bliss, the golden sun with its beams brings us a heart-warming, delightful light. Forty-five little girls, standing upright between their benches, were singing a pagan hymn, and when I recited it Marianne crossed herself and said 'Jesus and Mary, what sort of prayer is that?'

The song to the sun was Fräulein Jung's only expression of joy, but she may have had her own way of being happy. Her happiness was expressed through the red marks she traced on our exercise books. Those red marks, whether underneath a guilty word or beside a line muddied by error, were a source of palpable pleasure to her. And there were errors aplenty in the exercise books which ink-stained fingers used to fill with signs, and in pages which the little girls hesitantly submitted to her pitiless pencil, while their eyes fastened on her lips, which were pressed tightly together as if they were gripping the pencil. The worst thing was when she used to walk between the benches, while we were writing, and I would sense her behind my back; it seemed to me that she saw the mistakes before they had even been written down, and that she was silently urging me to make them, simply for the joy of marking them in red. I found her presence behind my back so unnerving that I hardly remembered how to write my own name. I felt as insecure as I'd done that first day in Dr Wallatz's study. Now, however, it was not the *naja* leaving its trace but Fräulein Jung's pencil recording her rebukes in red words at the foot of the page. My homework would invariably have at least one such rebuke: 'Your writing is untidy'; 'Your spelling is poor' or 'Your grammar leaves something to be desired'. To round it off, there'd be an exhortation to do better, which implied a far from flattering appraisal of my commitment: 'Try harder!'; 'Buckle down!'; Do some spelling exercises!' and 'Read!' I despaired, though Dr Wallatz did his utmost to console me. Perhaps in his heart of hearts he wondered why my parents had insisted on sending me to school, when I could perfectly well have gone on studying with him, even up to adulthood perhaps. He imagined a very private school, in the style of Rousseau, which would be adapted to suit the needs and abilities of the pupil, instead of which I was having rather desperately to adapt myself to a school which in no way suited me. My mother was adamant: 'Naja must go to school with the other little girls. What'll you be thinking of next, a private school indeed, that's for princesses!' I therefore tried each morning to drown my disgust in the cup of sweet tea that Marianne used to make for me, and I angrily sank my teeth into the slice of bread and marmalade as if it were Fräulein Jung's thigh. Then I left the garden path behind me, went down Goethestrasse, crossed the avenue and let myself be swallowed up by the tedium of the morning. In the afternoon I used to step through Dr Wallatz's garden gate. I so needed to tell him about my failures that I did not even have eyes for his vegetable geometries; I needed his words of comfort as much as his plants needed water. He listened to me with garden shears in hand, or else with his pipe when the cold made it impossible to use shears. He shook his head, said how right I was, and as he helped me with my homework would endlessly criticise schools, teachers and syllabuses, so that, to hear him, one would never have understood how he had lasted thirty years among the very same teachers, in schools very like my own and with syllabuses which may well have been even more absurd than the ones I had to swallow.

'Try harder!'; 'Buckle down!'; 'Do your exercises!'. Even at night I was harried by Fräulein Jung, her mole and her red squiggles on my pages. Now it was she who visited me in my dreams, and oddly enough she would appear to me with yellow hair, in twisted strands growing close to the nape of her neck, and she had empty, pendulous breasts which she slung behind her as she said 'Try harder!' and 'Do your exercises, exercises, exercises, exercises . . . !'

Fräulein Jung was brutal with her judgements but Herr Braun, who taught us mathematics, was brutal with his ruler. He patrolled the benches like a policeman, turning his wooden weapon over in his hands, behind his back. At the least mistake or failure to pay attention he would appear from behind you and, suddenly, before you even realised, the ruler left its red trace on your fingers. He was known as 'corporal', and it was said that he was even more brutal with the boys and that with them he used, as well as the ruler, his fingers, with which every now and then he would attack the ear of some wretched little boy, and he would pull so hard that the others at a certain point seriously began to think that it might remain in his hand. I was horrified, and I was still more so when one day I turned round to ask for a piece of blotting paper, felt a swish in the air and immediately afterwards a sharp pain in the head. I was about to raise my arm when I exchanged a glance with the corporal. I read an expression of triumph on his face and I realised that he hated me. Perhaps he also hated the other children, the school and even those who had sent him there to be white-washed and purged of his 'brown' past, and who had demoted him to a junior secondary school although he had been a teacher at the grammar school. Perhaps he hated everyone in equal measure, but I noticed his gaze fall on me and I felt that he hated me more than the others and that it was actually on me that he wished to be revenged. The following day I refused to go to school. My parents pretended that I was ill and let me stay at home for a week but would then accept no excuses. Marianne accompanied me as far as the school gate and did not move until she saw me disappear inside. They did not trust me. My mother perhaps feared that from one day to the next a subversive energy might develop inside of me, and that I might try to run away, rebel and cause them trouble in some way. For trouble was the only thing they expected of me.

As it turned out, I did not cause them trouble, at any rate not deliberately. In the end I adapted to school. My instinct came to my aid: bend low, let the wind pass over you, raise up your head again when it is far away in the distance. That's what I did. I bent my head to save my neck. I studied and I improved so much that Fräulein Jung was obliged to write on my exercise books: 'You are making good progress!', 'Keep up the good work!', 'Keep going!', 'Very satisfactory!' The corporal, after a conversation with my father, stopped clipping me with his ruler but ignored me, did not call me up to the blackboard, never asked me any questions, did not grill me, and did the grades and reports in his own way, but they were adequate and served me well enough.

There certainly were other teachers who walked among the benches of 2C or sat at the desk in front of the assembly of scared little girls. Among them there were no doubt some fair and tolerant persons, who did not delight in marking mistakes in red or in hitting distracted pupils with rulers, but they must have been dull, grey and stooping figures, such as the people one saw toiling amidst the ruins, who, like the other teachers at my secondary school, have left no trace in my memory. It is not them I remember, but a man who walked around the streets and filled the ruins with his singing. He must already have been old, although I am not certain about this, but anyway his voice was not; it was powerful, pleasing and perfectly matched his accordion. He sang just one song, always the same one, *Man schenkt sich Rosen in Tirol*, In the Tyrol one treats oneself to roses. You could tell from those roses that he was coming, even when he was still a long way off, and people knew it and got some small change ready. Once he was directly beneath the windows of the school; it was spring and the song climbed up from the street to us, filling the classroom with roses, ruffling the exercise books open on the benches and causing the pencils to roll. Soon everything in the class was in motion, as children swung their plaits, linked arms and mouthed the tune. Then a sharp rap drove roses and music back into the street, as if they had been flies imprisoned between the walls of the classroom. Window panes shook, mouths fell silent, plaits lay motionless along the backs of the seats and exercise books were carefully re-opened. Only the hair in the mole on Fräulein Jung's lip still moved, still shook with rage, in time with her voice as it resumed the interrupted narrative: 'Rumours of the most beautiful virgins could now be heard on the Rhine . . .'

It was May 1950, I was twelve years old and my breasts were starting to swell under the light sweater that Marianne had made me; I sat in the middle row, third bench, and the place next to mine was empty. Of the forty-four little girls around me, who shared the same fate day after day, not one of them in those seven months of school had addressed so much as a word to me. No one had asked me where I lived, or invited me to skip with them in the playground, or let me into the secrets they told each other, in little groups. They sometimes cast glances at me, covertly, but when I looked at them they directed their gaze somewhere else; sometimes I felt that they were talking about me behind my back, and that they were making fun of me, but they were probably not doing that. They simply did not notice me.

* * *

The situation improved a little the following year. On the first day back at school I had not dared to sit next to one of the other pupils and the place next to mine had once again remained empty. Then Grete arrived, found the empty place and sat down. She was new and didn't know anyone. She simply sat down, turned towards me and asked: 'What's your name?' 'Naja?' she immediately remarked, 'I've never heard a name like that. At home no one is called Naja.' She started at me, as if searching for a clue as to my having such a strange name: 'Where do you come from?' I blushed. It was the first time someone had asked me that question, just like that, directly, as if she suspected, just by looking at me, that my origin would be as unknown and strange as the name I bore. 'From far away,' I stammered. 'And where might that far away be?' Grete asked, refusing to abandon the chase. 'Places you don't know.' 'How do you know I don't know them?' 'Because nobody knows them.' 'If you don't want to tell me, don't tell me, see if I care. But I come from Königsberg, a place everybody knows.' She said it with pride, as if so regal a name, the king's mountain, implied that anyone coming from that place was of equally illustrious stock. Grete's family was certainly not of royal blood but from what she said it had been noted for its wealth in Königsberg, for it had owned a farm with a thousand hectares of land, and in the summer Poles had worked there as agricultural labourers or taken on other, more responsible posts. Before the war the Poles had come of their own free will but during the war they came as prisoners and worked as they had done in the past but were paid less. According to Grete, the country around Königsberg was a paradise for everyone, aside from the Poles who worked there, infinitely vast and infinitely rich, and no one would have ever dreamt of going away if the Russians had not arrived. From what Heidi and Marianne had told me, I had already understood that in each and every story the Russians always played the part of the killjoy and that when they arrived everyone ran away.

I too had met some Russians when I went with my grandfather Bairqan to Safapol kolkhoz, which was in the cotton fields, on the plain between the Amudar'ya and Termez. The president, who was Russian, invited us into his house, offered us tea and biscuits and was very kind. I just couldn't imagine him raping women and killing children. I could only think of him as I remembered him, a kind man who had patted me on the cheek and offered me a biscuit. My grandmother Martha had not had bad experiences with the Russians either, indeed quite the reverse. A Russian had been in love with her and she would have stayed with him if her father had not forbidden it, and if they had not gone back to the Rhineland. How could these benevolent images be squared with the terrifying accounts of the Russians one heard in Cologne? Perhaps a uniform and a cap with a red star sufficed to turn peaceful men into a bloodthirsty horde, before which the only rational thing to do was to flee. Grete's family, consisting of her mother, the grandparents and five children, had indeed fled. The only one not to have taken to his heels was Grete's elder brother, who was then a soldier. Although he was only seventeen, he'd been called up, at the very last moment, but had not had the time to fight for, as Grete explained, his war had lasted just two days. On the first day he had reached the front, and on the second he had been captured by the Americans. After a year he was sent home. Now the whole family, the mother, the grandparents and the five children, were in Cologne, save for Grete's father, and they knew only that he had been at Stalingrad, nothing else. Grete used to tell the story as if it had nothing to do with her, investing no emotion in it and still less embroidering upon it. Heidi too would speak in very much the same way. Their stories were normal enough and there was no reason not to tell them. That's how it was, and there was an end to it. Grete anyway tended to be a little brusque about everything, did not stand on ceremony or flatter, in the way that little girls usually do. And it was not surprising, given that her house was full of brothers, and her mother, who had got a job as a ticket collector, had neither the time nor the energy when she returned home in the evening to teach her daughter how little girls ought to behave. Grete, although she had her plaits redone every morning, behaved just like a boy. She was brilliant at whistling and liked to do it whenever she could. She would whistle on her way into school and she did not stop until she was told to shush. When someone in the street yelled out: '*Mädchen, die pfeifen und*

Hühner, die krähen, denen soll man bei Zeiten den Hals umdrehen!', girls who whistle, and cocks that crow, should have their necks wrung without delay, Grete would just laugh and whistle all the louder. It was already clear that it'd not be so easy to force her to bend her neck, which she held very straight on her slender shoulders.

Grete was the very first to turn up to school one morning with a handsome pony tail instead of plaits. Her friends looked at her as if she had dyed her hair green or given herself a porcupine hairstyle like Struwwelpeter. She looked round provocatively as she shook her head from right to left and back again, as if responding to a refrain that she could hear within her, and the tail dangled this way and that like a reddish-brown plume brushing against her thin neck. It would be none too easy to bend a neck like that.

I admired her. I admired her pony tail, her whistling and the proud way in which she used to say 'at home'. It was not that I cared about the thousand hectares of land at Königsberg, or that I was particularly interested in that place. It was the sheer ease with which she boasted about it that made me admire her. I would have liked to have been like her, to have her brown hair with the red highlights and her freckled cheeks, to live with five brothers and to come from Königsberg. For my part, when someone looked at me, the very idea that they might ask me where I came from made my heart sink. In actual fact no one ever did ask me, perhaps because they all regarded me as so exotic that they supposed that the place I came from was definitely, inexorably unknown, and so much so that there was no point in pursuing it any further. But it was an episode at school which brought it home to me just how ashamed of myself I was.

We had a biology teacher whom we called *Herr Reichskäferführer*, or Führer of the beetle kingdom, because he had a collection of beetles that had been the finest in the entire Third Reich, or so he claimed. This *Käfer*, as we called him for short, was obsessed by the genetic inheritance of characteristics. One of his favourite assertions ran as follows: 'People can reel off the pedigree of a poodle but if you ask them when their grandmother was born they won't know.' In order to prove his theory about people's lamentable neglect of their own genealogical trees, he would ask someone in the class, where do you come from, where do your grandparents come from, and so on? When he came to me, he looked at me with an air of scientific detachment and asked: 'And what about you, do you know where your grandparents are from?' It would have been very easy for me to answer, for I knew my family's genealogy by heart, and could recite it. I could have recounted the story of Bairqan my grandfather, of Bairqan's grandmother who used to sing in a language which only existed in the land of the thousand monasteries, of Urus Khan, who had left the land of the seven rivers, and of his wife Sagatai, who wept for the sons that the Great Wind had scattered across the steppe. I could have gone back to Mongotai, who had been the first to reach the banks of the Volga, and to Muchor Lousang with his one thumb, who had defeated his enemies with a whistle. I could steer the history of the Tunshan against the current until I reached the great ancestor Alcidai, who had returned from the kingdom of the eight *Naga* kings, and go back to our springs, and to Sigi Quduqu who knew how to transcribe Genghis Khan's orders as blue marks. I could have recited the entire genealogy of the Tatar-Tunshan from memory, and used their names and the names of the places in which they had lived to fill the cold space of the huge classroom, where forty-four little girls, who knew nothing whatsoever about me or about the Tunshan, and a teacher nicknamed *Reichskäferführer* were looking sceptically at me, let's see how she answers this one, who knows where she's from, she probably doesn't even know herself. I could have done all that but I didn't dare to expose those names to their mockery, or to subject them to Herr Käfer's scientific theories, in part out of modesty but also out of shame. My first impulse was to lie, to say the first thing that came into my head, to appropriate Heidi or Marianne's family, to turn myself into one of those little girls who were looking quizzically at me and awaiting my answer. Instead I opted for a different kind of lie and said: 'I don't know.' 'There,' commented Herr Käfer jubilantly, 'what did I tell you? They don't know what genetic material they derive from. With dogs you take care that they are a pure breed and that undesirable crosses don't occur.' He turned his back on me with a gesture of contempt. I felt ashamed, not because of his gesture but because through that lie I had repudiated my family. My betrayal brought about the disappearance, once again, and more painfully than before, of everyone I held dear, of Bairqan, Mai Ling, Malik, Haysce, Ul'an my father and Börte my mother. Grete too was different, for she spoke a language that the other girls sometimes couldn't even understand, she behaved oddly, and she was an alien. But not as much as I was. There was no one in the entire school who was as alien as I was. It was pointless trying to hide it, to deny my origins and to say that I came from a mysterious faraway country, to cloud reality; it was enough simply to look me in the face in order to understand. I was irremediably different, and what was worse, I was ashamed of it.

36

I FOUND MYSELF looking in the bathroom mirror more often than usual. It was an oval mirror with a gilt frame lit from both the right and the left by two bronze lamps shaped like the calyx of a flower. To begin with I had looked long and often at the two lamps, so beautiful did they seem to me. Now I no longer cared about them, since I had eyes only for myself. Taken overall, I would have found nothing to criticise in my appearance. If I had been with the Tunshan I would certainly have been judged to be a pretty girl, even though I knew that where beauty was concerned I could never compare with my cousin Haysce; perhaps, who knows, someone would have sung rhymes in my honour. I could have borne comparison with the other girls. I was tall and lithe, with an oval face, and with eyes that were dark and almond-shaped but not as slanting as those of Mai Ling or of my father Ul'an. The rest of my body was passable, and it was just my nose that betrayed me. For the Tunshan there was nothing exceptional about it; it was merely a Mongol nose such as so many of them had, short and rather flat. Now, however, when I looked at it in that oval mirror, my nose seemed markedly too small. The fact is, I was no longer able to look at myself through Tunshan eyes. Now I saw myself through the eyes of those who were around me and who assuredly judged my nose to be too little. They would never say such a thing to me openly, but they intimated as much, for I had learnt not only to see myself through their eyes but also to read in their eyes what they thought of me. Once I plucked up courage and asked grandfather Berger: 'Do you find my nose too small?' My grandfather was busy impaling a worm on a hook and did not answer straightaway. Then he looked attentively at my face, as if he were observing it for the very first time. 'I wouldn't call it long,' he answered, 'but it suits you.' It was nothing but a kindly excuse, I said to myself, plainly my grandfather thought as others did or rather, saw me as others saw me. I would have preferred it if no one at all saw me. If someone looked me in the face I would immediately bow my head and say to myself, they're looking at my nose and they're certainly thinking, how short her nose is.

Once Marianne caught me contemplating my nose in the mirror. 'What's the matter,' she said, 'aren't you happy with your nose?' 'You can see very well that it's too short!' 'If that's all that's bothering you, noses nowadays can be changed.' 'Changed? How?' 'They put a plastic one on.' I looked at her in horror, but the idea intrigued me: 'How ever can it be plastic?' 'I read about it in the paper. There are surgeons who do it.'

My grandfather laughed when I told him about our conversation. 'They don't give you a plastic nose, it's not like acting the clown at Carnival. There really are surgeons who can change the shape of a nose but they use your own skin, not plastic. But I,' he continued after a brief pause, 'I wouldn't have my nose changed even if I had one like Cyrano de Bergerac. An operation is still an operation, and if it's not strictly necessary why run the risk? And who do these surgeons think they are? Even if they believe they can remake nature at will they are not gods, for us to entrust ourselves to them with our eyes shut. Do me a favour, stop thinking about your nose; there are worse things in the world than a nose that's too small.'

I don't know if what my grandfather had said convinced me, but events shortly after that made me forget, at any rate for a while, my worries about my nose.

That very same summer, 1952 it was, my grandmother fell ill. She became more and more yellow and had pains in her side. They took her to Cologne, operated on her and when she came round they showed her a glass with five stones in it, on her bedside table, and everyone said to her: 'Have you seen, we told you so, they were stones. They've taken them out now. Here they are.' My grandfather said nothing and kissed her on her forehead, which was still yellow. My grandmother, when there was no one else there, turned to me and said very quietly: '*Rebyonok*, my child,' and she winked, as if she wished to entrust a secret to me: 'they think they can fool me with this story about stones', and she gestured towards the bedside table, 'but I wasn't born yesterday. There's something else involved.' She shut her eyes and I noticed that her eyelids were yellow too, her whole face was, and even her hands, which stood out all the more against the white of the sheet. *Ach ty bedny rebyonok*. I stroked her forehead, and she smiled. 'You have cool hands, my child. I am closing my eyes because then I can feel your hand better. Like a cool wind blowing across the steppe.' She opened her eyes more and more rarely until one morning they told me that she would never open them again. I ran my hand over her face one last time, her forehead was like a frozen steppe. She'll have thought about the Volga, I said to myself, about the land she trod as a small girl and about the Russian officer. *Ach ty bedny rebyonok*, I said very quietly, bending over the bed so that she alone could hear.

It was a terribly sad summer. My grandfather understood that he'd not get over his loss, said barely a word and became thin and stooped. My parents tried to persuade him to stay on in Cologne, in our house, for what would he do on his own in Daun? It's even sadder on one's own. And what if you fall ill? But he was stubborn. I can look after myself perfectly well. And then there's Lucifer, who's expecting me. Would you risk your health for a dog? For a dog, yes, you bet I would! He was a stubborn old man and they did not manage to convince him. I wanted to accompany him but they would not let me go. I would have ended up tiring him still more. It was not the right moment for a holiday.

My grandfather never really recovered. He didn't go fishing any more, and he stopped visiting his patients. 'Come the autumn he'll get better,' my father would say, but he plainly wasn't convinced, 'we need to work out how to get him to close down his consulting room. Besides he could have begun to draw his pension some time ago.' We didn't have to wait until the autumn. One afternoon, my father, while up on a visit, found him outside the house, on the wicker armchair, asleep. Lucifer lay in front of him in his usual position, with his long paws on my grandfather's feet, and he did not move, not even when he heard the car arrive and when he saw my father getting out. There was no greeting, nothing at all; he did not move from his post, but just turned his head, whimpered and panted, while his pink tongue dribbled on my grandfather's feet. It was then that my father understood. Thirty years are no small thing, so how can you separate yourself from someone after so much time spent together? You'd have to begin a whole life from scratch, on your own. My grandfather had not felt up to it and he had died. He had died gazing out over the lake which had been a volcano, over the river where he had been a director of the dragonflies, and of the junipers which used to stain the meadows with violet; he had died in the midst of all the things he loved but which, without Martha, were not enough to keep him in life. 'He's been lucky,' my father said. Everyone thought so.

There was still Lucifer. He too was in mourning, whimpered, refused his food, got up reluctantly when I arrived and licked my hands, sought my affection. It broke my heart. 'Let's take him with us,' I begged. My mother said our house was not suited to such a big dog. My father shook his head: 'You'd not be doing him any favours. Lucifer is used to going in the woods, to running free and to hunting rabbits. What would he do in a city? Poor creature, can you imagine him on a lead!' I retorted that even for a dog woods and rabbits were not enough, and that Lucifer would certainly have preferred being with me in the city to being in the country with people he did not know. My father did not agree. Lucifer was given to the peasants who had cared for my grandfather towards the end. The house on the eye of the volcano was sold and we never went back to Daun.

In the space of a single summer I had lost a grandmother who understood my fear of confined spaces, and who used to say 'We are used to the steppe, you and I, we can't be shut in by walls,' and to call me *rebyonok* in a kindly voice; a grandfather who understood fishes; and, finally, a dog who had reminded me of the happy carefree times when I had roamed about with my cousin Malik. I would see Lucifer again leaping around me; I would call him and he would suddenly rear up and run towards me with his long black legs which seemed barely to touch the ground. He too had gone, and that summer I again took to hiding beneath my eiderdown, in my soft cave, and it seemed to me that I would not stand firm, that I would do as my grandfather had done and not leave my refuge again. But I was made of the stern stuff of which nomads are made, and I stood firm.

'You need a whole lifetime to learn Latin, but French can be learnt in three weeks. What of English? Any old negro knows how to speak English.' Such were the linguistic theories of Herr Zepp, the new teacher of German, who wanted first of all to instil in us a sense of his superiority as a teacher, and a perennial student of Latin, a language that wasn't studied in our school. His theories had no effect on us, though, because we particularly liked 'the negroes' language', and because we'd often find notes under the benches saying things like 'How are you? My name is Werner. What is your name?' The messages were written by the pupils who attended in the afternoon, and who were male. Because there was a shortage of classrooms, the school buildings were in continuous use, with girls in the morning and boys in the afternoon, which was why polyglot notes were sometimes to be found underneath the benches, to which the girls replied in their preferred language. Meetings out of school were planned in German or in English. I too once found a note of this kind, written, however, in German and in a fine hand, very different from the scrawls used by the other writers of messages. The contents of the note were original too. He did not begin with a request that one reveal one's own name but got straight to the point: 'I know you. I've seen you many times and I like you. I'd like to meet you after school. Daniel.' It was a brazen declaration to say the least. This Daniel must be a bit of a show-off, I thought, and Grete agreed with me. But I was intrigued, and so I waited a few days and then wrote on a scrap of paper: 'How have you got to know me? Tell me who I am!' It was a test to see if he were lying. The answer came soon enough, written like the earlier note in a painstaking script. He described me, said that he had set eyes on me several times, reiterated the invitation to meet up after school and ended up by saying 'I love you'. I did not answer, but only because I did not know what to write, and whether I should say yes or prevaricate. Just a few days later, however, when I was already on the way home, I was approached by a tall, pale boy in a jacket which hung off him and which still bore traces of the colour of the military overcoat from which it had been made. In other words, he was just a boy like all the rest, and I would very probably not even have noticed him, had it not been for the note. Yet I immediately grasped that it was Daniel. May I accompany you? He was very shy, as I had imagined he would be. I remembered my cousin Haysce and her adventure with Batu, and ever since then I had been convinced that boys who are bold in speech are in fact awkward and very shy. So it was with the one walking beside me, wrapped in his olive green jacket, who did not dare to say a thing to me. I felt our embarrassment grow. 'Aren't you going to school?', I asked him, for we had already gone a fair distance and I was afraid that he would accompany me all the way home. He did not even answer me but took to his heels, as if he had realised that he was fearsomely late, while I knew perfectly well that he was early because the afternoon lessons only began at two o'clock. He's a strange one, I said to myself, and I felt relieved when he'd gone.

But he reappeared the next day and this time he had prepared what he had to say to me. It became a habit. He would accompany me every day, for a few hundred yards, then turn around and go to school in his turn, always very early. On Friday he asked me if we could see one another on Saturday, and this time far from school. Now it was my turn to be flustered, for I simply did not know how to behave on such occasions. But Daniel looked imploringly at me, and so we settled on a date beside the river. However, when the time came to go I hesitated; I was afraid he wouldn't come or that he would behave like my cousin's admirer and run off if I so much as dared to touch him.

Yet he did come, and he didn't run off when I touched him, indeed, he held my hand so that I wouldn't run off. Both of us were so afraid that, to overcome it, Daniel began to speak. He was Polish, he told me, and his whole family had remained there. Why? I asked. They had been taken away, eighteen of them, his whole family, and they had not returned. And why had they been taken away? Because we are Jewish, Daniel replied abruptly and I stopped asking questions. Very gradually, however, those strolls beside the river helped us to confide in each other, and Daniel, a little at a time, told me his story. When they had taken his family away, he was seven years old and was on a farm, where he stayed. After the war his aunt in Cologne had tracked him down and had brought him back to live with her. The aunt was Jewish too, and had survived because her landlady had hidden her in the cellar. In the cellar? Yes, actually in the cellar, and she had stayed there the whole time. She only came out at night. And had no one seen her? They had in fact seen her but no one had said anything, and so she survived. However, as you can well imagine, she had been so scared all those years hiding in the cellar that she had turned completely white. Not like an old woman, for she was not yet an old woman, but white like someone who has lost the colour of their skin, when the pink has gone away and the skin no longer has any colour. That's horrible!, I said. The idea of that white aunt gave me the creeps. Even her eyelashes are white, Daniel said by way of conclusion, looking into my eyes. The idea of having to live with that white aunt disturbed me. What about her eyes? I asked and then immediately felt ashamed to have asked it. Her eyes aren't white, Daniel laughed, eyes can't change colour; they are black, just as they were before. If one day you come to my house, you'll meet her. I had no desire whatsoever to meet Daniel's aunt and, besides, I still did not understand why the poor woman had had to stay hidden all that time in a cellar, until she went completely white. But it was just one of those stories everyone preferred not to tell, the children because they knew nothing about it, the adults because they did not want to know anything about it, and Daniel because he was faced each day with an aunt who was as white as a ghost, and he had no desire to recount so many details. I really didn't want to meet Daniel's aunt.

Yet I did meet her. Daniel was very keen that I go to his house. His aunt was a friendly lady dressed in black, in the old style, with her blouse buttoned up to the neck, which made her seem even whiter. She was not just white; she was transparent. She seemed to be made of air and when you stood beside her you could smell an odour of damp walls, as if she had not got rid of the mould from the cellar. She sat me down on a velvet sofa, similar to those in the Berger household. 'Luckily the house was not bombed, and so at the end of the war it was handed back to us. There were still some things left inside.' In the meantime she offered me a cup of tea and I noticed that her hands shook. I thought that the cellar must be to blame for that too. As if she had guessed what I was thinking, she said: 'Since the war ended, I've not been able to control my hands.' I said that I'd help myself. She let me do this, sat down, with her pale hands in her dark lap, and looked at me from beneath her white eyelashes. Daniel sat beside her. There seemed to be a kind of silent understanding between the two of them, a complicity between adults and not between a boy and an aunt whose whiteness made her seem so very old. The aunt had taken in her nephew because he was the sole surviving member of the family, and not because she had wished to adopt him or educate him. There was no need anyway, for Daniel had educated himself. His aunt did not mind what he did, and reckoned that he was mature enough. Perhaps she thought that anyone who had suffered such a monstrous injustice in their childhood would know how to distinguish between good and evil. On Saturdays I would bring my homework, and we would work together sitting at the living-room table, while his aunt sat in the next room in complete silence, so that I did not even realise that she was there.

We did our homework, or else we pretended to do it. We fooled around. Once I came up to Daniel, took his hands and put them on my breasts. He didn't run away even that time. By then I no longer feared that he would behave like Batu. But I never had the courage of my cousin Haysce. Perhaps I wouldn't have had it in the *ayil* on the Amudar'ya either, where everything was infinitely simpler, or so it seemed to me. For at fourteen, the age I was then, I would already have had a husband, which is what I had a right to, and perhaps even a baby. Here on the other hand I lived a kind of extended childhood, in which everything seemed still to be an apprenticeship and nothing was done entirely seriously. Daniel and I would awkwardly rehearse the part of adolescents who don't know what they want, when in fact we knew perfectly well; history had made us older than our years, but we lacked the courage to take for ourselves what we had a right to.

Once we were both sitting in his aunt's sitting room. The spring light was streaming in through the window onto the table; I turned my back to the window, while Daniel was in front of me and bent over an exercise book. As I raised my eyes from my own book I noticed how a ray of sunshine, passing close by him, pierced his throat. It passed right through, as if skin, tendons and bone were no obstacle. I was horrified, for it seemed to me that Daniel was becoming transparent like his aunt. I couldn't help crying out 'Daniel, you're made of glass!' Daniel looked up without even smiling and held a long, white hand up to the sun so that the sun passed right through his splayed fingers and the skin seemed transparent. 'It's true', he said, 'I'm made of glass.' He let his fingers glide through the ray of sunshine, dividing it into streams of light. 'I've nothing to hide,' he added.

What could one have to hide at the age of fifteen?, I wondered. But even if Daniel's soul was as transparent as his skin, I found it difficult to peer into it. That shy and gentle boy sometimes seemed odd and incomprehensible to me. It is true that I had no terms of comparison, for at that time I knew no other boys aside from him, and I already knew that it was pointless to compare him with those I had known beside the Amudar'ya. Yet the way in which Daniel, as he touched me, used to start, while his eyes asked me to forgive him, seemed odd to me; his gaze too was odd, for it seemed to go through things and persons alike, as if simply by looking at them they became as transparent as he was. His way of talking about himself was odd too and quite unlike Heidi and Grete's idle chatter; it was as if nothing could surprise him any more. He told me about his mother, and about the last time he'd seen her; he remembered her in her summer outfit, with her blonde, wavy hair, just like his own was now. They had gone by car to the farm, so that he could spend the holidays in the fresh air, or that was what they told him. The peasants were standing deferentially in front of the gate, with a throng of children round about. Daniel was scared and had clung to his mother, and she, just before leaving, had kissed him on both cheeks and had said to him 'Have fun!' They were the very last words his mother said to him. 'Have fun, she said to me, as if that were such a simple thing to do!' He said this sarcastically. He regarded her urging him to have fun as her last will and testament and he was not able to execute it. What did having fun mean? I ventured a reply. Perhaps, I said, it was a state in which one would be happy to remain. We too, as we walked along the river, were having fun, when all was said and done. Daniel shook his head. It wouldn't do; the task left him by his mother was too exacting to be reduced to walks hand in hand beside the Rhine.

How was one to have fun, I wondered, if one had to live with an aunt who watched you from beneath snow-white eyelashes? And as for me, could I have fun with a mother who watched me and yet seemed to be unaware of me, in a place which was still stranger to me than his aunt's house was to Daniel? Daniel did not ask me questions, and did not want to know where I'd left my mother and if I had left her. Though he was but fifteen years old it was as if the world no longer had any secrets for him, and he therefore had no need to ask anything. I was grateful to him for this.

He used to hold my hand and we used often to walk along in silence. I was grateful to him for this too. My story paled by comparison with his, and was not even worth telling, or so I thought. Besides, would I have found the right words to recount things that were unfamiliar to him? For instance, the right words to describe a yurt. As time wore on, I too found it hard to recall all of them. What exactly did we call the central post inside the yurt, or the rope used to close off the opening in the roof? Even the part of the yurt where the children slept had a name I no longer remembered. Gradually words left me, turned pale and slowly disappeared, until in their place there remained an object without a name, a void in that part of the yurt in which the children slept, a void where the rope for closing off the smoke hole hung from the roof, and the central post too no longer had a name. I realised it in fits and starts; an image from back then came into my mind and I searched in vain for the names of things, and when I failed to find them, I felt frightened. The same thing must happen to those who lose their memory and realise that it is just the beginning of an evil which will end inexorably in their forgetting all the words. The same despair must strike those who suddenly forget the names they have known since childhood and who see, while their mind is still lucid, the abyss into which they are about to plunge. I became aware of how words were abandoning me, and so tried to avoid thinking about it. I did not talk about my past for fear that I might have to worry about searching for lost words. Daniel did not want to know anything and anyway I understood that not even my story could have surprised him. One particular episode confirmed this.

We were in his aunt's living room studying. I was revising my latest geography lesson. The distance between Sebastopol and Archangel, it said, is 2,300 kilometres; Moscow is 2,000 kilometres away from Cologne. An aeroplane covers that distance in six hours. Turgay, Charkov, Karaganda and Alturbulag are on the fiftieth parallel, while Vilnius, Moscow, Chelyabinsk, Omsk and Libinsk are on the fifty-fifth parallel. Daniel leant over my exercise book. At school I had copied out the map of central Asia which Frau Weigel had hung on the blackboard. Due to lack of space, my map had a somewhat elongated shape, since the whole of central

Asia could never fit on a single page of an exercise book, but it was clear enough. At the top, next to a disproportionate Caspian Sea I had written 'Kazakhstan'; directly beneath I had drawn the Aral Sea, from which there ran two blue lines, the Syrdar'ya and the Amudar'ya, which resembled veins coming out of a blue liver. The names of the mountains were underlined in brown, and included the Talas range, the Altai range and the Hindu Kush, which then met up with the blue curve of the Amudar'ya. I had carefully set out the cities too, and had marked Kiwa, Karaganda, Alma-Ata, Kokand and Bukhara with red dots.

When Frau Weigel unrolled the map and hung it on the blackboard, I was not really moved at first. The only atlas I remembered was the one Bairqan used to draw with the little bones on the rug in the yurt, and I had never seen the places of my childhood drawn on a map. Yet the names Amudar'ya and Bukhara had struck me and, little by little, with real astonishment, I had grasped just where the geography lesson was taking me that day. Of course I didn't say anything, but diligently copied central Asia into my exercise book, and even though it had turned out so elongated, it nevertheless had rivers, mountains and cities on it, which, although they bore different names to the ones known to me, were the same as I had known and now recognised.

Daniel leant over my exercise book. 'Do you want to know where I come from?', I asked him. I ran my finger along the blue vein of the river and stopped at the bend, where it met up with the brown strip with Hindu Kush written above it. 'I come from here.' Daniel leant his head further over the page, tried to make out where my 'here' was, pushed my finger aside so that he could read more easily and then shook his head. 'So that seems far away to you?', he asked me in an ironical tone of voice. He put his little finger on the point I had indicated and stretched out his hand across the exercise book until his thumb reached the place on that imaginary atlas which might stand for Cologne. 'Look,' he said. 'The distance from there to here fits into the palm of a hand.' The distance which Daniel was measuring with his palm, through the mere fact of being measurable, became shorter. While the distance that separated him, Daniel, and his snow-white aunt from the others was not reducible to metres or to outstretched hands. It was as if Daniel's Poland were unreachable and his aunt's cellar, instead of being beneath the house or a few blocks further on, were light years away.

My places were shut up, it was true, in a page of an exercise book, but they continued to seem very distant. And by now they may well have had very little in common with the places I had known. The whole of my past might in a short space of time have become, just like my drawing, naïve, crude and out of proportion. Only the tiny pile of true names I remembered served to keep that past attached to reality. When I thought in this fashion I felt as if I had a void beneath my feet. It was better to think about something else. So many things ran through my head: school, homework, Dr Wallatz's study, then school and homework again, with all too little time for walks with Daniel, and too little time too for Heidi and Grete. Too little time. We used to pull in our dresses around our waists in order to seem slimmer: Heidi sewed herself protective oversleeves with frills; Grete had attached a rosette, and I secretly imitated her. We were growing up in a hurry. 'How you've grown,' Marianne used to say to me as she measured with astonishment the distance from the cardigan sleeve to my wrist, and to think that just a year before it had fitted me perfectly, indeed she had deliberately made it a little on the large side. We were growing in a hurry, like the city round about us which was throwing proud new bridges across the river Rhine, and which was becoming taller and more modern, like the hastily built apartment blocks. There was not so much time to think, for the important thing was to grow, taller and more modern; there was no time for the past, and even the words to define it had been forgotten.

'I don't have the time,' I would say to Daniel, but sometimes I did, and then we would kiss beside the river, in a place we knew, where there was no one about.

37

MY MOTHER TOOK an interest in me in much the same way as she took an interest in the rest of the house, in other words, every now and then, when she remembered to do it, and with the tacit understanding that everything went on perfectly satisfactorily without her. Which is in fact how it was. Marianne would consult her but more for form's sake than for anything else. 'Madame, isn't it about time we washed the sheets?', she might ask, or 'Don't you think the floors need polishing again?' My mother would pretend to have noticed: 'Yes, yes, I was just about to tell you.' Everything thus went ahead with her implicit agreement, and according to the routines of the household, without anyone feeling any need to change them. I fitted in with the routines, and got along well enough, so my mother had no real need to take an interest in me. Marianne and Kathe were there to prepare meals for me and to wash my clothes and when they said to her, 'Don't you think that Naja has grown a bit, and needs some new underwear?', she it was who went to buy them for me at a shop where she was a regular customer, or passed on some of her own or, just once or twice, accompanied me to the dressmaker. We didn't squander money in those years either, but I didn't want for much and took my bearings from the other girls my age who had nothing.

Usually, when I had to turn to my mother for something, I would find her in her bedroom lying down on her peach-coloured bedspread, with the curtains drawn because the light troubled her, and then I didn't dare to disturb her. Sometimes, though, I would find her in the sitting room on the ground floor, reclining on her Empire-style chaise longue and reading. When in that relaxed pose, with her chestnut hair draped softly over the embroidery covering the back of the chaise longue, and her wide skirt hanging down to the ground, deeply immersed in her book, my mother resembled one of those ladies who appear in nineteenth-century portraits, whose suffering but resigned air she shared. What she lacked, however, was their sweetness, and their expression, in the canvases at any rate, of renunciation. My mother did have a quality seemingly resembling sweetness but it was in fact an absent-mindedness, towards both persons and things. I cannot recall my mother ever having praised Marianne or one of the servants, expressed an opinion on a dish or a pudding, or observed the special effort made by someone or other. She was probably not observant enough to take note of the intentions of those around her, or, if she did take note, she did not deem it necessary to waste words on them. My mother was too indolent ever to pass judgement on anything. As the years went by, I was ever more persuaded that my mother's silences were in large part due simply to an ingrained, invincible indolence, which had become a matter of habit, way of life, and intellectual inclination. It cost her an effort to speak, to adapt to the person to whom she was trying to make herself understood, or to construct a sentence that went beyond what was strictly necessary. As time passed, everyone had grown used to her parsimony with words, and it must have seemed a pointless exercise to her to disappoint their expectations. She would merely have startled, and even irritated those who had long since grown accustomed to her silences.

Every so often, however, my mother would have bursts of loquacity, but her dialogues were with roses, not persons.

The garden, in theory at any rate, was her domain, although the artistic passion of a man like Dr Wallatz, the shrewd pedantry of our neighbours, and even the most minimal notions of horticulture, were equally alien to her. The upkeep of that large garden had been entrusted to her, much as the other household affairs were, on the tacit understanding that she, as the lady of the house, should have expert knowledge of it or at least take an interest in it. And that house was not one in which skills would be called into question or at least checked from time to time. Every now and then my mother remembered about the garden and then, as if gripped by a sudden mania for action, she went about with gloved hands and armed with shears. When plants grew in their own fashion or were a little slow to produce shoots or buds, or came up crooked, or thwarted her in some way, my mother didn't stand on ceremony but attacked them with her cutting tool and reduced them to bristly little stumps and truncated branches. On the other hand when they grew in the way she wished, she was sweetness itself, as with the magnificent rosebush growing on the right-hand side of the entrance, a riot of gold, so that going up to it was like approaching an altar. The roses were called *Gloria Dei*, appropriately enough, and were yellow with a copper-coloured border. My mother went into raptures over them, praised them, stroked them, and was forever putting her nose inside them to breathe in their perfume. She used to talk to them too, at great length, and dropped into the golden calyxes the words she denied to others, and heaped praise on the fleshy petals. She never went very far in praising those around her, who waited on her. I do not remember that she ever touched me, and yet she might often be seen stroking the corollas of her flowers. That's just how my mother was, mean with feelings and arbitrary in the way she dealt them out, utterly incapable of accepting anyone who did not bend to her will, whether plants or persons, indolent, and yet beneath it all she nursed a haughty desire to dominate.

The garden soon recovered from her fits of enthusiasm; the mistreated plants put out buds again at will, and at the beginning of May an assortment of grasses and flowers which no one, aside from the wind, had ever dreamt of sowing, sprouted again in the meadow. The secret of that garden, which made it so very beautiful, was neglect.

Every now and then it was I who became the object of her sudden and unexpected attentions. She'd ask me, where are you going? She would cast an eye over me: that skirt's a bit too short for you, get Marianne to lengthen it, or, what are you going to see at the cinema? Have you told Papa? And when I'd got back, if she was still on her chaise longue, she would call me, put the embroidery in her lap or put down her book on the side table, open at the page she was reading, and she would say, tell me all about it. What was the film like?, but she never expressed the slightest wish to come to the cinema too, with me perhaps. Once I asked her: 'Why don't we go together, on Sunday?' I felt very bold. But she shook her lovely chestnut hair. 'No, no,' she said, 'my movie-going days are over.' This upset me and I did not ask her ever again; indeed, I became reluctant to tell her about the films I had seen and she became aware of this. She stopped asking me to tell her about them.

I didn't understand what my mother meant by saying 'my movie-going days are over', given that in those days we talked about nothing else; cinemas were springing up faster than houses and it seemed that people needed films more than butter on their bread. For my part, I often went to the cinema with Daniel, with Grete, and sometimes with Heidi. But Heidi always got to see films before I did. We were crazy about Marika Rökk, who according to us was very beautiful, in fact 'divine', and whenever a film was on somewhere or other with her in it, we'd hurry over to see it. Heidi had her own system for going to the cinema without paying for a ticket. She had remained small and thin, and so could easily blend in with the crowd and get in unobserved. Moreover, since it was not enough to see a film just the once, she would hide in the toilets before the end of the first show and only come out when the second one had begun, and in this way she managed to see the film twice in a row. It often turned out that her mother was already back home and she got thrashed. But more than that was needed to get Heidi to give up Marika Rökk and the cinema, and her mother, realising that she was powerless, first thrashed her and then wept, saying what ever had she done to deserve a daughter like that, and that she was sure to die of a heart attack. No doubt she said the very same thing the day she received a postcard from New York in which Heidi simply let her know that she had married an American. Her mother didn't die of a heart attack but wept at the news and said that it was all the fault of the films Heidi had seen. I don't know if she particularly blamed Marika Rökk but I gathered from the way in which Ingrid recounted the whole affair that she still felt some bitterness towards her sister for never having taken her to the cinema with her, with the excuse that she was too small. Perhaps because she had not seen so many films, Ingrid did not run away with an American, and a negro at that, but married a confectioner from Cologne who worked as she did at a patisserie called La Bonbonnière. They then opened a shop together, in which Ingrid amused herself by building the boldest towers with chocolate boxes and by peopling the shop window with whole families of chocolate Easter bunnies, and with countless baskets of coloured eggs.

I generally went to the cinema with Heidi, since Daniel turned up his nose and said that it was all kitsch, which took away the fun of it for me. Grete, however, was easy to please, especially if it were a love story; the keener she was on a film, the more quickly she would fill her mouth with the sweets we had brought with us and which as usual I had paid for. I used to pay for the cinema too, in that my father never asked me how much I had spent and on what. When I asked him for money he got out his wallet and gave me some. It was good fun, and I was grateful to him for it. I used to take the tram and meet Grete at the stop before the cinema, and then we would go into the corner store that sold cigarettes and sweets. Which bag should we have? The big one, Grete said as if she were the one paying. I had mine filled with *Bärendreck*, the liquorice twists that inexplicably were known as 'bear's number two', even if in my opinion bears had nothing to do with it. I unrolled them with my teeth, so as to reduce them to string and then eat them with small bites, because I enjoyed both the consistency and the taste of the liquorice. But Grete was more demanding and could never choose. Hurry up, the film's about to begin. Then she took a little of everything, small coconut squares with coloured bands, peppermint balls and sugar twigs with, she used to say, flowers inside. She used to see the flowers of course, and sniff them before making them disappear in her mouth. I paid and then we would run over and queue.

The new cinemas, springing up from the ruins, were magnificent picture palaces, swathed in velvet, with monumental entrances and with gilt ornamentation protruding from the walls. It is perfectly true that often not even a glimmer issued from that magnificent array of lights, and the great entrance halls were left in shadow. The toilets too were almost always sunk in gloom. 'What would you have us do?', answered the man at the counter, if someone complained. 'We install the lights and they make off with them.

Are we supposed to search everyone as they go out?' In those days people thought that cinemas didn't need lights, since the films were watched in the dark, and they didn't think twice about unscrewing bulbs and slipping them into their pockets. That type of theft was regarded as a crime of honour, even though Cardinal Frings had never absolved bulb thieves from the pulpit, as he had done years before with coal thieves.

Once I remember we were at the Rex and *Niagara* was showing; the cinema was packed, Grete and I were queuing and to pass the time we had already begun to dip into our respective bags of sweets which we held tightly against our chests in order to protect them. What a lovely flower, what a sweet perfume, Grete said in a loud voice, talking about the sugar twigs of course, and in response two boys who were just in front of us turned round and said: 'Leave some for us!' They laughed, then one of them looked at me and exclaimed: 'Where did you find this one then?' He was addressing Grete but referring to me. He must have been a joker, always ready with a quip, because he immediately came up with a rhyme: *Sie kommt aus dem Mongoleneck / und frisst Bärendreck*, she comes from the land of the Mongols and she eats bear's number twos. Everyone, both in front of and behind me, burst out laughing at the bizarre rhyme, even Grete, and all eyes were on me. I stood there with my liquorice twist half in and half out of my mouth, without daring to go on chewing it. I swallowed it and hid the rest in my pocket, where Marianne found it weeks later, sticking to the cloth and covered in dirt. I felt myself flare up with rage, even at Grete, who was laughing with the rest of them, and I would have run away if I had not reckoned that to do so would attract still more attention. I stayed where I was, in the queue that was slowly advancing towards the counter, and hoped that they would say, I'm sorry, there are no more seats, but the person at the till said how many seats did we want, and Grete hurriedly replied 'two, circle' and waited for me to pay. I did not dare to say anything, for fear that everyone would turn round and make comments, perhaps about the way I spoke. When we got to our seats, Grete offered me her bag of sweets. I pushed it away in a rage. Then, to make me feel better, she said: 'Don't be upset. With that nose everyone's bound to think you're a Mongol.' She actually said 'think you're a Mongol' as if I were not really one, and as if the fact of being taken for a Mongol, or the very insinuation that I was one, could constitute an insult. And all this was because of my nose. At that moment I would readily have grabbed the bag of sweets, which Grete still clutched tightly to her chest, strewn them on the ground and trampled them underfoot. I don't recall a single scene from *Niagara*; I only know that Marilyn Monroe was dressed in red, that I caught the tram at the first stop instead of walking part of the way with Grete as we usually did, that I didn't go to the cinema with her again, and that never again in my life did I eat a single *Bärendreck*.

That evening I was still so distraught that my father immediately noticed. 'What's the matter, Naja, is something wrong?' I ended up telling them everything. I was afraid that they too would laugh, but neither one of them did. My father looked seriously at me and said: 'If that's all it is, if it's just the nose, there is a remedy.' 'I seem to remember that we already spoke about this before', my mother said, 'and that Naja did not agree.' 'She's grown-up now, she's a big girl. A nose does count for a lot. It'd certainly make things easier.' I knew where such talk led and I also remembered my grandfather's words about those people who thought they had god's hands and could remake nature at will. But my grandfather was no longer there to tell me that my nose suited me very well, because I'd been made like that and couldn't be remade in a different fashion simply because in the country where I now was people wore noses of another shape. I couldn't imagine myself with a different nose. Yet the episode at the cinema had destroyed the last vestiges of my self-confidence. I no longer even dared to look at myself in the mirror, I did not risk going out, I avoided even Daniel, and I had stopped speaking to Grete.

One day my father called me into his study. A fug of cigarette smoke hung over the Biedermeier furniture and obscured its gleaming surfaces. My father was wearing his ash-blue smoking jacket, and the tables and armchairs were as always covered with sheets of paper, scattered among the overflowing ashtrays and the empty glasses. He seemed to me to have aged, or perhaps it was I that had grown and was beginning to notice changes in adults too, which before I had not heeded. He had lost weight and deep eye-sockets made his nose look thinner. Only much later did I understand that there must have been some relation between the cigarette butts, the empty glasses, the purple shadows on my father's cheeks and the pages scattered about his study; at that time I only sensed the characteristic disorder of the study, steeped in the habitual odour of tobacco, and my anxiety, as I waited, standing beside the desk, for him to tell me why he had called me. 'I have had a word with Dr Schönhuber,' he said, 'he was a friend, an acquaintance, of your grandfather and he works as a surgeon here in Cologne. He has told me that it could be done, that it's not a difficult operation. He does of course want to see you.'

Dr Schönhuber received patients on Tuesday afternoons between three and six, but my father and I had an appointment outside of normal hours. I was a private patient and Dr Schönhuber had known my father's father, Dr Berger. I doubt that he could ever have imagined what my grandfather thought about his hands. His hands, though, were the first things I looked at. They were white, tapered and beautiful. They were a god's hands, which worked with skin as if it were clay; they remodelled disfigured faces, shortened drooping eyelids as if they were muslin curtains, and reshaped noses. He too had a catalogue, just like at the hairdresser's, and one could choose, would I like this one, yes please, no thank you, or would this shape of nose suit me better?

'It's just a question of shape, and in your own case it's solely a matter of an external defect; in other words, the nasal septum is not defective but merely the shape, that is, the nasal cartilage. It is obviously this that we should work on, performing an intervention of a corrective nature which will affect neither the respiratory apparatus nor the external structure, given that every phase of the operation will be done from the inside, without any visible incisions. We will need to insert a small scale implant to achieve the requisite length.' Here Dr Schönhuber paused, looked me in the face, smiled faintly and asked me: 'What do you say, Fräulein, we could make you a French-style nose, of the kind the young men like?' It was a joke but I didn't understand it and so didn't laugh. Dr Schönhuber became serious again and concluded with a summary: 'Her face is oval rather than broad. A longer nose would suit her very much better. Let's make her the nose she deserves.'

There was thus supposed to be a kind of fundamental right as regards human appearances too, and perhaps there existed canons to establish shapes and measurements to which every individual had a right, to which he had a right because he deserved it. This at any rate was what Dr Schönhuber's words implied, and one gathered that for him it was an incontrovertible axiom. Each person deserved a specific nose, a specific shape of ear or a specific type of breast, and it was his right to have it made to measure, if nature had denied it to him.

I don't remember if I said yes, but in any case Dr Schönhuber, like my father, would have found the very idea of me refusing altogether unthinkable. The date of the operation was discussed. The day after the end of the school term was agreed upon, to give the skin a chance to recover during the holidays and to enable me to appear the following year at school with a new nose.

'At your age wounds heal quickly,' the surgeon said as he held out his beautiful hand and we said goodbye.

We went back outside into the street. In front of the clinic there was still a heap of ruins, across which a large tarpaulin had been extended, in order to prevent storms doing still more damage to the walls. Before getting into the car, though my father was already at the wheel and waiting for me, I looked at the people walking along the pavement, who were normal, misshapen people, with bodies which had turned out more or less well, who had never however, had the good fortune to pass through Dr Schönhuber's hands; people who knew nothing about the canons of beauty and did not have the slightest idea what form of nose or ears they deserved. Even the man I saw pass by leaning on a crutch, a disabled ex-serviceman, assuredly did not know about his natural right to get his lost leg back. Even if he had known of it, what good would it have done him? It was far, far simpler to remake so small and insignificant an organ as a nose than to give back legs or arms to those who had lost them in war. For this not even the white, highly skilful hands of Dr Schönhuber, not even all the hands of all the Dr Schönhubers in the world, would have been enough.

When I got home from the clinic, Marianne brought up her hands to her face and said, 'Jesus and Mary.' My father looked daggers at her; I was covered in plasters, but neither Marianne's exclamation nor my father's reproachful glance escaped me. Aside from the olfactory, all my senses were highly alert; indeed, they seemed sharper than they had been before the operation. I became attuned to the subtlest inflections in a voice or to the tiniest flicker of an eyelid, insofar as it might be interpreted as a negative judgement on my nose. When the nurse removed the plasters, so that Dr Schönhuber could assess the success of the operation, the latter said to me: 'What do you reckon? Take a look at yourself. Take a look in the mirror. The discoloration will go away, and then you'll have a completely new face.' He was obviously satisfied, but I refused to look at myself in the mirror, fearing both my own reaction and the response of the others to it. Days passed and still I didn't dare to look. When I went into the bathroom I would place my hands in front of my face so as not to be able to see myself in the mirror, and I would then find myself peeping through my fingers, like a child playing hide-and-seek with itself. Marianne, on the other hand, would study the improvements on my face each morning and say: 'Better and better; you'll see how beautiful you've become!' But when I stole a glance or two at my face, all I saw were the purple and then yellow marks on my cheeks, and I did not dare to submit to my own judgement, let alone to that of strangers. Since coming home from the clinic, I had not left the house, and only went into the garden when I was sure of not meeting anyone. If there was a ring at the gate I simply went and hid.

'Come on,' my mother said, growing weary of the game, 'stop hiding and take a good look.' I locked myself in the bathroom, stood bravely in front of the mirror but immediately ran away. The face I saw was not my own. It was another girl who was observing me in my terrified state, a girl with a thin, prettily turned-up nose, but one who had nothing to do with the one I had known, Naja, who had come years before and all on her own from the Amu-dar'ya, and who then had had a black plait reaching down to her knees and now no longer had that and had a nose that did not belong to her. I understood now what my grandfather had meant by saying 'they believe they are gods and can remake nature'. You could not alter a person's form without also changing their essence, which lay beneath the form. No one had told me that with a different nose I would become a different person. They had simply thought that I would be the same person, with a more beautiful nose, and that was where the error lay, for the outside and the inside are the same person, and once the outside had been changed I was no longer the same inside as I had been before. I was a being that I did not recognise, and I did not know whether I would be able to get used to the stranger that I had become.

38

THE YELLOW MARKS on my cheeks gradually faded, and anyone who saw my nose would have said that it had every right to be where it was. The incisions, as Dr Schönhuber had explained, had been done solely on the inside, so the epidermis had not suffered lasting damage and was gradually beginning to recover from the trauma. My skin was adapting more easily to the change than I myself was. I felt as if I were divided in two: between my face, which was eliciting compliments from all those who had known me before, saw me in my new guise, and said 'how beautiful you are, how good you look, that surgeon's a veritable magician, what miracles medicine can perform nowadays'; and my inner self, which was just not interested, which told me that it did not care what others thought, which wanted me to be just as I had been when growing up and which refused to recognise me. The compliments I received, instead of delighting me, filled me with a motiveless rage, which I would then regret, and feel myself to be ungrateful. From the way in which people spoke to me, I gathered that, second only to the surgeon's skill, it was my father's generosity that met with general approval. 'I dread to think what an operation of that kind costs!', Marianne would whisper to Käthe. 'He does all he can for his daughter, while she . . .'

Yet I was far from happy. I didn't want to look in the mirror and I had got it into my head that I was no longer able to breathe, as had happened when I had first arrived in that house, but this time it wasn't because I had too little space or because the roof threatened to fall on top of me. It was because I missed my nose. 'It isn't possible, it's pure suggestion,' declared Dr Schönhuber as he shone a light inside my nasal septum. 'The nasal fossae are perfect and besides, the plastic surgery hasn't harmed the respiratory function in the slightest, as I believe I have explained to you more than once.' My father was embarrassed; Dr Schönhuber could not conceal his irritation, and I for my part was ashamed, yet I could not be persuaded that it was suggestion alone. Perhaps it really was. Even at the beginning, when I felt that the roof was falling on my head, it was suggestion, but I truly felt a knot in my throat, as if the air could not go any further down. Now the air was no longer coming up my nose. It was just suggestion. My nose was perfect, inside and out. A very lovely nose, thanks to Dr Schönhuber's skill and to my father's generosity.

Yet I no longer wanted to go to school. 'This girl's getting hysterical.' 'It must be her age.' 'Yes, it must be.' 'But school, not wanting to go to school?' 'How can we hope to understand, who knows what's going through her head?'

I didn't feel that I could face the whispers of my schoolfriends – what have you done to your nose? What is that yellow? Has somebody punched you on the nose? – the sidelong glances of my teachers or their comments on my recovery from the surgery, although as likely as not no one would have said a thing. Yet I feared their silence too. I was allowed to stay at home until the yellow shadows had totally disappeared from my face.

One day Heidi turned up in our garden. I heard her coming up the stairs with Marianne and hid in my room; she knocked timidly, appeared in the doorway, sat down on the edge of the bed, into which I had crept, pushed aside the eiderdown and looked carefully at me. 'Do you know,' she told me after a moment's thought, 'do you know that you resemble Gretl Beck? Except that she hasn't got your eyes. Do you remember *The King's Admiral*, where she plays the part of . . .' It was not like Heidi to lie just to flatter me. In her eyes my nose was wholly acceptable, indeed, better than the previous one. This was what Marianne reckoned too, as did the other servants, my mother, my father, and it was what my fellow pupils at school would also have thought. The problem was mine, and mine alone. I had once and for all to learn to see myself through others' eyes, not through those of the Tunshan, whom I had left behind me, somewhere in Asia, and who could no longer judge me; and not through the eyes I had had before, which saw me in a mistaken fashion. I could not go on hiding myself in my cave of feathers just because I had a nose I did not like, when everybody else found it beautiful.

Heidi persuaded me to go to the cinema, at the very end of September. The air was delightfully soft; a damp warmth hung above the banks of the Rhine, a last trace of summer, and the river was bearing it away, leaving behind what had been.

My schoolfriends didn't say anything, while the teachers for their part were new or if old seemed not even to recognise me. Grete had kept the place next to her free, looked at me and said: 'Is this why you've been hiding away all this time? You've got a supernose, lucky you for being able to get your nose changed. Goodness knows how envious Irmgard must be, with the one she's got! Think how happy she'd be if she could change hers too!' Irmgard sat three rows back from me and had a nose with a bump on it, a nose that jarred with the rest of her face and her slender body, that gave her an unfortunate profile and caused her a great deal of suffering. But no one would ever have thought of making her a new one. Irmgard's envy was no comfort, for I felt a rage inside me, much as on the day on which Grete and I had sat next to each other watching *Niagara* and I had seen none of the film. But on Grete's bench there were just exercise books and a completely gnawed pen, and in front of us there was Frau Meyer looking sternly at us. She certainly did not think a nose a sufficient reason to deny her the attention that was due to her.

I wondered what had become of Daniel, for he was not there waiting for me. He had not left me any note; there was no trace of him at all. I did not even know if I cared about him or not. I had become someone else, and was different now from the girl who used to walk with him beside the Rhine, or who used to sit in his aunt's sitting room. He might perhaps have seen that difference solely from the outside, but to me it seemed likely that he no longer cared about me. He was another milestone in my past life, and each time I also left behind, as if I were slipping out covered in a new skin, the people I had known in the old skin. I was new. No, I just didn't want to know what that strange boy, who was gradually becoming transparent like his aunt, who seemed to be made of glass and yet was quite inscrutable, thought of my nose. I stopped seeing him. But one day I did come across his aunt, and it was when I was strolling with Grete, for we were in fact seeing each other again, because my need for friendship had proved stronger than the resentment I harboured on account of the episode in the cinema. All of a sudden I was facing Daniel's aunt in the street, swathed in her black dress, with a black umbrella to shield her from the sun, which otherwise would burn like fire, Daniel had once told me. Just a single ray of sun would bring her out in red, itchy blotches. She stopped, and I could see that her umbrella was shaking in her hands, as if she were cold but, as I knew, it was her permanent tremor. Yet to see her outside her house, with her umbrella shaking as if the wind were up, and with her dark eyes scrutinising me beneath her invisible eyelashes, was petrifying, and I could not even manage a simple greeting, not a thing. The aunt stood for a moment and looked at me, then went on her way, with her umbrella quivering, and I was astonished that she even left a shadow behind her. 'What did that spectre want of you?', Grete asked. 'I don't know,' I lied. I could still feel myself shivering.

Hush, don't grieve out aloud, in case a servant of Erlig Khan should hear you. For if a servant of Erlig Khan should hear you, grieving for no good cause, if he should hear you, he might tell Erlig Khan, the lord of the nether world, and Erlig Khan knows how to satisfy someone who is not content with life. Erlig Khan will send a servant to seek you out. And he'll take you or someone close to you and then he'll return, because once he has learnt the way, Erlig's servant will return once again. One must not let him find the way, but when he has found it you must make him forget it! So be quiet and light incense sticks before the seven spirits of the hearth, the seven spirits of the fire and the seven spirits of the earth, and may Erlig Khan not hear you, may he not hear you!

Erlig Khan's servant must have heard me, when I said that I couldn't breathe. Erlig Khan's servant must have read my thoughts, when I said to myself that I would never be able to get used to the stranger that I had become, and Erlig Khan's servant must have been nearby when, instead of being grateful to my father, I avoided him, and when he called me I ran away, when he spoke to me I replied in monosyllables. For Erlig Khan's servant found the way to the house in Schillerstrasse and I it was who had called him, for I was grieving within and my lament was loud enough to be heard by Erlig Khan, the lord of the shadows.

In February it was my father's turn to be operated on. He came home, went to bed and did not get up again. Relatives and friends were forever going up and down the stairs, for short visits, followed by much whispering and tinkling of coffee cups in my mother's living room. No one spoke to me. The servants spoke among themselves, with Kathe saying 'it was the smoking that did it', and Marianne contradicting her: 'No, it was the war. You couldn't come back from war as if it were just a picnic. War gnaws at you from within, and you can't shake it off as you can a stomach ache. There are those who die in wartime and those who wait until peacetime to die, for war doesn't end when peace comes.' Marianne knew what she was talking about. After her husband had returned from prisoner of war camp, the previous year, she would repeat over and over again, 'He's just not the same, he's just not the same.' This wasn't her Franz, this gloomy, emaciated man who hung about the house picking up all the objects and staring at them, as if he found it hard to remember what they were called and what they were used for. He was no longer the man who once upon a time used to rub his great big hands together, happily, and ask 'Alright then, what shall we do now?' Now Franz hung about the house without being able to do a thing; in bed too, Marianne whispered to Kathe, nothing doing. Five years of war and ten years of prison could not help but change a man. My father was one of those who had waited until peacetime to die.

My grandmother passed by me and went straight to her daughter. My mother wept and did not want to see anyone. My grandfather was often around in those days, but he had a gloomy air and if by chance he came across me, he seemed not even to notice me. I hid myself away and went up to my father's room only when I was sure that no one else was there. After school I would hurriedly eat whatever Marianne had prepared, for my mother no longer appeared at the dinner table, and then I would go up to my father's room, quietly approach his bed, in the submissive way in which I had approached his paper-strewn desk. My father opened his eyes and smiled faintly. Sometimes I would sit beside him with a book and read silently. My father found it hard to speak. Sometimes I thought he was asleep, but he would open his eyes and ask: 'Naja, how's the nose? Are you happy with it?' 'Yes, Papa,' I lied. 'I've always tried to make you happy, Naja.' 'I know, Papa.' I squeezed his hand, and hoped that I would be able to forgive myself for my own ingratitude; he really had tried to make me happy, and it was not his fault if he had not succeeded. But was it my fault if I wasn't happy? Forgive me for my ingratitude, Papa. I gently squeezed his hand. You could not know. I was too young to understand.

You gather branches and bushes, you make a neat pile of kuraj, you make plans and then the wind comes and disturbs them, drags them somewhere else, abandons them where it chooses. Who can know what the wind's plans are?

By April my father had become so thin that his bones seemed to be held together with skin. 'I was thinking again about your father, about Ul'an,' he said to me all of a sudden. 'How strange all of that was. How very strange. One should never nail fate to one's own words. Words have their own weight, Naja, do you understand what I mean by that?' 'Yes, Papa.'

Words have their own weight and draw fate behind them. And what of fate, who can draw that behind himself? The wind blows as it chooses. Who can know what the wind's plans are . . .

'Once you've entered a war you never leave it. You should never start a war. They always say that they end in a hurry.' My father found it hard to speak. That thought tormented him, and beaded his forehead with sweat. Marianne was right to say that you don't return from a war as if it were a picnic. War forgets no one. It takes its victims when it chooses. And it gnaws at you from inside, up until the very end. 'There are no just wars, or holy wars, and no weapons are blessed. It's all a farce, do you understand what I'm trying to say, Naja?' 'Don't tire yourself out, Papa.'

I sprinkle my weapons with kumiss, may Qormusda be on my side. I sprinkle my arrows with kumiss, may Qormusda protect me from my enemy. Tengri of the earth and of fire, may my weapons sprinkled with kumiss be holy. May I defeat my enemies and return unharmed to the ayil *Tengri of the seven mountains, I offer you my kumiss, blessed be my weapons!*

Was that a farce too?

One day, in fact one of the very last days, he opened his eyes wide and said to me: 'Look after your mother, Naja. Of the two of you, you're the stronger.' 'I will, Papa,' and I touched his hand as it tried to clasp mine. A grip with no strength left.

I have lit perfumed incense sticks / I have offered them to the monastery of Erdeni Juu. / As I prostrate myself before you and make offerings, / have pity on me, my Erdeni Juu. / I have lit incense sticks that smell of musk, / I have offered them to the sandalled Buddha. / As I prostrate myself in prayer, / have pity on me, my sandalled Buddha. / I join my hands above my forehead / and pray to the Padma Sambhava. / The sickness for which there is no remedy. / Once again I join my hands above, / I entrust myself to the Padma Sambhava, / may he grant me grace and protection!

Ügedelegü the shaman could do nothing to save my mother Börte, had been powerless before the bite of the *naja* that had killed my brother Ginchin, and had not known how to heal my father Ul'an's wound; his prayer, the very last I retained any memory of, failed to save my father. He died in May.

The family tomb was at the outermost edge of the cemetery, where the enclosure wall turned at right angles. The funeral procession was therefore crammed into the space between the wall and the tombs, and waited sorrowfully for the coffin to be lowered into the grave, which had been made ready. I felt my mother's gaze directed at me from beneath her back lace veil, which framed her face; with the whole family assembled, she suddenly felt responsible for my behaviour and feared, despite her tears, that I might cut a sorry figure. I would have burst into tears too, so stricken was I by grief, and by rage too. My father was doing me an injustice, for he it was who had me brought here and now he was going away and leaving me without support. How cruel it was that all those who had loved me should go away, one after the other, my grandmother, my grandfather and now my father. Just like my father Ul'an and my mother Börte. And the Tunshan too, who knew where they were, they too, they might as well have been dead. I was just about to give vent to my sorrow in tears, but I resisted. I feared that once I had begun I wouldn't be able to stop, and so I resisted. I felt my mother's gaze directed at me from beneath her black veil; she certainly thought it odd that I was not weeping; perhaps she feared what the relatives might say about me, and out of rage I might then have begun to weep . . . When, all of a sudden, a blackbird alighted on the cemetery wall and began whistling so gaily that everyone turned around, though no one even thought to silence it. The priest was reciting the prayer for the dead and there was that impudent blackbird coming down and singing so loudly, without heeding the people in mourning gathered there beside the wall, directly below it. The priest looked witheringly at the blackbird over his glasses, but it was unperturbed and continued its irreverent song, as if it had been hired to accompany the ceremony and had misread the score. It was too joyous a music for so sad an occasion. I threw into the grave the little bunch of roses which I had been holding all that time in my sweating hands, and I looked up. The blackbird flew on a little way, alighted on a bush and started whistling again, directly above my father's grave. Then an absurd idea struck me. Not a new idea but one that had been buried deep within me somewhere, and the blackbird with his joyous notes was bringing it to light. It is not by pure chance that it is singing directly above my father's grave, I said to myself, and so loudly too. Souls have wings, just as birds do. My father's soul had not remained beneath the earth that had been thrown on top of him in handfuls. I had been taught that only the purest souls, and they were rare indeed, went straight to heaven, while the others had to wait a while before getting there. Why could they not be turned into birds and, once they had been purified, use their wings to reach paradise? It was no more absurd an idea than any of the others, but it was more charming, far more charming, indeed, than the sad waiting-room in purgatory. I had to smile despite myself as I noticed my mother's reproachful look from beneath her black veil. She was clearly thinking that I was downright odd and that I would never become a girl like all the others. But I was reconciled once again with my father, and with those who had left me. I no longer felt any rage and even the desire to weep had gone. The blackbird went on whistling and I in turn looked at my mother, her face stricken with grief beneath her black veil, and I thought about what my father had said. He had been right, of the two of us, I was the stronger.

* * *

In the months that followed my mother did nothing else but weep. I did not understand how she could grieve so for a husband to whom in the final years she had given only silence. But perhaps within her silence a love had been hidden which I had not succeeded in understanding, and which only came to light now, in the form of tears. She was unapproachable. Only Marianne and my grandmother, when she came, dared to enter her living room and bring her something to eat. I avoided her, and even despised her a little. To let yourself go seemed to me hardly dignified, thoroughly offensive to those around you, and a sort of selfishness too. My mother refused to take an interest in anything whatsoever, while everyone took an interest in her. The only people to take an interest in me were Marianne and, as far as school was concerned, Dr Wallatz.

School ended, and that year it really did come to an end. I passed the secondary school exam, the *Mittlere Reife*, and brought home a report on which Herr Zepp, my German teacher, had written: 'This pupil has overcome the initial gaps in her knowledge and has proved to be capable of diligence and application in her studies. Her participation in lessons has always been satisfactory. She has shown a real aptitude for languages.' Herr Zepp had not been overly lavish in his praises but his judgement, though succinct, was positive. I showed my certificate to Dr Wallatz. He had good reason to be proud of me, for he had betted on the right horse. I had managed to reach the finishing post at the same time as the other girls of my age, although I had set off so much later. I had confirmed his theories on the uselessness of public schooling. I had gained very good marks even in German, despite the notorious severity of Herr Zepp. But Dr Wallatz was incorrigibly ambitious, and the idea of me wanting to give up studying tormented him. 'It's a great pity. You'll regret it. Such wasted talents. You could go on, three more years and you'd take the higher certificate.' He was prepared to help me, but I didn't want to have anything more to do with school, with benches, with teachers who wanted only to catch me out, and with schoolfellows who just ignored me, for my new nose had not made me any the less excluded. No, I regarded my five years spent at school as more than sufficient. Heidi and Grete did not continue either. I would do as they did, and look for a job. Like the others. I didn't want to be different.

39

MARIANNE IT WAS who came up with the idea. The three of us were sitting in the kitchen, Grete, Heidi and I, and we were tucking into a fruit cake, on top of which Marianne had put a generous dome of whipped cream. Once she had carefully cleaned the bowl and licked the spoon, Marianne sat down next to us: 'And what do the young ladies plan to do now?' We shrugged our shoulders. We were sixteen years old, and with only the vaguest idea of what we might do in the years that lay ahead, aside from going to the cinema and getting engaged. 'I read that they're taking on new staff at the Telephone Exchange. There's a more modern system now and they need some young people they can train up.' She went to find a copy of the *Kölnische Rundschau* and showed us the advertisement. There was a photograph of smiling girls in dark overalls, sitting in front of upright panels full of holes. The telephone operators in front of the new illuminated switchboards. I couldn't imagine what such work involved, but Heidi and Grete were suddenly very enthusiastic. 'Just suppose if someone on the telephone should say to you "what a lovely voice you have, Fräulein",' and then Heidi tried to counterfeit the 'lovely voice'. We laughed so much, and then the next day all three of us turned up at the Telephone Exchange in Mühlheimer Strasse, opposite the fairground, in Deutz.

They called us 'tail-enders' because we were the new girls, the ones at the bottom with everything still to learn. To begin with, we had to learn how to speak. Frau Maus would stand in front of us and show us where to put our tongues when pronouncing an *r*. Not so deep in the throat, further forward, on the tip. Frau Maus pushed her red-painted lips forward as if she were blowing a soap bubble.

We used to recite poems: Röslein, Röslein schön. 'That's not bad at all,' she said to me. The others had a much stronger accent. 'You can speak like that at Carnival,' she said, 'but you don't speak in dialect at the Post Office.' Frau Maus was from Hanover and had no difficulty in pronouncing her *r*s and her *sch*s correctly. 'Now say "*Die saueren blauen Trauben*",' the sour blue grapes; just saying the phrase made one's tongue feel blue and on edge. We stood up one after the other to recite the tongue twister and heaven help anyone if they got in a muddle and out came 'sour wine', as Frau Maus used to say. She'd be left on her feet repeating and getting ever more confused, and mocked by the other 'tail-enders'. Then there were the numbers, which we had to pronounce in such a way that no one on the other end of the line would ever have to ask 'Pardon? Could you repeat that, please?' We had to become masters of our own vocal cords. We had to attain a clarity that was automatic but somehow courteous at the same time. Frau Maus was adamant that we were supposed to smile with our voices. We were employed not by the Post Office but by the obscure interlocutor known as the 'subscriber' or even the 'user', who from a great distance gave us orders to execute with the greatest possible precision and courtesy. Without swallowing letters, pronouncing our *r*s clearly. Impersonal and very courteous. Genuine 'young ladies of the telephone exchange'.

After the six weeks of the tail-enders' course all three of us were taken on. In order to buy the blue overall with the little white collar and a row of buttons down the front, the uniform worn by the young ladies of the telephone exchange, Grete dipped deep into her savings, Heidi asked for a loan, while I was given it as a present by my mother. Our seats were lined up along the wall; behind us were the tables at which the clerks supervising us sat, and behind them, in the middle, was the table at which the controller of the whole room sat, who was a man. We had shifts; it turned out that Heidi and I were on the same one, and we would meet Grete in front of the doors of the metal lockers, where the overalls were hung up, or in the cafeteria, or else we would not meet at all, or would greet one another hurriedly as we passed in the lift.

The lift was the central organ of the building in Mühlheimer Strasse, a kind of heart that pumped employees from one floor to the other without ever stopping. The name paternoster was particularly appropriate to its motion, which was jerky but continuous, save for brief stops on the ground floor, and on the first, second and third floors. You had anyway to hurry to reach it. Those inside would cheer you on, 'Go on, make a dash for it, you'll make it', as if it were the last run of the day. Sometimes it seemed as if the paternoster did it deliberately. You would arrive out of breath and very close to that doorless lift, but, just as you were about to cross the narrow gap between the floor and the cabin, and with the others already pushing back to make room for the newcomer, the mocking paternoster would suddenly shake a little and start to move again, leaving you disappointed, and with your nose level with the legs and feet of those who were getting in, or, conversely, with the arms, faces and hair of those who were getting out.

The cafeteria was on the second floor, and every three hours we had a break of half an hour, when we could recount to one another all that we had not been able to say in the previous hours, spent side by side but speaking only with unknown persons. Our sole means of communication were gestures and meaningful glances, or even, in those rare moments when the pin was not inserted and no one was calling the numbers for which we were responsible, half-whispered words. It was agonising having to wait so long in order to know what Grete's gesture or Heidi's grimace may have meant, or for my part to tell them something about Hans. 'Discipline is the be all and end all at the Post Office,' Frau Maus had taught us. We were very much aware of the double line of supervision behind us, consisting of the women who supervised our work and the man who supervised them, and indeed the entire room. And, to cap it all, Frau Schrumm's voice would sometimes worm its way into our ears, from central control on the second floor: 'No, my girl, that won't do at all. Clearer pronunciation, and more courtesy in your tone of voice, please.' Sometimes she would also add, peremptorily: 'Come to my office at the end of the shift.' At such times one would wholly forget what one wanted to tell Grete or Heidi, for from the expression on their faces one just knew who had an appointment with Frau Schrumm on the second floor, at the end of the shift.

It is true that, so far as the Post Office was concerned, we were creatures endowed only with voices, and yet postal discipline extended as far as our appearance too. The young ladies of the Telephone Exchange were supposed to display decency and decorum at all times, even when they were not seated in front of the switchboards, even when they were in the cafeteria. 'Eccentric modes of dress, which might in some way cause annoyance or disruption, are to be avoided.' Those who contravened this rule might easily incur serious penalties, ranging from suspension to dismissal, or so Herr Kröber, chief supervisor in our room, informed Grete, as he looked sternly at her fingernails, which were green. That day Grete had turned up for work at the Post Office with her nails painted with green nail varnish. It was unclear whether she had been out to provoke, or whether it had simply not occurred to her that the colour of her nails could give rise to annoyance or disruption, but Herr Kröber anyway did not allow for any extenuating circumstances and suspended her for a day.

Once it was I who caused a scandal, though wholly involuntarily. It was summer and at the end of our shift we had gone to eat an ice-cream. I had changed into my new dress, which mama's dressmaker had made for me. It was a dress made of crêpe de Chine, with red poppies, a narrow waist, with puffed sleeves and a rounded, very low neckline. 'Doesn't it strike you as a little too much for a girl of Naja's age?', my mother had asked. 'Why should she have to hide anything?', the dressmaker replied. In order to placate my mother, however, she had stitched some thin strips of the same material above the neckline, but these had the effect of a piece of gauze which, when placed on a Venus to cover up her charms, instead of hiding them serves to display them. My mother and the dressmaker were agreed though that the dress really suited me, and it was true. The red of the poppies flattered me; I had long hair reaching down as far as my shoulders, the skin of my arms was dark, the dress emphasised my thin waist, and my back was almost bare. At the Post Office I made haste to conceal myself beneath my overalls, but just as I was taking them off two colleagues standing by the lockers gathered round me: 'Let's have a look, oh what a lovely dress!' Grete was admiring it too, and I was standing there a little flustered, with the overalls which I'd just taken off still in my hand. I was about to hang them up in the locker, when Herr Kröber's voice stopped me. I turned round in embarrassment; Herr Kröber was not alone, for Herr Koch, the deputy director, was next to him. 'We'd like to take a little look at this dress,' said Herr Kröber in an unctuous voice. Both of them were indeed looking at it and I felt my face turn the colour of the flowers I was wearing, while the myopic eyes of Herr Kröber and those of Herr Koch, which were shadowed by his bushy eyebrows, looked through the strips of cloth on my chest, and Herr Kröber gave a snort and said: 'Don't you think this dress is cut a little too low, young lady?' I felt naked, and it seemed to me that their eyes were touching me in a quite brazen fashion, but I did not dare to go away until Herr Kröber had dismissed me, saying 'Let's dress with a little more decency when we're at the Post Office!' But they were the only ones who had been indecent.

Yet we, the young ladies of the Post Office, were not schoolgirls and the Post Office was not a college run by nuns. Once we had taken off our blue uniform and were outside the building on Mühlheimer Strasse, we would expose ourselves without undue shame to the gazes of the city, which in its turn offered itself to us none too shyly. After work, when we were on the afternoon shift and we got out at seven o'clock, we would dress up. I used to put on my dress with the poppies and the little strips of material and go out with Heidi or Grete, with Ingrid or Katharina, or with all of them at the same time, depending on the shifts, and Jürgen, Helmut and the others would be waiting outside for us. I worked, and my eighty-nine Marks a month all went to me, not like my friends, who had to hand them over to their mothers, and so had nothing; I did night shifts and felt more grown-up than ever. In the months that followed I was to grow up still faster.

* * *

Deaths never come singly, the Tunshan said, and I still remembered this. When someone died, one had to behave in such a fashion that Erlig Khan would not find his way back and come to take another soul. To obstruct him, one could employ spells and the lamas' prayers, but sometimes they were no use, and Erlig Khan found his way back all the same and paid another visit to the yurts. Not only on the Amudar'ya but also in the city on the Rhine, the angel of death willingly took the same road a second time. He had done this when he bore off my grandmothers, one after the other, and when, after my father's death, he likewise bore off my mother's father, Georg Schifferl, the proprietor of the Modern Living furniture factory, in which during those years my father had been both technical director and architect, adviser and partner.

When they told me that my grandfather was dead, I was not surprised and I was not grief-stricken. All I remembered of that grandfather was fleeting appearances, glances that seemed not to include me, and a persistent failure ever really to concern himself with me. He had never regarded me as part of the family. I followed his coffin out of a sense of duty, but I was thinking about other things. I never imagined that the death of a person who when alive had been so alien to me would change my existence far more deeply than that of the persons who had been close to me.

There was nobody left to run the furniture factory, for not one of the husbands of my mother's sisters, who were civil servants with steady jobs in the new state or reputable professional men, understood furniture or had been party to the secrets of the factory, which my grandfather, either because of a whimsical fondness for my father, or because there was no one else, had shared with him alone. Perhaps he was the only person who had managed to adapt to his authoritarian ways, and who in some way managed to stand up to him. But when Erlig Khan's servant took both of them away, there was no one to take their place and the Modern Living furniture factory had to be sold.

When the time came to sell up, we learn that the business had not been as flourishing as the lifestyle of its owners, and especially that of my grandfather, might have led one to believe. When the accounts were done, it turned out that we had debts. My father's inheritance was simply debts. It was also papers, sketchbooks full of designs, drawings, models in plastic or in metal, furnishings for the houses of the future, coloured and lightweight, furniture without a past, conceived for the houses that were going up in those years, houses which were still in large part frameworks of wood and metal. After the war my father had discovered an artistic bent, and art proved more congenial to him than philosophy and his earlier, never completed studies had been. But even his furniture designs remained unfinished, paper projections of his imagination only the most minimal part of which were destined to become concrete geometries in metal. Many of the drawings which later passed, after wearisome argument between my father and my grandfather, into the hands of the workers at the Modern Living factory became furniture which remained unsold in the showrooms and was never put to the use for which it had been intended. Perhaps they were too cold, as my grandfather maintained, or too impractical, as my grandmother said, or not comfortable in the slightest, as everyone said. In my father's view the people of Cologne were too *spiessig*, too petty bourgeois, to buy furniture which looked to the future. In my opinion, the shortcomings of the designs which filled my father's sketchbooks and covered the shining Biedermeier surfaces in his study were that they had no history and never had the time to have it, because they existed only on paper or as unsold objects in the Modern Living showroom. They became my inheritance but as an inheritance it was no use, and certainly not in paying off the furniture factory's debts. To do that the Biedermeier pieces, the house itself and the garden had all to be sold off.

My mother needless to say knew nothing of all this. She had never been aware, not only of how much the factory brought in, but even of how much money her husband had, or of what it cost to run the house, to pay the servants and to maintain the life she pretended to administer and which in her naivety she believed would continue just as before, through a kind of instinct, sustained by some altogether mysterious income. The precise nature of this income did not really concern her. When she was made to sign the papers, my mother dried her eyes and signed, in a resigned kind of way, and without understanding what it was all about. She found it hard to grasp that the villa with its overgrown garden couldn't be kept on, that the three women who worked in the house, and who in reality did very little, given that they never received any orders, could no longer be paid even the wretched wage that they had received up until then; that, in short, the mysterious sources of money had dried up and that they would now have to adapt to another way of life. There was now an expression of dismay on my mother's face, but she did not weep for the house that was no longer hers and for the possessions she had to abandon, or even when Marianne cried as she said farewell and made us promise to look her up in Bonn where she had a married sister who had found her another job, in an ambassador's house, she was careful to let slip, as if to say that she was bettering herself, but in the meantime she was crying, packing her things, hugging me again and again and crying some more. My mother's eyes remained dry, but that shadow of dismay remained imprinted upon her face like a mask, and never really left her. In reality, however, I knew that my mother was not surprised by anything. If for the majority of the city's inhabitants the most important milestone had been the currency reform of 1948, after which, to judge by what people said, everything had gone better, for my mother and me, the major change came afterwards, in the mid-fifties, and it was precipitated by those two deaths in combination. As far as my mother was concerned, it was a change for the worse, but for me it was another step towards the normality which I craved.

My mother's relatives helped her to buy a flat in a quarter which had only just been built, in a decorously elegant area of the city. Those pieces of furniture which could not be fitted into the new apartment were given away or sold. We arranged the rest in the freshly whitewashed rooms, in which the antique furniture seemed out of proportion, in that it took up too much space, got in the way and even seemed to take the air we needed to breathe. Now I understood the meaning of my father's designs and insisted upon reclaiming some of the pieces piled up in the Modern Living storeroom, which shortly afterwards would have both a new owner and a new name. The new house felt more like mine than the old one had ever done. In the villa on Schillerstrasse I'd always been an intruder, who had had nothing to do with the cherrywood furniture and the silk rugs. It had always seemed to me that they were checking to see whether I had made a mess, that they sought to erase the marks I left, on the floor, on the door handles, everywhere. The new house, on the other hand, was mine as well. There were no trees round it, but there was a terrace from which you could glimpse the Rhine. I arranged the white furniture from my old room in the new one, and finally I got rid of my dolls. In the course of moving house I came across the old leather bag, which no longer seemed so bulky, and which had faded, although it still had a vague gamy smell mixed with moth-balls. What a stink, I said, thrusting it away from my nose. I shoved it into a trunk and stored it in the attic. Moving house cheered me up no end.

The women would roll up the felt covering from the yurts, dismantle the wooden latticework separating and closing off the various rooms, so as to reduce them to bundles of planks, then they would load them onto oxen and camels, taking care that the load was balanced, and put the wheel used in the opening on top, lashing it on with ropes. Ropes would also be used to tie on furnishings, utensils, bags and whatever else was in the yurt. As they worked they would step round the children who were obstructing them, and everybody was busy and cheerful. Moving house was a festival, and the women would put on their finest clothes and jewels and paint their cheeks and eyes. We would leave the well-trodden ground of the old ayil and the hearth-stones, but we would take the fire with us. Moving house was a festival, among the Tunshan.

My mother did not laugh as she roamed around among the trunks and supervised the servants who were helping her wrap the china in tissue paper and plunge it into the straw. She had a serious, bewildered expression on her face as she checked the packing of the furniture, to ensure that the corners would not be damaged in transit. She roamed anxiously around the garden and I saw her stroke the roses as if she were saying farewell to a person who was very dear to her. She looked so wretched that Dr Wallatz said he would move the roses to the new house too. He transplanted them himself, with great care, so as not to damage the roots, in a large terracotta vase with putti all round it, and so the bush of *Gloria Dei* moved house, along with the furniture. But while the furniture, though generally ill-suited to the new surroundings, could somehow be fitted in here and there, the roses simply refused to adapt and so died. Plants are like men, in that they cannot be forced to take to a land that is not their own, if they do not wish it. Every day my mother would bend over the plant to check for any sign of recovery, but when she saw that the youngest shoots were withering, that the bush was losing all vigour and becoming stiff and gaunt, she interpreted the refusal to survive as a betrayal and took no further interest in it. It was me who uprooted the dead trunk from the vase and replaced it with a wisteria. The little shrub was well satisfied with the soil I had given it and grew, covering the wall of the terrace with its branches, and gaily taking in the June light through its violet clusters. My mother would sit on the terrace and look with bewilderment at the exuberant foliage of the hanging garden, but she would never bend down and water, if I were late and the afternoon heat rendered the tiles too hot to touch and the plants were suffering. My mother did not know how to read a plant's thirst in the condition of its leaves. She had never learnt to look after others, my mother, and the days when she had learnt domestic economy, at the English misses' school, were too far in the past, furthermore they had been lessons for well-to-do housewives, who had been administrators rather than workers in their own houses. My mother had never provided food, or darned, or ironed. No one had taught me either, but I learnt fast, for I had skilful hands and imagination. I knew how to bow my head and adjust to the new wind which was blowing on us. As for my mother, the wind would have torn her up by the roots and rolled her wherever it chose, if she had not summoned up all her strength and attached herself to me. She marvelled at the progress I made, how quick my fingers were, how tall my flowers were growing, and how lovely the house was, which, at long last, was my own house too. My father had been right: of the two of us I was the stronger.

40

'THE WIND SEEMS to have confused his eyes.' 'The wind? You mean the war,' said Jürgen, correcting me. 'What's the painting called?' 'It's written as *Guernica*.' 'And what does *Guernica* mean?' Jürgen shrugged his shoulders. 'I don't know but you can see that it's war.' People were thronging in front of the pictures, for it was Picasso's first exhibition in Cologne. We were trying to make our way through the crowd and get a little closer to the canvases. I was bewildered and confused. I was familiar with the oil paintings in Dr Wallatz's house, portraits, landscapes, and the child in soft pastels. On the walls of the house in Schillerstrase too, there had hung landscapes and portraits, and calm, somewhat dark interiors. I had never seen anything remotely like *Guernica*. 'The wind has blown through everywhere,' Jürgen said. 'Or the war,' I said.

Jürgen had already wearied of the art; he dragged me outside, into a city which was in search of order after the disorder of war, and which was swiftly reclaiming the past from which it had been excluded for so long. We walked a while in silence, beside the river. I felt that I could still see *Guernica* in front of me. 'My father says it's Jewish art,' said Jürgen. Daniel's aunt came into my mind. I thought again of the paintings we had just seen, and wondered if anyone could remind me of them more strongly. It's true, I thought, she too had been confused by the war, for the war had taken the colour from her skin, and had distorted her, as it had the women in *Guernica*. I did not understand the comment of Jürgen's father, that it was a Jewish art, but yes, perhaps the Jews did have something to do with it.

* * *

We discovered confusion and disorder in music, in the tortuous sounds that could be heard at the Taboo. The night-club itself smelled somehow of mystery. We would walk down the steps and sit at tables in the cellar, while the piercing sounds which crashed against the ceiling caused the candles stuck in bottles to shake. 'A negro music,' Jürgen said, quoting his father once again. 'Listen,' I said to him then, 'just don't mention your father again.' I thus brought the argument to a close, but the Taboo was anyway no place for having a conversation, except during the brief pauses, when the musicians mopped their brows and put down their instruments. I found that music electrifying and when we came out my head was so full of sounds that I would have said that I could see them gliding along the river, hear them echoing between the walls, like an echo that was lost in the midst of the houses. Jürgen's father was in a sense right: it was a music that came from far away, that did not belong to the city, and beyond the smoke-filled vaults of the Taboo it was an outsider.

Heidi had once again fallen behind, because she found it hard to pedal on the bicycle belonging to her mother's friend, which was too big for her. 'Come on, Heidi, hurry up.' Grete, Helga and I urged her on, for we had better bicycles, but as soon as she caught up, we pressed on again, without giving her time to catch breath. She protested and fell behind once more. The riverbanks were covered in green, and the boys, a fair way ahead of us, were already at the picnic spot. We went back in the evening with huge bunches of wild flowers and ears of corn.

Jürgen was crazy about the water. He had shifted crates of beer by lorry during the summer holidays, when there were no university lectures, which was back-breaking work, but he had saved enough money to buy a boat, a collapsible wooden canoe. When he spoke about it, his eyes lit up. There was nothing like gliding along the river, going with the current and drifting over the swaying water weeds, really, I had to try it. I let myself be persuaded and one Sunday in July we arrived at the Moselle. I was given a short theoretical lesson in the art of using the paddle, and then we were on the water. Yet the boat did not obey us, and no matter how much Jürgen yelled 'to the right! to the right!' or 'to the left!' or 'harder!', the canoe spun round, following its own rebellious impulses and defeating our attempts to control it. We bore down forcefully on the paddles, splashing each other with water; for a while we managed to follow the direction of the river, but then the current took hold of us again, carried us straight towards a foaming mass of water, where it rose into swift little eddies, and went on more rapidly still, at the gallop, causing our boat to leap about. I was drenched and frightened; Jürgen was behind me yelling orders but the sound of the water was now so loud and my anxiety about using the paddle so great that I could not even hear them. 'To the bank! To the bank!', I heard from behind me, and clung on tight to the paddle. It was all very well saying 'to the bank' but the racing waves were taking us somewhere else and the branches hung so low that one had to bend down to avoid being entangled. I tried to hang onto them but they snapped off in my hands.

Perhaps I had been very unskilful, perhaps the current had been stronger than we'd anticipated, or perhaps it was the fear, I don't know, but what is certain is that the canoe did capsize, with us inside it, and I ended up upside down, being dragged to the bottom, with my mouth full of water and in a state of sheer panic. I managed to wriggle sideways and get my head above water; the bank, I was in the middle of the stream and was being borne along by it, I had to reach the bank. I grabbed hold of some nettle bushes and the stems came away in my grazed hands; I clutched at a more robust branch, pulled myself up, slipping on the mud, and then I was out. The bank was a jungle, and my legs were scratched and reddened by the nettles. Where was the road, where was Jürgen, and where was the boat? I waded through another stretch of water, the river bottom was soft and I sank in. Up on the bank again, and another jungle. There was a path beside the river, which I followed, dripping, scared and shivering, until I reached the road, at long last a road.

* * *

On that road I met the other shipwrecked person, muddy and scratched as I was, but with thoughts only for his lost boat. He had tried to swim after it but had seen it rush onwards, capsized, dragged along like a bare tree trunk. A branch will stop it, he had thought, but the stream swept away boat, rucksacks and clothes, and left us in a sorry state, me in shorts and with my blouse clinging to my chest, Jürgen with just one shoe, which he took off, because he could walk better barefoot. I didn't know whether to laugh or cry at our shipwrecked condition, but Jürgen was weeping only for his boat and blamed me and my lack of skill for the accident. I felt humiliated; I burned at the injustice of the accusation, and I shook, with cold and with rage at one and the same time.

I was still shivering when the car took me home. When my mother saw me come in shaking all over, in sandals, she said: 'For heaven's sake, Naja, you'll catch pneumonia!', and ran to fetch one of those very large towels. I took off my still damp clothes, and stood there naked; my mother hesitated, with the towel held out between her arms, and I felt embarrassed. 'I'll do it myself, thank you,' I said. My mother withdrew, closing the bathroom door gently behind her.

I used to tell my mother the bare minimum. When I came back she would ask me with a distant politeness, 'Where have you been?', but as adults or colleagues do, out of politeness rather than curiosity. I did not have to get in at a specific time, as my friends did, and heaven help them if they were late; I did not have to face a barrage of threatening questions, where had I been, with whom, what had I done. My mother simply asked me out of a sense of duty, and I answered out of a sense of duty, saying only as much as was necessary. I would tell her my girl friends' names, though prudence dictated that I pass over those of my male friends, and modesty prevented me from speaking of Jürgen. We rubbed along well enough, we didn't raise our voices, issue orders or criticise, nor did we give offence. Heidi's mother hit her if she got in late, while Grete's brother had seen her out with a boy and had told her mother, who had called her a tart. When I went out, I'd say, I'm going to the river with Helga, today it's hot, we're going swimming. I'll be back late, don't wait up. OK, my mother replied and smiled faintly. Have fun. Sometimes she too went out, and visited her sisters, for she didn't have any friends. I would tell her about work, about Herr Kröber and Herr Koch, and sometimes I complained about them. My mother nodded in agreement and sided with me. Late one afternoon, I came back when she was still out on the terrace, with some work in her hands, though she was no longer sewing, and it was almost dark. I greeted her and said: 'I'm getting married.' My mother looked up and for the very first time I saw a look of real astonishment on her face. I anticipated her question and announced: 'To Jorgios Papatsónis.'

Jorgios Papatsónis had been introduced to us by Herr Koch as an engineer who had come from Athens to study the new telecommunications systems. We were assembled in the cafeteria, in the interval between one shift and the next, and when Herr Koch arrived, accompanied by his guest, the girls politely stood up, looking both serious and well-mannered in their uniforms.

Herr Koch walked into the middle of the room, with the grey contingent of male employees lined up in the front row, in a compact formation, while behind and alongside them stood the blue group of female employees. Herr Koch gestured to his guest to stand on his right, took a moment or two to assume a sufficiently balanced and relaxed posture, put his hand in his pocket, thought better of it, let his arms hang down framing his abdomen, cleared his throat and finally began to deliver his prepared speech: 'Cologne is at the forefront of European telecommunications. As employees here, we have good reason to feel proud.' Grete nudged me in the ribs, winked and immediately assumed an exaggeratedly demure air, clasped her hands together and swung them to and fro at the level of her groin, and at the same time shifted from one foot to the other, imitating the orator, who continued as follows: 'What device is better adapted to curtailing distance than the telephone? But the telephone brings together nations as well as individuals. It is through technological exchanges that nations, nowadays, meet and communicate. Telecommunications and progress recognise no borders . . .' Grete, who was protected by the shield of blue overalls and white collars, continued to mimic Herr Koch, while the girls around her imitated her in turn, compounding the effect, so that there were endless stolen glances between us and stifled giggles, while Herr Koch scrambled up to the summit of his speech, and attempted yet bolder oratorical flights: 'It is the rapid exchange of technological information which is enabling us to open ourselves to new horizons. It is no accident that our contacts with the other European countries should begin with Greece, the country that can boast the most ancient technology of telecommunication.' Here Herr Koch smiled in anticipation of the joke he was about to tell: 'You only have to think of Mercury, the winged god, and symbol of the new technologies . . .' Herr Koch looked around to see what impact the reference had had on his audience, but no one, either among the quite motionless grey group of men, or among the women, where an imperceptible breeze was causing the blue creases of the overalls to shake, gave any sign of having picked it up. His gaze had only to sweep the room, however, for even the slightest trace of a smile to be extinguished there and then.

Herr Koch felt disappointed and hurried on to the concluding part of his speech. 'Engineer Jorgios Papatsónis', and here Herr Koch gestured emphatically towards the man next to him, as if he were Mercury in person, 'will remain with us for a year, in order to master the technology and telephonic organisation of our Central Exchange.' At this point he stopped, extended a welcome to the engineer, in the name of all the employees, men and women, at the telephone exchange, and wished him a pleasant stay in Cologne. Someone initiated a round of applause but in the general embarrassment it died away. Those of us wearing blue overalls looked at one another, failing to understand quite what the speech had had to do with us. Our role had probably been simply to listen, as it usually was, even though for once the object of the speech had not been an abstract interlocutor but a person of flesh and blood, who even smiled at us, standing there demurely in his blue suit and red-striped bow tie, with a bronzed face and dark moustache. Jorgios Papatsónis was young, handsome and an engineer; it seemed as though he had come down from Mount Olympus to receive the offerings of mortals, a god who indulgently laid himself open to the gazes of the women in their blue overalls, who were delighted by the apparition.

Herr Koch motioned to us to make ourselves comfortable, and we therefore returned to our places and to the cups of coffee we had left on the table. Grete nudged me still more sharply in the side and whispered '*temperamentvoll*', an epithet which summed up as far as she was concerned all the qualities of the man who had just been presented to us. The fact that she had not even heard his voice did nothing to undermine her conviction that Jorgios Papatsónis was a 'highly passionate' man. It was the definition routinely used for those from Mediterranean countries, the advance guard of the armies of unskilled workers who would follow on in subsequent years. They merely had to have black and perhaps curly hair for them to be attributed a sanguine, exuberant and passionate character, as if they were one and all bullfighters, Calabrian bandits or at any rate tenors. However, the word *temperamentvoll* did not refer just to the appearance and character of the person so described, for it also reflected the speaker's admiration for and astonishment at qualities deemed to be wholly foreign, and it therefore contained an implicit self-assessment and even a touch of envy. So general a judgement was of course quite devoid of any individual reference, and was really a matter of pure cliché, yet this Jorgios Papatsónis seemed altogether to merit the epithet *temperamentvoll*, and not only because of his black wavy hair and moustache. For he was also a sociable fellow, who sat with the regular staff in the cafeteria and recounted, in a rudimentary but effective German, tales from his own country, so that all those around him laughed, nodded and repeated to one another, *temperamentvoll*, he really is *temperamentvoll*.

But Jorgios Papatsónis must also have had some other mysterious quality or have been able to call upon a very special degree of international backing; or at any rate have come with a solid recommendation, since technological fervour and the progress of telecommunications were not enough on their own to justify the high regard in which the young engineer was held, and the respect which the other employees of the male gender accorded him. The staff at the Post and Telecommunications Office were for the most part female; the few men would have escaped observation altogether had they not served as supervisors and departmental heads, for their appearance and dress should really have condemned them to an irredeemable greyness. Jorgios Papatsónis was in all respects their opposite. He was handsome and elegant, and flaunted silk ties and lordly ways. More than one young lady of the telephone lived in the hope that, even when dressed in her blue overalls, she might attract the attention of the *temperamentvoll* engineer Papatsónis.

One day we were sitting directly behind him, when the cafeteria was not at all crowded. Jorgios Papatsónis winked at me. 'He was looking straight at you,' Grete pointed out, 'didn't you notice?' As if I hadn't noticed! 'He probably does that with all the girls,' I replied with a shrug, you shouldn't make too much of a mere wink. But inside I felt all churned up.

'I like you because you are so different,' he said to me. At the beginning I took this very amiss. I was trying so hard to be like the others, and all I wanted was a normal life, so how could I be different? I did in fact have a normal life. I was like the others, and ever since I had begun working I had lost any sense of being considered different. What mattered in the Telecommunications Office was not your appearance, still less the genealogy of your family, but how you did your work, and I did mine well; I had already gone up a grade and had had a wage rise. And now this Greek engineer came along and reminded me that I was different. Thinking about it again, I saw that it was a compliment. I was no longer of an age to regard equality as a condition of my own identity and I could now understand that being different could be something to be prized. Where appearance was concerned, and that was what Jorgios was referring to, I was indubitably different. I began to be proud of my difference. I realised that my girl friends envied me my dark hair and my perennially tanned skin, while they found it hard not to look too pale, and even my almond eyes were admired. Yet what they envied above all was my being chosen by Jorgios.

We arranged to meet two stops further on from Mühlheimer Strasse, so that the girls would not gossip too much; he took me by the arm and led me to the Akropolis, one of the very first Greek restaurants in Cologne. Jorgios entered the premises with the air of a lord returning to his palace. He greeted everyone in a loud voice; then the owner's wife came out from behind the kitchen counter. *Kalispéra*, *kalispéra*, she said, and immediately alerted her husband. Dimos Serafis appeared in his turn from the kitchen, covered in sweat, wiped his hands on his apron and held out a plump hand to Jorgios and then to me. He showed us to a table which in his view was quieter than the others, shielded by a wooden trellis on which a plastic ivy plant was climbing vigorously. It was by no means the only fiction on the premises, since the Akropolis was itself a kind of stage set on which everything, save the actors and the food, was sham. Thus there was a discus-thrower and an Artemis in fake marble, an amphora made of plaster and pretend nets with pretend fish in them. Dimos Serafis was by his own lights an avant-garde director, who was offering a public eager for novel tastes a still unfamiliar staging and an unexplored cuisine. At his tables there sat along with the Germans some of his fellow countrymen too, a little uneasy in a milieu which to their eyes must have seemed still more contrived than it did to the Germans, who did not know the original. Dimos talked at length with Jorgios, and together they chose the dishes we would have to eat, which was never an easy task. In between the ouzo, the hors d'oeuvres, and the dishes which would arrive after lengthy preparation in the kitchen, and which would be served to us by Dimos Serafis in person, Jorgios would talk and talk. I would hear about his house in Pirgos, in the Peloponnese, his dog, the hunting expeditions with his father, his sisters, Athens and the Acropolis, the real one, at sunset, or in the early morning. He sounded like a romantic with a hunger for ruins, a man prepared to stand and gaze for hours at the sunsets at Cape Sounis, to follow the fauns across the mountains of Arcadia and, in his own language and among his own people, a poet.

I would listen entranced, for not since my childhood had I heard anyone telling stories in that way, and in Jorgios's tales I couldn't really tell where the boundary lay between fantasy and reality, indeed, I suspected that there wasn't one. Jorgios Papatsónis was someone who would have known how to bewitch listeners even when he was wholly ignorant of their language, just through the flow of his speech, his gestures and his charm.

When are you going home?, I ventured. Don't think about that now. Yet I was thinking about it. He would be going back to his house in Pirgos, to the most perfumed garden on the Peloponnese, or to Athens, to introduce the new telecommunications technology he had learnt in the building on Mühlheimer Strasse. Jorgios was only passing through Cologne, like Dimos Serafis, who was only there so that he would be able to build a house on his native island. Dimos was building his house on Cephalonia as he worked in the Akropolis, in the kitchen; he was sweating blood and tears for a house that was still a meadow, while the one he had lived in as a child had collapsed during the earthquake, years before, along with the other houses on the island. To judge by the way he sweated, you'd have said that he was in Cologne to rebuild all of them himself, all the houses that had fallen down in the earthquake, and not just to put up his own. From the way Dimos talked, you'd have said that just one or two more years and the Akropolis would be sold, with the plastic ivy, the discus-thrower, the amphorae and all, and he'd be going back to live in the house he was building, in the kitchen. Yet he never did go back to his island, either because the house in Cephalonia took too long to build, perhaps he had planned it on too grand a scale, or because as time passed he had become fond of the Akropolis, or because of his children, whom I saw doing their homework at a table in the restaurant, or because of his wife, who fell ill and stayed for good in a land that was not her own, or for any number of other reasons. The fact remains that when, years later, I chanced to go back to the Akropolis, Dimos Serafis came out of the kitchen wearing his apron, which was as greasy as ever, his face bathed in sweat, and almost wept when he set eyes on me. It was then that I understood the difference between us. He too had not gone back, save for a short while, to Cephalonia, and perhaps he would not even manage to stay there, but what matters is not so much the fact of going back for good as the illusion of being able to go back for good. Dimos had that illusion and I did not. I had no place to return to. I had no other place to be in except the city that was flaunting its new-found youth, much as I was flaunting mine; I had no other house except the one with the terrace from which I could catch a glimpse of the river, and even the river, beneath its new bridges, had by now taken the place of the one I had known as a child, among the Tunshan. City, river and house were all mine, but when I sat behind the pretend ivy of the Akropolis and Jorgios held my hand and told me that I was not like the other girls, but different and better, I believed that you could change your place of residence much as you changed your clothes and that places left no trace inside you. I thought that I would be able to wrench myself away without any difficulty, whenever I chose, from the places I was in, and that I would have no regrets.

The evening that Jorgios Papatsónis told me that his father had written to him asking him to come home, and that his stay in Cologne was over, I felt as if the Acropolis, the real one, columns and all, had fallen on top of me, and as if the discus-thrower, Artemis and the amphorae from the Akropolis had begun to whirl round me like the figures on a carousel. 'It's the ouzo,' I said to Jorgios. 'Your face is actually the same colour as ouzo,' he replied, and asked me if I wanted to go to Greece with him.

41

HELENI PAPATSÓNIS WOULD often sing. But they were sad songs which, even if you did not know what they meant, brought tears to the eyes. '*Otan pezáno na min me klapsis . . .*', Heleni sang. It was her favourite song. 'What is your mother singing?', I asked Angeliki, who was the youngest daughter and who was often with me. Angeliki tried to translate: 'If I should die, do not weep for me and do not visit my grave, because it's you that killed me, it's you that killed me.' 'She wrote it, words and music,' said Angeliki. 'My mother writes her own songs.' 'Why does she sing such sad songs, Angeliki?' The girl didn't know why or didn't want to say, or did not know how to say it. When I came up to Heleni she smiled at me with her lovely sea-green eyes, which already had crow's feet around them, and stopped singing. 'Please sing,' I said to her, 'I like your singing'. I had learnt the phrase just for her.

When their father was out of the house, the five sisters were happy. You'd hear them chattering away in the living room as they did their homework seated round the big table, and it seemed like a kind of school when you saw them in the midst of their books and exercise books, or else they'd be in the garden, perpetually coming in and out of it, calling and being called. When their father was at home, they would whisper, the comics would disappear and the radio would be turned off. All such things had been banned by Kostas Papatsónis. Heleni stopped singing and concentrated on her sewing or knitting and fleetingly raised her perpetually reproachful eyes to look at her husband. When Kostas Papatsónis arrived, his daughters made a slight curtsey and kissed his hand, while he in turn would kiss them on the forehead, all five of them, or in fact six, since I too received my kiss of greeting, like a daughter.

I got on well with the sisters, and they treated me like one of them. I envied them a little. How lovely it must be to be so many; I had no brothers or sisters and therefore envied them their friendship, which seemed indestructible, strong as it was through the shared, tacit agreement of those who have suffered, and suffer, the same fate. 'There's a wall of five sisters in front of me,' Kostas used to say, 'as stubborn as mules and all of them against me.'

Jorgios and his father, on the other hand, understood one another very well. The two men were alike. 'We are cut from the same cloth', Kostas would say, as if that son were entirely due to him. He had had to wait ten years for him, since Heleni had brought thirteen children into the world and seven of them – the boys – had died. It was natural enough for a father to love that single male, who had withstood the fate of his brothers, more than all the sisters put together. They had of course spoilt him, out of fear that fate would carry off that unique being too, who in some way justified the exorbitant number of sisters. Thanks to Jorgios, Heleni no longer had to hear again and again what she had heard after the first seven pregnancies, there's no point, you don't know how to make them. She had managed one at any rate, and a handsome one too, like his father twenty years before, and like him vain and tyrannical.

But I did not know that. Jorgios had started to work in Athens and was looking for a house for the two of us. When he got back home he was happy and affectionate; he would grab me by the waist and dance me round the room; he was a fresh breeze that blew all our cares away. 'Even in Athens there's no one to compare to you.' But then he would disappear. There were his friends and, once the season started, the hunting. Then he and his father talked of nothing else, made preparations, discussed, and arranged to meet their companions at dawn.

I was jealous of the friendship between father and son, of the intimacy from which I was excluded, of male pursuits that kept them away for so long, and for which there was always time. Once, on the eve of a hunting party, I plucked up courage and asked him to take me along. Hunting? Yes, hunting. But it's not for women. Why not? They looked at one another, and did not know what to say. Then I dug my heels in. I told them how often I used to go hunting as a child, how my grandfather used to take me, really, my grandfather, and not just trifling animals like hares or pheasants, but gazelles, for instance. Once Bairqan had handed me a rifle. I was a child, certainly, but I was not afraid. There was no risk of me getting tired; it took much more than that to tire me out. It was the first time that I laid claim to rights in the name of my past. Kostas was the first to recover, though a little unsure if he had understood me correctly, and perhaps offended at being taken for a hunter of small game, he said: 'Here, however, women don't go hunting.' My request was quite impossible, like so many other things in that house. I felt stifled. I was like the jasmine plant which grew out into the street but without ever leaving the soil of the garden; the space allotted to me lay between the rosemary bushes by the door and the bougainvillea at the front of the house, and that was all. The girls came in and out, but took care never to be caught outside of the agreed routes, while their mother rarely ever left the garden. She placed no limits on her own inventions but respected boundaries which were not real and treated them as if they were.

Sometimes I went out on my own. Where do you go?, they used to ask me. Outside, in the mountains. What is there to do in the mountains? Nothing, just things to see. What is there to see? There were so many things to see on the Erimanthos mountains: the plain far below, where the mist was slowly burnt off by the sun, the sea in the background, marred only by specks of white. There were trees weighed down with figs, which were sweetness itself, and I chose the ripest ones, which were dark purple, and ate them whole, so that only the stalk oozing with milk remained stuck to my fingers. I went on my own. How did I manage not to get lost? If you were a woman going out on her own, you were bound to get lost; even the old man who hailed me from the bench in front of the entrance, and the shepherd asked me, are you on your own? Don't you get lost? I didn't used to get lost. I had always found my way, without getting lost, for I was someone who came from far away.

I did not yet know why Heleni sang such sad songs and why the daughters fell silent when their father entered the house. I knew nothing and thought myself happy in the house with the reddish-purple bougainvillea, with its marble floors that felt so cool in summer, its wickerwork furniture and lace covers. I loved the Easter sweets and I loved the sea. I did not miss the Central Telephone Exchange. When I handed in my notice, Herr Koch had said to me: 'You have my very best wishes. We were very satisfied with you, and if by any chance you were to come back, there'd always be a place for you here.' It had been a strange leavetaking, as if it was assumed that my marriage would not last very long. It had never occurred to Grete, however, that I might come back, not with a husband like that; my mother had run her thin hand through her already greying hair and had asked, as if it were a little daring of her to do so: 'Can I come and find you?' I was touched, and I hugged her. It was the very first time I had hugged my mother.

That summer, the second I spent in Pirgos, Barbara, the eldest of the sisters, got married. Heleni's songs became sadder still: you take away all I possess, even my daughters you take away from me. Why do you say that, Heleni? Do you not know that a woman is not destined to grow old before the hearth where she was born? Heleni knew that, but even that normal distancing, which in her opinion had come too soon, was adding yet more sadness to her already sad fate. Yet when you saw her bent over her embroidery, like a Penelope who no longer expected anyone to return, and when you heard her sing, you understood that her fate was dear to her.

In the autumn the family moved to Athens, to the new house in Kolonaki, in an elegant quarter above the old city and the Acropolis, in a wide street but with a garden that was more modest than before, though still with purple climbers. I and my husband had two rooms, but Jorgios used to get back late at night when I was already in bed; I would hear his footsteps on the garden path and, because I felt that he was treading softly so as not to wake me, I'd pretend to be asleep, in order to put off an encounter which I feared would prove painful. My father-in-law was also only very rarely to be seen in the new house, and did not come back for days at a time. More and more it was a house of women.

At the beginning of autumn my mother came to join us. Up until then her letters had been very brief, and I could not really gather from them how she was coping, what she was doing, and whether my absence weighed on her. In August, however, a letter arrived which left me speechless. 'I so long to see you. I want to come and find you. Write to me as soon as possible.' No one had any objections, neither Heleni, nor the sisters, nor the men, who did not really care who lived in that house. I went to the port with Melissanthi to meet her.

We were early, the ship was not yet in sight or perhaps it was delayed, and so we walked up and down the quay, sitting down every now and then on the bollards, around which the anchor chains would shortly be wound. Melissanthi, I didn't know to what purpose, began to speak about Jorgios. She had run into him by chance in the city centre, and he was not alone. She looked at me. I didn't understand. Don't you understand? He was with a woman and they were walking arm in arm.

I concentrated on looking at the green water, which was lapping against the quay; a film of oil was floating on its surface, with a rainbow trapped within it. Shoals of little fishes swam busily about in the rubbish. There was still no boat on the horizon. Why did my mother have to be coming just then? Why then, when she would witness my humiliation? What was I doing on that jetty, waiting for a mother who likewise, in her own time, had not really loved me? What was I doing in a country which, once again, was not mine? The little fish went on feeding greedily on the refuse, in the middle of the diesel oil rainbow, and still there was no sign of any boat on the horizon. I would have preferred it if Melissanthi had not been there, watching me, a little coldly, and perhaps feeling a little superior. Because at that moment, sitting on the bollard like some siren, her lovely hair falling over her shoulders, a flicker of scorn in her eyes, I felt her to be both superior and hostile.

Now I understood why Heleni sang such sad songs. Kostas, as everyone knew, often had other women. Beautiful young women, who appeared in the newspapers. Women who did not sing sad songs and did not know how to embroider. Jorgios was like his father, and imitated him in all things. Was I to end up like Heleni?

There was a whistle as the boat docked. My mother came down the gangway wearing the beige overcoat which I knew so well, and although it was no longer new she was as elegant as ever. I watched her come down, a lady in the middle of a throng of people carrying bags and tired children, a lady who, because of her high heels, paid careful attention to the steps and clutched her glossy leather handbag, her chestnut hair streaming in the wind. My mother was no longer young, but the grey strands could hardly be seen. She looked around for me, and once she had spotted me she could not stop smiling.

The two mothers had no need for words. I would find them bending down to inspect a piece of sewing or a rosebush. 'How lovely,' my mother would say, 'to have roses that are still so fragrant at this time of year!' Heleni designed a piece of fabric for my mother, with large flowers on it, and for the very first time I saw her embroider a tablecloth that was gaudy and used all the colours. What good would a common language have been to them? They were linked by something that could not be expressed in any language, the sense of loss, suffered as an injustice by both of them. Such was the common fate of Penelopes. Heleni sang and my mother hummed the tune. Just like two sisters. Whereas we, the actual sisters, smiled at one another when we saw them, with the indulgent smile of adults watching children.

My mother followed me onto the Acropolis, around Plaka, everywhere. She flourished in the light. She had been shut in for too many years; she had fed her grief behind drawn curtains, in the monotony of the muted colours in the villa on Schillerstrasse. At last she had decided to draw the curtains and breathe in the colours. Gone from her face was the expression of fear with which for years she had observed me, and the indifference with which she had treated me. She heard me speaking a language she could not understand, and she saw me moving easily around a city she could not master, and using a guide book to explain the landscape and the ruins. My mother now admired me.

Yet I was in agony. In order not to be always waiting for Jorgios, I went around with Melissanthi. In the afternoons we went to the café Exarchia, in the quarter of the same name, which was a long way from our house. It was a haunt of students, foreigners and officers. It was a fashionable place, where they drank instant coffee, and if you wanted Greek coffee you had to ask for it, and the waiter would look askance at you; you sat on red and blue plastic armchairs and listened to modern music. Modern here meant Western, English and American. There were many Englishmen in the café Exarchia. They were handsome boys in blue uniforms, with good manners, like gentlemen, and they courted us. We used to put on close-fitting jumpers which clung tight to our chests, and which were so short that you only had to raise an arm to catch a glimpse of skin, and we used to make up our lips with red lipstick; Melissanthi added colour to her cheeks and had more than one man circling round her. But they found me attractive too. David, for instance, with the gold braid on his uniform and the shy smile. The language we'd used on the notes left underneath the school benches came back to me as I spoke with him.

It was David who took me to Cyprus. It was a swift departure, planned in secret. He had come to collect my mother and me at night, one evening when there were only us women in the house. We left in silence, without saying goodbye to anyone, not even to Heleni. I felt remorse for not saying farewell. My mother used to maintain that she had seen a shadow at Heleni's window just as we were about to leave the garden, a shadow that had given a wave of the hand. And she had given an answering wave. I wonder if it was Heleni and if she had seen that salutation in the darkness. There were crickets in the gardens of Athens, and the car, as we set off, had made a terrible racket. It was as though the street had suddenly filled with noise, and as if everyone had come out of the houses and looked out of the gardens full of crickets, to watch us flee.

The ferry weighed anchor at dawn, and up until the very last moment, until I saw the port disappearing into the distance, I was still beset by anxiety that someone had followed us and boarded ship, and would bring us back to the gardens full of crickets, to the marriage bed which had been dissolved by me alone.

I was going away and I did not even know where I was going and who I was going with. My leavetakings had always been like that, in that I let myself be dragged hither and hither rather than deciding myself which road I should take. I wore what was most precious to me, but I also had two suitcases instead of a leather bag. This time I was taking my mother with me too. She had followed me without protest, and she had not even asked me if she could go back to Cologne. I could not tell if it was out of trust in me or want of trust in herself, incapable as she was of leaving on her own; she would have followed me anywhere, and I didn't feel that I could leave her behind. It was my duty to think for her too, for of the two of us I was the stronger. I was becoming more and more so. My mother had been scared when she boarded the boat, but she had had a look of admiration on her face that she increasingly reserved for me. She stayed with me in a boarding house just behind the port, and then in the two rooms above the café Desdemona. One of the rooms was for her, and the other for me and for David, when he arrived, and they both had Art Nouveau floral carpets, and chipped shutters, but when you opened them the sea entered the room too. I did not want for anything, for the two rooms overlooking the sea, the Desdemona, David and my mother, her too, were all I needed.

42

THE WALLS OF Famagusta were at my back, the quayside in front of me; I was on the same latitude – or perhaps a little further down, although that hardly mattered – as Birbesc, where I was born. If I looked straight ahead, beyond the sea there lay the Asia from where I had come. The tip of that oddly shaped island pointed in the direction of the journey I had made fifteen years before; on the other side, on the mainland, the Baghdad Railway touched the point nearest to the sea, before reaching the last station on Turkish soil, Nusaybin, where Bairqan, my uncle Borrak and I had boarded. But the sea could not be seen from the train; I still remembered how I had leant out to try and see it, and yet did not see it until Izmir. I would have liked to get to the very last outcrop of Cyprus, which seemed like a spear aimed at the mainland. Just to get there, to see the sea breaking against the rocks and to think of myself as being at the point nearest to my past. 'Why won't you take me there, David?' 'What do you hope to see down there? There's only goats. And besides it's dangerous to go down there.' David was convinced that there were partisans hidden behind every ruined castle, inside every abandoned chapel, and in the shelter of every bush. 'There aren't any more partisans,' I retorted, 'they have driven you English out.' 'Not altogether, not altogether. There are still two prints of the Queen's little finger in Cyprus,' David smiled at his bizarre comparison, 'and many who are biding their time before erasing them.' David only felt safe inside what he defined as the Queen's fingerprints, and heaven help anyone who stuck their nose outside. 'What are you doing then in Famagusta, aren't you outside the print there?' 'It's just a short way from the English base to Famagusta. Besides, you're worth the risk.' But I didn't believe that the risk was as great as David said. My clients were nearly all English and they didn't seem to be reckless types, prepared to risk their skin for a glass of wine in my bar. When they were off duty they came to the café in the port. I had rented it from the Englishman who had run it since the annexation and now, having grown old, wanted to go home. Go home where? they would ask him. To my home, to York, he used to answer. After so long? Does it strike you that I've become a Turk? he would say resentfully. To some degree, yes, it seemed so, but out of kindness they wouldn't say so. He was just 'the old sailor', as his café was called, a name which it had kept until I rented it. It was a familiar haunt, and not only to the English, since everyone passed that way. It stood beside the gateway to the sea and against the walls of the old city, but separated from it by those very same walls, with just the sea and the docking or departing boats in front of it. It seemed a pity to close it down. David made me a loan; I rented the café and renamed it Desdemona. Let's go to Desdemona's, just as before they had said let's go to The Old Sailor. The interior still preserved some traces of bygone glories: mirrors with gilt frames, bowl lamps, made of glass and protruding from the walls, with the electrical wires twisted round like snakes, and armchairs that had once been pink velvet. These faded items shared an atmosphere of decayed colonial splendour and equally ancient layers of dirt. I had everything cleaned, arranged new wicker chairs outside in place of the old, and put new cushions, made of a red fabric, on top of them. I hired two Turkish lads, a waiter and a dish-washer. My mother lent a hand, collected up glasses from the tables, made sure that everything was going alright in the kitchen and that the cups were washed as well as they should be. The English approved of the changes and came in still larger numbers. Cypriot merchants stopped to drink coffee at my tables, with Turks and Greeks taking it in turns to sit on my wicker chairs; the uniforms of many nations came and went, and there was chatter and laughter in many languages. Among so many different peoples, I was no more different than any of the others. I grew my hair long and from time to time I plaited it; I was proud of my appearance, which was neither Turkish nor Greek nor English. I was the girl at the café Desdemona, or else just Desdemona. That's how they knew me, and the men came readily to my café; it was rare for women to pass that way but sometimes a Greek merchant would bring his wife or his whole family and they would come to watch the ships. The women tended to look at me a little distantly and even suspiciously, for they did not know what to make of me. When in doubt, they judged me to be no better than I should be, but they were mistaken. The café Desdemona was a respectable place, and anyone whose hands strayed when I passed by with a tray, or who tried any funny stuff with me, would immediately be shown the door, for there was the Turkish waiter to defend me and besides, everyone knew that I was with David, and they respected the fact.

I was happy with my work and with my appearance, indeed, I would gladly have recovered all of it, and been what I had once been, with the nose I had had then, the same as it was then but of course bigger and grown-up. 'Don't pay it any mind,' David said as he tried to console me, 'we all lose a part of ourselves as we grow up, be it a nose, a leg, a head or a dream. Everyone leaves a piece of themselves behind, it is the obol we pay in order to become an adult. Besides,' he added with a laugh, 'what would your real appearance be? Are you not a mixture of a little of everything,

Turkish, Mongol and others besides? We are all of us thoroughly mixed up, some a little more and some a little less. Take me, for instance, I have the blood of a Kashmiri great-grandfather in my veins.' 'It may well be, but you can't see it.' 'Blood normally can't be seen,' David retorted and smiled. He had fine features and thin lips. When he smiled, the whole of his face smiled and not just his mouth or his cheeks. He was one big smile. He might well have the blood of a Kashmiri great-grandfather, I told him, but he indubitably had the skin of his Scottish grandfather, which went red at the slightest hint of sun, as he himself said. 'This island doesn't suit you,' I teased him, 'you can't take the sun.' 'Do you think that is reason enough? Do you think my ancestors could take it any better than me? Yet they went to the most sun-baked countries on earth, where, logically speaking, they wouldn't have been able to take anything at all. Had it been up to them, they would still be there now.' We were sitting in the wicker chairs, after the clients of the café Desdemona had left; David was sipping a brandy, and I a liqueur, and the damp sea air was making us a little drowsy. I drew my shawl tighter around me.

'We English,' said David, who liked to advance the most outlandish comparisons, 'are the last of the Crusaders.' He took pleasure in combining the most disparate elements, so as to produce an odd history of his own fashioning, which I did not always understand. 'Fundamentally, your ancestors and mine resembled one another. Yours crossed the steppe on horseback, mine the sea in boats.' He spoke very readily about ancestors; my own past intrigued him and he used to ply me with questions. I feared that he liked me more for my history than for what I was in the present. Sometimes I even regretted having recounted it to him, and would have preferred to leave it hidden, to offer up to him the enigma of my past, and to hope that he would give up trying to decipher it. But that would never have been possible. David was too curious and too keen on investigating. How, he said, could one ever hope to understand a person if one knew only their present? I, however, did not so much want to be understood by him as to be loved by him. But for David sharing his thoughts with me was a way of showing love, by revealing to me his innermost way of being. He followed his trains of thought as others follow their obsessions, so that when an idea had got hold of him he could not let go of it again until he had explored it in depth, no matter how outlandish it was, and he used to embroider it, sew embellishments onto it, and would often arrive at entirely unforeseen conclusions, which were sometimes highly original and at other times downright peculiar. He let himself be dominated by his thoughts, and while he rode them it mattered little to him whether others could follow him or not. 'They used to cross the steppe and occupied countries that they didn't even know; it is incredible how far they got. And what of the English? They too ventured into every part of the world, the difference being that they got there by sea. Of course they went there to get hold of other people's wealth, but ended up settling in those distant countries, taking up with the most beautiful girls and staying put. Just as those who came before them had done. And their children grew up with something from one side and something from the other, so that there's no point in distinguishing between what they owe to each. They had fused and there's an end to it. That's how it was in Cyprus too, where so many peoples passed through and left their genes here. How is one to distinguish between the various groups, you tell me? It is pure chance what language each one of us ends up speaking. If languages were innate, we would all of us together speak twenty of them at most, which had been learnt at birth. How can you really say this man is Turkish, that one Greek and that one English? It would be like taking Famagusta cathedral and claiming to be able to separate the Gothic façade from the mosque inside it. One would risk bringing the whole thing crashing down.' I drew my shawl more tightly around me, for the air was growing cooler, though the old city behind us seemed to be radiating heat. I thought about the bizarre nature of the comparisons advanced by David, who continued his train of thought: 'I don't finally know why they've got it in for us English, for we have never tried to separate anything, and if it had been up to us, they could have continued to live together, Greeks and Turks. And if it hadn't been for us,' David broke off and squashed a mosquito on his arm, 'we would not be here at this hour of night chatting, because the mosquitoes would already have devoured us.' I certainly agreed with him about this last point, for the English had generously flooded the entire island with DDT; I had found a few empty canisters inside the café and I could still almost smell it, as if it had got into the old velvet chairs and never gone away, as if it had permeated the dust itself. There was a similar smell in the old city too, a smell of disinfectant which would suddenly emanate from the houses and mingle with others, which were familiar to me, and which I came across as I walked along the winding alleys, between the dilapidated buildings on my way to the covered market. The smell assailed me there in particular, roasted meat and smoke mingled with fat and cumin, and I felt that I was in Bukhara, in the spice market, which had the same smell, a smell that I knew, that I knew only too well! I felt at home. Even the music I heard in snatches and the words I did not understand were not wholly new to me, and the ragged children playing in the alleyways, the women leaning out over their thresholds and quickly arranging their scarves on their heads were not alien to me either. In their eyes, however, I was an outsider and it was as an outsider that they scrutinised me, the children pointed at me, and the men glanced furtively at me. It was strange. It was as though I was returning to the country where I had been born and where I had passed my childhood and where I recognised everything, and yet the people did not recognise me and believed me to be a foreigner. It was vexing to feel myself both at home and an outsider, although the same thing might well have happened in Bukhara.

Famagusta was, like Bukhara, a city of ruins, save that here it was the facades of churches that towered above the hovels, like pretend cathedrals, designed to mislead the eye. The city also reminded me of Cologne in the first years after my arrival there, when the remnants of churches and apartment blocks rose up from the rubble. Famagusta's ruins were not so sad as those of Cologne, either because they were ancient, and no one is ashamed of ancient ruins or even thinks to hide them, or because poppies grew wild there and cats walked through them, and I'd never seen a cat in the rubble in Cologne. There had been no cats in Cologne. In Cyprus, on the other hand, they were everywhere, thin, wild, frightened but at the same time proud animals which had a regal air and would spy on you from on top of dilapidated walls. We had adopted two white cats, which used to walk between customers' legs or curl up on the wicker chairs and shed white hairs on the red fabric of the cushions. My mother grumbled, but they were a part of the household; they were Desdemona's cats and people were used to them.

'Now I'll let you hear how Othello dies; climb up and play the part of Desdemona applauding him.' I climbed the steps of the theatre, in Salamis, and sat down on the top step, with my back to the sea. David's voice reached me, confident and clear; stressing the syllables and scanning them, in order to heighten the melodramatic tone, he recited: '*I kissed thee: no way but this, / killing myself, to die upon a kiss.*' 'Bravo,' I said, applauding from above, and I said to him as I recited in turn: 'I prefer you alive, O my Othello.' 'Prove your innocence to me, Desdemona,' David declaimed from down below.

We embraced among the ruins; there was no one there to disturb us.

The café was full, in the summer beneath the umbrellas, and in the winter beneath the open sky; people preferred to sit outside, even if the wind blew dust and rubbish through the port, and whipped the paper tablecloths off the tables. I served coffee and drinks, chatted with the customers and smiled at one and all. My mother sang my praises, how clever you are! I was clever too. I spoke Turkish as if it were my own language. I brought round trays and mixed cocktails as if I had done nothing else my whole life. In the evening I opened the till and the accounts balanced. A real businesswoman, David said, and kissed me. And so I was. I had shaken off the lethargy to which I had been condemned in Greece and felt an irresistible need for activity and for approval. The officers who smiled at me, the Greeks and Turks who ordered first one drink and then another, the chairs which were almost always taken, and the full till were cause enough for pride. If anyone asked me where I was from, I told them the truth. I was not ashamed of my past. From my little corner beside the gateway to the sea, Cyprus seemed to me to be the calmest place in the world. It was very far from being that.

'*O bloody period!*' David said to me, one evening in December 1963. But this time he did not laugh, for the tragedy was real, and there was no need to heighten it. It was close to Christmas, and just then the struggles between Greeks and Turks began again. 'How could it be otherwise,' David observed, 'in a state that has a flag that no one likes, where each side wants to hoist its own, blue and white for some, red with the crescent for the others, in a state that does not have a national anthem, and how could it have one, if there's no people to sing it? In a state that has a history in common but refuses to accept it?' This was one of David's characteristic judgements, which made him seem more profound than he really was. After all, it's not flags that make peoples, or national anthems that make them agree. 'But this time you'll not be involved,' I said. 'We're always involved, even if only as cops,' David replied. I could hear the water lapping against the quay, and the sea wind getting up. Even in Cyprus the cold weather was coming. David was looking at the waves, but was plainly following another train of thought: 'I don't want to end up like Bragadino, who left his skin in Cyprus, quite literally. They flayed him, stuffed his hide with straw, and exhibited it in public, and he was not far from here when he watched his own embalmment.' David looked around, as if to find the spot where the terrible event had occurred. 'Stop it, stop it!', I begged. 'In any case,' David added, 'I think that I'll be spared such an end, for I have orders to return to England.' The wind was blowing more strongly and I felt a great tiredness wash over me. If I was tired, it was not only the previous day carrying trays and supervising the kitchen. David's words too suddenly made me feel drained.

David's announcement threw my plans into confusion. Even though I had foreseen and feared his departure, it came out of the blue, as if a sudden gust of wind had slammed shut the shutters to the two little rooms above the Desdemona. David hesitated and then asked me: 'Do you want to come?' 'To England?' Yet again a country that I did not know, a language that was not my own, a house in which I was an outsider. I would have to create a new way of being from scratch, and get used to a sky that could never be as bright as this one was. 'There's the sea, too, where I live,' David said as he tried shyly to persuade me. But the sea would certainly not have the same colours. 'You won't find a sea like this anywhere else. It's not for nothing that Aphrodite was born in Cyprus and not on the coast of Wales.' Why was he not staying in the land of Aphrodite, why was he not taking me to the furthermost tip of the island, where it points to the east, why were we not looking together for a place to be, beneath that light and beside that sea? But David shook his head. 'I can't take up being a goatherd, it's a fine occupation, but it won't do for me. Or would you have me fish, so as to be at sea as much as possible? I wasn't born to be a fisherman; one could get used to anything, even to fish or to goats, I know that, and perhaps I still have a little of my grandfather's blood in my veins, and he had a flock of five hundred sheep, in Scotland. But that blood must become diluted as time passes, and now there's not enough of it for me to become a shepherd. Or would you have me sit all day in an armchair watching you work, like a pasha, with you as my slave?' 'Don't joke, David. The truth is that you set great store by your uniform.' 'Perhaps, at any rate I know what I'm going to do tomorrow, I know where my country is, even if it's only the Queen's little finger.'

He could not persuade me to follow him and I could not persuade him to stay. He preferred a sky with unreliable colours, but which was his own, to one under which he would always have been a guest, and where he would have had to re-invent himself every day. I wasn't prepared to follow him. Should I go home? I don't know.

When the *QE II* was so far away that waving out to sea seemed absurd, the more stubborn among us remained on the quay looking at the wake, as if we had lost the ship. My mother then turned to me. She had an anxious look on her face, one that was all too familiar. What now?, her eyes said. What shall we do? What do you plan to do, you know that on my own I can't do it, so shall we go on together?

I know, mama, I know you're afraid. I'm afraid too. But we've grown up, don't you see, both of us, we've become adults, you too, not just me. We don't any longer need someone to lead us by the hand. Together we're strong, you and I.

In March the café Desdemona filled up with soldiers wearing blue berets. They were Canadian, Danish, Finnish and English. They had dropped out of the sky or else landed in front of the café's wicker chairs. They came in waves, disappeared again and sometimes came back. They had the sympathetic look of boys who did not really know what was expected of them.

'Who are these ones then?' 'They are the peacekeepers.' 'Peace? Since when did soldiers bring peace?' 'Come on, mother, don't pretend to be in another world. They are coming to keep the peace in Cyprus.' But my mother was stubborn: 'They will do as the Americans did on the Rhine, when they brought us peace.' The remark astonished me, for my mother never talked politics. 'In a way you're right, for those soldiers brought peace too.' 'A fine peace that was, built on the ruins of our cities!' I was increasingly surprised and vexed, and went so far as to say: 'Had it not been for the bombs, the Nazis would never have accepted any peace.' 'And do you suppose the fanatics from around here will submit to peace just because soldiers in blue berets are bringing it to them? They will plant bombs in the streets just as they did before and blow up your peacekeepers!'

Let's hope you are wrong, I said to myself as I watched that cheerful internationalism in uniform which paraded through the port in front of us. Let's hope that they really know how to guarantee peace, and that they know how to hold together this state that nobody wants. Let's hope that they don't force us to leave. '*Oh bloody period*!' David had said. Let's hope that a bloody epilogue is not in store for us.

If we did go away, it was not because of the conflicts between nations which did not love their own flag and which did not have a national anthem in common. If we did go away, it was because of a strictly personal conflict, which I thought I had left behind by fleeing from Athens without saying farewell. I had thought my leaving Athens had made me invisible or at any rate untraceable. How would you set about tracing someone who had fled by night on a ferry to an unknown destination, fetching up on an island, whose name was not known either? Who had noticed our flight, who had realised what direction we were going in, who had betrayed us, in the house that had been my own, in Kolonaki? It certainly wasn't Heleni, who anyway knew nothing about it. Beware of the sisters, Angeliki had said to me once, beware of the real sisters and of the acquired sisters. It had clearly been one of the sisters, for how otherwise could Jorgios have traced me to Cyprus? Without a trail, even a professional detective is at a loss. Someone must have talked. But why had they done it? And why was Jorgios trying to track me down? What was the point of hiring a spy to find me in that labyrinth of islands, and to follow my every movement incognito? Perhaps he had sat down in the café, with the others, put his hat on the next chair, and gestured to me. What can I get you? An ouzo, please. Fine weather today, isn't it? It's always fine in Cyprus. Would you like anything else? Nothing else, thank you, how much is that? He must have observed me in his own good time, while I was talking with David or joking with the other officers; he must have studied me closely while he was sipping his ouzo, then he must have paid, goodbye. Then the very first thing he'd have done was to phone Athens: I've found her! Now a letter had arrived, from the chambers of Counsellor Sinaris, using phrases that I barely understood, but which sounded like an indictment, an indictment which fell upon me like an insult. Why did Jorgios want me to return, and what inexplicable and brazen arrogance had led him to believe that I would have obeyed, thrown myself at his feet perhaps and begged for forgiveness? He threatened me through a lawyer and ordered me to come back, but what lay behind the order?

I got hold of the name of a Greek lawyer. I requested an appointment, was granted one straightaway, kept it, and so for the first time since I had come to Famagusta, made my way to the new city, to Varòsha. I felt somewhat disorientated, for I had become unused to the geometry of modern blocks with wide, straight streets and hotels running down to the sea. Counsellor Pavlos Becatoru's chambers were not far from the coast. There was a lift, an entrance hall, a secretary wearing high heels who told me to make myself comfortable, the Counsellor would be able to see me in a minute or two. I felt intimidated. On the walls of the waiting-room there were some prints of Famagusta and old photographs of Cypriot peasants. Were they Turks or Greeks? Puffed-out trousers, large moustaches. Turks or Greeks? The caption just said 'Cypriots, 1878'. Perhaps they were not so bothered about fine distinctions then, I thought. But the secretary was already ushering me in, opening the door for me, please, take a seat. Counsellor Pavlos Becatoru rose from the black leather armchair, sat down again, what can I do for you. He listened carefully, read the letter closely, asked me a few questions, then drew the black leather armchair back and said to me: 'Do you want my honest advice? Pack your bags and run, leave Cyprus, go away. As soon as you can.' I was terrified. Was I in any danger? The lawyer shook his head, he didn't want to overstate the case, but in a certain sense, yes, I was. A lawsuit would not be decided in my favour. But I was in a different state, how could a judgement in Athens hold good in Cyprus? 'A different state? Yes, in a strictly legal sense you are right, they are two different states, with different legal spheres. But in practice our two states are very close, didn't you realise? And people might resort to other means aside from justice. If I were in your shoes I would not trouble my head about legal borders. For territorial borders are far easier to cross.' But what about the letter? What did my husband hope to achieve by it? The lawyer pushed himself even further backwards in his leather armchair, interlaced his fingers and set out patiently to explain, as if starting from scratch and talking to someone who knew nothing at all: 'Your husband wants to frighten you. He wants you to come home, for a divorce case can drag on and besides, from what I understand, your father-in-law would probably not agree to it, for political reasons I suppose. A scandal could well bring other, more scandalous facts to light, and neither the father nor the son could allow that. They have their place in society to consider. On the other hand, they cannot allow the daughter-in-law or wife, that is, you, to be in Cyprus on her own, when she has already been married in Athens. Should she refuse to go home . . . they will now know where to find her . . .' I was still more frightened. 'What could happen to me?' The lawyer shrugged his shoulders: 'I cannot say for sure, but, as I have already said it would seem to be highly imprudent to stay. When it comes down to it, you are on your own in Cyprus. That too is the height of imprudence.'

I felt the ground give way under my feet; I was so upset that I wrung my hands, ran them through my hair and bit my lip. '*O bloody period!*', David had said. If only David were still with me, if only I had gone away with him, even though to an unknown country! Desdemona, a name that brought bad luck, David had said, but it was going to bring me only good, I was sure of it, it was a fine name all the same. Desdemona's end had not been a beautiful one; even though not as horrible as that of Bragadino, her end was nonetheless not to be envied. Images from tragedy ran through my mind, with an assassin hanging around the café chairs, attacking me from behind. Desdemona, a name that brought bad luck. I was sweating so much that I felt as if I were stuck to the armchair. The lawyer noticed and asked me: 'Are you hot? The air-conditioning is not working too well.' I was embarrassed and answered in a low voice, to myself rather than to him: 'It doesn't matter.'

The ferry for Venice left from the other part of the port. The Turkish boy loaded a trolley with our suitcases and the wicker basket containing my mother's tablecloths, some crockery, objects bought in Cyprus and a few mementos. In closing the shutters in the room above the Desdemona some flakes of green paint had been left on my hands; I had long been planning to have them repainted but had never got round to it. We made our way downhill. At that hour the port was empty, save for a flock of birds that were moving about at the end of the quay. The front door to the café was shut, and I looked at it as if it had not been I who had opened it every morning. The chairs were still upside down on the tables, where the waiter put them before going home, in order to protect them from the damp, and then he would tie them all up with an iron chain. I didn't like it but I had been advised to do it, what with all the people passing through the port, you never know, they said. The waiter therefore chained up the chairs every night, but brought the cushions in. Seen thus, at dawn, with their feet in the air, their backs leant against the tables, the white wicker chairs seemed to me like bound sheep, made ready for transportation.

Suddenly a cat leapt down from beneath one of the chairs, whining spitefully at having been woken up. I was terrified. It was not one of my cats, but an unknown, wild animal, with a large, purulent wound on its back.

The part of the port from which the *San Marco* was to sail was very crowded. We joined the throng, me, my mother and the boy with all our stuff. I did not have time to think of anything at all until the boat had left the port behind. Only then, when I saw the boy growing smaller on the quay, did I grasp that the leavetaking was for good.

I believed that I was descending into the despair I had felt back then, and that I was falling into a black hole, as I had done then. I felt as if I were huddled up in a corner of the bridge, clinging to a big leather bag, my face buried in it and with darkness all around; and on the rare occasions when I looked over the side of the boat even the sea too was dark. I had an emptiness inside which prevented me from thinking, a kind of dazed lethargy which I tried to shake off, in order to return me to my present-day self, which was not the same as it had been back then. In this I failed. I was inextricably linked to the child I had been then; the two images were intertwined and I had to call on inner reserves of strength to separate them. I was another, and yet I was the same, how could everything be repeating itself, just the same? My head was spinning, I had nausea and a knot in my throat that left me feeling as if I were suffocating. How could I be suffering from a lack of air with all that sky above me? I refused to watch the wake behind the ship. It's the same, exactly the same, I thought, I am living out the same story twice.

Yet it was not the same story, for how could the wake behind the boat be the same? The proof of this lay in the fact that this time I was not travelling by myself, for my mother was with me, and she was looking intently at the waves and the seagulls, as if all her thoughts were suspended from their wildly beating wings. She was holding her hair back with her hands, to stop it lashing her face. 'Do you know,' she said to me all of a sudden, 'I am basically happy to be going back. I missed Cologne.' 'Lucky you!' I replied.

Lucky you! What about me? Did I miss Cologne? Could you miss a country which was not your own? But was it really not my own? Perhaps, I found myself thinking, much to my surprise, perhaps it was mine too. Perhaps it was mine too, the city I had seen destroyed, with the bridges plunged into the river and the pile of ruins around the Gothic towers of its cathedral, and which I had seen grow up again, which had grown up alongside me. I had seen the city shyly attempt to open up to all that was new, just as I had been learning in those years to be different from what I had been before. And wasn't the river which could be glimpsed from a terrace purple with wisteria mine too? I had swum in its water; I had wandered along its banks; behind its bushes, near to the embankment, I had let a boy's hands touch me. That river was mine too. The city on the river was a part of me. It belonged to me. Even an acquired land can become one's own and be beloved. I am not coming back just because I have nowhere else to go. I am coming home, I thought to myself, and the thought surprised me. And I let my eyes sink into the ship's wake, as Cyprus disappeared into the sea which had seen the birth of Aphrodite.

Cologne station was much as it had been when I had left, with the iron rosettes in the arches of the roof. We got off, and as if there had been some understanding between us, sat down on a granite bench, with our suitcases and our wicker basket in front of us. We sat there, watched the empty platforms and neither of us dared move. I almost jumped when someone asked us: 'Do you need anything?' I noticed the cross on her chest before I saw the mouth from which the voice came. 'No, thank you,' I replied. 'We don't need anything. We come from here.'

Epilogue

'WHAT WOULD YOU like for your birthday?' Peter asked me at breakfast. My fortieth birthday was drawing near but up until then I had avoided thinking about it; I had not yet decided seriously to weigh up my life, as is appropriate for so momentous a recurrence. Peter seemed to be more interested in what he was reading than in any answer I might have given, and yet that question asked in passing, between a cup of coffee and the newspaper unfolded like a screen between us, brought me face to face with the date, raw and unalterable, that I would have preferred to avoid, perhaps by falsifying the calendar or simply by forgetting it. But Peter never forgot birthdays and, even though he was reading the newspaper so intently, did not forget that I owed him an answer. 'What would you like then?' 'I've not yet given it any thought,' I replied, truthfully enough.

Why was I afraid of that date? Partly because I felt a sort of awe when faced with numbers that end in zero; besides forty is a multiple of eight, the sacred number par excellence. It was sheer foolishness, I said to myself, to yield to such superstitions at your age, after all the years you've been here. But it was not only the magic number, there was something else which caused me to fear that birthday, namely, the memory of Mai Ling and her completion of forty years.

Amongst us a woman at that age was old. She had finished her reproductive cycle, her children had grown up, the wind off the steppe and the sun had dried up her skin, her back was bent from carrying excessive weights, and her mouth, when she laughed, was just a black hole. At the age of forty the time had come to give way to the younger wives, who were still able to enrich their husband's yurt with children; the older women settled themselves in a corner of the yurt, in an enclave reserved entirely for them; if they were rich they got their spouse to give them a yurt to which they retired, like pensioned-off queens, finally removed from children and grandchildren, and free from the obligation to minister to the wishes of all and sundry. Many women of forty would cut their hair; it was as if they were once again severing an umbilical cord, but this time it was their own. In truth Mai Ling did not actually resemble the other women of her own age, whether because, thanks to her privileged position as the wife of a khan, she was spared the hardest work, or because of her nature, or because she took more care with her own appearance than the others did. I remembered how much time she devoted to smearing her skin with various oils that Bairqan used to bring her from the bazaar in Bukhara. In no respect did she seem an old woman, for she looked slender and upright as she walked around the village, using the little steps her mother had taught her, with her chubby, pink cheeks and her smooth neck. Nonetheless, when she turned forty she wanted a yurt of her own, as was her right, and she got it. They pitched it on the edge of the village, on high ground, as she wished. She decorated it with rugs and with silk, and when it was ready she went there, followed by a small procession of women. The men were excluded from that ceremony.

Before two days had passed, the whole *ayil* heard Bairqan's voice shouting 'Mai Ling, Mai Ling!' It was the tone of one who brooked neither objections nor delays, and it was the voice of the khan, who gives orders and treats all the others as his subjects. In reality Bairqan no longer had any rights over Mai Ling, who as a retired wife no longer had to obey any husband. It was a right by which older wives set great store, indeed it was the only right they had. Mai Ling therefore did not stir from her yurt, even though Bairqan's cry had created an uproar in the village. She did not even stir when I was sent by my grandfather as his messenger, and panting I reached her yurt and brought her the order: 'Bairqan wants to have you back, Mai Ling.' Mai Ling smiled, let him come and tell me that himself, if he wants me. Bairqan was not the kind of person to bide his time, and so he tied his blue belt around his *chalat* and mounted his horse. Mai Ling's yurt was not far off, and Bairqan could easily have reached it on foot, but my grandfather, like all the Tunshan, deemed it not only pointless but even unbecoming to walk, when a horse was to hand, and still more so when a ceremony was involved. A quite particular ceremony was in fact unfolding before the Tunshan who were lining the path along which Bairqan rode, for what he was doing was quite outside the ordinary run of things, an act of homage never before paid by a khan to his lady. Mai Ling was led back to the yurt as if she were a new wife, on horseback, and she laughed a little at the strangeness of it all, yet she was clearly proud of the honour, though in truth she regretted a little her yurt of peace, from which she had been torn away by Bairqan. She was brought back to his orders, which had to be carried out without delay, to his rages, which had to be assuaged, to his sudden and pressing desires, to his weakness, which only Mai Ling knew how to conceal. What did it matter to him if she were forty or even older. Bairqan was not one to be intimidated by numbers, no matter how magical; if they got in his way he would sweep them away with the angry gesture with which he would chase a tiresome person out of his yurt. Bairqan, my grandfather, who loved Mai Ling and me too, but who had sent me to the other side of the earth in order to stay true to his word. Because words have their weight and cannot be dismissed with a wave of the hand, as importuners can.

Now I too was forty. I had not been married to a khan, and I had never worn the jewels which I had brought in my leather bag to wear at my wedding feast. They were too showy, too heavy and too valuable, so I had kept them locked away in my safe, until one day I had given them to an Afghani girl who was going back to her own country to get married. I wished her to take them back where they came from. Those jewels were intended to make one's neck, ears and forehead more beautiful, but if they were shut away where no one could see them, they had no more value than a cast-off ballgown. I was only too glad to give them to the Afghani bride; I imagined her with the red carnelian earrings brushing her shoulders, the sapphire necklaces around her neck and on her forehead the turquoise diadem which I would have worn if fate had not decreed otherwise. I gave these things to her willingly, for they were a part of my past for which I had no further use.

I had not had any children. Mai Ling had not had any either, but my father Ul'an had entrusted my brother and me to her, and after the *naja* had taken Ginchin, I was left as her daughter. For the Tunshan it was a grave misfortune not to have children, and they would go to any lengths to have them, so that my husband would not have hesitated to take another, more fertile wife. I had been spared that humiliation. Peter did not regret the children that had not come, nor did it occur to him to take another wife, who might give him children. We got on well together by ourselves anyway. I had no cause to fear turning forty. The life I had led, when all was said and done was comfortable and well shielded from inclement weather, had not left any especially deep marks on my face. Like Mai Ling, I still had smooth skin, which was not dried out by the wind or by age. My hair had not yet lost its black, shiny colour, and I knew how to go about concealing the few white strands. I was well built, moved gracefully, and was aware of my male colleagues watching me as I walked. I had had a career. After my first job as a telephonist, I had attained to the upper floors in the new telecommunications block. I had a desk piled high with papers, a telephone that was always ringing; the director and deputy director readily came into my office to consult me and to speak with me.

After my mother's death I married Peter and we lived together in the flat with the terrace from which you could catch a glimpse of the river. Our friends envied us our home, and its magnificent position, who in Cologne could afford such a house! I tended the plants on the terrace and Peter said I had green fingers. When I paid a visit to Dr Wallatz, we would exchange tips and secrets on how to make our plants flourish still more.

There was nothing particular about my life, nothing to make it seem different from that of any other woman of my age; even my way of speaking was no different from that of my neighbours on the floor below or of colleagues who worked in the office next to mine, for it was the Cologne accent, which we laughed about but were proud of too. What did I have to fear then? The only thing in me that was different was the past. I still kept a leather bag in the attic and inside it there was a silver inlaid box; there were little boxes full of amulets and little silk scarves, but I no longer remembered having opened that bag. I had simply taken the precaution of running strips impregnated in lime oil, green and off-white ribbons, round it to protect it from moths, carelessly tied around a bag that was itself very rough and ready. But from then on I did not remember ever having changed them, and the moths might well have already begun to attack them. Somewhere or other, in a trunk, there was also a red box with a severed plait inside it, a relic that would have dissolved into thin air just as soon as I had untied the ribbon and set about opening it. By some odd association of ideas, Mai Ling turning forty, the bag with the anti-moth strips, the red box, and Peter asking me what I wanted for my birthday all came into my mind at once, and the answer arrived as if unprompted: 'A journey to Bukhara.' Peter put down his newspaper and I saw through his glasses the look of astonishment on his face. To Bukhara? Yes, really, to Bukhara, it wasn't so hard to get there, a little expensive perhaps, the journey might be a little long, you'd have to go by way of Moscow, book in advance, request a visa, perhaps in April then? 'Why not? We'll take both our holidays in April.'

The interpreter had bright blonde hair, puffed out as if she had stuffed straw in it, and pink lipstick on and said that she had studied German in Leipzig. She was forever emphasising the fact, especially when she did not understand something, as if to reproach us for not speaking as well or as clearly as in Leipzig. She never forgot a measurement or a date, so that by dint of dates and measurements I no longer knew what the use of minarets and domes might be, if not to have their heights or diameters measured. Assembled beneath the Gur-e Mir, we had obediently admired the wise work of the Soviet archaeologists who had restored it, and the still wiser work of Tamerlane's architects, who had built it. We had wandered around Registan with our noses in the air, without ever straying very far from our own little group; we had walked in a line along the Scha-e Sende, the road of the tombs, and of all the names that came tripping off our guide's pink lips we only managed to retain those we already knew. There were fragments of blue glazed pottery lying on the ground around the tombs. We secretly filled our pockets with them, and to assuage our guilt, said to one another that there was so much that the archaeologists would never have put the puzzle together again, but would have made new tiles, a quicker and more practical method. That's how it was in Samarkand, which we were visiting as tourists. But the Tunshan had rarely gone as far as that. The only ones to have been there were Bairqan and my father Ul'an, when he went to enlist, but the *ayil* knew little of that. And even if I looked around, as I walked through the old city and the children interrupted their playing to shout out to us 'one pen, one pen', which was more a greeting than an actual request, even if I tried to peep into the courtyards, every time that a door in the clay walls chanced to open, I could not really imagine where the Austrian, the man who had sent my father off to find the Wehrmacht, could have lived.

Bukhara, however, was just as I had remembered it. Nothing had changed. There were notices announcing restoration projects, but the latter were only at an early stage. Bukhara was the same, even if delivery vans, lorries and vehicles with varying degrees of horsepower and in varying states of repair were parked outside the bazaar, in place of horses, donkeys and camels. Yet the lay-out of the market was just the same. There were benches lined up against the city's clay walls, and goods laid out on the ground; there were displays of velvets and damasks, fabrics stitched with gold thread, shoes and caps decorated with gold charms, and then there was the covered market, which sold fruit, spices and meat. Crouched down among the goods I saw an Uzbek selling ropes. He wore a stiff, embroidered cap on his head, and a blue embroidered coat; lower down, on the collar of the jacket there gleamed a row of medals which he wore in the correct manner. It could be him, and anyway it looked like him. The ropes, for their part, looked like those used to tie the foals to the rail when they were feeding.

They were ropes made with particular skill, and my grandfather Bairqan used to buy them from an old Uzbek who, according to him, was the only one to make them as they should be made. We would find him among his ropes, and Bairqan would bow respectfully to him; the Uzbek would lay them in his open palms, as if they were silk, and whisper the price, half reluctantly. Bairqan, with the same air of complicity, would offer him half, then shoulder the new ropes of twisted cotton, which gleamed white as if they had been dyed in *kumiss*. I bent over the ropes. The Uzbek, when he saw me looking at them so intently, handed me one. I took it. I stood there with the rope in my hands, as the seller sang its praises. There was no need for that, since I knew its merits. I paid for it, although I felt a little embarrassed.

'There you are, try one,' the woman behind the pyramid of crystallised sugar said to me. As she offered me the paper bag, she would smile and show the gold in her teeth. Inside there were ten sweets in the form of marbles, coated in a white sugary crust with a toasted almond centre. I put one into my mouth immediately, for I knew how delightful it was when the sugar melts bit by bit until there is just the almond left to be chewed, and you have to make it last a long time. They had to last the whole journey back to the Amudar'ya and every time I had to decide whether to eat them all at once, one after the other, or to nibble little bits and perhaps leave some of them for Malik, at least one anyway . . .

The Uzbek guitar player, who rolled his eyeballs up towards the sky when he sang, was there too. They were the dimmed eyes of a blind man, with the pupils hidden behind a white curtain, and when I was a child I would try not to look at them and listen just to the voice and to the instrument. I would tug at my grandfather's arm and refuse to move until Bairqan had thrown a rouble into the Uzbek guitar case.

I tossed in a five dollar bill and moved off smartly to rejoin the group, feeling ashamed because I feared throwing in dollars in the midst of small change was the act of a braggart and a tourist.

* * *

We were seated beside the Lab-e Haus, the last remaining example of the many fish-ponds of Bukhara, beneath the mulberries which, according to the guide, had been planted five hundred years before. They too were the same, then, as they had been when we used to sit on the steps, beside the water's edge, and my grandfather would divide up one of the watermelons he had bought at the bazaar, after he had haggled long and hard, tested the hardness of the rind, put it to his nose, and pressed it against his ear as if it were a patient in need of auscultation. He cut it open swiftly, with rapid gestures, and I sucked at its spongy flesh, which was dripping with sugar and dotted with black seeds. A nomad child, her plait reaching down to the ground, a slice of watermelon in her hand and a ring of seeds all around her. That was me, then.

In front of us, on the table, a row of teapots was drawn up; their style had not changed, red flowers against a green ground, a simple, modest, homely art, which did not pretend to rival the magnificence of the faience ware so much admired in those days. The green tea was boiling hot and the little cups steamed; we were waiting for them to cool down, and in the meantime the guide was drawing our attention to things to right and to left. To the right stood the Nadir Diwan-Begi madrassa, and to the left the hostel for pilgrims. While we were sitting around the tables beneath the mulberry trees, an episode occurred which, when recounted, seems incredible, and yet it was merely a matter of accident, and everything accidental has something incredible about it, always.

This is how it went. Around the square there were Uzbeks playing chess and drinking tea, sitting down cross-legged on raised wooden platforms. There was also a small cluster of men closer to us, but my back was turned to them and I was listening to the guide. She was continuing with her explanations, which for once had to do not with monuments but with the people living in the midst of the monuments. 'For example,' she said, 'there's a group of Tatars right beside us. They are few in number, because most of them have left. You can distinguish them from the Uzbeks on account of somatic features, language and customs. They are a difficult people;

they keep to themselves and don't integrate with others. As you can see, they still wear a part of their original dress, the tunic laced up in the Mongol style, on the right shoulder.' I too turned round to look; the men seated at the table looked at us in their turn. Our guide was quite right, they were different from the Uzbeks, taller in build, with broader faces and narrower eyes. We looked at them and we realised that they were talking about us. Then one of them stood up, approached the guide, began to talk to her, and both of them looked round at me, as they spoke. 'Have you been here before?' the guide asked me. 'This man maintains that he knows you.' I heard the name of the Tunshan uttered, and Bairqan and Ul'an mentioned. I then tried myself to work out who this man looking at me could be. He seemed puzzled, as he spoke with the guide: 'He says that you could be a cousin, but that you seem to him to be too young to be that, yet at the same time too old to be a daughter of that cousin.' I felt embarrassed; my fellow travellers did not understand, and the guide grew suspicious. But then all of a sudden the man, as if he had discovered some proof, pointed at my arm. My arm was bare, the mark around the elbow stood out against my skin, and the last few days' sun had made it still darker.

What have you done to your arm? You have a black mark below your elbow . . . That's the reward you get from your famous godhood . . .

Malik, my cousin, was not really surprised at seeing me beside the Lab-e Haus. It was only to be expected that if I came to Bukhara, I would meet him, and it was only to be expected that I would come back. What of the other Tunshan? What of Bairqan and Mai Ling? They had all gone away, to Sinkiang. My departure had set in motion plans that had been laid long before. They had all gone away, and only Malik's family had remained. At the very last moment, just when they were about to leave, they had decided to stay, and now they lived in Karakul, in a kolkhoz on which they reared sheep. He, Malik, was its president. The guide translated what he said into her stereotyped language, but it wasn't easy for her to find the words for so unusual a matter. It was a shame that I couldn't communicate directly. I heard Malik speaking with the other Tunshan, those still at the table, who were now nodding and smiling at me, but not knowing if they should approach me, because they were a little confused by the strange people around me. I too didn't know whether to stand up or not. Peter watched me, amused; my travel companions still didn't understand, and the guide was visibly ill at ease. Malik came up to her, asked her to translate, and said: 'Now you are forty. It's time for you to come back home.' The guide translated what he had said as if it were a formula in an initation; I didn't understand at first, and I got him to repeat it. It's time for you to come back home, that is precisely what Malik had said. At the age of forty it was normal to return to the place from which you had come. After thirty years in distant lands. What are thirty years on the steppe? The city, as I could see for myself, had not really changed, the steppe still less; the Tunshan had gone away, it was true, but Malik was standing there before me, had recognised me immediately, even before he had found the proof on my arm, and he was speaking to me in all simplicity about going back home. So it was still my home then.

Now I understood why I had come. I had come to find out whether there was a place that was still my home, a place I had the right, the duty even, to return to. In all those years I had envied the foreigners who lived in Cologne because they had a place to go back to, and now I too had one. It did not matter that it was a land in which I would no longer have been able to live, for the important thing was simply the illusion that one could go back.

Malik looked at me and waited for an answer. The guide remained silent; my travel companions observed me, without understanding at all. Peter smiled at me. From the nearby table the Tunshan nodded and gestured to me to come back.

The kuraj *does not return to the place from which the wind has torn it. That is what I would have told you, Malik, if I had not forgotten my own language and the words we used to call to each other when we were children, among the yurts of the Tunshan, to the north and to the south of the great river whose sources are in paradise.*

GLOSSARY

afghanetz: a wind that blows from the north into central Asia and into Afghanistan, very hot and dust-laden.

Albasty: a female demon that features in the myths of the Turkic populations of central Asia.

arang: a jinn that lives in the rivers, in the myths of the Turkic populations of central Asia.

arrak: alcoholic drink produced by distilling *kumiss*.

ayil: village of yurts, or family.

bodhisattva: enlightened Buddhist sage who, though he has achieved liberation, renounces nirvana in order to remain in the world and guide men to salvation.

chalat: tunic or shirt worn by the Mongols, buttoned on the right, up to the neck, along and beneath the shoulder, and cinched at the waist by a belt, cut in the same way for both men and women.

Erlig Khan: in Buddhist doctrine he is the lord of the other world.

garuda: in Indian mythology he is the king of the birds, the opponent and enemy of the snakes.

Great Wind: wind from the north-east, which blows to the south-west of the Alatau. It was known by this name as early as 1259.

jinn: in Arab tradition, a general term used to refer to many different kinds of spirit. Jinn are also mentioned in the Koran.

julag: pre-Buddhist ceremony known among the Mongols, held in honour of the sky and of local deities, to which were added lamaist and Buddhist deities. The ceremony consisted of a series of libations with mare's milk.

karaburan: strong wind that blows from the north-east into Turkmenistan.

khaghan: leader of all the khans.

khan: title of sovereigns in the kingdoms (khanates) of central Asia (Mongols, Persians, Turks, Indians).

kumiss: drink made of fermented mare's milk, slightly alcoholic, known to all the peoples of central Asia.

kuraj: a Kyrgyz word referring to the bushes which shed branches and roots in the winter and are dragged along by the wind, thereby scattering seeds, *Salsola kali*, across the steppe. In Russian *kuraj* is called *perekatipole*, or 'running field', in German *Steppenhexe* and *Windhexe*, or 'witch of wind and steppe', and in English 'tumble-weed'.

madrassa: a type of building in Islamic architecture which housed a school of theology and which consisted of a square courtyard with four iwan (rooms with a dome) and with cells for pupils.

mingan: group of one thousand soldiers in the Mongol army.

Moghul: population of Afghanistan of Turco-Mongol origin.

Momo: according to the beliefs of the peoples of central Asia, the 'grandmother' who lives in the sky, and who watches over the family and over childbirth.

Naga: In Indian mythology, the *Naga* and *Nagini*, kings and queens, are the protective genii of the household altars, half-human or wholly human figures, with a large hat in the shape of a cobra. The *Naga* were incorporated into the Hindu pantheon, in which gigantic snakes expand their necks so that they form canopies above the heads of the gods. The *Naga* reappear in Buddhist legends and iconography, first and foremost in the case of the famous Muchalinda, the gigantic king of the snakes, who used his fanned-out neck to protect the Buddha sunk deep in meditation.

naia (or *naja*): a genus of colubrid snake to which the cobra belongs, widespread in Africa, India, south Asia, its bite can cause death in a matter of minutes. It lives close to springs and has a fairly varied diet (with some exceptions: for example, the *Naja melanoleuca* and the *Naja oxiana* lives solely on frogs). One metre forty to two metres fifty in length. In some species (the *Naja naja*) the back part of the scutum takes the form of spectacles or of a monocle.

obo: among the Mongols, a heap of stones erected in honour of local spirits.

Om mani padme hum: Sacred syllables of Buddhism and lamaism. The formula means literally: 'You jewel in the shape of a lotus flower.'

Oxus: ancient name of the Amudar'ya.

Padma Sambhava: name of the Indian missionary who introduced Buddhism to Tibet, whom Mongols and Tibetans revere as a saint. In Sanskrit it means: 'born of the lotus'.

Pashto: Indo-European language belonging to the Indo-Aryan group, derived from ancient Iranian languages. In 1930 it became the official language of Afghanistan.

Qormusda: god of 'the eternally blue sky' and prince of the *Tengri*.

quriltai: among the ancient Mongols, the assembly of all the khans.

Stupa: in Buddhism, a religious monument consisting of a large dome on which sits a square structure surmounted in its turn by a rod with horizontal rings, generally intended to hold relics of the Buddha or to illustrate his life.

tengri: term used to refer to the deities of the Mongol shamanistic pantheon.

Tsong-kha-pa: Tibetan religious reformer, founder of the so-called 'Yellow Hat' sect, or Gelugspa (1357–1419).

tümen: group of ten thousand soldiers in the Mongol army.

ulus: among the Mongols, a territorial arrangement of tribes.

yurt: felt tent of the nomadic Mongols of central Asia with cylindrical walls and a spherical covering.

Sources and Acknowledgements

MANY DIFFERENT WRITTEN sources, many voices and many fellow travellers have contributed to the making of *Kuraj*. To mention every single contribution to the novel would be to rehearse the whole history of the book. I will begin by referring to authors and works which have played a crucial role in deepening my anthropological and historical knowledge, or from which I have derived information or valuable documents which, whether translated or re-worked, later formed part of the novel. I ought therefore to mention, in its entirety, Professor Walther Heissig's massive oeuvre on the history and literature of the Mongols. The conversation between Genghis Khan and Sigi Qutuqu has thus been taken, albeit in a loose translation, from the *Geheime Geschichte der Mongolen* published by Manfred Taube (1989). The polyglot inscription found on the banks of the Ili has been translated and adapted from the account given in Erich Hanisch's essay: *Zwei viersprachige Inschriften zum Dsungarenkrieg aus den Jahren 1755 und 1758* (Miscellanea accademica Beroliniensia, Berlin 1950). The prayer recited by the lama during the *julag* ceremony is taken from Henry Serruys' essay: *Kumiss Ceremonies and Horse Races* (Wiesbaden 1974). From the collection *Testi dello sciamanesimo siberiano e centro asiatico*, edited by Ugo Marazzi (Turin 1984), I have taken the spell against bolts of lightning, the one about the nails of the dead, and the prayer of the shaman Ügedelegü. The camel driver's poem, sung in the language of the Moghuls of Afghanistan, is drawn from an essay by Michael Weiers: *Die Sprache der Moghol der Provinz Herat in Afghanistan* (*Sprachmaterial, Grammatik, Wortliste*) (Opladen 1972).

I wish to thank Dr Rudorf Kaschewsky of the Zentralasiatisches Institut in Bonn, whom I have consulted in person, for providing me with very useful geographical information, and Dr Sachro H. Sakirova, lecturer in Central Asian Turkic Studies at the University of Bonn, who also made some practical suggestions as regards my journey in Uzbekistan.

I would also like to offer my thanks to Professor Inojatullo Schukurow, who patiently guided me through government offices and archives in Bukhara.

The chapters on the Turkestan Battalions are based upon the following books by Professor Colonel (retired) Joachim Hoffmann (whom I also consulted in person and wish therefore to thank): *Deutsche und Kalmyken, 1942 bis 1945* (Freiburg 1974) and *Kaukasien 1942/43* (Freiburg 1991), from which I took Asimov's poem to the Don and the circular by Count Stauffenberg.

For discussion regarding the Italian presence at Stalingrad I wish to thank Professor Manfred Kehrig, the director of the military archive in Freiburg and author of *Stalingrad* (Stuttgart 1974), who has been of great assistance to me. I would also like to thank Dr Peter von Gosztony, the author of *Hitlers fremde Heere* (Düsseldorf/Vienna 1976), for his suggestions, and Dr Marina Rossi of Trieste for information on Italian prisoners in Russia and in the Soviet Union during the First and Second World Wars.

For information regarding prisoners in the Soviet Union I have drawn on interviews with Italian and German veterans. Of all those who recounted their painful experiences in prisoner of war camps I would like to mention in particular Hermann Eder, Joseph Geiger, Alois Konrad and Wilhelm Wächter, Josef Meier and Helmut Schnell, who made available the manuscript on Karaganda camp, from which I took the poem *Abends wenn der Mond am Himmel steht*. I wish to extend my heartfelt thanks to Mario Belardo, Alessandro Cattaneo, Pierino Gandolfi and, above all, Melchiorre Piazza, President of the Unione Nazionale Italiana Reduci dalla Russia.

I wish to express my gratitude to the employees of the Ufficio storico dell'aeronautica in Rome, and to General Antonino Zancla, for information on meteorology, and to General Letterio Curcuruto and Ugo Gissi, former airman and military photographer, for very helpful details on aviation during the Russian campaign.

I am grateful to all those who shared their experience of post-war Cologne with me: Rudolf Ast, Gertrud Devidtz, Sigfried Heringslehner, Frau Goebl, Bruno Melchert and his wife Henriette, Dietrich Neuhaus and his wife, Philipp Reitzel and Maria Scholl.

I would like to thank Lydia Spötter, who was born and raised on the Volga, Ingrid Weyermann of Telekom and the former employees of the Telephone Exchange with whom I conducted a collective interview. My thanks also go to Heleni Salzmann, who recounted her childhood in Greece to me, and to Alla Heimgärtner, who found the word *kuraj* in an old Russian dictionary.

My thanks go to Rosanna and Bartolomeo Columbu of Ollolai, in Sardinia, for their linguistic advice.

I would like to thank Elisabeth Stadler and Gertraud Allgaier, who showed great care and patience in transcribing the German-language interviews.

My gratitude also goes to all those who laboured so hard to bring *Kuraj* to publication, and in partiular Anna Maria De Palma. My thanks to Alberto Rollo and to those at Feltrinelli who taught me that producing a book is a collective act too.

My thanks to those close to me: to Gabriella Portinaro Untersteiner, who encouraged me to write, to my sister Rosalba, who was my first reader, to Christa Vogl, who put her old school exercise books at my disposal, to Gerhard, who lavished advice on me, and to Claudio, who listened again and again to Naja's story.

But above all I wish to thank Naja, who, in telling me about the Tunshan and about her childhood, gave me, as she herself said, 'a few fragments' but fragments of the utmost value nonetheless. Thank you, Naja, for letting me turn them into a novel, a novel that in some way belongs to you.

A NOTE ON THE AUTHOR

Silvia Di Natale was born in Genoa in 1951 and moved to Germany in 1973, where she lives with her husband and son, and teaches and works as an ethno-sociologist. *Kuraj* is her first novel.

A NOTE ON THE TRANSLATORS

Carol O'Sullivan is Senior Lecturer in Italian Language and Translation Theory at the University of Portsmouth. In 1998 she was commended for her translation of stories from Stefano Benni's *Il bar sotto il mare* by the John Dryden Translation Competition.

Martin Thom is a freelance writer and translator, whose *Republics, Nations and Tribes* was published in 1995. He has translated works by, among others, Alain Corbin, Elisabeth Roudinesco and Moustafa Safouan.

A NOTE ON THE TYPE

The text of this book is set in Linotype Sabon, named after the type founder, Jacques Sabon. It was designed by Jan Tschichold and jointly developed by Linotype, Monotype and Stempel, in response to a need for a typeface to be available in identical form for mechanical hot metal composition and hand composition using foundry type.

Tschichold based his design for Sabon roman on a font engraved by Garamond, and Sabon italic on a font by Granjon. It was first used in 1966 and has proved an enduring modern classic.